I, MARTHA ADAMS

One of the most widely and favorably reviewed books of the year.

"In this high-voltage thriller, Winslow creates a 20th-century Joan of Arc who, almost single-handedly, saves her country from domination by the Russians. It is an immensely readable, fast-paced novel that satisfies because it captures the cynicism of the invader as well as the passions of the patriot."—*Publishers Weekly*

"If Jeane Kirkpatrick were to write a Harlequin, this might be it."—*Washington Post Book World*

"Shame on your Ludlum, Forsyth, Maclean! Your ilk in the all-male army of bestselling thriller-writers has been upstaged by a charming young lady in New York. Mrs. Pauline Winslow has written what I rate as blockbuster of the year."—Melbourne *Herald*

"America cowed—invaded by the Russians and suffering under the snow-capped jackboot. This is the unusual but gripping theme of *I, Martha Adams*, in which author Pauline Glen Winslow paints a scary picture of what life would be like under a Communist regime in a country used to more freedom than anywhere else in the world ... a good read."—*Evesham Journal*

"Pauline Glen Winslow, an established mystery writer, introduces readers to her talent for writing about politics and issues of the day in this fascinating page-turner."—*Pittsburgh Press*

"The many inferences and references to philosophies and actions now prevalent in America which make the original Soviet takeover quite simple makes this novel instructive as well as entertaining."—*News and Views Magazine*

I, Martha Adams, do hereby demand that all troops of the USSR and its satellites, together with their civilian personnel, begin at once to evacuate the United States of America and its territories. Such evacuation is to be completed within forty-eight hours of the receipt of this demand. Any delay or failure to expedite and complete the said evacuation will result in the annihilation of the USSR from Smolensk to the Kolyma range. Only total and immediate compliance will bring about Magnanimity.

PAULINE GLEN WINSLOW

I, MARTHA ADAMS

BREN
FICTION
BOOKS

I, MARTHA ADAMS

Copyright © 1982, 1984 by Pauline Glen Winslow

A Baen Book

Baen Publishing Enterprises
260 Fifth Avenue
New York, N.Y. 10001

First Baen printing, May 1986.

ISBN: 0-671-65569-8

Cover art by Melo.

First published in Great Britain in 1982 by Arlington Books (Publishers) Limited. This edition published by arrangement with St. Martin's Press.

Printed in the United States of America

Distributed by
SIMON & SCHUSTER
TRADE PUBLISHING GROUP
1230 Avenue of the Americas
New York, N.Y. 10020

With thanks to the US *Air Force*
for their very kind and prompt cooperation

"Should a President, in the event of a nuclear attack, be left with a single option of ordering the mass destruction of enemy civilians, in the face of the certainty that it would be followed by the mass slaughter of Americans?"

Richard M. Nixon, 1970

BOOK ONE

SURRENDER

Behold the curb; it is ready to hand

☆

I

Later, people said that the United States woke up one morning to find itself defeated, but that was only true on the East Coast. The news came at 7:30 a.m. Eastern Time and in the western states most people were roused from their beds. Some had been wakened earlier. There were those who would never wake again.

Martha Adams, in her New York apartment, was already up. She had been on the telephone, trying to reach her husband, but the lines were out of order. Josh Adams had called the night before from Grand Forks. He had been fussing about his life insurance. The premium was due and he wanted the amount of the policy increased.

"Call the broker, honey," he had urged, as he had done before, but she had forgotten. "The inflation makes that seventy-five thousand look very small."

Martha didn't really agree. She had a job of her own and Buzz was starting college next week. His expenses had been settled years ago. But she rarely argued with

Josh and promised to do as he said. Sometime during the night or in the early hours, when it was uncommonly noisy even for New York, she woke, remembering that the life insurance bill now came directly from a computer center, not the broker's, and that it would go to Josh at his company's headquarters. She would need the long string of numbers that had become more important now than a mere name and address, and she had decided to catch Josh before he left for the site, and have him send the papers on to her.

The telephone operator was sympathetic.

"There's been a breakdown on some of the Western connections," she said. "It's being worked on. Why don't you try a little later?"

Not much later, Martha thought. Grand Forks was only an hour behind New York time and Josh always left for the site early. Really, though, it was hardly urgent. Blinking in the morning light she wondered why she had jumped up out of bed in such a rush. Insurance . . . She had had a restless night; that made little things grow out of proportion. And she was overtired, probably. Yesterday had been a long day.

The previous morning she had tidied the Connecticut house, raked the gravel on the drive, and left to catch the 11:10 train to New York to do a few days' shopping. There had been no place to park the car at the Waterbury station, and she had had to race to the next station at Naugatuck where there was more parking space. Fortunately the rest of the way was without incident and she had arrived in the city in time to get her hair done by her favorite man at Bergdorf's, and, by giving up lunch, managed to do quite a lot of shopping.

She had bought underwear and sweaters for Buzz, who was starting his freshman year at Yale. Jeans he bought himself. A smart-looking blazer caught her eye and she bought it on impulse, knowing it might have to be returned. Boys of seventeen had their own rigid standards now, not always clear to the maternal mind.

Luckily Buzz was far easier than most. She also bought two pairs of slippers for Josh. None of the department stores had had the material she wanted for new living room curtains and she had gone to a very special place and paid far too much.

Martha liked to keep the country house as it had been in her mother-in-law's day, with New England spareness and simplicity. Materials that had once been used for economy were now most expensive and the only fabrics that had caught her eye were the hand-woven lengths she had found in the little shop in SoHo. She had decided to get a loom and begin weaving herself. There was room in the big barn. Buzz didn't need all the space for his radio equipment, and he wouldn't be home much from now on.

Having quieted her conscience, she had telephoned friends, Birdie Maynard, an old schoolmate and now a lawyer in a city poverty program, and her stockbroker husband. Together they had dinner and went to a play. The play had been favorably reviewed but it seemed to be about nothing in particular and her attention had wandered to Buzz, staying for a few nights with his friend Robbie. Josh, far away in North Dakota, she didn't need to worry about; he had more good sense than anyone else she knew.

In the intermission, Birdie had asked about Josh. These days she was very much the smart New York woman, sleek and bright. Despite her marriage, she was always frank about her admiration of Josh Adams. "He's such a—a restful man," she often said. Rumor had it that Greg Maynard was an energetically unfaithful husband. Then she asked, "So Josh will be out West a whole year? Again? Won't you miss him?"

"A year at least," Martha had replied. "But that's his work. And he's glad to have it. The Columbia Company was lucky to get the contract. They're few and far between now."

Since Carmody had taken office, Martha might have

added, but she didn't. Birdie and her husband were
ardent supporters of Carmody, and they had applauded
when he canceled all the Reagan military projects.
Since then engineering firms had laid off even their
best men. "Repair and maintenance," Josh had said
about the work at Grand Forks, and not much else. The
old ICBM silos, Martha had guessed, but she hadn't
asked. Secret, of course. After so many years she was
used to that. The bedroom habits of the three people
on the stage could not hold her interest and she had
begun to feel sleepy in the theater.

Birdie and Greg had insisted on taking her up to her
apartment on Madison Avenue, to Martha's slight embarrassment. She had not planned to return for another
two weeks and the cleaning woman had not been in for
several days. The place needed dusting and it was hot
and stuffy, the air conditioners taking a long time to do
their work. But Greg had been inclined to linger over
his nightcap. He enjoyed watching Martha dispense
hospitality. She moved swiftly, without bustle, and was
a favorite partner on the tennis court. He liked her
long legs and the arrogant lift of her head; the way she
looked as good sailing as she did in evening dress. With
her copper-colored hair and green eyes she was an
exciting contrast to the petite, brunette Birdie, with
her carefully arranged city style. Back in the Seventies
Greg and a previous wife had belonged, briefly and
discreetly, to a wife-swapping group. He had remembered that when he met Martha, but even if Birdie
could have been persuaded, Greg didn't think he could
have approached Josh. A dull old stick to his mind, and
the friendship had remained principally between the
women.

At last Birdie had taken Greg away. Martha tidied
up, had a bath and went thankfully to bed. From the
long habit of a woman who was much alone, she switched
on the bedside radio and heard the murmur of the
news. More trouble in Panama. Josh had always ex-

pected it. England's Princess of Wales had given birth to a daughter in a Toronto hospital. Would her children continue to bear royal titles, the announcer wondered, or was royalty itself likely to pass into history? The inflation rate for the month had been up a frightening four per cent. No wonder everything had cost so much, Martha thought, turning the radio off.

Then Josh had called. "I have to take care of you," he had said, "since I got you to marry a broken-down old wreck of an engineer." The fifteen-year difference in their ages was one of his standing jokes. She had gone back to bed, smiling, and then thought of the cloth she had bought, soft and sturdy, subtly patterned in the pale, muted New England green so right for the house. Sighing with satisfaction she had fallen asleep, only to be woken a few hours later.

In their twelfth-floor apartment the usual New York noises were not too penetrating. When Josh was there he muttered about the wailing sirens of police cars, ambulances, and fire engines, but then, he loathed New York. Martha thought that the barking of a dog on a quiet night in the country was just as bad. But in the early hours of that morning, the noise did seem to be worse than usual. Car horns were hooting and people were shouting, drunks, doubtless. In the old days the doorman would have got them to move on. Now the building had no doorman, only a buzzer system. She had yawned, quite awake, and turned the radio on again.

The late night show was still in progress, but it sounded very dull. A panel of experts on homosexuality in the public schools. Martha was about to switch off when the hour struck and there was the usual abrupt switch into the newsbreak.

"There have been reports, unconfirmed, of large explosions in desert areas in several western states from Nevada to North Dakota. One story has come in of possible sabotage to power stations. An early report

claimed a missile facility near Denver was involved, but
this has been checked out and found to be totally untrue. We repeat, the story about the Denver facility is
completely untrue. Mr. Watkins, head of the Environmental Protection Agency, made a statement on that
after a check within the hour. Mr. Watkins, who was
roused from his bed in his Georgetown home, says he
has heard nothing of any explosions in any missile or
energy plants, nuclear or otherwise. Tune in for a full
report on the explosion rumors on the eight o'clock
news. Now, to other news. Police last night were hunting for a man who held up a delicatessen at Fortieth
Street and Lexington and shot the owner in the head.
The man was wearing jeans and a windbreaker and was
observed leaving the scene and running towards Forty-
Second Street. The owner was dead on reaching Belle-
vue Hospital. Tickets for the Bones concert at the
Coliseum are totally sold out and Bones fans without
tickets are asked *not* to appear at the doors. The police
are preparing to put up barricades to keep any crowds
at least a block away." The station cut back to the show
in progress.

Martha had switched the radio off and tried to rest a
little longer. She had had a nasty pang when the announcer spoke of explosions and mentioned North Dakota. But she soon convinced herself that it was nonsense.
Rumors had been springing up for years, ever since
Three Mile Island, but they usually turned out to be
nothing very much. The anti-nuclear people, she suspected, liked to keep the pot boiling.

But when she rose and couldn't reach Josh on the
telephone, she had to wonder whether some explosion
might have been the cause of the trouble on the line.
Not in the silos, though. Josh had assured her years ago
that they were safe from accident and in the very unlikely event of sabotage, the worst contingency would
be disablement, not explosion. Her mind ran over the
possibilities. Liquefied natural gas, perhaps? Oil refin-

eries? And didn't the telephone company use a lot of microwave transmission these days? Could that be interrupted by an atmospheric disturbance? She didn't know. Most likely it was just some trouble at a switching station, she told herself, as she filled the coffee pot.

Rubbing her eyes, she got a sudden image of Josh's face with a characteristic expression, affectionate, concerned. "You drink too much coffee, Martha. No wonder you can't sleep." His gentle chiding touched his wife, knowing that he looked on the woman of thirty-seven, office manager, mother of a grown son, as if she were the girl at Connecticut College he had fallen in love with eighteen years ago.

While the coffee was brewing she watered the plants. Rose, the cleaning woman, had given the African violets too much water, she noticed. They were all leaf. Restless, she tried Josh's number again, but with no luck. Not that she was worried, she told herself. It would be absurd to start worrying now, after all the projects he had worked on. In the Reagan days he had been working, she was sure, on the missile sites, although he had never told her about it. The jobs were more hush-hush than anything done since SALT III. But she was fidgety and turned the kitchen radio on. As she padded about she was aware that her feet were aching a little from all the walking the previous day in her city shoes, but the broadcast had most of her attention.

"We repeat," the usual host for the morning show was talking, "the President will be making a special broadcast at 7:30 a.m. Eastern time. It will be carried on all radio stations in the area, and on all television networks. The broadcast will be repeated, but it is urged that everyone who can do so, tune in."

The telephone rang and Martha rushed over and snatched the receiver but it was Birdie's voice on the line. "Martha, did you hear the news? Have you heard from Josh?"

Birdie liked to be first with the news, good or bad, but her voice was concerned.

"No," Martha said, "but I expect everything is all right. A fuss about nothing."

"We repeat again," the announcer was droning on. Martha, irritated, wondered why the usually casual announcer had now taken to using the royal "we". "Carmody is going to speak," she told Birdie, knowing that she would rush off. Just then Martha didn't feel like talking about Josh.

"I must catch him," Birdie said at once. "I hope you hear from Josh soon." Martha could hear Greg murmuring in the background.

The coffee was done and she poured in the cream she had bought in the Night Owl delicatessen the night before. She felt more cheerful when she'd drunk the first cup and decided not to tune in to Carmody. Like one of his predecessors in office, he loved to hog the air waves, especially when the polls showed his popularity was slipping. What was his excuse this time? Panama, probably. Or the inflation figures. It wouldn't be about the reported explosions. He couldn't wring any glory from that, unless he made an "evils of big business" speech. But then the Environmental Protection Agency would have set the ball rolling. Strange, though . . . 7:30 was hardly prime time. A new ploy. Shock value, getting people before their eyes were quite open. Carmody, who seemed unable to handle any real problems, had taken lately to manufacturing little crises and solving them with great parade.

The program went back to the usual light music, traffic announcements and weather reports. "Stories about heavy lightning in the west, causing fires and other damage, have not been confirmed. But we can tell you, right from here in the studio, that telephone service has been interrupted, because we haven't been able to reach our own Ron Mundy who is vacationing in Montana. Seventy-five degrees and sunny, another fine day like yesterday. Traffic was normal, except for delays at the airports."

That was the ground crews, no doubt. They'd been having a job action for the last week. Josh was due in next month for a few days and she hoped it would be over by then. "It's 7:25. Traffic is now flowing normally on the George Washington Bridge. The Holland Tunnel is bumper-to-bumper. In honor of the Bones concert tonight at the Coliseum, we will listen to their version of 'O Happy Day'."

Martha tried the telephone again. This time it was worse; she couldn't get a dial tone at all. The line wasn't dead, but it was full of odd sounds and clicks, the way it had been in the power black-out and the awful day when the bomb killed Reagan and Bush. Everyone and his mother must be calling up about the Carmody broadcast. Cheap publicity hunter. Josh had said he would be a disaster, and how right he was.

Seven twenty-nine. Annoyed with herself, she switched on the television set. It was a very old set and the picture took some time to come into focus. It was, of course, the Oval Office. Carmody loved to see himself there. Rumor had it that he kept a film of every broadcast, and ran it over and over for his own delight like a fading movie star. An official whose face was familiar but whose name she couldn't remember was mouthing something. She turned the sound up. Then Carmody entered, flanked by aides. The camera zoomed in on him and Martha was shocked.

It was just two weeks ago, up in the country, that she and Buzz had watched the President make a speech. Buzz, as usual, had been silent, but she had made a running commentary on Carmody's absurdities. He had been sleek and beaming, as he announced his conquest of the gypsy moth problem in the north-east. He had solved it, everyone in Connecticut knew, by permitting the aerial spraying that he had forbidden two years before.

This, however, was a very different man. Carmody
now looked drawn and old. The sleekness was gone,
and she guessed that he had done without the atten-
tions of his make-up man. Perhaps he had decided not
to run again. But even as the thoughts whirled in her
head, she felt a brutal clenching in her gut.

His voice, when he began to speak, was low and she
had to turn the sound up further to hear clearly.

"You may have heard some rumors during the early
morning about explosions," he said. He stopped, fumbling with some papers on his desk, and looking at the
camera helplessly. Carmody, a handsome man, always
called the camera his friend. Martha was sweating despite the air conditioning. There *had* been a nuclear
explosion. North Dakota, they had said. Josh . . .

"Everything has been thoroughly investigated. Please
do not panic. The radiation damage is minimal, confined to small areas, and comparatively little loss of life
is expected."

An aide thrust a sheet of paper before him and the
camera showed clearly the President's trembling hands.
He read slowly, and for once the dramatic Carmody
was without expression.

"At five a.m. Eastern time, Soviet missiles launched
from Panama and Cuba by-passed our Early Warning
System and struck our major missile sites in the west. A
second, simultaneous strike was launched against our
bomber fleets and submarines. The Chiefs of Staff have
informed me that our capacity to retaliate has been
rendered substantially ineffective. At the same time an
ultimatum was received from General-Secretary Ulyanov
of the Soviet Union. The whole text of the ultimatum
will be read later and will appear in the morning
newspapers, but in substance it called for an immediate
and unconditional surrender of the United States of
America. If such surrender did not take place, a third
strike would be aimed at our population centers, and
these weapons would not be 'clean'."

He paused. "Consultation with the surviving Joint Chiefs and their seconds in commands, as well as the nations of the former NATO alliance, has made it clear that we were left with no choice. No choice," he repeated, in the manner of an old man whose mind has begun to wander. He sounded as though he had taken a heavy tranquilizer. "At seven a.m. this morning, the signing of the Instrument of Surrender took place in the Pentagon. Marshal Borunukov has asked me to say that the American people should go about their normal business. No great upheavals will occur."

His face was in close up and his eyes, facing the camera, were like those of a dead man.

"The Soviet people send a message of good will. There can be, now, peace in our time."

— II —

A key sounded in the door and although the steps were soft, Martha jumped. She had been staring at the set blankly. Carmody had left the Oval Office but the television camera crew, apparently expecting more, left the cameras trained on the empty chair.

Rose came in looking frightened. In her haste she had left the door to the apartment open, and voices drifted up from the usually silent hall. "What's goin' on, Mis' Adams? The Super downstairs, he said . . ."

The network, suddenly aware that there was nothing but confused-looking White House officials in front of the cameras, switched back to New York. Jason Purfleet was already in his seat, his face wearing its usual expression, both serious and benign, though this morning more serious than usual. His voice was not noticeably agitated.

"Well, we have all had a great surprise, and a great shock. The actual terms of the surrender have not as yet been delivered to the press, but we are expecting them at any moment. For any of you who have not seen President Carmody's announcement, it will be repeated at eight o'clock."

An arm cut across his face with a fluttering piece of paper, and he grasped it, slightly flustered.

"Well. One piece of good news has come in. The Environmental Protection Agency has been monitoring the missile site areas that were destroyed in the Soviet attack and the radiation is the minimum we could have expected. It was a surgical incision. There should be comparatively little loss of life due to radiation. Our large population centers have been spared. That's a great relief, isn't it, Mel?"

Mel Kranks, the anchorman for the morning news program, had joined him.

"You bet," he said, thankfully.

"Of course," Purfleet went on, "we don't have much specific data as yet. But Canada has been heard from, and naturally they've been worried. At Manitoba, which is not far from one of our biggest sites and downwind today, they say the count was no worse than we had at Three Mile Island after the problem there."

Manitoba. Close to North Dakota and Grand Forks. Grand Forks. Martha closed her eyes for a moment. When she opened them, Mel Kranks was tugging at his hair. It was flat and thin, not fluffed out to its usual pompadour style. "What a morning. I've been trying to get Johnny Lind in Vegas—he's singing at the Sands this week. Wondered what's happening in Nevada—we used to keep a lot of stuff down there in the desert, didn't we?"

"I think all those sites were abandoned after SALT III, Mel. When we got rid of most of the bomber fleets. Those old B52's weren't worth a damn. And nothing has come in about any strikes in Nevada. Not to us, anyway."

"Well, I guess those high rollers out there won't even be awake yet to know what didn't hit 'em," Mel offered, with an imitation of his usual broad grin.

"Most citizens of the United States have woken up to a great shock," Purfleet said, with a note of reproach for the levity, "though some of us have not been entirely surprised. On this very station we have warned President Carmody that reactionary elements in the military were breaking the SALT III agreements. In this day and age, that sort of thing could not be hidden, and the Soviet government, with its undoubted military superiority, obviously would not tolerate that much longer.

"And there were those rumors that some of the crazies left in the CIA were planning to do a job on the President."

"A military and intelligence operation," Purfleet said heavily. He gazed into the camera. "In an effort to maintain responsible standards, we have not developed that story in depth on this station. Public panic would have done no good. But we know that not only the Soviets but the European governments have been worried about it for months—maybe longer."

"We were wrong, Jase," Mel said. "Maybe this could have been avoided. We should have leveled with the public. That responsible journalism stuff was a lot of bull. We forgot our duty under the First Amendment."

"There's a lot to what you say, Mel," Purfleet said with a nod, "but we have to go on from here. A meeting has been called of the Security Council for ten o'clock this morning. I've already spoken to some people over there and they're not too worried. In fact they think the world situation will calm down. Now that the Soviets won't feel threatened, we can really get down to the problems of peace. We may have had a military surrender, but we will become partners now. Not only, as Carmody said, for peace in our time, but for our children and grandchildren."

Martha, who could bear no more, jumped up from the chair where she had been crouching, and switched off the smooth faces.

Rose still peered at the blank screen. "Have we

really surrendered to them Russians?" she asked, uncertainly. "What do those two mean?"

"Carmody has surrendered, as have those two gibbering idiots," Martha answered. "Not the United States. There are plenty more people to be heard from."

"Will—will Mr. Adams come home now?" Rose asked. She was still clutching the bag in which she brought her apron, her head scarf and her working shoes. An immigrant from the Virgin Islands, she had worked for the Adamses in New York for many years. She had gone to Martha for help with practical problems, but she had taken comfort from Josh's quiet, solid, masculine presence.

"Mr. Adams is dead," Martha said, the words scarcely a whisper. She had been almost certain from the beginning; quite certain once she had known that Grand Forks was definitely gone. Whether the warheads were clean or not, none of the men out there could have survived the heat or the blast. Josh could not have been saved, for he had been staying in a reconstructed, old army base, less than a quarter mile from the site.

Tears welled in Rose's eyes and spilled down her cheeks. The woman who had been widowed long ago took the new widow's hand and pressed it painfully. "It's the boys we must think of now," Martha said after a long silence. "Luther and Buzz." Luther, Rose's son, was a year older than Buzz and a student at City College.

Martha went to the telephone again to try to call Buzz. Nothing had been said of any strikes in the east, but there was the New London base, with whatever submarines Carmody had allowed to remain. The lines were still choked. Everyone calling everyone else, and vitally important calls, no doubt, disrupted.

Rose, shaking, had gone into the kitchen and poured herself a cup of coffee. Turning on the kitchen radio, she stared at it intently. The announcer was giving the traffic report. "Confusion on most of the major arteries going out of the city," he said. "Looks like a lot of

commuters decided to turn round and go home, but the
lanes are set for the incoming traffic. The George Washington still has only two lanes open going west and cars
are bumper-to-bumper from Ninety-Sixth Street. This
report isn't quite up to date, I'm afraid, because unfortunately our helicopter got into an accident earlier this
morning. I don't have the details, but it seems that the
'copter smacked into a plane that was off course. There's
a lot of confusion today, folks. Those who can stay home
are probably better off doing just that. No report yet on
Cheerful Charlie, our Whirlibird Man, but I'm not too
hopeful."

Off course? Or non-scheduled air traffic? Martha wondered. As if in confirmation she heard the sound of
heavy air traffic grunting overhead. The old building
that she lived in vibrated slightly from the noise. Not
just the odd 747 going into Kennedy. "There'll be another news update in ten minutes," the announcer was
saying. "But in the meantime I'd like to say, keep cool.
My guess is that inside of a week we'll all know a lot
more and things will start to shake down. Hell, this
attack might turn out to be not much worse than Pearl
Harbor and we lived through that one."

Martha grabbed Josh's binoculars from the closet shelf
and went to the window. She gazed up into the cloudless sky, where a formation of huge transport planes
with red stars on their fusilages were swooping downward and eastward in the direction of McGuire Air
Base.

III

The announcer was wrong. In a week's time the public did not know much more, and the amazing thing, to Martha, was what little reaction the news appeared to bring. Where was the Congress, the military, everybody? When she first heard Carmody's announcement, she had been caught up in her own loss. Yet she could not believe that the country would tamely accept what he had done. What about the troops overseas, the ships at sea, all the country's allies? The whole of America seemed to be in a lingering state of shock and—far more worrying—submission.

The morning the news came Martha and Rose both thought of their sons, of military age, the first to be affected by war. Rose had rushed home. "I'll get there if I have to walk," she said, but that day the subway was still running. Martha had not been so lucky. There were still taxis on the streets and she managed to get to Grand Central Station, though there was a lot of traffic. But Grand Central was crowded to the limit, with a

29

mob up the great flight of stairs spilling over to Vanderbilt Avenue.

"No use trying to push through there, lady," a sweating policeman said. "You can't buy a ticket and you can't get on a train. If this keeps up the station will have to close down. God knows where they're all going," he went on. "They'll be trying to get back in a couple of days. Lookin' for their pay checks." A child, separated from its mother, was screaming. The policeman lifted her and pushed through to the anxious woman. "Can't stay on vacation forever."

Vacation? His word struck an odd note, yet Martha understood him. In the warm weather, the crowd was mostly in leisure clothes, whites and bright colors along with the inevitable jeans. The scene below the great balcony was like a holiday mob in some usual civil crisis, a strike or an electrical failure on the railroad. Small children carried toys; the lost child had dropped a doll which was crushed at Martha's feet. Teenagers with backpacks carried sportsgear, and one tall, towheaded youth was trying to maneuver a canvas dinghy through the mass of bodies. Some of the youngsters wore headsets; others carried portable radios and the blaring rock music drowned the shouts of passengers who were trying to greet, inform or merely to curse each other.

A youth in sneakers, with a woman's leather bag in his hand, became stuck in a crowd. He dropped it hastily. The policeman retrieved the bag but let the youth go. "Can't mess with bagsnatchers now," he said. "Looks like a lot of old biddies are going to lose their life savings today."

Penn Station, she learned from a taxi-driver, was just as bad. She was annoyed with herself for not bringing the car. But it was a nuisance in the city and she rarely drove all the way, unless Josh was in New York. Josh. As she extricated herself from the mob, a truck pulled up on Forty-Second Street and dumped piles of newspapers at the vendor's stand outside the south entrance. Martha rushed to buy one. The banner headline was simple. US SURRENDERS! An exclamation mark, not a question. There was no other real news, merely comments on the President's speech, and a conjecture about a special session being called at the UN. The front page had obviously been substituted on a paper already set up. She threw it aside, failed to get another taxi, and went round the city on foot, trying the car rental agencies. They were mobbed almost as badly as the station.

"Try us in a couple of days." A grey-haired woman at a small local agency recognized Martha. "It's just the panic. Most of them will soon be back. Where do they think they are all going?" she asked, in an echo of the weary policeman.

Martha searched in her bag for change and tried to call Buzz from a public phone, without success. She stopped in a small coffee shop to rest for a moment. A radio was playing, tuned to an all news station, traffic, weather. "A spokesman at the White House says there are no new announcements at the present time. General Cumberland, who has been in Washington for talks on the Panama situation, cannot be reached for comment. Our Washington correspondent went over to the Soviet Embassy, where a statement was given that the Ambassador, together with President Carmody, was preparing to meet a diplomatic mission due to arrive from the Soviet Union. Here in New York, the Soviet Ambassador to the United Nations is about to attend the Security Council meeting this morning, but he has promised that a full text on the Soviet intentions will be issued after the meeting has taken place."

Still nothing was said about any Russian strikes in the east. It looked as though they had been spared that. The few people in the coffee shop listened without speaking, except for a white-haired old man muttering at the end of the counter. "I don't believe it. They can't do it. It's against the Constitution. Roosevelt didn't surrender after Pearl Harbor, did he?"

"Quiet, Pops," the waitress said. "I gotta hear the news. I've got a sister in Omaha. She's got three kids."

Martha paid for her coffee, which she left on the counter. She was not due back at work for two weeks, but she would go over to the UN anyway. There would be news, even if it wasn't couched in a way she'd like to hear. And maybe they would have some special lines that she could use to get through to Connecticut.

The guard on duty nodded to her, but he had no time for his customary greeting. There were a lot more people than usual in the halls and corridors. A sign was up, saying that all tour parties were canceled.

In her office everything seemed normal except perhaps that no one was surprised to see her. The girls were busy, and the word processors all seemed to be functioning. Miriam Weiss, who took her place when she was away, was not at Martha's desk where she should have been. Instead, Madame Paul, head of personnel and scourge of the young employees, was standing beside it, just replacing the receiver on the intercom. Her enameled face and smooth hair were totally unruffled by the events of the day, to which she did not refer.

"Glad to see you here, Mrs. Adams," she said. "Can you stay for a while? Mrs. Weiss hasn't arrived, or been heard from. And this work has to be ready for a Council meeting this afternoon." Martha agreed, though in the circumstances it seemed absurd to spend a day like this checking for accuracy in statistics on the five-year curve in pulmonary disorder of the under ten-year old group in Botswana. Madame Paul motioned her outside and once the door was closed, handed her a list.

"This is for your section, all American citizens, I see. They should report down to the Post Office at 12:30 p.m. for ration cards," she explained. "All UN employees are to receive special cards. Probably they will be used in stores set up here, but that is not arranged yet."

Martha noticed that her name was not on the list.

"You, of course, are on the schedule for the British Mission," Madame Paul said, already walking away. "You can collect it over there at any time."

She disappeared into the next office.

Lucy Kander, a plump, fair girl from New Jersey, was standing by the door and closed it behind her. She was flushed.

"The old cat, she said she'd put me on report for being late. It took me two and a half hours to get in. You'd think nothing has happened."

Martha's usual words, designed to soothe the girls without infringing on the other woman's authority, could not be spoken.

"I think you should try to keep the job, as long as you can, Lucy," she said. "They're issuing ration cards here."

"Ration cards?"

While Martha was explaining the likelihood of food shortages, she wondered what confusion had put her on the list with the British. Twice she had received a paycheck for a very important Adams and had looked somewhat enviously at the large figure before she had handed it in to Personnel. But he had been an American.

Lucy, who lived near some of the best farm land in Jersey, and had listened to the farmers complaining that the bounty of the crops was flooding the market, could hardly believe her, but she and the other girls agreed to go for the cards.

"Will it count for our coffee break time?" one of them asked anxiously. The Post Office was in the bowels of the building and a ten-minute walk. It would probably be crowded.

"No," Martha said, absently. Everyone knew she was American. Probably some mistake had been made when the records went over to the computer system. She had been born in the United Kingdom and there was often confusion because of her name. The former Miss Martha Adams.

"Miss Adams, I'm Josh Adams," he had said, smiling.

A Saturday-night dance at the church hall in Litchfield, but Josh couldn't dance. It hadn't mattered. Josh. Before she could remember her father had been killed, with her mother, in a car accident. Now Josh was gone too. She tried again to call Buzz, but without success.

At 11:45 a.m. word came round the corridors. "The meeting's up." The Security Council hadn't taken long. Martha found herself impelled to go to the office of the Times correspondent, where a report of the closed proceedings was just being delivered. Bob Postern was staring down at it. He was sitting as usual, shirt-sleeved, his shoulders bowed over his manual typewriter that he refused to change. A grey man, with a mop of curling, grey hair, his face was marked by the pain of a persistent stomach ulcer. Now he was grey in complexion as they read the reports together.

The People's Republic of China had condemned the wanton aggression by the Soviet Union on the United States of America. The Soviet Union replied that it had acted in self-defense. It had responded to an urgent threat of an attack on the Soviet Union itself by a group of dissident CIA and military personnel who had also intended to overthrow the legitimate government of the United States. Reactionary elements based in Florida had at the same time been planning an invasion of Cuba and Panama, and both of those countries had appealed to the Soviet Union for assistance. Now that the crisis was under control and the danger of nuclear war had been averted, relations between America and the Soviet Union would be returning to normal. Any disagreements still pending would be handled through the usual United Nations channels. The British Republics deplored the use of nuclear weapons and asked that the interests of American workers, who could have had no part in any aggression contemplated by the military, be protected. The People's Republic of China called for a resolution condemning the aggression of the Soviet

Union. It cast the only vote in favor of that resolution. The United States, together with the British, abstained.

"I wish I could have a drink," Postern said. Martha knew that Bob, who had once had a drinking problem, had been a teetotaler for years.

"Bob, have you heard anything about New London?"

"Not directly. But there are no reports of radiation coming from there, thank God."

He turned for a moment to say something to the girl in his office, and then looked again at the report.

"Will the General Assembly do anything?" Martha was thinking aloud.

"Yes, they'll talk. If there *is* a General Assembly. There probably will be, if only because they like the display."

Martha had known the Posterns for many years, through the Alsop family in Avon. Josh hadn't cared for him much, partly because of the usual, mild contempt of the engineer for the tribe of writers, partly because of what he considered a pro-Soviet bias in his reporting. But Bob looked worried and ill enough now. "Where's Josh?" he asked.

Suddenly Martha couldn't talk any more.

"On a job," she murmured and moved away. Bob, staring at a blank piece of paper in his typewriter, went on speaking.

"We all knew something had to happen. Things couldn't go on as they were. The danger to world peace. The nuclear race. There had to be some lessening of national autonomy. We've advocated it for years on the economic level. Now we should show a cooperative spirit and try to create a safer, saner world society . . ."

He had already started to type, pecking away at his old keyboard.

— IV —

Martha, who up until now had been able to feel nothing, was suddenly swamped with the acid taste of disgust. She had to get out of this place. Downstairs the staff entrance was choked as the normal traffic was held up for all passes to be checked and re-checked. The public entrance should be clear now that the tours were stopped, and she walked through the long corridors. It was strange to see them empty.

A guard who usually directed visitors was standing at the entrance and he looked at Martha inquiringly. "Sorry, Mrs. Adams, this door is closed. You'll have to use the other entrance."

"We're awfully busy upstairs," she said, "and I have to slip over to the British Mission about my ration card. Some idiot in Administration has jammed up the front entrance; the guards over there are going crazy."

He nodded and opened the door for her. As she left she noticed a long line of telephone trucks outside and men hurrying into the building carrying equipment. She had expected something like that, but she hadn't seen such an array of telephone people since, so many years ago, she had watched on a television screen the little town of Plains, Georgia, being transformed into a center for national communication.

A crowd was waiting in the streets around the UN complex, waiting for news, no doubt. She could have told them to expect no help there. People were milling outside the building that housed the British Mission on Third Avenue. The new Union Jack was flying over it, much buffeted by the changing breeze, garish in its bright red border. Inside the Consular offices there was a long line of employees from the Mission itself as well as the English Secretariat people, waiting for the ration cards which were obviously not yet prepared. "Half the staff aren't even here," a voice was muttering. "They're still on summer holidays." Puzzled-looking men and women were leaving, clutching bits of paper resembling supermarket receipts.

The Consul, a neat little man with bright silver hair, peered out of his office at the crowd and spotted Martha.

"Mrs. Adams," he said smiling. "Come straight in. What can I do for you?"

They had met the year before when the United Kingdom had suffered a cholera epidemic, a new, unique strain that had been difficult to control and caused much loss of life. He had been personally concerned, as his grandson had been stricken, and she had managed to get him one of the first samples of a new American drug which had proved effective. The child had lived, and Martha had received cards from the consul at Christmas and Easter.

"I won't trouble you, Mr. Aspey," she said. "I'm only here for one of those documents. I was sent here," she added, "though I know it's a mistake. I'm an American citizen."

"Come into my office," he said.

Inside, with the door closed, he motioned her to a seat.

"You don't have to wait in line; I can give you the document. If I were you," he said, with a slight hesitation, "I would take it, and say nothing."

His face was very pink, very clean and well-shaven and his eyes were bright and sharp as a bird's. "I saw your name on the computer list and left it there. You were born in the former United Kingdom, weren't you?"

"Yes," she said, "but both my parents were American, working in the Foreign Service there. They died and I came to the States when I was two years old."

"Well, I suggest you leave things as they are. *We* will say nothing. With so many on the list, we can easily let it slip by. There may be, after all, many difficulties to come and things will be easier for you with a British card."

Martha frowned. "I don't want to be treated differently from any other American."

The Consul looked impatient. "Dear lady, you simply don't know what you are saying. I assume you wish to survive, and that you want your son to survive. A document means nothing to you now, but you will find things very different in the future. You've heard the statement of our Ambassador at the Security Council," he said, in a different tone. "Here, we can do very little. Let us do what we can."

He stared at the wall opposite his desk. There was a light rectangle on the paint where a picture had been taken down—a portrait of the Queen, no doubt. The British government had ordered that all representations of the Royal Family be removed from public buildings after the passage of their Citizenship Act. The blankness of the wall was reflected in the blankness of the Consul's expression, but he recovered himself and rose.

"I must see what I can do to expedite the distribution of these papers." He pressed a slip into her hand. "I hear that some of the United Nations garages are being changed into a food storage area and these slips will be honored there. I wish you luck, Mrs. Adams. Come and see me again, if I can help you in any way."

Outside the building, Martha hesitated. She had said she would stay in the office that day, but she was very reluctant to do so. At this time she should be with Buzz. Grand Central might have cleared a little. She walked to Lexington and got a taxi down to Forty-Second Street, but the street was so jammed she had to get out on the corner. The sidewalk was packed with people and she bumped into a girl leaving a hamburger place. It was Beverly Green, one of the girls from her section.

Martha apologized. "I hope Miriam has arrived," she said. "I want to go to my son in the country."

"She won't be coming back," Beverly replied.

In front of Grand Central, barricades had been set up, guarded by policemen. The station had been closed.

Beverly, usually rather loud and truculent, dropped her voice confidently. "Miriam and her husband went right out this morning, after the broadcast. They went to her sister in Canada. She told me they would catch the first plane. Just said good-bye to me real quick when I went over as they threw stuff in suitcases. Guess she was smart."

Martha wondered how many Americans the Canadians would let in. American refugees. Was that what people were going to do? Run?

"We were going to Hawaii next week," Beverly added. "But now I don't know. Even if they let us go, who wants to fly over the West? Say what they like I bet some of it's still cookin'. I'm not ready for the lilies and the casket."

> ". . . the lilies there that wave
> And weep above a nameless grave."

The lines, long forgotten, rang in Martha's head. She had forced away the thought of Josh. Now it returned with such violence that she had to bite her lips not to sob in the street and she tasted blood.

With a great effort of will she turned her mind to
Hawaii. What was happening there? The fleet was an-
chored at Pearl Harbor, surely. Would it just tamely
surrender? She bought an afternoon paper. The first
page was news of the official surrender. The editors
stated that the full terms of the treaty were not yet
available. Martha noticed the euphemism; it sounded
less abject than the truth, reminding her of the treaty
after the defeat in Vietnam. But the principal term was
certainly that all military forces, by order of the
Commander-in-Chief, were to lay down their arms. She
stood still, not noticing the people jostling her. Surely
the military would not lay down their arms.

The rest of the paper was full of the same stories as
the earlier edition, except for some update on local
news and jams at airports. Kennedy had been closed for
private travel at noon, Newark International was expe-
riencing some difficulty, La Guardia, still operating,
was under heavy usage and might be closed down later.
The Deputy Mayor had made a statement, pleading
with people to stay where they were and not to panic.
There was no danger of further atomic warfare, and the
Environmental Protection Agency, after an emergency
monitoring program, assured him that there was no
significant radiation on the winds from the West. On
the eastern seaboard, only Savannah had a level high
enough for evacuation plans to be considered. There
was no reason for people in the northeast to throw the
transportation system into chaos.

"The Deputy Mayor?" Martha questioned.

"Just Hizzoner's luck," Beverly said, pushing through
the crowd. "He's on vacation in Israel."

"I wonder how lucky," Martha said. Suddenly she
missed the feisty, outspoken Mayor.

The last item in the paper that caught her eye was
that the Bones concert would go on as scheduled. Johnny
Hogger, leader of the group, stated, "We have come to
the USA to give these concerts, and we are not going to

disappoint our fans. Our message of love and peace will
bring people together."

A woman, carrying two heavy suitcases and wearing a
backpack, trying to keep close to three small children,
began to cry.

Over on First Avenue the telephone trucks still waited.
Surely with all that equipment she could manage to get
through to Buzz.

"We'd better get back, I suppose," Martha said. There
was still a long line of people from the Secretariat
Building to the gate and beyond, inching very slowly
forward. "We can try to slip in the other way," Beverly
shrugged, "I'll take my turn," she said, in no hurry.
Martha couldn't blame her. She saw Beverly plunge
into talk with another girl from the office, but what
could they tell each other? No one knew anything. A lot
of the women, she noticed, were wearing chains with
the old anti-bomb emblem, which they called the peace
sign, and then she saw them on some of the younger
men, too, prominently displayed under their open-necked
shirts.

She walked up to Forty-Fourth Street, where the
doors were open, but the one guard was now reinforced
with two fellows. Giving a quick smile to the one who
had let her out, she stepped inside. She was about to
walk on when one of the guards caught her and held
her with his arm against the wall. Before Martha could
voice her indignation there came a sound of marching
feet. A column of soldiers filed in, carrying full equipment including field rifles. The dark khaki of their
uniforms was unfamiliar, as was the sword and shield
insignia on their caps. The officer murmured something
to a UN official who led the men to a stairway. Their
boots squelched and heavy splashes darkened their pants.
They must have come up river in launches to the dock
built recently with the reluctant consent of the City and
the Coast Guard.

"Sorry," the guard said, letting her go, and she made her way to the elevator bank.

A man stepped forward from the shadow of a broad column, where he had been observing the arrival of the soldiers, and spoke to the guard who had admitted Martha.

"Who was that woman?" he asked.

"A staff member," the guard said, apologetically. "A nice lady and there's a terrible crush in the front."

The observer was a pale, plump man with a large head whose hair had receded to a fringe round his skull, giving him a tonsured look. His monkish air was enhanced by a belly that his well-cut, grey business suit could not hide. With his heavy jowls and impassive expression, he was not, at first glance, intimidating, especially to the guard, a tall strong West Indian who did not revere authority.

"Your orders," the man said coldly, "were to permit no one to enter or leave through this doorway until the Special Force arrived. Do you understand that?" He turned to the other two. "This entrance will remain closed except for people with special documents about which you will be instructed."

He turned back to the West Indian. "You are relieved from duty at this post. Return to the guardroom."

The guard was about to argue, but something made him pause. It was not only his remembering who this man was: Virinsky, Under Secretary for Political and Security Council Affairs. Rumor had it that he was the senior KGB officer in the Organization. The guards called him, derisively, Father Three-Thumbs, because of the deformed, forked thumb on his left hand. The UN prostitutes called him something else.

No, it was a change in the demeanor of the man himself, a cold assumption of power that was now so daunting. If the guard had any doubts, the appearance of his own chief, usually assured enough, now pale with anxiety, was decisive. He left.

Virinsky murmured a few words into a walkie-talkie and stood, still and impassive, until two of the soldiers returned. After speaking a few words to them in Russian, he reverted to English to address the guards.

"These men are here to assist you, to make sure no unauthorized person enters here, or leaves. Now, what was the name of that woman?"

V

When the terms of the surrender—now referred to as "the Instrument"—were made known, most people seemed relieved. It referred purely to the military. Ships of the navy had been ordered to Soviet ports. All other commands, including installations overseas, were to be placed under the orders of the Soviet army.

Nothing as yet was said about any changes in the political structure or civilian life. The newspapers and the television commentators were cautiously cheerful. Carmody, still in the White House, made statements urging people to remain calm. Martha, in whom a sense of unreality persisted, thought they were all too calm. Except, of course, for the rowdies.

On the night of the surrender there had been a huge disturbance at the Bones concert, when several hundred fans, angry that they could not get tickets despite the publicity, broke the police barricades and attempted to enter the already full Coliseum, pulling those already seated from their chairs. A fight broke out and in the melée there were several hundred injuries and over thirty deaths. The next day the morning papers seemed glad to have this event to fill their pages, and they moralized on the general lawlessness.

Martha heard the news first on the radio. Her set was tuned to the program of a usually acerbic commentator, but that day Pete Greco did not explode with his usual fury. Instead, he read the Instrument in a calm, measured voice. "Any failure to comply completely and immediately with the terms of the Instrument will be considered an act of war."

He paused. "That is to say, I suppose, that we would again be under the threat of annihilation. This possibly accounts for the strange silence on the part of officials and members of our free press, while it is still free. Yet I find this silence pitiful and obscene."

Next a group of commercials were aired, then a traffic and weather report. Because of the confusion at the airports, all international flights were canceled until further notice. La Guardia had reopened, but passengers should be prepared to find no seats available on outgoing planes. Then there was the news, with the same story of the Bones concert that had been given earlier.

Greco's voice did not return. Martha turned from one station to another. Music, weather. A discussion panel, ". . . only the defeat of the military . . . perhaps the whole military-industrial complex." "Just as in Vietnam," the moderator remarked. "Exactly," her guest warmed up. "If we keep our heads there is no reason for our lives to be affected, except perhaps for the better. The ruinous expense of keeping up those so-called defense weapons—whose value is now shown for what it's worth—can be used for social programs, as so many of us have advocated in the past."

Another station, to which Martha normally did not listen, seemed to be having a celebration. Disgusted, unable to believe what she was hearing, she walked over to the Maynards' apartment on Park Avenue and had herself announced. The Maynards were not surprised to see her. Other people, it seemed, had dropped in without warning the night before. Suddenly Manhattan had become a village.

Birdie was already fully dressed in a tailored suit and a tiny hat that was for her a kind of trademark. Greg, who got up to give Martha a cup of coffee, was still wearing a silk dressing-gown and slippers and his hair was rumpled.

"The exchange won't open today," he said.

"I expect it will soon," Birdie said cheerfully.

Greg did not look convinced. He switched on the television.

"We lent them twelve billion last year," he said. "They must realize the value of the financial community."

There was a brief flash of President Carmody, together with the Soviet Ambassador, welcoming a delegation of Soviet officials at Andrews Air Force Base. Carmody looked somewhat recovered. The Soviet Ambassador, a large, chubby man, was smiling. The officials were expressionless. The cameras moved off quickly.

"The delegation was small," the anchorman in New York said approvingly. "It looks as though there will be little interference."

"Why did the cameras leave Andrews?" Martha said, fuming. "What was going on there? And why aren't the crews out at McGuire? I saw big Soviet planes heading in there yesterday, and if they weren't troop transports, I'll be very much surprised."

"Oh, Martha, you are always so suspicious of the Russians," Birdie said.

"Well, I know a uniformed soldier when I see one, I think you'll allow," Martha replied. "And an armed column of Soviet troops marched into the UN yesterday. In wet boots; they'd been brought up by water."

"It sounds like one of those panic rumors from the

First World War," Birdie looked amused. "Russians with snow on their boots, wasn't it?"

Greg was more practical. "You'd expect them to move in some troops to make sure the terms of the surrender were complied with. The fact that they didn't take out all the military airfields suggests that they intend to use them."

"But nobody's saying anything. Nobody's *doing* anything," Martha burst out. "I think Greco was taken off the air this morning for talking about the surrender and . . ."

"Oh, him," Birdie broke in. She had collected her bag and was getting her briefcase ready for her office. "I'm surprised he's lasted this long. There have been a lot of complaints about him. He's one of the rabble-rousing warmongers that got us into this, in my opinion. Terrifying the Soviet Union with the constant talk of rearming. You'd think Reagan was still President. The owners of that station certainly won't want to start off on the wrong foot."

Martha put her coffee cup down, murmured something and left.

Birdie looked up from her briefcase over to her husband, who was twiddling a pencil aimlessly over a blank sheet of paper.

"Poor Martha," she said. "Repressed hysteria. She didn't say a word about Josh, but she must know. Can't face the truth, so she has to be angry at the external world."

Her husband usually stopped listening when she analyzed their acquaintances, but this time he responded.

"Are you sure Josh was working on a missile site?"

He glanced at the newspaper where the stock market pages usually were. For a moment they looked normal, but the date above the columns was that of the day before the surrender.

"He was at Grand Forks," she said briefly. "But his firm has been working on site construction for the Air

Force since the Robert Moses projects ended. No wonder there was never any money for civic improvements,
with everything going to the military. I couldn't get a
taxi last night, and I tried the subway. You wouldn't
believe how bad it's got. I came up again and managed
to get on a bus. That's why I got home so late. D'you
think it would be better if you drove me downtown,
Greg?"

Husband and wife discussed transportation and domestic matters and forgot about Martha until Birdie was
leaving.

"Poor Martha," Birdie said. "It's going to be tough
for her."

"She'll get over it. Widows do."

The thought of Martha as a widow took his mind for a
moment from that ominous page of newsprint. He recalled their last game as partners on the grass court of
his house out at Quogue. Her eyes had gleamed a
green excitement after her winning shot and she had
laughed, that rather husky but pleasant laugh.

"Not only Josh," Birdie said, hardly noticing his last
words. She had never suspected Greg with Martha,
though there weren't that many women she felt confident about. It was one reason why she had kept up the
friendship with the country-loving, staid Adamses. "It's
this whole thing. The trouble is, she won't be adaptable. You'll see," she said as she hurried off.

Her husband had to agree. It was just as well, in the
circumstances, that he had married a woman who *was*
adaptable. They were probably all going to have to
adapt a lot more than they liked and quickly at that.

Martha still had no luck with the telephone in her
efforts to reach Buzz. The Deputy Mayor kept asking
people to stop trying to use the system and give it a
chance to get back to normal. Her office phone was
replaced by an intercom, and another instrument that
went through a switchboard.

"Like they had years ago," Lucy Kander told her. She looked rather rumpled, as if she had spent the night on a friend's sofa. The Path tunnels had been closed due to panicking New Yorkers, crowding and fighting on the trains. The buses could not cross the George Washington Bridge for the stalled traffic.

Martha found where the switchboard was now located, and spoke to the operator.

"We have the lines here," the girl explained. "We can make calls and we have direct linkage to places of importance, for our use only. But a lot of localities are blocked off by their own usage."

"You mean I could get Moscow but not Connecticut," Martha said.

"Well, we can get the Governor's mansion, Mrs. Adams. We have links with all the governor's mansions now and the state executive buildings. It's called Regional Linkage. Hartford is Region One. Would you like me to get Hartford for you?"

"No, thank you," Martha said. Buzz would be at Robby's in Litchfield, over twenty miles from Hartford. In a couple of days things should quiet a little. She would be able to get a car. Or perhaps a train. Lights winked across the switchboard, teasing her mind with the memory of another call she must make. Then she remembered Josh. She was supposed to call Josh about the life insurance. *Life insurance.*

Her eyes were blind with tears and she bumped into Madame Paul on her way back to the office. The Frenchwoman, oblivious to her distress, handed her a slip of paper. "A directive has come through, stating that all Secretariat employees will take their luncheons within the building. Too much time was lost yesterday by the people who went out. Arrangements have been made to accommodate everyone. You will see the assigned times listed."

"Most of the staff already do eat in the cafeteria," Martha said, as she looked at the staggered hours. A small thing, but the girls wouldn't like it. They couldn't eat together.

"So it will make little difference," Madame Paul said. "And it is just as well. The restaurants are running out of food; suppliers are having trouble getting through. There were fights this morning at the coffee shops around Grand Central. By the way, Mrs. Adams, I thank you for coming to our assistance while you are on leave. You are still entitled to your full six weeks. In a day or two, we can make arrangements so that you can leave for at least a week, and as a token of appreciation for your help, I will arrange that you get a travel pass immediately. They will be issued to all Secretariat employees as soon as possible. There are trains running, but just now seats are only for people on work with priority status."

She glided off.

So that was what was happening at the station. Martha remembered the woman with the three children. Much as she wanted to go, she felt like a collaborator.

That night the American public was treated to a videotape of the Joint Chiefs, together with Carmody as Commander-in-Chief, conducting a Marshal of the Soviet Union into the War Room of the Pentagon. Surprisingly, General Cunningham, who was supposed to be in Washington, was not visible and Admiral Parker was represented by his second-in-command. Perhaps the Admiral was at sea, but where was Cunningham, the Air Force Chief? Could he have escaped in the command plane that was always airborne? Unlikely. The victorious enemy would have shot it down.

"This is like Lee handing over his sword at Appomattox," the newscaster said solemnly. "Perhaps today, like that day, will be the beginning of a new, better era. Lincoln saved the Union. Perhaps President Carmody has saved the world."

Martha wondered how long Carmody would last. She said as much to her neighbor, a Mrs. Furness, whom she met in the hall the next morning. The woman sighed, the pinched, anxious look on her face oddly at variance with her well-groomed hair and the rich elegance of her clothes. At the end of summer she wore a suit of linen and silk printed with leaves of bronze, and thin-strapped lizard sandals of the same color. "The Vogue Woman," Josh had always called her. He had never got to know the neighbors.

"Oh, I do hope we have no more killing. After all, what else could the President have done? I have a nephew in the Navy," she added. "I believe he was at sea. What will happen to those boys, Mrs. Adams? If they do sail into Soviet ports, will the Russians send them home?"

Martha knew it was unlikely, but did not have the heart to say so. The New York apartment building was quiet. Many people who had been away for the summer had not returned. Martha found herself glad to talk to this neighbor, though they had never conversed before except for a few words during a Red Cross drive. Her friends now seemed far away without the telephone and even those in the city, like the Maynards, had become hard to reach. Last night cabs had been scarce, buses overloaded, and the police had warned would-be passengers of unruly mobs at many subway stops. Martha herself had seen fighting in the streets. Not with the Russians, who were scarcely yet in evidence. New Yorkers were fighting each other.

"And can you believe the shops," Mrs. Furness went on. "I'm expecting my husband back from Cincinnati and I went to Gristede's yesterday and they had almost nothing, and the other supermarkets were just as bad. Panic buying, the Deputy Mayor says, but the manager of Gristede's said that supplies haven't been coming in . . ."

The two women parted and Martha made her way to the UN, walking more warily than usual; the short, unexpected bursts of violence were frightening. Two cars, unable to pass because of double-parked vehicles on either side rammed each other with a sickening crash of bumpers and grilles. Neither driver was badly hurt, but one had a bloody nose and hurled himself on the other in a mindless rage. A drunk woman staggered from a doorway and clutched Martha's shoulder. Her breath was rank and her red-rimmed eyes glared in hatred. "It's your kind that got us into this mess, you and your kind."

Martha pulled away. Your kind. What did the woman mean? A group of teenagers were in a wild melée. This violence would be a good excuse for martial law. And who would administer it? Her mind went back to the unexplained absence of General Cunningham and Admiral Parker. She wondered, with a swift pang of hope, if Admiral Parker was somewhere in an atomic submarine, perhaps gliding into the Black Sea or the Gulf of Finland, to fire a missile or make a demand on behalf of the United States.

But Admiral Parker was not at sea. He, General Cunningham, and other senior officers were being held under heavy guard at Andrews, pending arrangements being completed at Bethesda Naval Hospital. Among the Russian "officials" already flown in was a small but efficient group of doctors, all trained at Moscow's Serbsky Institute in "socio-psychiatric" medicine.

─── VI ───

At the office Martha had a surprise. Seated at Miriam's desk was a Vietnamese girl, neatly dressed, composedly typing, with a large stack of forms already growing at her side. It was not yet nine o'clock. Madame Paul looked in at the door.

"Oh, Mrs. Adams, this is Nguyen Thu Thuy. She will be taking Mrs. Weiss's place. You will find her completely fluent in English and French, and she knows the work. She has been with the World Health Organization in Geneva. If you fill her in on the details, you can probably get away tomorrow."

"But when Mrs. Weiss returns?" Martha said. She had not been officially informed that Miriam had left the country, and after all, no one knew what might have happened on her attempted flight.

"She deserted her post at a time of crisis," Madame Paul said. "She has been dismissed."

Martha frowned. Miriam might find that she needed her job badly.

"Surely, Madame Paul," she retorted, "these are exceptional circumstances and our work is not urgent. Besides, we have never dismissed anyone for a day or two's absence. Procedure would forbid it."

"All our work is urgent, Mrs. Adams," Madame Paul said, coldly. "Procedures are being revised. And American citizens in this Organization are particularly required to show loyalty and diligence if they are to remain."

Before Martha could reply, she glided off with only a slight tapping of her heels on the marble floors. Beverly Green swore under her breath, "Old cat." It was the usual resentment of the young worker against the sternly-efficient Frenchwoman. The hardly-veiled threat had not been understood, yet it puzzled Martha a little. The Russians undoubtedly would control the Organization now. Madame Paul, if she wished to keep her post, would probably have to knuckle under. But this was very quick. Like the order for the ration cards.

"I'm going for coffee," Beverly said, although it was neither her usual break time, nor the time slotted on the new list. Martha wondered if the girl would be allowed to enter the employees' coffee bar. Probably not. The public one in the basement had been closed. Beverly would have to go outside. "Don't be too long," she said. Usually, she would have said nothing about a small infraction of the rule, but now she had an impulse to warn the younger woman. Am I getting like everyone else, she wondered. Going along. Playing it safe. Making it easy for the new masters.

At eleven o'clock a memo came round. Ration cards would be honored today. Attached was a list of times when cardholders could go down to the parking garage. Beverly, who came back late, missed her turn. She was already indignant about her treatment. "When I came back in those creeps wouldn't let me pass. I've never seen any of them before. They grabbed me like I was a bundle of washing or something, hands all over me, and hung on until someone came down from Madame Paul's office. I want to sign a complaint . . ."

She caught Martha's warning glance. "Well, so what? The Russians always say they want to help the workers, don't they? Last year their delegates said they favored our request for a cost-of-living raise."

The third level of the garage had been partitioned. Martha, presenting her paper from the British Consulate, was directed into a section where canned goods were piled on a counter and baskets of produce sat on the concrete floor still smelling of gas. A young man wearing a business suit and heavy eyeglasses handed her a thin paper sack bulging with heavy cans and some green stuff, inexpertly packed. Her preference was not to be consulted, it seemed. "How much do I owe?" she asked. "It'll be deducted," the young man explained. She saw him make a check against a number on a computer readout.

As she went out she passed the length of the garage and met two of her girls coming out of the American section, with the same kind of goods but in much smaller bags. A man walked past with a large leg of lamb sticking out of his paper sack, next to a carton of eggs and there was some murmuring, quickly hushed. Martha took the food with her, though she could hardly eat. It would keep and it would probably be needed. Since the morning of the surrender she had hardly been able to hold food down and had been living on canned soup at home and coffee and croissants at the UN. Even the act of putting a toothbrush in her mouth brought on nausea.

But food was obviously going to be a problem. When she tried to buy cream in shop after shop there was none to be had. A supermarket manager, whom she had known for three years, told her that although most of the shops had tried a voluntary rationing scheme it would be of no use unless supplies started coming in. "I'm not opening for customers tomorrow, but I'll be here with two of the men to take deliveries, if any arrive."

He looked at Martha's paper bag. "Do you mind if I ask where you got that, Mrs. Adams?"

"Of course not," she said. "I work at the UN and they've collected emergency supplies for the staff."

Martha felt uncomfortable carrying the bag while other customers drifted up and down the aisles, staring at the shelves empty of almost all foods. There were still housewares, pot-holders, spatulas, egg-whisks dangling from hooks, light bulbs in cartons, kitchen scissors and packets of needles and thread. Racks by the checkout counter still held magazines and a stack of astrology books.

"Only for the staff, and the diplomats, I suppose," the manager said. "Well, the days of the locust are upon us. Mrs. Adams, I suggest you get home quickly with that food. Let me bag it for you."

Deftly he put the telltale sack into a sturdy bag with handles and covered the top with rolls of toilet paper.

"Maybe you'll make it now," he said. "Good-bye."

He spoke as though he didn't expect to see her again. Looking back, she saw the gates going up outside the windows, the customers leaving, and the doors being closed, locked and padlocked.

Outside her neighbor's door she paused a moment, mindful of Janet Furness's husband returning, perhaps, from Cincinnati. She rang the bell, to see if she needed food. The woman ran to the door, red-eyed, and though gracious to Martha, was obviously disappointed that the arrival was not her husband. "Well, I didn't really expect him. There are still no civilian flights coming in. Though everyone says there was no real trouble out that way. You haven't heard anything, have you?"

"No," Martha said. "Not even a rumor."

"So I'm sure it's O.K. But it's awful not being able to talk . . . I don't know whether to try to get down to Bucks County or not. This morning I walked all the way to the 59th Street bridge, because I heard the farmers' market was still there. The farmers get in somehow. I paid ten dollars for a lettuce. I said I thought it was ridiculous but the farmer said there are rumors that the money will be changed and it won't be any good anyway. And he said it's getting harder to get gas and he doesn't know how much longer he'll get in. He's seen a lot of people just walking out of the city, carrying their things, but no one wants them up in Mount Vernon or New Rochelle. If Phil doesn't get back soon I think I might go to my brother-in-law in Saddle River. That's not so far and I'm afraid to be here alone. When I came back from the market two boys jumped me and took the lettuce and my purse."

Martha gave her what comfort she could, including some of the cans, frankfurters, and corned beef, the kind of food that neither woman would have touched a week before. Martha herself had some cream of tomato soup from a supply she had kept in the apartment for emergencies. The taste, reminding her of childhood, was oddly soothing. Then she lay in bed in the New York night that was never really dark, thinking that tomorrow she would go home, to the country, to Buzz. She did not think she would return. The words of the supermarket manager stung. She had no wish to be part of a special group, a locust.

New York had long been just two steps ahead of chaos. It was no wonder that now New Yorkers should be concentrating on personal survival; there was no time to take true measure of the calamity. Up in the country things would be quieter and there were friends who would know what was going on. Colonel Fairfield should be at home. He had recently retired after a long posting in West Germany. And Bill Webster, an old friend and a US Senator. He would know what stomach for resistance there was in the Senate. There were plenty of anti-Carmody Senators.

The next day at the office the atmosphere was strained.

Beverly did not appear. Madame Paul's assistant told Martha that she had been dismissed for insubordination and rowdiness. A Cuban girl was sent in to take her place, and in the afternoon three more Cuban girls arrived. There were not enough desks and chairs, and three American girls were told to give up their seats and explain the work to the new employees.

"Rearrangement," Madame Paul said, but no one believed her. Two of the girls cried and Lucy Kander, who had been there longer than Martha, refused to explain her work and left. As she swung out of the door she gave Martha a look that made her feel uncomfortable, as the supermarket manager had done. Madame Paul's private office, separate from the big room that housed Personnel, was small and plain. Martha followed her there, ignoring her assistant outside.

"Do we have to have these changes?" she asked. "Miss Kander is one of our best workers."

Madame Paul was seated, her long, thin hands resting on her desk top in complete composure. "It is not in my discretion," she replied. "The orders for a change in the number of American nationals per office came from a higher level. And Miss Kander, by her behavior today is obviously one of the least adaptable to the new situation."

A flare of temper shook Martha for a moment out of the numbness that enveloped her. "According to the Instrument of Surrender," she pointed out, "the new situation, as you call it, is supposed to affect only the military."

Madame Paul's thin eyebrows were raised.

"We are not discussing the military surrender of the United States, Mrs. Adams," she said. "This is a world body. But now our tasks have been much increased. The Secretary-General is lending his good offices to promote the civil recovery after the Soviet strike. As to which nationals could serve best in any capacity is a matter between policy-making and the requirements of

Personnel. But while you are here," she handed Martha a document case. "That contains your travel papers, including a WHO special pass. Secretariat people will get passes in due course, but I hurried that through for you personally. Thu Thuy will be able to take over. I hope to see you back a week from Monday."

Martha took the documents and left. She wondered what had happened to Madame Paul's predecessor. Those who remembered her said she was a woman with understanding and compassion.

Madame looked after her speculatively. Then she took a leather-bound book from her desk and opened it to a half-filled sheet. There, under the names Miriam Weiss and Lucy Kander, she wrote *Martha Adams*. She paused for a moment and added the note, British. Then she looked up. The porters had come to move her personal belongings and her files to her new quarters. She went ahead, examined the large corner room with a view of the river from two sides, the sizeable outer offices, and nodded. Two men brought in a fine Aubusson rug and unrolled it, placing it to her satisfaction. This would be a suitable accommodation for the performance of her new duties. When her desk came, she put the leather book in her top drawer and locked it. Soon she went to report at the office of Constantin Virinsky.

Grand Central was still barricaded on 42nd Street and on Vanderbilt Avenue. Martha showed a policeman her travel pass, and he caught her elbow and took her aside, out of earshot of the people still waiting, questioning, at the barrier. "There is an entrance on the overpass," he said. "You can get on it from Park Avenue. Be careful walking; stay close to the buildings. You will see a door on the left-hand side; there'll be an officer there. Just show this to him."

He handed the paper back. Martha found her way around to the ramp and then walked south on the elevated roadway. A few taxi-drivers zoomed past, snapping at her heels. Three police officers stood guarding a doorway she had never noticed before. One of them examined her pass and gave a quick look to the man at his side.

He spoke anxiously. "World Health—is there trouble, lady? Radiation sickness, maybe?"

"Not that I've heard," she said, and saw the relief in their faces. Honesty compelled her to add, "But my office hasn't received much data yet. Too much confusion."

As she said it, she wondered why she had not received any information. If the switchboard could reach the governors' mansions, some of the new data should be coming in. Perhaps another office was receiving it first. One of the officers guided her down the stairs and through a doorway that led onto an upper level of Grand Central. It was familiar. There was the café where she had sometimes drunk a cup of coffee or a glass of wine; now it was closed. The officer turned to go, and then looked back. "Any other sicknesses that you know about?"

"Nothing unusual, but as I said, it's too early yet. But there's no reason to expect any," she added, with a mental proviso, *if we've been told the truth about the limit of the strike*, "once the food supplies start moving."

The man gazed at her. He had a square, Irish face; not too many like that in the NYPD any more. "I hope to God—I've got three kids, and four boxes of cereal left in the house—and that's it. There's not a market around Bay Parkway with anything in it."

Martha had brought two tins of the frankfurters to add to her emergency stock. Taking them from her bag, she pressed them into the man's hands. "I hope things get better. They have to feed the police—but take these."

She walked down to the main hall with his thanks in her ears, still feeling oddly treacherous. It was a strange scene before her. The large, lighted photograph of white sails on a blue lake at the east end blazed over an expanse of floor, dimly lit, with only a scattering of passengers. There were no lines at the ticket counters. The betting windows, of course, were closed, as were the shops.

Her train was waiting at the track, but there were remarkably few people on it. Only some business men of the usual sort, commuters carrying briefcases, taking the train home rather than risking the roads. One of them carried a newspaper she hadn't yet seen. The headline read, CARMODY TO STEP DOWN? She sat directly behind two such commuters, just to be near somebody. Perhaps to talk . . . but they were deep in their own conversation as they waited for the train to start.

". . . no chance Mary will be there to meet the train at Westport. I couldn't get through and I didn't know this morning when I would be back. But the 7:35 isn't running tonight. And there was no sense staying in the office anyway. Not much I can do with half the staff missing . . ."

His companion nodded. "I thought the passes would be a good idea. Stop the panic rush. But it's no good giving them to the executives if the workers can't get in. Most of our people come from Jersey, the Island or Westchester—not many New Yorkers any more. I wish the board had moved the offices to Stamford, I've proposed it half a dozen times. I suppose someone will make travel arrangements soon."

"I'd like to know who. No one seems to be in charge at City Hall, and try to find out who's running this railroad!"

He looked round and Martha caught a glimpse of an irritated, well-fleshed face. "This line has been a disgrace for years. Look at those windows, they haven't been washed in a decade. And Mary will probably expect to meet the 7:35. It's a hell of a walk to Springview Drive and I've brought all these papers home."

The other man grunted. "At least you're in the right business. No matter what, people always need oil. But I don't see anyone rushing to buy cars. Never any good news for us."

"Detroit might be getting different kinds of orders. Wouldn't surprise me at all." He looked at his watch. "We're five minutes late. How did you get your pass?"

"Kay, my secretary, found that top execs were getting them. She's worth a million, that girl. Supposed to be from someplace downtown, in the World Trade Center, but it's so much grief getting down there, they set up a booth in the UN building. First time that place is making itself useful. But they wouldn't give it to Kay; I had to march over myself."

"You were lucky. Tom Lewis went over with me. But they wouldn't give him a pass: publishers not on the essential list. He was screaming away about their educational line, but the girl behind the desk came from Sri Lanka or somewhere and I don't think she understood much. He went back to that fifty-story, glass tower his company owns with his tail between his legs. Says Caravelle is just about out of fresh food."

"Maybe he'll get rid of that publisher's paunch before things settle down. And it's true when you come to think of it. God knows, most of the stuff his house prints isn't exactly what you'd call in the national interest. You smoking again?"

"Nerves acting up. For me, I wouldn't have most of Lewis's books in the house. But he did tell me a funny one about the phones. The Deputy Mayor was screaming that none of the City Hall lines were working, and somebody told him priority went to essential manufacture. So the municipal authorities have zilch, but a steambath down on Greenwich Avenue called the Steel Balls was allocated six lines."

The train began moving. "Say," his companion said. "The bar car is on. What about coming back for a drink?"

The two men walked back through the car. The train got up speed quickly, much faster than usual. A new engine driver? Martha wondered. They would have to slow down sharply at 125th Street. They came up out of the tunnel still at a good speed. The name of the station went past quickly and at the same time a thump came from overhead, and another and then another. Outside the smeared window was a dark shape. A foot in sneakers, a leg in jeans, was dangling from the car roof. As the train sped on, the foot kicked with a sickening thud against the glass and the boy fell to lie somewhere out of sight.

Martha screamed. Several men in the car looked round.

"The kids have been doing that," one man offered, "since they closed the station. I guess there's a couple up there."

Martha was running to the emergency brake. "That boy must be hurt . . ."

The conductor appeared suddenly and caught her arm.

"We can't stop the train, lady. He'll be taken care of. The cops'll pick him up. They try to keep the kids out but somehow they get up on the station roof and bore through. Ingenious young devils. Not that there's anywhere for them to go. They'd only be held and sent back when they got off."

The boy might have been Buzz's age. "What's the *sense* of all this," she cried. "Why not let them on? There's plenty of room."

"Not for me to say, ma'am," the conductor replied. He was an older man, and he looked unhappy. He clipped Martha's ticket. "Change at Bridgeport."

Martha, shaken, sat silently until she reached Bridgeport. Her legs were trembling slightly when she stepped onto the platform to wait for the connecting train. The harbor that lay below the station was more crowded and busier than she had ever seen it before. Two large merchantmen were being loaded while seamen were at work, hanging on the scaffolding, painting out the names. Both ships now flew the Soviet flag.

Not far off, the *Murmansk* was riding the choppy waters. With its twenty-four guns it looked menacing enough but many of its crew were gawping like tourists. A quarrel broke out on one of the merchantmen as a loading crane dipped perilously over the men working on the side. The sound of cursing between seamen and longshoremen rose to the station platform along with the shrieks of offended gulls. The single car pulled in; the passengers boarded, and the little train jerked out of the station on its way to the Naugatuck valley. The passengers complained about the grime as they always did.

— VII —

It came as a relief, at Naugatuck, to see Josh's Chevrolet still sitting under the trees in the small space in the parking lot reserved for passengers. And there was still gas in the tank. It was lucky, after all, that she hadn't been able to park in Waterbury. That city had long been plagued with vandalism and now even this shabby old car might be tempting. The newspaper office, which took up most of the station building, was already closed for the day. She was alone. No other passenger had gone so far and the fashionable, commuter towns were behind her. She swung out through the town with its long-shuttered factories onto the road that led to Bantam.

The small towns and the countryside showed no signs as yet of the frantic chaos that there had been in the city. The only reminder of the disaster was the sign up on many gas stations which read, "Out of gas." The general store at the crossroads was closed, but then it would be at this hour. The advertising that covered the windows screened the shelves, full or bare. The grade

of the road increased; water fell in a sparkling rush over
the dam, and in the center of the reservoir a flock of fat
ducks floated in formation. Soon she made the turn,
and to her right was the lake, glistening in the last light
of the afternoon sun, blue and rippled only by the
breeze. No boats were out; no humans were in sight.
The houses were hidden by the trees along the shore,
still in full leaf, the rich green of the maples bordered
by the dark spires of the pines reaching up from the
hills. For one moment it could have been the lake as
the Tunxis Indians saw it, before the white man came.
It was the lake that Josh had loved, and her throat
tightened.

Then the houses came into view and it was time to
turn off the road. Two cars were parked before the
Webster place; the Senator was probably at home. Tomorrow she would go over but now . . .

The white house, with its two red barns still stood.
Home. The back door was unlocked, but no one was
about. An empty glass, washed clean, was draining at
the kitchen sink. She walked up the drive and over the
grass to the big barn. The heavy door stuck a little, she
pulled hard, and there in the gloom was Buzz. Slices of
light came through the cracks between the old planks,
picking out his sandy head, craned forward, the metal
pieces of the earphones, motes of dust and Buzz's sturdy,
young shoulders in his thin, denim shirt, and the slight
sheen of his bare forearms, firm and freckled. He was
wrapt in concentration before his tranceiver, an acolyte
before his altar. For a moment she wanted to cry.
Instead she sneezed and Buzz turned.

He gave her his usual, laconic greeting. "Hi, Mom."

She blew her nose, hard. "I thought you were with
Robbie," she said.

"I was. But I came home thinking you might manage
to get up. I hear things are a mess, down in the city."

Of course. The ham radio. Buzz murmured something into the microphone and his mother caught a

glimpse of his expression, a blank innocence that suggested he was up to something.

He gave her a hug that could have been casual, but Buzz wasn't given to hugging.

"They took out Grand Forks."

"Yes." She could say no more. Buzz knew what that meant. For a moment she kept him close, tears pricking her eyes.

"Hungry, Mom?" He eased away and went to the kitchen. "The electricity is still on so the stuff in the freezer's good. Over on the other side of Litchfield they've been having a power cut, nobody knows why."

Together they put a meal on the dining room table as they had so often; hamburgers, salad and squash from the Swenson farm down the road. Usually, Martha talked and Buzz listened, or didn't listen. But that evening it was Buzz who talked.

"I think it's a line, all that stuff about so few people killed. I haven't raised a soul in Omaha, and you can make a darned good guess what happened there."

There was no way Omaha could have escaped, even if SAC had been carefully targeted. But Martha felt sick just the same, picturing the stricken city. They had left the lamp unlit and their reflection in the looking glass over the sideboard was dim and strange as if they had moved into another world. A world where they sat and talked of the destruction of Omaha.

Buzz was putting a pickle on his hamburger, placing it exactly in the center as he liked to do. Of all people, she had expected Buzz to match her feeling of outrage. Yet, she remembered, he had always been a self-contained child. She had never been sure what was behind his preoccupation.

"You'd think someone would have done something," she said bitterly. "The airborne bombers, the armed subs. They couldn't have got them all. Surely they didn't all just turn themselves in to Russian ports."

Josh had said that of the submarines at sea, most

would survive any Soviet attack. But he had also said, she remembered, that they carried small inaccurate warheads, useless against military targets. Only the *Ohio*, the lone remaining carrier of the Trident missile . . .

Buzz glanced up at her. "I got through early that morning to a ham in Stockholm. Couldn't raise him after that. But he'd heard rumors that something had happened alright. Wasn't sure exactly what. I guess one of ours got through. But Carmody signed us over anyway."

She didn't have to ask what morning. One ship, or perhaps one aircraft had attacked. Ignoring the surrender, or not waiting for it. Or maybe there was just an error on the communication lines. What had happened to the missile carrier? Were there any others?

"I'm not hearing much from abroad now," Buzz said. "Either the guys are scared or there's been a crackdown."

"Perhaps you'd better move your stuff down to the cellar under the big barn," Martha said.

Buzz gave her another look.

"You can always run up an antenna when you need it," she suggested. "From the road no one would even realize that cellar's there. Not many people are likely to go tramping through the long grass in the back."

After dinner Buzz took the big jug down to the Swenson's to get more milk. They were already in bed but he could help himself from the milk room. While she put it away, he went back to his equipment and she didn't see him again until he tapped on the door of her room, hours later.

"Same as I've been hearing all day," he told her. "Rumors of fighting on the Mexican border. They say there are Cuban troops in Florida. Trainloads of bodies are being moved from towns and villages round the strike areas. Robbie raised a guy near Little Rock who saw them himself. A kid near St. Louis saw troops moving, our troops, but it was just a burial detail. Some people are sick in Duluth."

It was the first real news she'd heard since the surrender. She lay in bed that night, the old brass bed she had shared with Josh and which had belonged before that to his parents. Watching the moon come up and listening to the frogs quacking in the pond, it was as though life were still normal, as though Omaha and Grand Forks were not charnel houses. Later she could not have said for whom she cried that night: for all the nameless dead, or simply for Josh, alone.

The feeling of coming home did not last. She was moved to go to Sunday morning service, but it was no comfort. The Adamses had always been supporters of the church, but Josh had disliked the present incumbent, more politician than clergyman, and their attendance had lessened. That Sunday was no different. The sermon could have come from Carmody in a cassock. No one seemed to want to fight.

The beginning of the fall term at schools and colleges was postponed, but Buzz disappeared most of the time to Robbie's. Unaffected by the gas shortage, he went off on his bicycle. Martha took to using her old bicycle to pay visits, but to her dismay the neighbors, whom she thought of as more independent-minded than New Yorkers and certainly less detached from the affairs of the United States than the officials at the UN, seemed just as acquiescent. "Nothing to be done," was the general response.

She hurried over to see Bill Webster, who was getting ready to go back to Washington and didn't have much time to talk.

"I have to be there, of course. There's a lot of work to be done. Bristow has to nominate a new Vice-President and we all have to feel out the new way of things."

Carmody had resigned. His health had broken down under the strain of the crisis, his staff had said, and it certainly seemed likely. That had made Vice-President Bristow, quite a popular former Senator but an old stalwart of the left, the next President. Perhaps Webster hoped to be chosen as Vice-President. Vice-President of what?

She stood in his study, a pleasant room that had once been the sewing room of the Webster house. As he stuffed papers hurriedly into a briefcase, his handsome head bent over like a clerkly lion, he seemed no different from what he was in his campaign, vigorous, purposeful, impatient. Josh, an old friend, had always liked him well enough, though he raised his eyebrows sometimes at Webster's politics. They were not only old schoolmates, but skiing and boating enthusiasts, which had kept their friendship alive.

"Might be just as well that Bristow is President. I'm going to see him at Blair House. I spoke to him from Hartford. Connecticut has been very lucky, by the way. They could have taken out New London, but they laid mines instead. Neutralizing, they call it. I think Bristow will get along with them better than Carmody. Carmody was always wishy-washy, but they'll trust Bristow."

"I daresay they will. He was always for unilateral disarmament, wasn't he?"

"Well, Martha," Webster looked up, his face a little flushed, perhaps from his exertions. "I know that you and Josh always disagreed with Bristow's group, but now you can see there was a lot in what they said. I mean, when it came to the point, we could do nothing anyway. And Carmody, though the man was always a bit of a fool, was right. What was the sense of having the country blown to cinders, just for the satisfaction of doing the same to the Soviets and murdering every last child in a city like Vladivostock? My God, I remember when scientists first hypothesized a cobalt bomb, until they found it might tip the earth off its axis, and poison the winds of the world. The country will get together under Bristow and make the best of a bad job . . ."

His car was waiting and he was off. His wife came in to offer Martha a cup of coffee. She looked out of the window. "It looks so stark out there," she said. "It used to be lovely, with all the elms. There were as many birds as you have, Martha. Bill is always meaning to plant some more trees, but he never has the time and I don't like to have it done without him here. I wonder if they'll have a session this autumn or if he'll be back. The Carmodys have already left Washington, I hear."

Cynthia Webster was a domestic woman, who hated Washington, but always got to hear the gossip. "When Bill came back from Hartford, he said that Bristow wasn't going to move into the White House. He's going to get some repair work done first and anyway, you know how he likes to seem the simple man. Dolly Bristow will be furious."

"The Trumans did that," Martha said. "But I thought the White House was in good condition now."

"Magnificent, I would say," Mrs. Webster agreed. "But that's politics."

"There are Russians in the White House," Buzz told her, that night. "Marshal somebody and a lot of soldiers. And some other guys."

Soon it was announced that President Bristow was opening part of the White House to accommodate members of the Armistice Commission. Among the members were Marshal Borunukov of the Soviet Union and Raoul Perez of Cuba. Little was known of Raoul Perez, though there was speculation that he was a military man. In fact, only two men in the western world knew who he was: Marshal Borunukov in Washington, and Virinsky in the United Nations building in New York.

—— VIII ——

The Swensons, an old couple, had never talked politics, except local matters, but Henry was moved to say, "Russkies in the White House. Wonder what my old man would have said."

He went on with his milking. His hands were red and swollen with arthritis but gentle enough still as he cleaned the cow's udders with warm water which smelt slightly of disinfectant. The cow stood placidly in her stall as he attached the milking machine, flicking her tail at lazy intervals against the droning flies. Martha remembered that old Karl Swenson had been an immigrant from Sweden; his people knew the Russians well. She remembered him as a rough yet courtly old farmer who had much admired her mother-in-law and brought her gifts of hard cider as strong as brandy, and sheaves of roses. The roses were all wild now, turned to a briar patch. Henry could only do so much and his sons had no interest in farming. They had moved away long since.

"I wonder if I'll be able to sell off some of the land," he speculated.

It was natural he should think of that, Martha told herself. The zoning regulations had forbidden the selling off of parcels of the Swenson farm, which was extensive. He could sell all of it or none, and Henry, who did not want to give up his home, had felt trapped with the acres he could not farm and without the cash he badly needed. The rent he received from letting the land hardly paid his taxes and he had been furious with everyone from the local Selectman to the Federal Government, all of whom he blamed.

"People are offering a good price for milk," he told Martha. "And for squash and onions. Now them fancy supermarkets are getting cleaned out, they're looking for local grown. All those folks who never looked for anything off our land except sweet corn."

Martha hurriedly offered to pay the higher sum; the Swensons had always sold their milk to their neighbors at the same price the big dairies paid.

Henry shook his head and nodded towards the house. "Betty has something for you. Why don't you stop by?"

Betty, surprisingly, was listening to the radio. Martha had never seen her sitting down at that hour in the morning. Even now her hands were working; a long knitted scarf was taking shape.

"We'll need warm things this winter," she said. Her face was pale under the remnants of her summer tan. "Martha, my Chris was out west. I'd had a letter from Nevada. What do you think?"

Chris was a drifter, and might have been anywhere. Martha tried to offer such comfort as she could.

"Was Josh . . ." Betty asked haltingly and stopped when she saw Martha's face. "I kept this back for you." She pressed a basket of vegetables into her arms. "There's some cheese there that I've been making. It's not the best but you can fix a sandwich." She disappeared for a moment into her big, slate-floored pantry and came out with two loaves. "I've baked these for us; we can't use them all."

Martha could only thank her good friend. It would save the stock in the freezer. The supermarkets up here were already empty of fresh food. One store manager was offering stamps to customers who regularly checked his bare shelves, to be redeemed when the expected supplies started to come through. Martha remembered the piles of green vegetables at the United Nations garage. That much had got through safely.

She was busy, for up in the country she had always done her own housework. Fortunately, Buzz had kept the place reasonably neat but there was a lot of outside work that needed doing. Then she found that chipmunks had been gnawing on the foundation and she set out traps and made repairs. But one morning an item of radio news drove her out of the house to walk down the lake road to the Fairfield house. She didn't need to go up to the big house with the stone porch. Colonel Fairfield, in jeans and a plaid shirt, was walking down the drive carrying a fishing pole and a box of tackle. He greeted her with a wave and a smile, but her heart was too full for the social niceties.

"It was on the radio," she said. "People are being asked to register for identity cards."

Fairfield sighed. "Yes, well. It might just be for the rationing scheme. They have to do that with transport broken down. In the cities . . ."

"And the next thing will be conscription," Martha said. "Why does everybody pretend that nothing's happening?"

He rubbed his forehead, as though easing off a cap that wasn't there, a gesture which was a sign of his distress. So Martha had seen him when he had learned of his son's death in Vietnam. He had seemed like a young man until then.

"People don't know much about what's happening.

They're just hoping for the best. Not much they can do after a surrender, except try to keep their heads."

"We seem to have lost some other part of the anatomy," Martha replied sharply. "How could Carmody have done it?"

"You can't blame the President." Fairfield spoke with the patience of a fisherman, but what he had to say was much the same as the driving Webster. "It's a wonder it didn't happen before," he added. "They've had the capacity for years now. Major-General Schweitzer was fired for warning the public back in the Reagan days."

"But won't we do anything?"

Fairfield looked at his rod. He seemed to be lost in some thoughts of his own. "If we could have kept NATO strong; gone ahead full steam with the Trident, rebuilt the bomber fleet. If Reagan had decided to go ahead with the plan to keep the missiles moving so that they couldn't have been pinpointed so easily—but that was impossible. Even Reagan couldn't have gotten that plan accepted, and he never really made the effort. Nobody wanted them shuttled round in his own state. Now—well, I suppose we could have launched under attack. Carmody must have had *some* warning. But considering our present capacity and the Soviets' defensive systems we could only have damaged them; we couldn't have stopped them. The retaliation would have been ghastly and our last state would be worse than our present one. We still have most of our industrial base, and they were careful not to poison the atmosphere. They want our breadbasket."

"You mean we're to be the Elois to their Morlocks," Martha said.

He smiled again. "So some people still read H. G. Wells," he said. "I wonder what he would have thought of all this."

Fairfield was no stereotype of a military man, and he had never fitted the popular concept of a missileer. His people were old Connecticut; he himself was a member of the Historical Society, his wife had been the chairman of the Library Committee and an ardent patron of the Goodspeed Opera Company. A distinguished-looking man, even in his worn country clothes, a fine pilot, a good administrator, they said. Once he had sworn an oath to defend the United States—now he was going fishing.

He must have seen her gaze on his hands, lightly holding the rod. "While I can," he said.

The lake was really too bright that day to fish. The sun in the clear blue sky gave comforting warmth but it was no longer the heat of high summer. Autumn was on its way.

"Fall will be early this year," he said.

Martha walked away, disconsolate. With her impatient stride, and her hair blazing red in the sunlight, she looked like a flaming rejection of everything he had to tell her. A fine woman, he thought. He was a chivalrous man and would have liked to offer comfort, but he had none. The night before a very senior officer—a three-star general—had appeared after dark, dressed in greasy overalls. All senior officers were being arrested, he told Fairfield. He would have been caught in the net himself, if it wasn't for the kids' CB. They knew more than anybody. He had got out of Washington, going from friend to friend, by car and on foot. "An underground, General Roche?" Fairfield had asked. "More a legion of the lost," the general said shortly. "How in conscience can you even try to form an underground, when they've got their fingers on the nuclear button?"

He was haggard, from exhaustion, fear or terrible decisions. Before dawn he was gone. "I don't want to make trouble for you. You're on the retired list."

From the water's edge, as Fairfield got out his tackle, he could see the houses under the trees on the other side of the inlet. A column of smoke rose from a backyard. Some die-hard was having a last cookout. It was still all there, not black and burned by the fires of a mad Prometheus. In Litchfield his daughters' children were alive and well in the white, frame houses. Except for Chip; Chip who was at West Point. He wished the boy were home, now. The academy would almost certainly be taken over by the Russians.

For himself . . . he was on the retired list, of course, but there were no guarantees. Nothing left but to enjoy the day.

He cast his line from the edge of the dock into the deep water. Soon he felt something on the hook. Not a fish, there was no tugging on the line. It was caught. The water was clouded with algae that hid the bottom. He jerked at the line, but the hook held. A harder jerk brought it flying up—with nothing on it but a scrap of stuff and he staggered back on the dock. Recovering himself he examined the scrap. A jagged piece of cloth, dark denim. In spite of its soaking, there was still a greasy feel to it as he rubbed it between fingers and thumb. Greasy denim. A mechanic's overall.

Kicking off his shoes, he dived into the water and searched the bottom. A large shape spread over the stones and rocks: he felt, before he could really see, the legs, the torso, the head. He rose to the surface, padded barefoot back to his garage and collected ropes and hooks. It was not the first time he had ever pulled a body from the lake, but he had never done it alone, and it took more effort than he had expected to haul the corpse up to the dock.

He gazed down. This was no accidental drowning. General Roche had not gone quietly; every bone was broken. But there were no bullet holes. His pursuers had wanted to take him alive no doubt. Not only a three-star general but he had worked closely with Cunningham.

The body oozed water over the bright white paint of the dock. Roche had probably been taken close by, and this was an easy place to dispose of an embarrassing corpse. If they didn't know now, they would soon guess who had given Roche a lodging the previous night; the census data, neatly computerized, would make that easy for them, as well as the Air Force lists. He looked back at his house that he had lived in so little and loved so much. For the first time he was glad his wife was dead.

In twenty minutes he had changed into dry, sturdy clothes, leather shoes, and had collected a duffel coat and a change of underthings in a rucksack. He added a package of food and a thermos, and, with the habit of a householder, he locked the doors when he left. That night, when the cars came for Colonel Fairfield, he had started his life on the road.

IX

Martha went home, to find a note from Buzz that he would be staying over with Robbie. Of course, after next week the boys would have less time to spend together for the postponed classes were due to begin, if they did begin. Probably the administrators would open the university, making what peace they could with the new order. Unless it was forbidden.

She had never felt more lonely and more desolate. As always when she was troubled, she worked, but the house was already shining clean, the grass mowed, the fence mended. She pulled out the long ladders and the paint bucket, and climbed up to the cupola on the big barn. Behind it, she noticed, Buzz had installed an invisible antenna. She spent the next two hours giving the cupola an extra coat of paint which it needed, and touched up some fading sections of the roof. Never before had she done this rather tricky job alone and the work, instead of easing her sense of loss, made it sharper.

From her vantage point she could see her neighbors, in their customary occupations: Betty Swenson, raking over her vegetable garden; John Simmons building up his woodpile. A car that looked like Colonel Fairfield's disappeared down the road, but it couldn't be. The Colonel was fishing. Over by the lake, some prudent soul was taking down his Stars and Stripes, left out, no doubt, since the Fourth. There had been no call to arms; there was no rebellion. Could it be possible, that the United States was quietly accepting its defeat?

The work done, she cleaned her brushes and put the ladders away. Her back ached, but she was hardly aware of it. As she washed her hands, the mirror over the basin reflected back the sunlight on her temples, revealing the first grey hairs.

In the kitchen over the refrigerator was a scroll that Buzz had brought home from school on the Bicentennial. In the living room, on the bookshelf, were the medals that Josh's father had received in the First World War. Her father had served in the Second World War, Josh in Korea. The bookshelves held her mother-in-law's books, the lives of Washington, Adams, Patrick Henry, Nathan Hale. If those men could see America today . . . Buzz was still making contacts by radio, here and at Robbie's, but nowhere had he heard of any resistance. One lonely drunk had thrown a bottle into the White House grounds and been arrested.

Buzz. He had rather an important air. His ability to get real news was an asset—until it got dangerous. She was *not* disappointed in her son, whom she had thought of as almost an adult. He was still a teenager, and it was folly to expect him suddenly to act like a man, to act like his father.

Fairfield had been her last hope, but of what? That he would tell her of some organized resistance, another chance? He, too, was accepting defeat. There must be other people, hundreds, thousands, perhaps millions who felt as she did, but where? The CIA, the FBI, they must still exist, but they most certainly would be on the victor's arrest list. Those who were free would not be looking for Connecticut housewives to console. She could not find a resistance if there was one, or many.

She had been staring without seeing out of the great window in the living room, across the stone wall and the briar patch down to the Swenson farm, with Mount Tom in the distance. Over the mountain there was something flashing in the sun—the new satellite the radio announcer had been burbling about that morning. It carried reconnaissance technology of a more advanced development than had ever before been seen on earth, or above it, the announcer had said, tittering. A new technological miracle. There were stories it carried laser weapons, he added cautiously, but that had not been confirmed.

Her spirits sunk to the lowest point she had ever known. Defeated. They were defeated. There was nothing to rally round, no weapon of their own with which to threaten the conqueror who had won by engendering the ultimate fear.

Outside the windows a flock of grosbeaks and mourning doves were twittering nervously. The bird feeders were empty, she had forgotten them. There were still seeds stacked down cellar and she went below, responding to the birds' call. She had always looked after them, with Betty Swenson's help when she was away, and would continue, as long as she could. In the cellar she switched on the light and looked about—the seeds were not there. Of course: she remembered. Before she went out yesterday morning she had moved some foodstuffs into the old pump room, in case of traveling prowlers. There were rumors of city folk drifting along the roads, looking for what they could find.

The pump room lay at the back of the cellar on a slightly lower level. Before she had ever come to the house, the water had been drawn up mechanically to the pump room and carried by hand to the rest of the house. Then the electrical system had been put in, connecting the pump to the water faucets in the kitchen and bathrooms, and the pump room had lapsed into disuse. The opening from the cellar had been bricked in, with only a small crawl space left hidden behind the boiler. This hidden room had been the delight of Buzz and his friends and a hiding place for objects too precious in a child's mind to be left in the barn.

A flashlight showed the sack of seeds propped, just as she had left it, in a corner. As she reached out, her foot tapped on the edge of a flagstone, and the careful householder noticed at once that it was loose. Another job. She had some cement in the cellar . . . and then she remembered. Of course, the family glory hole. Everything of importance was kept in the safe in Josh's study; she had had a dreary morning going through the folders that he had neatly labeled and filed. She looked at his will, the bank accounts, the stock certificates—searching for something, she didn't know what. Some personal note, jottings, a letter, a voice of comfort from the grave. There was none, except the proof of Josh's love and thoughtfulness. They had lived sparely so that she could have a comfortable widowhood—those fifteen years had always weighed on Josh's mind. He had even made arrangements for his own funeral, his grave and his memorial tablet. That at least could be raised.

Her hands, almost with an impulse of their own, lifted the heavy flagstone. Carefully wrapped in oiled paper were the family's really treasured possessions and she opened the packages, one by one. Who had saved a Captain Midnight secret decoder? Not Buzz, Captain Midnight went back long before. It must have been Josh himself. A sheet of paper, badly yellowed, covered with her mother-in-law's bold, firm hand. It was her recipe for grasshopper pie, the pie that had won the prize at the Four-H over redoubtable competition. No one had ever been able to pry the recipe from her. Martha's eyebrows arched. Brandy and creme de menthe. No wonder the ladies had loved it.

A stuffed baby shoe, the kid gently crumbling. Josh would never have had a shoe like this, it could have been his father's. That must be all. But under it was more paper. She looked beneath and at the very bottom was a large packet, so bulky that it was hard to lift out. She could not remember the hole as having been so deep. The package was carefully taped, but curiosity drove her to unwrap it there and then, sitting on the cold flags with the flashlight on her lap.

As she glanced at the top sheet, she was flooded with disappointment. What had she expected, she reproached herself. A diary, a journal, full of loving observations from Josh? Josh, whose letters read almost like business letters, whose love had always been expressed in actions, not words. These were papers to do with a job, like hundreds of papers he had kept in his office, and that he sometimes brought home.

And the paper wasn't new. The documents, Josh's originals, were dated '81, '81, '82. The waterworks project. She remembered during those years the Reagan Administration had kept him busy with waterworks projects in the west. Nothing secret about it, except perhaps the cost. There had been some sort of scandal about it, after Reagan's death. Money that had never been properly accounted for. It had all helped his opponents to keep the Presidency for Carmody, and to gain both houses of Congress. Nothing was proved against the Columbia Company, which Josh had worked for, but it had gone into liquidation. Its president, old Mr. Drummond, had died and there had been rumors of suicide.

She rifled through the sheets and the drawings, Project 198, Project 199, Project 200. None of the drawings, all made in Josh's own hand, looked anything like water conduits. Nor had there been anything like two hundred water projects. She forgot her cramped position and discomfort as she stared at drawing after drawing. No engineer herself, she had been married to Josh long enough to be able to read a plan fairly well and understand the specs. And she had seen plans for missile sites before. Josh had started on the drawings for Grand Forks long before he had gone out there.

These drawings and specs were for 230 missile shelters, similar to the ICBM sites at Grand Forks. But the country hadn't built, at that time, 230 missile sites, let alone that many completely new ones. Josh had built none at all in those years. And yet . . . there was his completion stamp on each and every one.

She sneezed suddenly and the papers stirred on her lap. For the first time she noticed the light corner markings: Ariz. Nev. Utah. Josh had certainly been working out west . . . on the water projects. Absently, she rubbed her back with her fist. Fairfield had reminded her of the Carter plan. She had heard some of the talk at the time. But that had been for a minimum of two hundred sites, each site comprising twenty-three separate silos—forty-six hundred altogether. The twenty-three silos would have been connected on a racetrack system and the missiles shuttled from one to another so that the enemy could not be sure where the missiles were if they planned a strike. Josh had liked the idea, with some reservations. But Reagan had not built them. Because it was Carter's plan, some said. Since no governor wanted them in his state, others had defended him. There was also the inordinate expense.

One of the missiles had a reference number different from the type at Grand Forks, ending with the letters MY. The project code? But it seemed to be the only one. At the bottom of the package, tucked in a fold of the wrapping, was a scrap of ruled paper with a torn-off edge from the sort of pad that Josh always carried in his pocket. There was his note:

MAGNANIMITY—completion of construction 11/9/82
Completion of installation ICBM's   11/12/82
Completion of installation ICBM MY   18/12/82

The flashlight failed, and Martha sat hunched in the dark room, unable to move. Her hands were shaking. No weapons, she had thought. No hope . . . A voice of comfort, perhaps, from the grave. But this was no voice of comfort: it was a call to arms.

BOOK TWO

THE NEW ORDER

*Weld fast the galling fetters; remember
that he who appraises is quick to exact.*

X

Virinsky was at his office in the Secretariat building frowning over reports from Washington and Hartford. It was still the modest-seeming office on the 37th floor, adjacent to the quarters of the assistants to the Secretary-General. There were no antique furnishings, fine rugs or other signs of an elevated position. Instead he had a metal desk with five telephones. The walls of this room and its annex were lined with banks of filing cabinets of heavy steel with locks that worked on signals from a computer that were known only to himself and adjusted on a weekly basis. His telex system was the best in the building; he had direct telephone lines to Washington, Moscow and Havana. A photograph of Lenin hung on the wall opposite the desk, and underneath it sat a bench of black leather and steel.

The Under-Secretary for Political and Security Council Affairs ran the First Department of the KGB, North America. He ranked as second-in-command to Kharkev, one of the most powerful men in the Soviet Union as

head of the KGB and also a full member of the Politburo, as Andropov and Lavrentin had been before him.
On that day, Virinsky should have been happy, for the
telephone call he had received the day before from
Kharkev had been the fulfilment of a long-cherished,
carefully planned goal. Virinsky had been told that he
had been named, along with Marshal Borunukov and
Ramon Perez, to the *troika* governing the defeated
country. Written orders were already on the way.

Kharkev had added the congratulations of his daughter, Virinsky's wife, who was still at her summer home
on the Black Sea. Elizaveta and the children never left
the Eastern bloc. This appointment was almost a guar-
antee that he would succeed Kharkev in time and that
the family would be reunited.

Virinsky had smiled his rare smile as he pictured the
heated conference at the Politburo that had come up
with this solution. The Marshal, who had been proved
correct in his plea for the strike as well as effective in
action, had an impregnable position, and there was no
doubt that he would keep the military command of the
United States. But the Politburo had been equally determined not to let the Army have matters all their own
way. The United States was too large; total control by
the military would endanger their own position in the
Soviet Union. The Marshal must share power with the
Party, but who could they agree upon who would also
have the toughness to stand up against the victorious
generals? Certainly no one in the pocket of any of the
sixteen ruling members; they would never trust each
other enough for that. And who else was there?

Perez had been the inevitable, if not popular, choice.
The most ruthless of revolutionaries, the organizer of so
much of the softening-up process in Central America,
he had the talent—up until now, at least—for keeping
himself in the background. A loyal party member all his
adult life, he was reliable; a guerilla leader who had

succeeded in Nicaragua, El Salvador, Mexico, he would not be awed by the Marshal. Virinsky remembered when the Americans had complained, years before, that Castro was exporting his revolution: Ulyanov had remarked that it was Perez who had delivered it.

There had been murmuring, however. Now that the main enemy had been subdued, guerrillas, though the most reliable of Party men, were not to be encouraged, even in the short run. Assimilation and consolidation were now the chief items on the agenda. And so it must have been easy for Kharkev, a smooth politician for all his brutish, Cossack look, to suggest that a third man be added to the governing entity; a man from the Committee for State Security, who had done such Trojan labor in the preparation years, who already had a system set up for the country's government, who could watch the other two and report directly to the Politburo, as only he was equipped to do.

This man need not be *named* to the American public or anyone else and in fact, with so much of the change in government flowing at this time through the UN building, it should give the rest of the world a comfortable feeling that the new regime was peaceful and harmonious: the New Economic Order and the New Political Order. The speech had been worked out carefully in the last meeting between the two men.

Kharkev had won. General-Secretary Ulyanov had agreed, Premier Tikhonov, his rival, had agreed, the Politburo had so voted. The Central Committee, nearly all Ulyanov men, had consented also. Virinsky's hour had come and it was sweet. He would be like a king in New York. New York, once, briefly, the nation's capital. He would like to see it so again.

But it was not all sweetness. Those Army fools, who had had all power at the critical time, had bungled. They had let Parker kill himself while under detention. There should have been a show trial of the Admiral. The nuclear submarine *Ohio* had escaped and inflicted

unpleasant damage on Riga. Nothing material: during
the danger period Soviet ships and submarines were all
in neutral waters and anyone of importance was in deep
shelter. But an example should have been made. As it
was, all that could be done was to send the officers and
crew to the firing squad after questioning, which would
have happened anyway. And General Roche had escaped. True, Roche had been found but he had been
killed in the attempt to take him. If Virinsky's men had
been with the arrest teams and had taken custody of the
prisoners, none of these blunders could have taken
place. And the military intelligence doctors had bungled almost as badly with Cunningham.

Virinsky tapped his desk in annoyance. He himself
should have been down there in the Special Wing at
Bethesda—a facility of his own planning—but the GRU
had been too impatient. And Cunningham had out-
foxed them. He held out too long. American generals
were not supposed to be used to questioning, by drugs
or other means. Virinsky suspected that Cunningham
had prepared himself; there had long been the possibility of capture by terrorists. Perez had made sure of
that. It was only when the general was broken in mind
and body that he had given anything. But by then he
was raving.

Virinsky slipped a spool of tape onto a small player on
his desk top. The transcript he had received from the
GRU had little value. Just the one word was clear . . .
Magna. If that was what it was. Fortunately, one of the
GRU men was a plant of his own and had smuggled out
a copy of the tape for him. He played it over and over,
but it was all meaningless screams and mumbles except
for those two syllables, breathed in the general's last
agony. Perhaps merely a prayer. But, though he checked
carefully, there was no reference to such a word in any
prayer of the Christian liturgy. The fools of the GRU
had not known, or troubled to find out, that Cunningham had been a diabetic. Another shot had produced a

few more words, mumbled, indistinct, and had killed him. The GRU interrogators had been sent home in disgrace.

Virinsky sent for tea and *ponchiki*, hot sugared doughnuts of which he was very fond. The kitchens now had orders to prepare them freshly, at any time, at his order. He played the recording over and over at different speeds and different pitches. The GRU would have had this analyzed already; any information it might contain would be in their hands and he wanted it. He could turn the tape over to his technicians, but there was another way. He buzzed for his secretary, and told him to summon Madame Paul.

Madame Paul, a trusted Party member, had served for a time in the translation section. She had the ability, from long practice, of listening to recorded speech that to anyone else was nothing but a harsh jumble of sounds or inaudible whispers and coming up with the contents. He had found this talent useful in many ways, and had rewarded her with several promotions. Madame Paul had proved to have many talents.

She came in quietly, listened to his instructions, and went at once to work, under his eye. That tape would not leave his room. He worked on other matters while she listened over and over, hour after hour, occasionally making a note on a small white pad. The lights from the river boats were already shining through the dusk when she turned to him with a small sigh.

"I am very sorry. I can only make out half a dozen words—there are only the half dozen words. The rest is not human speech."

He waited impatiently.

"The first is *Magna*—Magna something, I think, but it is impossible to say what. The others are more clear. 'Sleeping giant . . . will destroy you . . .' But that is all. Between 'sleeping giant' and 'will destroy you' there is a combination of sounds that might be *perhaps*. But that is absolutely all."

Virinsky didn't like it any more than Marshal Borunukov had done, or Perez when he had got it from his own spies inside Bethesda. Each man, separately, ordered a massive search of intelligence files but found nothing that corresponded to the code-word, if that was what it was, *Magna*.

Borunukov, who had taken over the private quarters in the White House, had tossed restlessly in the Presidential bed the previous night, fearing contingents of US troops deployed about the world in some incredibly stealthy fashion to escape all notice. He knew it could *not* have happened; but he had no rest until he ordered the sending up of the new satellite; ostensibly to celebrate the victory but chiefly to use its new photo-communications—so obligingly provided by the Americans—to ferret out any suspicious movements anywhere in the world.

Perez, who used the White House offices by day, for the sake of his Third World image slept in a shabby-looking house in the heart of Washington's black ghetto. It was well guarded by his own troops, but he, too, had an uneasy night. If any reprisal was possible by a group of American insurgents, what was more likely than an attack launched from Miami or Cuba, an attempt to take over the Cuban silos while her troops were dispersed around the globe? He rose early and ordered more troops into Florida, causing a sharp quarrel with Borunukov.

Virinsky, before he left his UN office that night, sent out a series of orders. All members of the US intelligence services were already on the arrest list, but now even the most minor employees were given top priority. He added instructions that in case of conflict with the GRU, his men were to arrest first and leave the explanations until afterwards. Thirdly, he ordered a list be prepared of Treasury officials and personnel, also to go on the immediate arrest list. Someone had to pay salaries and expenses of any organization, secret or not. *Magna* . . . sleeping giant . . . did not sound like a small and inexpensive undertaking. A new most secret, most urgent project file was set up and placed in his steel cabinet. It was titled Project Magna.

—— XI ——

The next day when Martha rose it was unexpectedly cooler. The furnace had not come on, although the thermostat was down to fifty degrees. When she tried the stove she found that the electricity was off. Down in the cellar she found old newspapers and kindling: started a fire in the old pot stove and put on a battered coffee pot. It took a long time to boil.

The freezer would have to be emptied soon. Of course, it *might* be a temporary "outage", which happened every now and again. But the telephones had not been restored. Up here, where there were so many summer homes, there were far more telephones than could possibly be in use at this time of year. The first confusion of panic calls had been followed, she was sure, by a systematic cut-off of private telephones. There were no more muddled voices, no buzzing and confusion on the line. Only silence.

The excitement of her discovery, that had kept her wakeful through the night, was dampened this morning by the practical difficulties. She knew, but what could she do about it? Whom should she tell? Bill Webster? He could be reached, perhaps, from Hartford. The governor's mansion would have a line to Washington; her UN papers might get her the use of it. But Webster had shown little stomach for a fight. Colonel Fairfield himself had been the picture of resignation. Once she gave up the secret of Magnanimity it was gone forever.

The back door clicked and it was Buzz.

"Thought you might need some help with the freezer," he said, casually.

She offered him coffee, but as usual he shook his head and took a glass of milk.

"It's cool on the back porch," she said. "But it will warm up later. The food won't last without ice."

"Pity they didn't wait until the lake froze," Buzz said.

"They?"

"Russian soldiers took over the plant at Haddam."

Martha had forgotten. The power came from the nuclear plant on the Connecticut river. But it had been part of a grid system that should have continued to operate if there was any failure. Buzz was probably right.

"I had breakfast at Robbie's," Buzz said. "Sausages. His mother said they would go first. The Colonel wasn't fishing this morning," he added. "He always says hello when I go past. His car wasn't in the garage, either. Mrs. Bruce at the Lake House was out fixing her pump and she told me three cars drove up in the night to the Fairfield place. The noise woke her up. Some men broke in, but the electricity was off already and she saw the flashlights in all the rooms. In the yard, too. But after an hour they went away. She saw the Colonel leave yesterday, she said."

So Fairfield *was* gone. She was glad he'd got away, but that was one less link with the old world. He had known people . . .

"Guess he won't be going over to his brother in

Avon." Buzz knew everyone's family connections. Full
as he claimed to be, he reached for a muffin and the
jelly. "He worked for Pratt and Whitney. They'll be
moving in there, I bet."

The Russians had already become "they", the mysterious power whose name must not be mentioned. She'd
forgotten Walt Fairfield, a good friend of Josh. Now he
would have to work for "them" if he wished to work at
all. Walt. It was Sunday again, he should be home. She
could drive over to Avon and get back before dark. To
talk. She need not *tell* him about Magnanimity, merely
sound him out.

Buzz took another muffin. Martha thought of Robbie's
mother.

"Alice can't go on feeding you," she said. "Can't you
bring Robbie here for a few days? And do you know if
classes are starting?"

"Put back a month. Students having trouble getting
to the campus. Waiting for things to settle, I guess. The
Admin's supposed to send out letters. I would bring
Robbie, but we've got a pile of stuff we're working on
over by the lake. Too much to bring down, and you
wouldn't want the mess."

"You mean you boys are in the cottage all day? It
must be getting chilly."

"We're O.K.," Buzz said. He looked excessively innocent, and Martha wondered what on earth the boys
were up to. Not girls, surely. Both of them were more
interested in anything electronic or mechanical than in
females. Born after the great sexual revolution, they
seemed not greatly concerned with it, at least not to a
point observable by a mother.

She was anxious to get going and did the domestic
jobs swiftly and then tidied herself to go out. She
paused at the barn where Buzz was working his radio
from its new home in the cellar that had once been a
chicken run.

"Martial law is being declared all over the place," he
said. "What *is* martial law exactly?"

"Troops can shoot civilians if they don't obey orders, or are suspected of illegal acts," Martha told him.

"No trials?"

"No. Shoot first, questions, if any, later." Martha frowned. "I shouldn't have thought they had enough troops for that."

"Some great supersonic transports have been flying into Bradley. Still no civilian traffic allowed."

As Martha drove to Avon, she wondered how long the hams would remain unmolested. They were licensed; someone would come across the FCC records soon enough. The only other news now would be from her battery operated radios. She switched on the one in the car. Bristow was making a speech. ". . . civilian panic. This is causing much unnecessary difficulty . . ." Martha remembered last time she had heard him speak. It had been one of his anti-nuclear speeches, no money for missiles or maintenance of missile sites. "Let them rot," he had said. It was a popular cry. "Citizens are urged to continue in their normal occupations," he went on now, in his rich, familiar voice. "As the overloading of transport facilities has made the new session of Congress impracticable . . ."

Bill Webster might just as well have stayed at home and planted trees. "For the handling of the emergency conditions, I have this day put into operation Executive Order No. 11490, signed by President Nixon for such a contingency and published in the Federal Register October 30, 1969, entitled 'Assigning Emergency Preparedness Functions to Federal Departments and Agencies.' This includes the provisions of the Executive Orders previously promulgated by President Kennedy. The Stock and Commodity exchanges will remain closed. The banks will open and depositors will be permitted to withdraw one hundred dollars in cash on a one-time basis only until the panic recedes. To assist the states in this period of commercial and financial confusion, the Interstate Commerce Commissions in cooperation with the Treasury, is setting up ten financial regions, as previously designated by the Internal Revenue Service. More information will come to you about this as operations begin.

"Be of good heart, my fellow countrymen." His voice took on the lyrical quality that had always moved his audience. "Peace is now here, and order will be restored. Some of you may have been alarmed by reports of rioting around military bases. In accordance with the Instrument of Surrender, our troops were temporarily confined to barracks. In some few, very few, places servicemen have broken out and there have been looting sprees. The use of illegal drugs is believed to be the cause. These outbreaks were quickly brought under control. A spokesman for Marshal Borunukov has stated that these incidents are not considered to be a substantial violation of the Instrument, and that peace-loving citizens can rest assured that they will not suffer as a result of this hooliganism."

He followed with more platitudes and Martha was about to switch off when the announcer's voice cut in.

"This ends the morning segment of our daily broadcast. Listen to the news on this station at six pm."

Twisting the tuning knob from one end of the dial to another, she could find no other program. The media had been worth little since the surrender, but even that little, apparently, was to be taken away. A gust of wind swept a leaf across the road, and then another, although the hills were still richly green. The road was almost empty of cars, but there were many bicyclists, with baskets strapped to the handlebars, mostly heaped with produce.

In Litchfield she drove by long habit through Old South Street to pass the old Adams house in which she had been raised, a large, gracious Colonial building with its fine portico and Palladian window. A large house that she and her grandmother had cared for themselves, but the expenses had grown too great for her grandmother's limited means and after her death the house had gone by special arrangement to the Historical Society. Martha had missed it, but Josh's house near Bantam Lake, once a small farm dwelling, was easier and much cheaper to run and it had always been a happy home.

Now two army trucks were parked outside the big house where a flock of black women and children, burdened with a quantity of household goods, were crowding through the doorway, sitting on the front lawn, and milling about. A similar scene was taking place by the Ethan Allen house up the street. A fat woman was arguing with the driver of the truck while she pulled at a large, overstuffed armchair, too heavy for her to handle.

"You weren't supposed to bring furniture. How the hell you got it in back there . . ." He was sweating, despite the brisk breeze. "Just your hand luggage."

"I ain't goin' no place without my own chair. I bet they ain't got one comfortable chair in the whole of that house."

A woman came to join her from the other house. "There's only one kitchen in that place, and they're sending in four families. I got three kids, are they crazy? I'm going back to Waterbury."

The first woman saw Martha slow down and appealed to her, hands on hips. "Lady, will you tell ole General MacArthur here that we wishes to return?"

A little boy began to cry. A woman darted from the porch to clutch his hand. "I tol' you not to let go."

"Don't you scol' that child," the fat woman said. "He got more sense than the lot of us." She turned to Martha. "They came round the project and said they was movin' us out to fine mansions. Beautiful homes in the country. And that house there has nothing but a lot of old books and papers and no beds or nothing. And mixing up all the families; I had a four-room apartment. I want to go home."

Some of the other children began to cry in concert.

The driver, a young sergeant, looked at Martha helplessly.

"We got the orders to move them out. They can't go back; that project is scheduled for another use. But this house isn't ready."

Martha wondered what had happened to the family who lived in the Ethan Allen house; she didn't know them, though Buzz probably did.

"I showed the orders to that secretary lady but she said . . ."

Millicent Reeve, a neat, grey-haired woman who was the volunteer secretary, came out, talking to another soldier. "I'll do what I can . . . Did you bring any food or blankets?"

"Just what you see," the soldier said. "That's what was in the orders." With a sense of shock Martha saw that he was carrying a rifle. "There's blankets and stuff in that house." He nodded to the Ethan Allen place.

"But the owners aren't there and . . ."

"I wouldn't worry about owners, lady," the soldier said. "Ain't much ownin' now."

The sergeant looked at the crying children and fumbled in his blouse pocket for a Hershey bar. To the mothers he gave his cigarettes.

"You're crazy, Joe, you know that," the other man said. "Ain't gonna be much in the PX, not to be givin' away."

Over the protests of the women, they got into the trucks and roared off. As though from another life, Martha remembered photographs she had seen once that she had first thought were fakes, but which had proved to be genuine after all. They had been taken at the end of World War Two in Europe. American riflemen had been herding refugees claimed by the Russians into army trucks to be transported back to the Eastern bloc. Unwilling, struggling, some had preferred death. But the soldiers had been obeying orders from their government, as these men were today. Operation Keel-haul, they had called it.

"I don't know what the Archers will do when they come home," Millicent said. "Right now I suppose I'd better go and see Dorothy Ives. She's Red Cross chairman now."

"I have to go to Avon," Martha said. "but I'll look in later on."

"I wonder if they'll send any more," Millicent said worriedly.

Martha pulled away. A moment later she heard a sharp crack at the rear window. Looking back she caught a glimpse of a child drawing away. He must have been about ten years old, defiant, frightened, throwing stones against an unbelievable reality.

In Avon the large supermarket was bare of goods. A service was beginning at the Methodist church and an unusually large congregation was assembling. She drove through the quiet town. Down the road near the river a cluster of maples hid the old house where the Walt Fairfields lived. As she swung round to the drive, to her relief Walt himself was standing, rake in hand, talking to a man she didn't know. Next to the broad, sturdy six feet of Walt he looked slight, a wiry man with dark hair partly hidden under a cap. He glanced up as she approached and, making a sketchy gesture of farewell to Walt, he walked off with a light tread, disappearing behind the tall screen of sunflowers, swiftly and silently as though the earth had swallowed him.

"Hi, Martha," Walt smiled, a warm and welcoming smile. "I'm glad you came over. I was thinking of you and wondering how you were making out. I have coffee on the stove—come on inside."

The coffee was brewing not in Ann's gleaming kitchen, nor in the dining room, but in a small sitting room where Walt had a Franklin stove. A large pie was set by the coffee cups.

"I have to try to eat all this stuff up," he said. "Can

you take some home, Martha? It'll go to waste, unless
we find some ice somewhere—we've still got the old
ice-house. I don't know what Ann would say."

Martha had noticed that although the house was neat
enough it didn't have the mark of Ann's presence. Ann
was an elegant woman and proud of her pre-revolutionary
house which had been featured in *Architectural Digest*.
Despite her immaculate smartness, she was a wonderful housekeeper, at least the equal of that notable
farmwife, Betty Swenson.

"She's away?"

Walt nodded. "I sent her down to her sister in Vir-
ginia at once, while the going was good. I wish I could
have got her to Canada."

His devotion to his still lovely wife, his pleasure in
her society that to him was the only pleasure that
mattered, was a matter of good-humored jest among
their acquaintances.

"Until we see which way things are going. Whether
people like me, perhaps Josh, if he has survived," he
gave her hand a squeeze, "will be marked men, or kept
for our continuing usefulness. Impossible to say yet.
The company is closed down temporarily anyway. Transport problems. If it goes the wrong way, at least Ann
won't be here when they come and get me. She should
be all right down there. I don't suppose they'll be
bothering tobacco growers for some time to come."

Walt was an aircraft designer. Martha remembered
what his brother had said. "John told me they would
want production. He's gone away, I think."

The Colonel was the elder of the two brothers. Walt
had admired and respected him. Now he shot Martha a
quick look. "He stopped by last night. We won't see
him for a while, I reckon. You have to expect, Martha,
that they're going to round up all senior military men,
as well as Intelligence. As for aircraft and missile production, they have good men of their own. It depends
. . . after all, their main battle is over."

"Battle!" Martha said.

"Well, they've got most of the strength of the world now," Walt said, calmly. He had the same practical outlook as Josh. As Josh had had. "Europe is effectively Finlandized. Even before this . . . I know John was worried and he was in Germany for years. No one over there had much stomach for a fight. The oil states will probably settle somewhat now they don't have the big powers to play off one against the other. There's only China, and China's technology is no real threat. Even if she linked up with Japan, they simply don't have the time. So the Soviets have a choice. They can use our military and aerospace production, or destroy it."

"They'll use it," Martha said. "Most of it, anyway."

Walt looked almost amused. "And what makes you so sure?"

"Because that's what they've always done. Produce weapons. Steal and use plants in countries they've taken over. And people tend to go on doing what they usually do—like rock fans going to the Bones concert after the surrender. We shouldn't give it to them," she said fiercely. "If we can't use it, we should destroy it. Though I don't know why we can't and don't use it."

"Martha," he said patiently, "they took out the missile sites. They got most of our bombers on the ground. What we had, which was precious few. As for the subs, those that escaped couldn't have been effective, not since the Navy moth-balled so many. The Looking Glass aircraft went out the same time as SAC headquarters."

Martha had to think for a moment. Looking Glass—it was part of the fail-safe command system. There had always been a General in a flying command post in case SAC was blown out of the earth.

"John thinks it was sabotage," he said. "But Carmody, like a lot of people, had too much reliance on the DEW system—the Arctic early warning. In a way it was our Maginot Line."

"But there was NORAD in Colorado—"

"It seems as though it was incapacitated. But no one in the East really knows."

"Walt," Martha said. "Suppose all the missile sites weren't taken out."

Walt looked up. "You think Carmody lied?"

"I don't know, but just suppose it was possible. If we still had the power to retaliate, is there anyone in the country man enough to stand up to the Russians?"

"If they missed one or two sites—and there's no reason to suppose they did—we could still inflict some nasty damage on them. But to what purpose? They're never going to get out now. They'd rather lose a couple of Soviet cities if they had to. And God knows what they'd do in return. They would have to make an example. But in any case, Martha, it was very clear they knew everything we had. Anything they didn't destroy, you can be sure they've occupied by now. It was impossible to keep secrets, and I think Carmody gave up trying."

Walt had always enjoyed his food and even now could dig in to Ann's blackberry pie. "I think Carter was the last President who tried to conceal weapons. The idea of rotating missiles might have worked. I was at Rocketdyne then and they were enthusiastic . . ."

He broke off. No doubt he thought it better not to say too much.

She pushed round her blackberries, leaving a dark smear on Ann's white porcelain plate.

"If he had built them, what should have happened, Walt?"

"I don't think the Russians would have made that strike. They would have had to take out every one of the sites—nearly five thousand. Our people would have launched under attack. The Soviets wouldn't have dared to take the chance. *I* don't think they would. But no President could do it; the danger wasn't real enough to people. Rocketdyne had plans on the drawing board for missiles with an unbelievable accuracy, but people were afraid of the whole idea. Missiles trundling about on surface transport or in underground tracks. And in the confusion of a first strike, who would know what was where? How many people would have access? If it was too few, the knowledge could be lost at the all important time—too many and the Russians would know themselves."

He put his fork down, very deliberately.

"Martha," he said, "did Josh ever talk to you about his work?"

"No," she said at once. "You know Josh wasn't a talker. I talked," she said. "About the house, and Buzz. Later about my job, the UN. I don't think he was much interested in the UN," she had to add.

"I wondered," he said. They were both silent for a moment. She tried to guess what was in his mind: could he suspect the truth? Did his brother? Suddenly, absurdly, she was afraid to speak. If Walt *was* arrested, they would find out anything she told him. No one could withstand them. And she realized with a sinking heart, that there had been nothing in the plans to say in which silos the missiles had been installed or what the rotation plan had been. That would have been on a need-to-know basis. Josh *may* have known the former, but certainly he had no need to know the rotation schedule. Another thought crowded into her mind: with the death of Reagan had the rotation taken place? Carmody, she was certain, had not been told about Magnanimity. If he had been, he would have given up the project under SALT IV. And Josh's plan would be filed with the office papers, and not hidden in the old pump room, to be found, after his death.

"Why do you ask?" she said.

"Did you ever become a US citizen, Martha?" Walt had stood, and was looking out of the window.

"I am a US citizen," she answered, startled. "My parents were American."

"Yes, of course. But you were born in England."

"I think my parents took care of it," she said, "at the American Consulate, in London."

She remembered the confusion on the UN computer, and mentioned it to Walt.

"I was wondering how you managed to get up here," he said. "Of course, with your UN pass and a neutral citizenship you have travel privileges. Martha, I think you should go back to New York, back to work. Up here you're known as the wife of Josh Adams who worked on military installations for the US government. He worked closely with NASA and Rocketdyne. Down there you're a British UN employee—much safer."

"They'll figure it out eventually," she said.

"Eventually can be a long way off. It's now that counts. They might come round and pick you up in the first waves."

"Buzz wouldn't come to New York."

"Buzz is looking after himself," Walt told her. "A lot of the boys won't go and register for identity cards. They don't stay long in one place. I think they plan to hide out and live rough if necessary. But Buzz is worried about you."

She felt the first pang of happiness she'd known since the surrender. Buzz had not, then, accepted the defeat.

"They'll look for him," the mother said, anxiously.

"Not yet. It will take them time. Registering makes it too easy. I think Buzz is wise. My guess is the ones that register will be drafted and sent abroad. God knows when we'll see them again."

Martha left, wondering as she went if she was being overcautious. Her knowledge was useless unless it was being shared. There was no one she trusted more than the Fairfield brothers. And yet . . .

Walt Fairfield watched her go. Martha's face was more open than she knew. Was it possible? He left the house by the back door, walked through the rows of peas, beans and tomato plants down through the marshy ground to the river, where the dark-haired man sat waiting. The nearest house was a quarter mile away, but they spoke quietly.

"So who was this Josh Adams," the visitor asked. "Tell me about him."

When Martha got to Litchfield, she found that more evacuees had arrived. Some were being put in the rectory of St. Michael's, a house she knew well. Old Mr. Reeve had lived there until his death and he had tutored her in the classics, her grandmother's wish. She gave Dorothy Ives most of the food she had brought from Avon; the children were tired and hungry. Many Litchfield women were helping and she went on.

By the time she reached home, she felt like turning back to Avon, though it would have used the last of the gas. She must trust somebody; she needed help, knowledge, the skill to evaluate her discovery, the ability to use it. Josh had said that Walt was the salt of the earth—she knew he valued him even more than his brother.

But while she sat in the car in her drive, uncertain of whether she should put it away, she had a sharp distraction. A state police car came down the road and stopped by the house. She looked up surprised, a little pleased, to see Kenny Rapp. He had married a cousin's daughter, the shy young Ellen, and lived in Northfield. But his expression quenched any pleasure. "Martha, I thought I'd better tell you. I just heard. Some boys were arrested by the Russkie MPs. They've got them under guard at Haddam's Neck. Robbie Deming, and your Buzz. Our people haven't been able to get to see them . . ."

— XII —

It was night before Martha got to see Buzz. Finding him was not easy, even with Kenny's help. As they sat and waited for information in the police station at Haddam, they talked in low tones. We're talking in whispers already, Martha thought. And the surrender only a week ago.

". . . and you're still working," she said.

Kenny shrugged. "As long as I can. Not much speeding on the highways now. Mostly directing convoys—a lot of foreign drivers. An order came down to pick up CB's. It's a felony now to use an unauthorized transmitter. All of our top brass seem to be missing. Like here," he added. He motioned his head towards the man in plain clothes who came out of the Captain's office. "That's not old Charlie Bennett. Charlie was here twenty years. Ask the guys where he is, they say retired. I was over here a month ago looking for a stolen car and he said nothing about retiring. We're getting some strange types moved in over our heads. The new Chief is supposed to be a Canuck."

The Captain came over and asked to see the identity card of the boy who had been arrested. Kenny had managed that morning to learn the charges, a difficult thing in itself. Buzz had been arrested for loitering in a restricted area and for vagabondage; he had no identity card. Haddam had become a restricted area because of the atomic plant and Buzz had been picked up, not by the local police, who would merely have warned him off, but by the military. Not American.

"Some Russians, not regular army. The rest are Czechs," Kenny told her. "Johnny Palacki heard them talking. He understands that Czech lingo, his dad could speak it and his gramps never liked to speak anything else. Cool-looking guys, they never seem to crack a smile. Martha, vagabondage is a felony under that damned regulation."

He had pulled out an identity card made out to Bruce Joshua Adams, stamped the previous day. "Tell them he left it in the pocket of his other pants," he advised. "Loitering in a restricted area is also a felony, and that'll be tougher to beat. We'll have to think up something."

Now the Captain looked at the card without speaking. He turned and had a few words with the man on the desk, who beckoned them over.

"The Captain wants to know what the boy was doing so far from home in the restricted area."

"I daresay he didn't know it was restricted," Martha said quickly. "He always visits Old Cart Road before he goes back to school. His great-aunt Sue lives there; she's ninety-two and bed-ridden. She had a nurse with her, but I don't know if the nurse is still there. I asked Buzz to go . . ."

"Why didn't he explain this to the arresting officer?" the desk man interrupted.

"I expect he did. Perhaps the officer couldn't understand him."

The desk man nodded and told her to sit down again.

Kenny had to leave but at nine o'clock he returned, bringing her coffee and baked beans warm on a plate.

"Don't worry," he said. "I still have some buddies here."

The Captain had left. Soon one of the men called Kenny over and they talked quietly. Kenny came back frowning.

"Buzz is in an area camp for juveniles," he told her. "The jails are full, so any kid that gets arrested ends up in an area camp awaiting trial."

"Trial?"

"Well, there's no bail, I can tell you. The hell of it is, it's under military regulation, so I don't know what we can do. But I'll take you over there."

The encampment, behind a tall, wire fence, was set up in the meadows near Greenfield Hill. "There's another one in Nathan Hale Park," Kenny remarked. "Bigger." Inside, rows of army tents were stretched out, a soldier before each tent, a machine-gun post at either end of each row. Lights were strung on heavy cables over the tents, blazing down on the American soldiers standing guard, and the foreigners, wearing the green shoulder flashes she had seen at the UN and on the guns. If the place was full of teenagers, the quiet was uncanny.

Inside the gate a military policeman asked their business.

"This lady's son got picked up for not having his ID on him. Hell, he only got it yesterday. The kid forgot." He presented the pass.

"Well, he sure as hell has got to carry it now. It is *the law!*"

The M.P. had a southern accent and emphasized his words carefully. "These passes have to be carried at all times. At *all* times. Just like in the military. Some of these spoiled, rich kids, they're gonna be straightened out. I'll take you to the officer."

He led them through the rows of tents. In the brilliant light the American guards were an odd assortment. A corporal wore fatigues with his trousers stuffed into his boots like a paratrooper, a private was in dress uniform with the insignia of the National Guard, a top-sergeant wore the khaki blouse of a summer uniform, as though a hand had scooped them up at random like toy soldiers from a box. At the end of the rows a small area was screened off with more wire. The cluster of tents in the enclosure bristled with more machine guns, and the only soldiers that could be glimpsed there were the foreigners.

"Transit camp, male criminals. They'll mostly be out by the morning," the M.P. remarked. "This is the lieutenant's office."

The office was a mobile home with most of the furnishings ripped out and replaced by desks, office chairs and filing cabinets. The kitchenette had been left as it was, painted a cheerful yellow with wooden birds dangling over the stove and the ice-box. The lieutenant, a sallow young man wearing glasses, was taking papers from one basket, stamping them and putting them in another.

"Yes?"

"State police," the M.P. said, cocking his head towards Kenny. "Wants this boy released. He'd forgotten to carry his ID, but he's registered. Region One, Southern Sector, Litchfield."

The lieutenant took the card and checked against the charge sheet.

"There's another charge. Restricted area."

"Visiting his great-aunt, Susan Booth, Old Cart Road, in Haddam," Kenny said. "The restricted area is not yet fully posted, and the boy went part of the way on foot across the fields."

The lieutenant went to the files, pulled out a folder

and ran a finger down a list. "Booth . . . Yes, I see. Scheduled for relocation."

"Where to?" Martha asked.

"The family will be notified. The area is to be completely sealed off. Just a moment," he said. Replacing the list in the file, he checked through a large, black book that lay open on a wooden table. It looked like the books on the immigration desks at airports.

"He's never been in any trouble," Kenny said. "A good student."

"You can take him out," the lieutenant said. "But don't let me see him here again."

The M.P. conducted them to the tent where Buzz was held.

"You'll have to come in and identify him before he can be released."

It was easy to see from the glare of the lights outside. Thin pallets lay on ground sheets and on each pallet was a boy, sitting up, quite still. Their ankles and wrists were shackled. Buzz was down almost at the end. He must have seen them enter but his face was expressionless.

Kenny identified him and the M.P. released the shackles.

"You're the first little bird to fly out of this nest," he remarked.

"What's going to happen to these boys?" Martha asked.

"I'm not the Justice Department, lady."

"Of course not," she said quickly. "Silly of me to ask. Only the lieutenant would know that."

He shrugged. As Martha had conjectured, he resented the implication that he knew less than his officers.

"Well, word gets around. Most of 'em will be inducted, I guess."

Buzz was silent as Kenny drove them home.

"You might at least thank Kenny," Martha said, exasperated. "He's been to a lot of trouble."

Buzz roused himself and thanked him, curtly. Martha added much warmer thanks and invited Kenny in when they arrived, but he said that Ellen would be expecting him. "I hate to ask you for another favor, Kenny," Martha said, "but will you try to find out what is happening to Aunt Sue Booth in Haddam?"

"It's no favor, Martha. Aunt Sue's a relation of Ellen's, after all. I'll find out. We can take her in our house if she wants to come. You know how she is."

Martha knew. Aunt Sue's fierce independence had been a source of quiet amusement and pride in the family. Kenny was good to make the offer. He had always been attentive to his wife's family, but this would be a considerable effort. They were lucky, she thought. There were those who had thought Ellen was making a poor match when she married a state trooper but her mother had encouraged the shy, timid Ellen to accept the man of her choice.

He drove off and Martha found that Buzz hadn't eaten since that morning. She lit the pot stove and warmed some of the stew that was already defrosting, found some candles and set the table on the back porch—the furthest point from the road. Buzz ate hungrily, drank some milk and then had a slice of Ann's pie.

By the light of the candle, Martha watched his face. When his freckles no longer seemed to be leaping from his face and his complexion returned to normal she gave him a fond look. "You might have been a bit more grateful to Kenny," she said. "You were rather terse."

"I was sorry you came," he answered. "I would have bust out, somehow. Now they know where I live. I wouldn't have told them. They only got my name from a note in my pocket. You'll be in trouble. Who let me go?"

"The lieutenant," Martha said. "He was an American."

"The geeks won't like it when they find out."

Buzz took another piece of pie.

"Geeks?"

"The Russians, the green tabs. They're KGB. The guys call them the geeks. Well, I guess they bit the head off the eagle all right. There was an argument when they grabbed me; one officer wanted me shot there and then, I think. After a while I was shoved in a van with some others. I wouldn't be surprised if they come after me; I'll have to get out of here. I'll spend the night in the woods. P'raps you should report me as a runaway, it might get you off the hook. Kenny I don't care about. If he's working for them, he's one of them."

His young face was hard.

He saw her gaze. "Don't worry about me, Mom. I can look after myself."

"It seems like it," Martha said. "What were you doing over at Haddam to get yourself arrested?"

"We needed something," he said slowly. "Robbie and me. And we guessed they'd be sealing the plant off entirely in a few days so we took a chance. New London's already an armed camp. We took Robbie's motor bike, went around back roads and did the last bit on foot. But it was lousy with soldiers; we didn't have a chance. We sneaked away from the plant but they spotted us on a road where we thought we were in the clear. I broke one way and Robbie another; I think he made it. The geeks handed me over to our own guys," he said bitterly, "and they shackled me and the other kids that went into the van. One of them asked which prep school I went to. They couldn't do it without our people, Mom. The geeks mostly handle the heavy prisoners. Webster is in that special section at the back of the camp," he added, "I got a look when he was brought in, after we were processed. He didn't look too good. The police chief from Haddam, a guy called Bennett, had been there, I heard, but he was already gone."

"How did you find this out?" Martha asked, remembering the silence.

"You soon find ways," he replied briefly. "The kids say there's screaming at night from the special section.

And firing squads are rattling off out in the fields. They say if you go out the front gate, like we did, it's a transfer. If you go out the back, it's curtains. Bennett went out the back."

Martha shivered. "Bill Webster . . ." She thought of Cynthia Webster, mourning her lost elms. "Bill was on his way to Washington."

"I guess the camp is handy for the people they pull off Route Eight and the trains: close to Bridgeport."

"But why Bill? He was always in favor of detente. He voted against every military appropriation."

"Maybe they don't want any Senators left around."

Martha looked at her son, drinking his milk as usual, but no longer a boy.

"*What* did you need from the plant?"

"It's best you don't know, Mom," he said quietly. For a moment he reminded her of Josh. She thought of the secret she was carrying, too precious to keep, too dangerous to share, and was tempted to share it with Buzz. But not yet.

"Uranium," she said. "What else would you want there?"

For the first time he looked startled, young and defenseless.

"Have you and Robbie been trying a build a *bomb*?"

"It could be done," he said. "Robbie and I machine-tooled a lot of our own parts. It's getting the uranium. We could have got it, easy enough, before the eagle died. What our people couldn't stop since the 1940's," he added in disgust, "It looks like the geeks have done already."

Martha had a rush of pride for her son, who was a fighter after her own heart, mingled with a dreadful fear for his life.

"Even if you got the uranium," she pointed out, "I think it would have been the wrong kind. Not the sort for a weapon, as it is. And neither you nor Robbie knows enough about nuclear physics."

Buzz looked down. "Maybe we know someone with access to a research reactor. P'raps we're not such dummies as you think."

"But even if you did manage to make a bomb," she said, forestalling argument. "If you could get close enough with it to destroy anything of importance, in the long run, what good would it do?"

"We could hold some of their bigwigs hostage," he said stubbornly. "We'll give them trouble. And there must be more like us. All over the country. We're not just going to sit back and allow them to take over, let alone help them to do it. Anyone who works for them should be shot."

Americans murdering Americans. They had come to it quickly.

"Buzz," she said slowly, "suppose there was something—something big. Something that might have a chance . . ." She stopped as he looked up, his eyes glinting with interest, with hope. "You might be needed," she went on. "If you're arrested for trying to steal uranium, how can you be useful? If you leave here, how can I find you?"

He thought, tapping his summer-tanned fingers on the white cloth.

"We might have to cool it for a while on the bomb. But I must go. No point in being a sitting duck. I'll have a last session on the radio, then I'll bury everything in canisters down in the briars. You'd better leave here for a while anyway, Mom. You don't want to be around if they come looking for me. If you need me, leave word with Robbie's mother, she'll know how to reach him. But what *is* this something big? Whose deal is it? How do I get in on it?"

"Buzz," she answered honestly. "I'm not sure yet. It's a possibility—perhaps more than a possibility. I have to talk to people. I might have to go back to New York. When anything happens, you'll know."

Buzz's eyes, as they met hers, had an expression very

different from the blank withdrawal of the last few days.
For the first time since the surrender they understood
each other, they were mother and son again.

Later, with only the light of a pale moon, she helped
him bury his equipment, while he gave her the news
he had gleaned.

"They're homing in on the hams already, but a lot of
the guys are still risking it. Word is out, induction has
started, boys seventeen and over. Reports from all over
the country of camps and firing squads. The ports are
busier than they've ever been. Food and goods going
out. Troops coming in. Some are Korean and Vietnamese.
Stories of armed resisters in the south and west, but the
geeks bring in heavy stuff and any Americans in the area
of the fighting get shot, women, kids, old people."

She passed on the warning about CB radios, but he
merely snorted.

"I suppose some guys'll turn them in, but if they
think we'll all give them up they're crazy. It'll be years
before they find them all, and by then we'll have built
more."

He threw some things in a backpack and left quietly
after giving her a rare embrace. She was choked with
emotion as he left and walked about the dimly-lit living
room in the silent house, unable to be still. Buzz. Buzz
and all the boys like him. They would risk their lives in
hazardous, mostly hopeless enterprises. The best of the
country could be killed; the worst would serve the new
masters, and the meek would accept their fate.

Yet, what did she know? The installations had been
built, not according to the Carter plan, but as two
hundred and thirty single silos, in Arizona, Utah, and
Nevada. The missiles, including the mysterious MY
missile, had been installed. How many missiles there
were, or where they were, she still did not know.
There had almost certainly been a rotation plan, and
once it was begun, they could be in any of the sites.
Doubtless all the information was programmed some-

where in a computer, but that computer could well
have been destroyed. It would take an army to occupy
all the bases; hundreds of missileers to check on all the
equipment, to fire if necessary.

Her mind shuttled back to the computer. Where it
could be, who might know. Then she hoped it had been
destroyed because if it could be found, the Russians
would most likely be the ones to find it. They would be
draining every computer in the defense establishment.
But if the sites could be found and taken, would the
missiles be enough to make a difference? Carmody had
had more than that under his command, but he had
chosen defeat.

Buzz had said that the soldiers might come here to
pick him up again. She couldn't take that chance. Down
in the pump room, by candlelight, she took the papers
out and made a list of numbers, states and dates. The
papers themselves she burned in the furnace until they
were black and gray. The ash she swept neatly into a
paper bag and went out to scatter it in the deepest
thicket of the briars.

The moon was hidden by cloud now and it was very
dark. No pale glow lighted the sky from the factory
down the lake road; it had been closed since the surrender. The briars caught her skirt, hands reaching out to
snatch and tug at her. She should have changed to
jeans, the housewifely part of her mind noted, while
the rest was fretting over the Magnanimity project and
the MY missile. If Josh had thought the missiles could
not be found, would he have risked saving the specifications? That package, now reduced to a slip of paper in
her pocket, was no sentimental memento. Perhaps Josh
had known, had somehow discovered the rotation plan.

He was—had been—a cautious man. If he had known
or guessed, and wished to leave her the information, it
would not have been *with* the specifications. He would
have left it *somewhere else*—in another place that only
she might be likely to find.

As soon as it was light, she would make a search. She would search through everything in the house down to the pockets of old clothes lying in the trunks in moth-balls. Perhaps she could start tonight, with a pair of candles. Turning quickly, a branch of a tall bush touched her face, leaving a sore scratch. She cried out, and then bit her lip in annoyance. The last thing she wanted to do was to attract attention to herself. Thank God there was no traffic on the narrow road; she was safe enough. The pounding of her heart lessened slowly.

A nearby branch snapped; two large hands grabbed her shoulder. A voice close to her ear murmured, "Don't call out . . ."

—— XIII ——

Martha broke away, but another figure came from behind a bush. The voice was reassuring. "Martha." It was Betty Swenson. Glancing over her shoulder, Martha saw it was Henry who had clutched her shoulder. "Don't be frightened. We've been searching for you. Katie Rogers sent her boy to tell us. An army truck with foreign soldiers has been down West Morris Road and they're asking for your house. They missed the way. She thinks they're looking for Buzz."

"Thanks, Betty," Martha said gratefully, and pressed her friend's hand. Swiftly she slipped away under cover of the darkness into the shelter of the orchard. There she hesitated. She had no wish to embarrass any of her neighbors. On the other side of Lake Shore Road there would be many unoccupied summer houses. She picked up a few windfalls for breakfast and headed for an empty house, not too close to home. There were no cars outside View Cottage but like most empty houses nowadays it was locked. Martha felt like a burglar as she broke a small pane of glass to open the back door from the inside.

It was odd to feel her way up to the bedroom of a woman she had never known and to lie down on her bed. And yet that night was not one of unrelieved misery. The moon broke from the cloud and she lay in its light and thought of the bravery of Buzz. Buzz, the giant killer, who hoped to defeat the Soviet military machine with a bomb made by his own hands. There must be many others like him, gallant young men, true descendents of the men who had made and kept this nation. The thought cleansed her memory of the American soldiers at the camp, the ignorant, the resentful, the first to be willing to do the enemy's dirty work, perhaps themselves to be eliminated soon after.

In the morning she found a boy and gave him five dollars—scarce now that the banks were closed—to look at her house and see if there were soldiers standing guard.

"No," he said, when he came back to report, "But the doors are bust in."

She made her way back warily but saw no one. Nothing except a neighbor's cat on the prowl, staring at a chipmunk caught in one of her traps. Chasing the cat off, she released the chipmunk and it hopped swiftly to the orchard. She threw the traps into the barn. There was no gasoline to take trapped animals to the woods, and she had no stomach for killing.

Certainly she had had visitors. The rugs were rucked up as though things had been dragged to the door; dragged down the stairs, the stair carpet was torn. Of course. She went up to Josh's study. His file cabinet and his big desk had been carted off. His books and his papers were gone. In the kitchen, the drawers were pulled out and thrown on the floor. Her domestic files of bills and receipts had been taken too. Someone would have the job of looking through all her bills for birdseed and household goods for nearly twenty years.

And not only papers had been taken. Her father-in-law's gold pocket watch that had sat on a shelf had disappeared. His medals were left. A fine, small clock had gone, and a portrait photograph of Josh's grandmother in a heavy, silver frame. Her mother-in-law's china birds, more valuable, had been left behind, though one was broken.

The looter had knocked it over, no doubt, when he reached past the big bible to the silver frame. The bible, too, was now on the rug, its gold lettering bright in the morning sun, unwanted as booty, an old religious artifact of little worth in this new world. It was an old family bible with floppy edges that had to lie down on its side. Martha preferred her own grandmother's bible and prayer book, and this one was rarely used, except to record births and deaths. Josh's death would have to go in there. His name would go after his mother's, Sarah Adams. The bible opened itself to that page. But the line was already filled in. Puzzled, Martha gazed down. The entry was in Josh's writing, like the previous one.

President Ronald Reagan. The date of his death. A scriptural reference.

No other president had ever been included in this purely family record. Certainly Josh had admired the late president, but . . . And the references: they were to the verses carved upon the graves. Sarah Adams, Ps 68:16. Martha remembered the verse from the psalm. Her mother-in-law had chosen it herself: the woman who loved her home on the hill. "Why leap ye, ye high hills? This is the hill which God desireth to dwell in, yea the Lord will dwell in it forever."

Had Josh known what was on the President's grave? She certainly did not. And yet there it was. Ma: 1:46. Ma—Matthew, Mark? It was not hard to decide; there was no verse forty-six in Chapter One of the Gospel of St. Mark. Matthew 1:46 then. "Who, when he had found one pearl of great price, went and sold all that he had, and bought it."

It was grimly apt. The awful scandal that erupted after the President's death about the missing money. The suicide of one of his chief advisors. Or could there be more? Her heart pounded as she searched her pocket for the slip of paper she had prepared the night before. Ma. Could that also be a reference to the Magnanimity project? Or the mysterious MY missile? Whatever that was? 1:46. 146. The Job 146 had been marked Utah. But that was all. Completion date of the installation was in October, '82. But why would that job number be next to the date of the President's death, years later?

A chickadee hanging from the bird feeder gave out an insistent cry. She looked up, blinking, into a shaft of light and saw again the mess in her sitting-room, with discarded bits and pieces carried from the upper floors lying just where they had dropped. One of Josh's pipes had tumbled onto the sofa; the stuff for the new curtains, much trampled, lay on the floor next to a radio, broken, from Buzz's room, by the Navaho rug it had been wrapped in. Mechanically, she picked up the debris. The Navaho rug, when had she last seen it? It had gone into the closet long ago. Then she remembered, suddenly and clearly as if it had been yesterday. The week the President was killed, Buzz had been home from school and ill with the flu. She had taken leave to go up and nurse him. His birthday came; he had been weak and cross and it was a dim celebration, until Josh had flown in to cheer him. He had brought the little rug, smiling apologetically. Buzz was not the age to have much interest in household goods. What was it he had said? It was terribly important to remember exactly. Something about his work? She heard his voice again.

"That was all I could find at the end of the world. Over fifty miles to Blanding, the nearest place to buy anything much. I could only find this at Barkham's, a

miserable excuse for a trading post." On this job, he
had told Buzz, his men all got rich from sheer inability
to spend a dime. Buzz had been promised a new transceiver of terrifying complexity; they had all laughed a
lot and Buzz had been cheered. The day after Buzz's
birthday Josh had flown back to the job and then the
tragedy struck. Josh returned soon after.

But why had Josh been on that installation? She
blinked again, the brilliant light was giving her a head-
ache. The project had been completed long before.
Repairs, was it? A modification? Something had happened, so Josh had had to know that one of the hidden
missiles—perhaps the mysterious MY missile—was at
the site 146.

It was hard for Martha to cut that page out and
destroy it, the record of so many generations of Adamses,
made by their own hands. Destroying history. A small
desolation. A lot more would be destroyed, before all
was done.

A boy on a bicycle came down the drive. The sun
shone on his fair hair and his bright, striped shirt. For a
moment he looked like any of the carefree children of
summer. But his young gaze was taking in the marks of
truck tires, the scattered debris, and he already had a
wary look.

She opened the door; he was relieved to see her.

"Mrs. Adams? A note for you," he said.

From habit, Martha went back for her bag to give the
boy something for his trouble, but when she returned
he had gone, peddling furiously. It occurred to her that
she had not seen the mailman since she returned. The
Post Office no doubt was in the process of change and
boys like these were filling its place.

The note was signed merely "W" but obviously it was
from Walt Fairfield. "I have been ordered to report to
work on Monday. Urge you return to work as we discussed. A friend may call on you."

A friend. Walt had guessed that she knew something.

A friend . . . an FBI agent who had escaped the net, perhaps, or someone from Rocketdyne? She looked about her, at her beloved home. When she arrived here, she had not meant to return to New York, to the United Nations. In truth, she had lost enthusiasm for her work, even before the surrender. Rather she had thought to throw in her lot with her countrymen. But now she had work of a special sort, and here she could find no one to help her. And Walt was right. Her chance of remaining free was greater there than here.

By 10:30 a.m. Mrs. Martha Adams, neatly dressed, was on the train bound for New York.

—— XIV ——

A parade was taking place in New York City. Soviet-American solidarity week had been proclaimed; festivities had already taken place in Washington and today it was the turn of New York, which some UN people were already calling the capital on the East River. Marshal Borunukov drove in the lead car, with Perez in the next. There had been some difficulty about the arrangements, causing embarrassment to the Deputy Mayor of New York, but the victorious Marshal of the Soviet Union ended in first place.

The Marshal did not need popularity over the conquered people. Alexander himself had not achieved a conquest equal to his; that was satisfaction enough for any soldier. Nevertheless it vexed him that on the few public appearances in Washington, Philadelphia and now New York, he was accorded a cool, sullen respect, while Perez, in his army fatigues, his Castro cap, sporting his black beard and surrounded by his entourage of African blacks and lackeys from Central America, obviously intrigued many of the young people. An occasional cry of "Ché!" was heard, which Perez would acknowledge, smiling, as if he had inherited a mantle from the bungling Ché, although as the Marshal well knew, it was Perez's people who had betrayed Guevara to the Bolivians.

Virinsky had remained in his UN office. He had no taste for public appearances. Despite the police and soldiers lining the route, (including the Mongolians who had been flown in for the occasion) there was always the possibility of trouble. Borunukov would stay in his special car that was armored like a tank, but Perez was no doubt showing off to the crowd, though naturally from the safety of a bullet-proof bubble. For the benefit of the television cameras, whose pictures would blanket the world by satellite, the parade had started on Wall Street, now under rows of red flags, bearing the golden hammer, sickle and star. On that bright day the gold was glittering.

The parade would end at the UN building, where the Marshal was to be received by the Secretary-General, who would commemorate the day as Peace Day. The speech was prepared, but a fuss was going on in the Secretary-General's office, where some of his third-world advisors had strongly suggested that Perez be given a separate and equal welcome. An addition to the Secretary-General's remarks was being hastily prepared on the theme of the dawning of an age of equality and plenty.

Even the Politburo, Virinsky knew, were not entirely pleased by this turn of events. Their ambivalence towards the military, their belief in Perez as the most able and dedicated of Party members, did not prevent a warning signal going off in those wary minds. Kharkev had called on his special line and had a few words to say that very morning. Virinsky was to join Marshal Borunukov in ordering immediate conscription of the entire 17-to-30 age group as he had requested, though the original plan, backed by Perez, had been to proceed more slowly. The Marshal had been delighted, and warmed towards Virinsky, his new ally. That would take care of the Ché lovers. They could be useful on the China border.

The barges on the river were hooting, which they had been ordered to do, as part of the celebration. An oversized kayak had been specially constructed to fly the flag of the newly-proclaimed Socialist Soviet Republic of Bering, named in honor of the great navigator, Vitus Bering. The Special Session of the General Assembly had returned Alaska to its Russian heritage with almost unanimous consent. Only Canada had abstained. As Bering was already occupied, the Resolution made little difference, but it was still good to observe the forms.

Cuba's request for the former State of Florida, the south-eastern peninsular of *Oblast*—that was Region—IV, was something else again. The Politburo remained undecided about how this was to be handled. Virinsky frowned at the thought of having to thwart Perez again so quickly. Perez had his own supporters, not merely the Third World rabble with their small socio-historical importance, but powerful men in Moscow itself. The Member for Foreign Affairs of the Politburo was a party comrade of long standing, and Ulyanov, the General-Secretary himself, was known to have said privately that Perez had done more towards the eventual defeat of the United States than Borunukov, so skillfully had he manipulated its leaders into strangling themselves. That, Virinsky thought, had been overstating the case, and did not give the KGB's Directorates S and A sufficient credit. Directorate A, with its huge success in *dezinformatsiya*, had made it impossible for the United States to arm itself for the modern world, and Directorate S, having purloined every worthwhile technological advance, had sent in continuous reports of the collapse of America's military might.

Perez had caused a lot of rabble-rousing. No doubt it was he who had encouraged Mexico, in return for her valuable cooperation, to ask for a large hunk of Region VI, the former states of Texas and New Mexico, and much of Region IX, the old Arizona and California. Neither the Politburo nor the army were willing to accede to this demand, but there was skirmishing along the border. Not against Russian troops—there were precious few there yet—but against Americans, who fortunately were doing the Russians' work for them.

Later, Perez and Borunukov were going to address the Assembly. Virinsky, however, had serious work to do. More than anyone else, he was responsible for implementing the New Order. It was imperative that the schedule be kept tight because of the plans for October 26, Ulyanov's name day, and the anniversary of the Revolution by the old calendar. Since Ulyanov's accession to power, the Moscow celebration had been changed to that day, and it was then, after the "honeymoon period" that the full plans for the New Order would be revealed. Ulyanov himself would arrive with other dignitaries, in great state, to address the Assembly and announce the final arrangements for the dissolution of the former United States of America.

And so far, the results of the interrogation of senior Treasury officials had been surprisingly disappointing. They had little information to give. In the world of bureaucracy that had been Washington, (so similar, in some ways, to the one in Moscow) it seemed the truth had been buried in the Bureau of the Budget. The Budget apparently was something that no one could fully understand or account for. And the Director from the Reagan years was already dead. He, like others, had committed suicide after the great budget scandal.

The door of the outer office burst open; there was a mutter from the secretary in the outer office, and Perez was at the inner door, still wearing the cap, the black boots and the olive green garments that had appeared

on the television screen to be army fatigues. Close to, it
was apparent that they were well cut and of a fine cloth
suitable to the season.

"What's all this about clearing out Harlem? Nobody
said a word to me. I find out about it when the parade
ends at Forty-Second Street."

No salutation, not one *"amigo"*, Virinsky noted, though
some called it Perez's favorite word. "I'm sorry you
were not informed," Virinsky said smoothly. "Naturally, you should have been appraised of scheduled
operations in Region II. I will look into it. But that has
nothing to do with the parade. Traditionally, I believe,
the parades end at Fifty-Ninth Street. In this instance,
the Secretary-General wished it to culminate here."

"To get his ugly face in front of the cameras again,"
Perez retorted. "He's certainly getting to like that." He
added a few more words on the subject of the Secretary-
General, and his idea that he was running anything. "I
had intended to stay at the Teresa Towers."

Of course, Castro had once stayed at the old Teresa.

"Well, you certainly can if you wish. Harlem as such
has not been cleared. There is only the general plan,
agreed on in council more than a year ago, that after
the taking of the United States the cities would be
cleared of their non-working populations and the workers brought in, to save the decaying transport systems.
It should have begun in Washington, but things are a
little behind there. It's no different than the policy for
Moscow. I expect the Americans themselves might have
liked to use such a policy but of course, they did not
have the means."

Perez scowled. Both of them knew very well that the
Americans could not have done it as it would have been
politically disastrous even to hint of such a thing. And
the political bosses of the ghetto areas had not wanted
to see their constituencies scattered to the four winds.
Now Perez himself was caught in the trap. His people
had their biggest support among the young and in those

very ghettos. Both of these bases were to be eroded while Borunukov would grow stronger. Yet he could do nothing. The United States must follow the same plan for conquered territory that each victim nation had suffered in turn.

Virinsky could imagine the coded messages that would go off that night to Perez's supporters in Moscow.

"Why not stay in the complex in Riverdale tonight," he said. "Their communication system with Moscow is superb."

Perez grunted what sounded like assent. He flung himself into a chair opposite Virinsky, his boots scraping the desk.

"Borunukov is taking over the Towers at the Waldorf-Astoria. Generals! I had to get away from the mob," he said moodily. "I'll have enough of them tonight."

The Soviet Ambassador to the United Nations was holding a reception after the Assembly meeting.

"You should have seen Borunukov on Wall Street," Perez gave a snort. "I think he was disappointed he couldn't have a ticker-tape parade. He actually suggested it might be a good thing to reopen the exchange for a while. Said it might be useful. I think he'd like to join the Union Club."

Virinsky gave a suggestion of a smile that might have meant agreement or mere lack of comprehension. His position was delicate. Although a full member of the troika here, in the Soviet Union he was merely Kharkev's second-in-command, controlling the First Department, the US and Canada. He did not rank there with a Marshal of the Soviet Union, nor with a brilliant Party man like Perez who had aided the group that overthrew Khrushchev and was a victorious guerrilla leader, the premier Cuban since the downgrading of Castro.

Nevertheless, Virinsky did not like the way Perez had swaggered into his office without a by-your-leave, as though it were the quarters of some local party secretary. The Russian's face, smooth and pale with its layer of lard, seemed without guile, though it did not for the moment deceive Perez.

"Another vodka-guzzling night," he said, as though deliberately provoking Virinsky to commit himself. "I think the Borunukov gang has disposed of enough vodka since the surrender to float the White House onto the Potomac."

"Surely they deserve some celebration," Virinsky replied mildly. His hands rested on his desk, over the covers of the files he had been examining when Perez had entered. There was no need to give Perez any hints about the Reagan budget. "They have gained a great victory for the Soviet Union, after all."

"*They* gained?" Perez's eyebrows shot up. "After all the work my people and yours did in softening the American eagle to a fat, helpless chicken? All Borunukov had to do was to point his missiles, with the aid of a few technicians and the information supplied by *your* department, *amigo*."

What did Perez want? He must want something to be sitting here passing out compliments. Certainly he was not just avoiding the celebration.

"Borunukov fired his missiles," Perez went on. "And the Politburo sent the ultimatum. But suppose that pompous ass has botched his job?"

Perez, now that he had emerged publicly as the real leader of the Caribbean group, was growing careless. The Marshal was pompous, but by no means an ass. And it was certainly unwise for Perez to say so to a man not securely in his own camp, unless he was acting as an agent-provocateur. After all, he must have no more liking for the KGB in the troika than he had for the army. Perez, no doubt, had had visions of the Americas as his own territory.

Virinsky made a deprecating sound that could have meant anything.

Perez apparently took it as an invitation to continue. "What if he missed a few missiles? If some American commander, still hiding out, could put a team together that could inflict unpleasant damage on Cuba, or the Soviet Union. The whole troika would be blamed."

"My information is that every effective installation was wiped out. The ICBM sites. The SAC bomber bases that still possessed nuclear weapons. The submarines, they have all been accounted for. The *Ohio* business was unfortunate, but one slipping through the net was always a possibility that had to be faced. And every missile site has been checked and rechecked. The accuracy was gratifying."

Perez paced about. "Not what the Canadians are saying. My friends up there aren't happy about Manitoba."

"Unfortunate, but inevitable. Reparations, of a sort, will doubtless be made. It was too close; the winds must blow somewhere."

"They'd like Pittsburgh," Perez said reflectively. "Historical pride, it was Fort Duquesne, you know. But anyway, you're speaking only of the *known* sites."

He strode over to the window, scowling down on the river below.

Virinsky's desk faced away from the window: he found the view distracting. Now he didn't like the feeling of Perez standing behind him and slewed round in his chair. Perez had heard something about Magna, of course. How much? Could he have learned more than he had himself? The KGB had more professional agents, but Perez had informers everywhere. "You don't suppose that any of their sites could have escaped our aerial reconnaissance?"

"Yes, they could," Perez retorted. "If their camouflage was good enough."

"Yet in Cuba in '62 . . ."

"Let's not play games." Perez wasn't noted for his patience. "You know very well we did everything we could for those missiles to be seen. It all ended, after Kennedy's brave words, with our having absolute con-

trol of Cuba; the US recognized it as a Soviet protectorate. We removed the old missiles, and the new ones
went in the hidden silos. And from Kennedy to Carmody
they were never spotted."

Virinsky looked at him. "American Intelligence might
have been poor, but it wasn't as bad as that. Carmody
knew. He just couldn't act."

"The last President of the United States," Perez said,
rubbing his beard. "Maybe I'll drink to that with
Borunukov. From Washington to Carmody. What a
decline in just over two hundred years!"

"There's Bristow," Virinsky said, wondering when
Perez would get to the point.

"Bristow can be President of something. Not the
United States. The Politburo will be meeting on that
this week. Ulyanov's coming over to make the announcement on October 26."

Virinsky grunted, slightly taken aback. Those plans
had been held closely. Only a handful of the most important men on the Politburo—all Ulyanov men—had
known these details that were to be announced at the
next meeting. His mind clicked over the names. Ulyanov
himself must have told Perez.

"Just look at those boats down there," Perez said
abruptly. "Any one of them could carry an atomic weapon
and blow us all off this rock."

The Great Hero of the Caribbean was jittery, Virinsky
could see, as Perez backed away from the glass wall and
moodily resumed his seat. The Castro brothers had
always said he wasn't fond of the smell of gunpowder.
In spite of his warlike costume, he was no more a true
guerrilla fighter than Lenin had been. His brilliance lay
in maneuvering and directing behind the scenes, but
now he also had the sense of theater suited to the
times. Virinsky sat impassively, waiting for what must
come. He became aware that his left thumb was exposed and he eased it under his palm.

"There are rumors," Perez told him. "Unsubstantiated."

The Cunningham tape. Did he have more?

"We should be in closer touch on this." Perez got to the point at last. But the nervous flick of the forked thumb had caught his eye; it was rarely exposed. Father Three-Thumb: Perez had heard the jibe. And other jibes. He wondered what was in the green file that Virinsky was taking trouble to conceal. "You've got a report on Magna." It wasn't a question.

Virinsky nodded.

"The Marshal's too sure of himself," Perez said. "Some people got away before we had secured all the airports. Some slipped over to Canada. We'll get them, eventually. Our organizations have worked together before. More closely than on the purely official level. Suppose we work together on this."

Virinsky said nothing. Silence, with such a volatile type of man, could be a useful weapon.

"I tell you, Virinsky, I have a nose for these things. I don't like the sound of this Magna."

Neither of them would give up everything, of course, Virinsky knew, but they could share more than they did now. Even if the Marshal learned about it, there could be no criticism of the troika working in harmony.

"I agree," he said slowly. "But I know no more about Magna now than I did when I got the report. No investigation has been fruitful."

His only hope was the financial records and that would be a weary job. And there might be nothing left to find. The bureaucrats had learned a good lesson from the Nixon mess, and by the time the scandal came to light the relevant documents had vanished into night and fog.

"The GRU made a botch of it," Perez summed up. "Cunningham. Roche. And the Intelligence people know nothing. Reagan must have known how heavily the intelligence departments had been infiltrated—by your people," Perez added, with a sudden grin. "Magna," he said, "should be a number one priority for both our organizations. Agree?"

Virinsky agreed again. He had now redressed the balance. Both Borunukov and Perez had come to him and been granted favors. When Perez had gone, he too, gazed out of the window, but did not concern himself with small atomic weapons. Borunukov had served in enough occupied territories to know how to secure it, territories that had showed a lot more fight than the United States. *Glavny rag*, the main enemy. A great prize. It was a large mouthful to chew. There would be those who would choke on it. And when the feast was digested, who would be in power in the Kremlin? The military? The politicals? Or his own people, no longer under anyone's command?

When the daylight faded, he continued working by the light of his desk lamp. On the day just passing into history, the United States had lost Alaska. It mattered little. After October 26th, the United States would be no more. The map he kept in the top drawer of his desk showed the plan he had worked out with Kharkev for the United Socialist Regions of the Americas. The Central American states were to be included and were already marked in black. The South American countries would be added one by one; the regional outlines were shown in dots. Kharkev was certain that he had the votes in the Politburo; Ulyanov could not resist the prospect of making the great announcement on his name day. Virinsky glanced at the space that was Canada, still left white. It would fall too, in good time, to join Alaska.

Yet he would give more than Alaska, he thought, to learn exactly what Magna was. Perez must know something already; that would account for his obvious fear. But what could his sources have found? Where were Perez's men more effective than Virinsky's own? Among some of the Caribbean madmen perhaps. Or in the wilder outposts of the PLO. The FLQ were much involved with Perez's people. Virinsky felt a moment's annoyance, remembering that Perez had already got his men into many police commands. But surely, if the full knowledge of this secret plan existed anywhere it would be here, in the Continental United States.

It was said that Perez, in times of stress, would quiet his nerves by having a string of prisoners brought out and shooting them himself. Virinsky was far more disciplined, but he drank hot, sweet tea until he sweated in the air-conditioned room as he drafted a note marked "Urgent!"

Reinterrogation of all senior military officers and intelligence personnel. No executions permitted until further notice, notwithstanding orders from the GRU, nor any other Intelligence departments. The thought of the too-hasty execution squads of the GRU caused his bile to rise to his throat. In his austere, practical office, the controlled Virinsky sat and swore. If there was one single living human being left alive who knew about Magna he, Constantin Virinsky, would get him in his hands.

─── XV ───

Martha had arrived in the city in time to be held up by the parade, though it had not been a simple journey. She could hardly have bicycled to Waterbury or Naugatuck and she had used her last few drops of gas making a round of the local stations to see if any had supplies to sell. As she drove into the large gas station on Route 109, she noticed that under the now familiar "No gas" sign there was an addition in small letters, "Except for holders of special permits."

The man on the pump was Andy Dickens, the owner, a pink-faced, fat and friendly man in a baseball cap, whom Martha had known slightly for years. She produced her travel documents. "Andy," she said, "I need gas to get to the New York train. And back, if possible."

He looked at the UN stamp. "You're on the list," he said. "I can fill you up."

She paid him and he took the money without his usual thanks. His eyes were cold and he looked at her as though she were a stranger. She glanced back uneasily as she drove away and saw that his gaze followed her, as Buzz's young stare had followed Kenny. A childish wish to explain swept over her. Her position, she saw, would be progressively more uncomfortable.

The road by the reservoir could have been a poster picture of late summer in Connecticut: a curve of tall trees, lush with broad green leaves, a dome of clear blue sky reflecting in the bright blue water. Birds still called from the branches, but the ducks were gone. People were running short of meat. She wondered what it would be like in the city.

At Naugatuck there had been no problem in parking her car. As she swung into the railroad yard, she was met by an armed guard. He checked her papers and led her into the newspaper office, where they were checked again. The former newspaper office was now occupied by State police. They looked apologetic, reminding her again of Kenny.

"Going through to New York?" the sergeant asked.

"It's O.K.," the guard said, "Pass good for Region II."

"Right." The sergeant looked quickly and handed the folder back to Martha. "There'll be another check at Bridgeport. Have your papers ready."

The guard escorted her to the platform and put her on the train. She saw other passengers going through the same process. At Bridgeport, and at Stamford, the State police were augmented by soldiers carrying automatic weapons. Again the train passed through 125th Street without stopping, and papers were given a final check at Grand Central. The doors to Vanderbilt Avenue had been reopened, though the subway entrance was locked and barred. Outside was a phalanx of guards. Somewhere close by a band was playing.

There had been few passengers alighting, and the number of cabs waiting were correspondingly diminished. The last one was snapped up before Martha reached the curb. The only cab left in the bay had a "radio cab" sign glittering. She was making for Forty-Second Street to try her luck there when the driver of the waiting vehicle yelled: "Your cab, lady."

So some New York cabbies were still picking and choosing their fares. It was faintly cheering that one bit of free enterprise was still undaunted. She would have thought that the lack of gas, and the tying up of money, had ruined the cabs by now.

"Lady," the driver told her, "there's always people who've got money. Don't ask me how. On Friday they started issuing redbacks to exchange for the hundred dollars in green, and on Friday night there were people blowing thousands of 'em in a big crap game near Times Square. But like you said, most of the cabbies are uptight. The big spenders now, they're mostly limousine types. If you ask me, the day a lot of these foreign wheel-jockeys learn their way about, most of the medallions are going to be called in."

With everything that had happened, she had missed hearing about the redbacks. Her money had been accepted in Connecticut.

"Don't worry," the driver said. "The green is good until the end of the month. For whatever it's good for. You'll see, permits are the thing now. The new boys on the block are permit-happy."

Because of the parade the traffic flows along the streets had been changed and there was a policeman at almost every crossing. It was strange, Martha remarked to the driver, that the streets were now full of New York City policemen, whereas in the old days they were not to be seen.

"The old days," the driver said gloomily. "You mean, like a couple of weeks ago. Still, you're right. It's a whole new deal."

With a wave of his hand, a policeman stopped the traffic.

"Better when the cops got lost," he added.

Helicopters were zooming overhead but the band

music could still be heard. Martha thought she recognized the anthem.

"Is it——?" she said.

"You'll get used to that. It's the Internationale. They play it every day on the radio when the news starts and when it finishes."

Traffic lights and signs were still operating: New York had its electricity. On the side streets there was a litter of furniture and household goods outside residential buildings. "Evacuations," the driver said. "A lot of people have been moved out. Retirees. People without jobs. They made a big sweep over the weekend and got all the bums off the Bowery, and the crazies off the streets in time for the parade. You won't see a shopping bag lady left in town."

To her surprise, after she paid the driver he picked her suitcase up and carried it into the foyer of her building and then went up with her to her apartment.

"I'll just look to see if everything's O.K.," he said. "Lot of people hiding out in empty apartments and they're not all senior citizens who don't want to move."

Martha was familiar with a certain type of taxi-driver who saw himself as a shepherd to his flock, and had started to thank him when they both heard a muffled sound from Josh's bedroom. The driver was moving towards the door, but Martha remembered Walt's message. If this *was* the contact, she couldn't have him discovered.

"Oh, that's all right," she lied hastily, "it's my housekeeper," and she bustled the man out. If it was a burglar, or a family of squatters, she thought, she would just have to deal with it herself.

He gave her an odd look, but accepted her dismissal.

"Here," he said, giving her a crumpled piece of pasteboard. "My card. Midtown cabs. Give us a call any time you want service."

She thanked him. As he left, it struck her that there was something familiar about him, the angle of his head,

tilted slightly under his cap, his light stride, but that was
forgotten as she turned towards Josh's room with a very
nervous clutching at her insides. Nonsense, she told
herself firmly. The muffled noise she had heard had
probably come from someone at least as frightened as
herself. She opened the door firmly and looked, surprised, into the ashen face of Rose.

"I hope you won't be mad, Mis' Adams," she said. "I
thought you was in the country."

Martha soothed her as well as she could, shocked
herself. Rose looked as though she had aged ten years
since the day of the surrender.

"They came round," Rose said as the two women sat
together in the kitchen. Martha had made the coffee as
Rose was trembling so much she had spilled the grounds
all over the floor. "They told everyone to git. We was
being moved to fine homes. But we couldn't take our
furniture nor nothing they wasn't room for in the trucks.
Miz Adams," she said, "I didn't want to go off with no
sodgers. I didn't like the look of it at all, for all they got
some of those young girls, laughing and squeaking.
Hightailing it off into the Lord knows where with a baby
under each arm. No, I didn't like it. Not nohow. But
there was no place to go with all my friends turned out
of they homes. So I thought that you wouldn't mind, as
long as you was in the country. 'Sides," she said, looking
down. "I just had no place else. I had your keys, and
Mis' Furness's next door, but they's people living there
now. Young folks. Mis' Furness, they turned her out
with no time to change nor pack nor nothing. She just
walked off for Saddle River in them high-heeled sandals, but she don't know if they'll let her cross the
bridge."

"The Vogue woman." Josh's joke. Martha had an
image of Janet Furness, limping across the George Washington Bridge in a St. Laurent summer silk, trying to
reach a haven that perhaps was still there, perhaps not.

Wondering what had happened to her husband in Cincinnati.

"Of course, you can stay as long as you like," Martha said warmly. "You can have my husband's room. You and Luther too if he wants to come."

Rose looked down at her hands that lay limp on her broad lap. "Luther went to register for his identity card with the police. He got the card and they told him he had to come back the next day to get it stamped. Mis' Adams, he has *never* come home. And no word. You know my Luther. He's a good boy; he wouldn't act that way. It's happening with all the boys. They take 'em and put 'em in the army and send 'em right off. I just have a notion I will never see my Luther ever again."

So that was what had aged Rose ten years. Not the loss of her home. Her Luther, her pride.

"Some of the boys, they went hiding out. But there's no place to hide. You can hardly get out of the city, and you don't even get in the subway without a special worker's pass. Some people hid out down there, but the police went down with guns and dogs. So the kids, they roam the streets and break in houses until they get picked up. My Luther, he wouldn't have done that."

Rose was weeping, silently, the tears rolling down her cheeks. What have we done, Martha thought, what *have* we done? The best were going first. Rose had put all the labor of a lifetime in one great effort to make Luther the young man he was. Her joy in seeing him one of the most brilliant students in his college class was reward enough. And now all that Luther had become was condemned to be an expendable unit in the millions of men under Soviet arms.

There wasn't much Martha could say. She couldn't comfort Rose with lies. Rose's own good sense had told her all there was to know. It was Rose who pulled herself together and began to clean the flat that she had already cleaned until it shone, although there was no hot water and there had been none all week. She left nothing for Martha to do, but Martha could not sit idle. Better to go to the office: she had been asked to return today and would be needed, even if it was late; almost certainly there would be an evening session. And there was Walt's mysterious caller: perhaps it was at the UN he was supposed to find her, not here.

The First Avenue side of the UN building was in a burst of splendor. An avenue of fluttering Red Flags marked where the victorious Marshal had ended the parade. A dais, much decorated, stood close to the doors. The principal actors had gone inside but the TV cameras still ground away as an assistant to the Secretary-General was explaining the ceremonies to a newsman. "And can you tell the viewing audience," the newsman was saying, "exactly what position Mr. Perez holds? Is he in the Marshal's suite?"

The Assistant Secretary-General coughed.

"Mr. Perez is a member of a Committee of Three which is overseeing the transition from war to peace. And now I must leave you ladies and gentlemen; in a few moments Marshal Borunukov will be addressing the Assembly."

"Thank you very much, Mr. Assistant Secretary-General."

The television crews packed up. Martha wondered what viewing audience they were talking about; how much of the country still had electricity. But perhaps it was the audience abroad they had in mind.

Inside the building she found changes: the Trusteeship Council had spread over most of the ground floor. The usual posters referring to South Africa had gone. In their places were portraits of American Indians, Hispanics and American blacks. The legend was "The End of Colonialism."

She went up to Bob Postern's office; angry as she had been with him, still she felt she should give him news of what was happening in Connecticut. He probably wouldn't know.

There was a new machine on Bob's desk; she recognized it from having seen an earlier model. It was a type of word processor that would take the material and translate it into the other official UN languages. The translations had often been ludicrous and it had been awkward to operate. Certainly Bob would never have used it. His chair was empty.

Bob's assistant, a Swedish girl who had been in the office for the last three years, told her that the reporter was down in the General Assembly Hall.

"Bob, down there?" Martha said. It was a well-known joke that the senior UN correspondent *never* went down on the floor, filing his stories from press releases, notes taken by his assistants, and his very occasional listening to the squawk box that was always on in his office. The English translator was murmuring, "the dawning of this bright new day for the colonized people of the Americas . . ."

"Bob retired," the assistant said, not meeting Martha's gaze. "It was easiest. The UNESCO regulation on the licensing of journalists was enforced and I don't think that Bob . . ."

"Why not?" Martha asked caustically. "He never made any waves."

The attractive, usually confident and brisk young woman, looked about furtively, though the door was closed, and the small office was empty apart from themselves. "I hear . . . it doesn't seem as though any of the former journalists are getting licenses. Or editors. A new broom . . ."

She seemed to take comfort in the old proverb.

"Not even James Reston?"

"You haven't seen the *New York Times* lately, Mrs. Adams. I don't think you'd recognise it. Bob called it *Pravda West*. There are no advertisements anymore, not even on Sundays. No fashions . . ."

She smoothed the pleats on her neat skirt. Martha knew that although the girl was always well-dressed in the latest style, she was no featherhead. She had been having an affair with Bob for over two years. No doubt it was easier to talk of a lost fashion page.

At her office, as she had expected, her group was scheduled to work late. When, with the advent of the new machines, the great typing pools had been broken up into smaller, flexible units, overtime was supposed to have been eliminated, but the plan had never succeeded, although the head of Personnel had returned from the offices across First Avenue to supervise the changes herself.

Now Thu Thuy was at Martha's desk, and work was up-to-date, though it looked rather odd. The statistics were poured into the neat language piles. The office was still working on the WHO overflow, she saw, but not on Kwashiorkor. It was collating figures on death by burn, blast and radiation. Her eye took in the headings: Grand Forks, Malmstrom, Whiteman, Warren, Minot, Ellsworth, and another name, garbled by the machine. Davis something—that would be Davis Monthan, and Little Rock. She flipped the sheets, under the cool gaze of Thu Thuy, and came to the total estimated dead: 265,944.

"I have been instructed to ask you to go to Personnel as soon as you return. Madame Paul is there now. Her new office is on the 36th floor at the southwest corner of the corridor."

Thu Thuy's English was perfect, if somewhat expressionless, with a faint French accent. Too young to have lived in the French occupation of her country, perhaps she had studied in France.

Martha was taken aback by the luxury of Madame Paul's new quarters. Not so much by Madame's sudden elevation—as some heads rolled others must take their place—but by the summons to all this magnificence. Adjustment of leave problems was always taken care of in the big, impersonal quarters of the Personnel department and not on the carpets of senior executives.

To her further surprise, Madame Paul motioned her to a chair.

"I thank you again for cutting your leave short. As you see, the Organization is busy as it has never been before . . ."

She stopped, gazing at the heavy scratch made by the briar on Martha's cheek. "What has happened to you, Mrs. Adams?"

"An incident in the street, as I carried my rations."

Martha, normally truthful, wondered at the lie that sprang to her lips before she had even considered her reply. She had been reluctant to mention her country life at all. If Walt was right, and he probably was, the less connection made between her and Josh, the better.

Madame Paul frowned. "Something must be done to stop these street attacks on our people. Both the civil servants and the diplomatic corps has suffered. The police have orders to sweep up the criminals and the penalty for attacking a member of this body will be death. I am sorry, Mrs. Adams, and I will arrange that you get a substitute ration. Supplies should be adjusted soon and you will get a greater choice. Do you speak any Spanish, by the way?"

"Yes," Martha said. "I took two years of the courses here, after work."

She had always been glad of something to occupy her time when Josh was away. That was why she had taken a job, once Buzz had started boarding school. In the years when Josh had been in New York, there had never been time enough . . . what had they done with it all? Talked . . . yet Josh was a quiet man.

Madame Paul nodded. "Good. Then you can stay in your old post. Some of the Cuban girls can speak good English, some almost none. Thu Thuy is most efficient, but I need her here. Personnel will be expanding, Mrs.

Adams, and I may need you here later also. But in the meantime you can pick up on the WHO material."

"The deaths from the missile attack, yes," Martha said. "Over a quarter million dead to date, from the 'clean' warheads."

Josh had said attack on the silos would mean dirty ground bursts.

Madame Paul's eyebrows arched. "Most certainly a limited strike. Or the deaths would have been in the tens of millions and you and I would not be here. A quarter of a million, very dreadful, but a small price for peace. After all, in this country, it is not more than five years' deaths on the roads."

She gazed at the woman before her. Mrs. Adams, a British subject, was on the protected list. Her work had always been excellent; she was a good organizer and she had the ability to make the decisions necessary in any office quickly, without the bureaucratic backing and filling of so many of the Organization management employees. She was liked by her subordinates while remaining very much in charge. Certainly she could have had promotion, but she had seemed without ambition and had no taste for office politics. Her social life was outside of the Organization.

Mrs. Adams had been a perfect employee, under the previous regime. But now . . . there was something Madame Paul did not quite trust. Nothing definite. Perhaps that arrogant lift of the head, so typical of American women for all her British birth. Not that Madame Paul liked the British any more than she liked the Americans. The British had killed her uncle, a naval officer, at Oran. Perhaps it was nothing more than her acknowledged dislike of that reddish hair, startling against the white, summer-freckled skin, which caught the male gaze among the many darker women of the United Nations.

But there had also been the outburst on the matter of the girl who had to be dismissed, Lucy Kander. She had made a note at the time, but it was not enough to justify going further. Now these remarks about a confidential report. It was not confidential as far as she herself was concerned, but still . . . Her own judgement would be to get rid of this woman as soon as she could be replaced. However, more than her own judgement was involved and she had had her instructions.

"We are making a survey of certain Organization employees," she said. "Those who have lived long in this country and have family or friends here. First, I wish to assure you that such connections do not prejudice your position with the Organization, necessarily. All that is required to advance in the Organization is loyalty to the Organization. I hope I make myself clear?"

Martha nodded. "Perfectly clear." She wished Madame Paul would get on with whatever it was.

Madame Paul did. She handed Martha a printed sheet. "Take this home with you. Read the printed questions, think long and carefully, and write in your answers. You will be interrogated on them later and your answers will be checked. It may be that you can give the Organization significant help." In truth the Secretary-General knew nothing of the survey, but Virinsky had assured Madame Paul that that mattered little now.

The cool-looking Head of Personnel had an inner glow as she remembered her last meeting with Virinsky in his office. She had always thought him one of the most brilliant men in the Organization. She even found him attractive, despite his plump body and balding head and the oddity of his forked thumb. In fact, the small deformity made him more attractive; it appealed to some protective instinct.

Virinsky, for his part, was well aware of her feelings. He spoke to her more freely than he would to many men highly placed in his own organization. Her psychological profile made her perfect for his purpose. A plain spinster—Madame was really Mademoiselle—she was devoted to him with the kind of devotion that expressed itself in service and desired only to move with him, in a reflected glory, to the highest levels of power. Her pathological hatred of Americans was convenient.

Her record, in his private files, made it all plain. Her father, a typical petit bourgeois of Lyons, had been well-known as a *collaborateur* with the Nazis during the French occupation, and the American lawyers later cut him to pieces. The family had lost most of their possessions. Then the Maquis (good French communists, though the Pauls did not know that) had taken his wife who had entertained the Nazis, shaved her head and paraded her through the streets of the city. Young Renée Paul had grown up in this shadow and it would take a long revenge to slake her thirst. A pity she was now old and plain, with her sallow skin and dark greying hair in its thin chignon . . .

"Our Stage One seems to have gone reasonably smoothly," Virinsky had told her. "Both the military and intelligence placed under control. Soon intelligence personnel will be eliminated in their entirety and all military officers. But despite all our preliminary work, a question has come up as to the completeness of our records: whether there might have been military personnel kept out of the known records for just such an eventuality. Rather as the Germans formed their Werewolf groups, but possibly more dangerous."

Madame Paul bowed her head in agreement.

"We are investigating from many directions," he continued. "A cumbersome, but thorough one is a check through the civilian population, which will be checked and rechecked through the computer banks. Who did they know in the military or in intelligence? What was the regular address of any such person? Where was the last known posting? This is to include friends, relatives, acquaintances; guesses and suspicions as well as known facts. I want you to begin with our own people here.

Only those who have been in this country before the surrender will be useful, of course."

Madame Paul had had the forms in a few hours, ready for distribution. Martha understood at once. Her heart sank. She tried to look impassive, nodded, and left. It was obvious what this was: an opening shot to make Americans inform on each other. Also it was obvious that she couldn't answer it. When Walt had suggested that for her own safety she return to the shelter of the UN, she had hesitated. She had done so, for the safety of her precious knowledge, and in the hope of finding *someone*, Walt's mysterious "friend", or anybody who might help her to use it. But now she realised that if she stayed she would be forced into the position of a collaborator. She remembered the look on Buzz's face when he had seen Kenny, still in his Connecticut State Trooper's uniform, walking among the guards at the juvenile camp. She would give no names.

In her office she worked, not mechanically, for the figures she was processing were not just numbers on a page, but the charred remains of her countrymen. Some of the figures had been compiled by American army units sent in to clear the areas of corpses. Other figures followed on the radiation sickness ratio among those troops, figures that were necessarily incomplete. The conquerors had not troubled to issue protective equipment. The men were expendable.

She looked round her office, now filled with foreigners, from Thu Thuy with her cold, lovely face, to the dark Cubans, rather sullen in aspect but working assiduously, and felt a dreadful sense of wrong-doing in presiding over the tally of her country's dead. Once Clara Barton had reckoned the dead of the North in order to send them home for honorable interment. But her own dead were buried in mass graves, the very grave diggers falling beside them, while she compiled statistics to be used for study, no doubt, in the planning of future strikes.

For the moment her hand shook and she could not write. Thu Thuy's long eyes were upon her, for once alive with expression: curiosity, satisfaction? Was she part of the official North Vietnamese contingent, Martha wondered wearily, or had she been slipped in with the refugees from the South, eager to play traitor to the country offering her haven? The hours dragged on and Martha felt again what she had felt there before, a sense of being slowly but inexorably stifled.

The form she had been given was not issued by the occupation forces. It was on the Organization's own letterhead, bearing the name of the Secretary-General. It was from this building that the travel passes had been issued; she remembered the two executives talking in the train. That already seemed like years ago. And on the day of the surrender, arrangements had been made for rationing. Preparations had been begun *before* the strike.

This place stank of conspiracy and betrayal. Outside the window dark had fallen, but the riverboats were brilliant with lights. At the landing stage, floodlit, the little kayak bobbed on the water under its bright red flag with the hammer, sickle and star.

——— XVI ———

"We've been betrayed before. We can be betrayed again."

In the hour before dawn it was cool in the desert outside the small Negev town of Mamshit. The group of men huddled in an abandoned hut, all wearing Bedouin dress that night, were not Bedouins or Jews. The speaker, Ibn Kafavi, called himself a Palestinian, like the rest, though he had been born in Beirut and had lived in many lands. They used no lights, for although they carried the papers of Israeli Arabs, they had no wish to draw the attention of the military police. Earlier, they had raided the old jail of Mamshit in an effort to rescue one of their people who had been taken prisoner. Two Jews had been killed, but the prisoner had died in the crossfire and they were in an ugly mood.

Kafavi paused, wishing he could see the faces of his group, a new splinter of the famous Black September force. Rather, he hoped it would be a splinter. The official policy of the force and the parent PLO, since the defeat of the United States, enraged him as it had enraged much of the Arab world who had so long supported them. Now Israel, that state which never should have been, was theirs for the taking. But the official word from the PLO command, presumably dictated by the victorious Soviets, was not to advance but to wait for orders. "What are we waiting for?" he demanded, and the group muttered in sympathy, though without an answer.

The eldest of the dozen young men who had assembled could have answered. At the moment he was very much aware of his discomfort at squatting in a drafty hut in the company of these armed youths, far too close to the Israeli patrols around the atomic plant of Dimona. But his orders had been to stay with the group and then make his report. He stayed, for he was a political officer under the control, through the Libyan secret service, of the KGB.

"We should rally our people and attack," Kafavi was saying. "Syria would join in at once. Libya. Egypt."

"That was the reason for waiting," the political officer, who the others knew as Ferooz, interrupted. It wasn't but the obvious reason would never restrain these hotheads. The digestive process of the Soviets was distended for a time with its North American conquests, while it still had to guard its China border, subdue any remaining recalcitrant Afghans and watch the Poles. The New Order in the Middle East was to come in orderly fashion, without the Arab countries rushing into battle on their own behalf.

"Syria and Libya have been good friends," Ferooz continued, "but friends in war become allies, and allies want rewards. And will Egypt, that fair-weather friend, assist us also? Should we let Egypt have the Negev, the West Bank? Will every Arab country come marching into our Jerusalem, to claim a protectorate of the holy places?"

His usual fervid outpouring was causing him to raise

his voice and he hastily softened his tone. The Israeli patrols here used sound detectors when they searched for terrorists.

In the darkness of the desert the ancient rivalries of the Arabs touched the youths as the nemesis of Israel, their common enemy, approached.

"Then we should take Jerusalem now," a voice muttered.

Kafavi didn't like the leadership of his group passing from him.

"It would make more sense to take Dimona," he said flatly.

The political officer could not disagree. Nor was he surprised. The unlucky prisoner whom this small group of youths had tried to free had been working before his capture as a helper in a flour mill there. The meeting at this place had had the earmarks of a scouting expedition and Kafavi was bright—perhaps too bright. Brilliance, after all, was no longer needed. The ability to follow orders was more important. All the men present knew that Dimona was not only an atomic plant but also an experimental station. It was there that the Israeli atomic bomb, if it existed, had been built. But it was precisely the Dimona plant that his own master, the Soviets, intended to occupy. But no matter how he tried, he could not dim the enthusiasm of the small group for the action.

"Twelve men can't take Dimona," he said. "It's the most heavily-guarded site in Israel."

"We can get hundreds of volunteers, armed and trained, thousands if we need them," Kafavi said. "Our people are longing for action. They see no reason for the waiting." The others agreed.

Ferooz could only accede and began, mentally, to prepare a report for his superior about this group that called itself The Executioners. He knew all of these men well, and he could arrange to have them detained, or if necessary eliminated, within two days. The broken door-frame showed a grey patch that would soon be dawn. The men filed out cautiously. Ferooz was the last to leave except for Kafavi. Ferooz paused on the threshold, his eyes straining to scan the wilderness, alert for the patrols.

All was quiet. There was nothing to be seen but the patchy fields of hemp growing in the sand. A few hours would see him back in El Karam. He could make his report, clean himself up and have a decent meal in the company of his wife. He was newly married, and the thought of young Leila caused his blood to race. It also made him careless.

A thud at his back took him by surprise, jostling him off balance. He never felt the knife that slid straight into his heart, only the impact of the barren earth as it rose to receive him.

The radio cab was waiting outside the employees' entrance on First Avenue. Martha recognized the driver as the man who had been so helpful earlier. "Quite a coincidence," she said. Her hand was already on the door but she hesitated.

"The guard is watching us," the driver said, sounding much less like a New Yorker than he had before. "Don't make a fuss. Jump in."

She wasn't at all sure that she should. Out of the entire population of the world, the only person she trusted at the moment was Buzz. But soon the guard would be at her side, asking questions. She got in. The man drove north rapidly, then turned onto the East River Drive.

"You're going the wrong way."

She felt a pang of fear. Perhaps she'd been a fool. The guard would have done nothing to her.

"Don't worry," the man said. "It's not a kidnap. But I don't want to go up to your apartment again; it might be noticed. We'll stop at a place downtown that's all right, so far. After we talk, I'll drive you back. Do you have someone there?"

"Yes," she said. "It really was my housekeeper."

Rose liked that title, though she had cleaned for half a dozen women. Martha's fear subsided though an excitement remained. When she had stood with her hand on the open door, the light had shone through the partition on the jaunty dark head under the peaked cap. When his voice had changed, she had suddenly made the connection. He was the man who had been talking to Walt outside the Fairfield house in Avon . . .

They stopped by an old warehouse building on Greene Street. There were no lights at the windows; this part of Tribeca was still commercial and the business day was long over. The street light wasn't functioning but the driver opened the heavy, locked door without fumbling and they went inside. Going up in the cumbersome, manually-operated elevator she stole a look at the man, but in the dim glow of the overhead bulb she could see little more than she had before, his hand grasping the lever as it had the wheel of the cab.

They got out into a dark loft with a lot of dust in the air and a rather familiar smell that she couldn't place.

"Stand still," he warned, "you might trip. I'll get a light."

There were wooden boards under her feet but his step was almost noiseless as he moved away. Suddenly needles struck into her shoulder and she shrieked.

"Quiet," he said brusquely. A flashlight, covered with a handkerchief, gave a small area of visibility. A furry tail flicked across Martha's face, and she laughed.

Her companion grinned. "I should have remembered. They call him Hymie," he added, "but it's a she. The pet of the floor." He drew up a carton. "Here, you can sit on this."

He sat on the floor cross-legged at her feet as Buzz might have done. Buzz. Where was he? What was he doing? She remembered the camp near Greenfield Hill and shivered, though the atmosphere was close.

"No one can see us from outside and they're not

patrolling down here at night very often—yet. Uptown almost every building has someone reporting comings and goings. They'll get here too before long. Methodical, very methodical. After that it will have to be out of doors and that's more dangerous. So you'd better level with me now," he said quietly.

The dim light showed the shapes of cartons and bulky old machines. Scattered about were objects that gleamed faintly. Brass, that was what she had smelled, simple things, door knobs, frames for lanterns, table lamp stands.

"No burglar alarm?" she said.

"It doesn't go off if you use a key. I have a key. I used to work here. I work in a lot of places."

"Who are you?"

"You want to know my name," he said. It wasn't a question. "I have a lot of names. You know who sent me after you."

"I have to call you something." She was stalling, and she knew that he knew it, but what else could she do? She had wanted to meet the man Walt had sent—he had good judgement—but now, when it came to the point, she could not blurt out the story of Magnanimity to a nameless man whose face she had hardly seen, in a factory warehouse.

On the workbench at her side, a lion-shaped doorknocker shone with a smug expression. How nonsensical I'm being, she thought. Who am I looking for, a general in uniform, on an army base, or in the Pentagon? All those places were in enemy hands. All those men were dead.

"Call me Daniel," he said. "After all, we're in the lion's den."

He smiled up at her. He was younger than she was, in his early thirties, she guessed. His eyes were dark and bright and he was an agile little monkey of a man. But his smile was attractive.

"The person who sent me told me you might very well know something useful. Something he doesn't know himself, but has suspected. Something you learned from your husband, who was killed."

She said nothing.

"God help us if they ever get you, lady," he said, in his New York taxi-driver's voice. "The trouble is, you've got an honest face. You don't have to say anything; it's all there. And they will find you, unless we get you off to Canada before the border is sealed. That won't take too long. Lucky for us it's nearly three thousand miles."

He paused, but she remained silent.

"Look, you would have been in prison or dead already if they weren't such bureaucrats. They're as bad as the Germans were. It's the plan, you see."

He instructed her, sitting with his hands resting on his knees, as though he were a counselor at summer camp. "It has to go in stages. Down the lists. First senior military men and intelligence people and their families, followed by the lesser lights. Next the politicians and then the communications people, though some of them might survive. Then they look at industry: who is needed, who can be trusted, and who goes on the list. They know very well that military work is done here by private industry, they've stolen enough. But in the Soviets all that goes through their boards of planning and design, and it affects their thinking. They were very quick in getting their arrest teams to NASA, the AEC, Defense's R and E, but a bit later to Rocketdyne, Pratt and Whitney, Lockheed, FRDC and the rest. Even now they haven't got to civilian contractors who worked on military bases.

"But they will. And when they do, they will look for the wife of Josh Adams, and they will find her. And if they really want you," he added, "your British birth won't help much. It just means that they would have to send an apology for your accidental death while in custody, written out in triplicate, to the British Consul. It's urgent," he said, very serious now, "because if they have any reason to suspect that you know what I think you do, it could happen tomorrow. Tonight."

She listened to him talking, knowing what he said was true. Hymie had got used to their presence. The cat went back to her sleeping place, a cardboard carton out of which a load of American eagles had been dumped. They lay in a heap on the dusty scratched floorboards. No market for them now.

"If there was—something," she said. "Could—could it be useful? Is there anybody, any army group, the right people . . ."

She broke off. It was hard to ask what she needed to ask, without giving away more than she wanted to tell.

The man saw that she was very wary. The designer from Pratt-Whitney had thought this part of the job would be easier than it was. Walt Fairfield had described her as a fine woman, a good wife and mother, slightly old-fashioned. She had been raised by a grandmother. Martha had lived in her husband's protection and then taken a small job to fill her time. She would be glad, he had thought, to unburden herself of this knowledge, useless to her, vital to her country.

Walt Fairfield was brilliant at his work; he was evidently not so knowledgeable about women.

Something about this Mrs. Adams reminded the man of women he had known in the settlements, also good wives and mothers, who had picked up guns and killed like furies when they were defending their homes, their children. They were tough-fibered, and they were suspicious. He wondered what Martha Adams would prove to be.

"I'll have to tell you something," he said, "though the less you know, the better. Back when Reagan first took office, my government made a trade. We had developed a technology we couldn't use. We traded it for the strong alliance we had with the United States, though since Carmody took office we were afraid we might lose that protection. We're certain that Reagan used that information to build weapons, at least one, and that one was installed. But after the assassination, we heard nothing. No cries of horror from outraged pacifists, not even one murmur. I was sent to find out what happened about the weapon. That was before the collapse. Now finding it is the only hope for us all. Enough? If you help me to find it I'll get the people. We won't need many, and I'll get them if I have to piece them together myself like the Baron Frankenstein."

She stared at him as the truth came. *Israeli* intelligence. Of course. She'd heard people say they were all over the world. With everything else gone, it was strange, almost funny . . .

He watched her face that was still a mirror of her thoughts like a child's. But it was a strong face and those green eyes were sharp. She was still a little unsure of him, why shouldn't she be? But there was so little time. He would have to risk a little more.

"The project was called Magnanimity," he said, slowly.

With an effort she remained poker-faced but a pulse beat fast in her throat. He had interrogated many people in his time and now he had no doubt. He was almost at the end of his desperate search, in the last faint hope for his country that was awaiting the pounce of the jackals. It was hard to believe: the only knowledge of the whereabouts of what his Prime Minister had called the Doomsday weapon was here, in the five feet, six inches of this slender, good-looking American woman. Fascinated by the incongruity, he watched, almost mesmerized for a moment by her long fingers with the unvarnished nails, as she bent and picked up mechanically, one by one, the fallen American eagles.

* * *

That night Perez did not, as Virinsky expected, stay in the Soviet complex in Riverdale, nor did he accept an invitation to the Ambassador's house in Glen Cove. Instead he took a plane from La Guardia airport, now open for travel to special permit holders, down to Washington which nobody remembered yet to call Hall City. There he stayed away from the White House, officially renamed the People's House, the change being made to wipe out the last vestiges of colonialism. This announcement in the UN speech had brought much applause.

Instead he went to the Soviet Embassy which had a splendid communication system of its own. From there, despite the hour, he had a long talk on a special line with Ulyanov himself, for the great man occasionally liked to bypass his subordinates. And so Perez became the first member of the troika to learn of the restlessness of the splinter groups of the PLO and the discussion under way to have the KGB wipe out the dissidents in a world-wide sweep. A "night of the long knives."

Perez was well aware that such an action would make it smooth and easy for the army to step in in due course, with all glory. And many of his own informer networks were part of those same splinter groups. "If the decision has not yet been taken, perhaps it will be reconsidered," he said. "Such an action would cause grave offense to many Arab states and make our future plans politically difficult. Of course, the military can do it all their way."

His point was quickly taken.

"Not everyone is in favor." The voice on the other end was guarded. "A few raids on Israel by small groups of hotheads might defuse some of the impatience. Just as raiding a village of Jews kept the Cossacks happy in the old days. Sometimes I think it would almost be worth keeping Israel in existence now that it can no longer be a real nuisance. It takes up the Arabs' attention while we get on with the important business."

The old cynic had amused himself. Perez hung up, mentally counting the votes. He believed his supporters would win. Kharkev would not like it, but the KGB head had too much power and the other members would be happy to see him cut down just a little.

Despite the late hour, Perez checked through the

reports given to him by his intelligence chief. They were sifted carefully and only items of unusual interest were placed for his immediate attention. But neither Virinsky nor Borunukov had made any progress, it seemed, in the Magna affair. His own people had found nothing.

He left the Embassy for his house in the slums, enjoying the awed glances of the inhabitants as his motorcade sped along their streets. The curfew made certain there were plenty of faces to press at the windows. He felt a dissatisfaction remembering that the relocation program would soon make his presence here unproductive. The people at the windows would be gone, replaced by others who would be careful to notice nothing.

The inside of the house he was occupying had been made as luxurious as the outside was shabby. The women who shared his bed brought him back to good humor, enhanced by the thought of Virinsky. Virinsky the unvirile. It was well known to all the intelligence services that Virinsky had problems of impotence and had brought small joy to his wife. In the morning he was somewhat reluctant to be awakened by a messenger. But he was too wily a politician to forget business, and two cups of strong Colombian coffee cleared his mind as he read. His aides had already got rid of the women and all his attention was sharply focused. Thus it was Perez who first noticed an obscure piece of data, perhaps of no significance: a KGB plant in a small PLO cell called The Executioners had failed to report after an expedition into the Negev near Kurnub.

—— XVII ——

Morning found Martha back at her desk. It was a relief to find that Thu Thuy was gone. A memo left on her desk merely stated that Nguyen Thu Thuy had been transferred to another department. She would not have to bear that cold hostility. The Cuban girls were not well trained and had trouble with the new machines, but their rather sulky looks were no worse than those of girls she had worked with in the past. Their muttered imprecations reminded her of Beverly Green, and she wondered, with sinking heart, how Beverly was managing to live, and Lucy Kander, and all the other Americans.

Madame Paul, who visited the office to watch the progress, would not have guessed that the crisply efficient Mrs. Adams had spent a sleepless night. It was just as well they had such a woman, she decided, putting aside her personal antipathy. The Secretariat was being stretched to the limit of its capacity. The dismissal of almost all the Americans had been summary. The re-

placements were not taking up the slack as easily as the
new masters had supposed.

Under-Secretary Virinsky must have contemplated
this possibility, but the plan had been put into operation nevertheless. Perhaps he did not have the last
word. In her many years with the Organization, Madame Paul had observed that the Russians were willing
to tolerate gross, embarrassing inefficiency for any political purpose. She recognized and accepted the strat-
egy. At the same time she was quietly proud of her own
department and disliked the sudden lowering of standards.

Besides, the work of the Personnel Department, with
all its new duties, had increased five-fold. She had
expected to have the highly-trained, politically suitable
Thu Thuy posted as her assistant, only to find this
morning that she had been co-opted by the office of the
Under-Secretary himself. This was surprising as his staff
was already very large. There was the usual staff of the
Secretary for Political and Security Council Affairs who
actually handled all the ordinary UN work; there had
been another office that assisted him in his intelligence
duties and there had been a third staff that she had
helped him set up to arrange for the post-war planning.
It had amused Virinsky, she knew, that the Americans
had paid so much of the cost of all this.

Madame Paul decided to make an appointment for a
meeting with the Under-Secretary—a foolish title, she
reflected, for him to use after his accession to power,
but it seemed to please him to keep it. There were
measures she must propose. Certainly the new work of
the Organization, dealing with the administration of the
country, must go forward, but many of its old activities
could be cut sharply. It had been a bureaucracy run
wild and about ninety per cent of its customary operations could be cut with no loss to anyone except the
department heads. It was a hoary joke that in working
to break up the colonial empires, the Organization had

formed one of its own. Under-Secretary Virinsky, she thought, would welcome and approve her ideas. She murmured a subdued acknowledgement of Martha's work and left in unusually high spirits. The sun shone dazzlingly on the river. It was a beautiful day.

Martha, if not elated, was not worn out by her sleepless night either. She felt a strength of purpose now that she had made her decision, and was prepared to accept the danger that followed. It had not been an easy decision. At eleven she took her break and went to the coffee bar overlooking the delegate's lounge. It was at present reserved for senior staff only, and quiet. She would have a moment to think: so much had happened in such a short time.

When the Israeli agent had identified himself last night in his casual way and spoken, very sketchily, about Magnanimity, she had not been able to assimilate his revelations. Instead of being flooded with relief at finding a longed-for ally, the only thing her mind had fastened on was the word "Canada." This "Daniel" expected her to hand over to him her country's greatest secret, and she was to be shipped off, like a refugee child, while unknown people did with it what they would.

Without having to make a decision, she knew that this was precisely what she would not do. If only Colonel Fairfield had been more encouraging, more organized, and less resigned to the new regime. Or if General Cunningham had survived . . . but Daniel had been certain he was dead. Daniel, that odd little monkey of a man. There was no reason why she should believe that he was who he said he was, though in truth she did. And Walt Fairfield had trusted him. Yet he, for good reasons no doubt, had told *her* very little. The real secret of Magnanimity. What was the "technology" developed by the State of Israel, that it couldn't use? It must be something of great import, and yet unknown to the scientists of the rest of the world. Could such a thing be possible? Probability said that it could not. And yet . . .

Last night she had told Daniel that she still needed time to consider what to do. He had been worried, urgent, angry, yet she had seen understanding in his bright monkey's eyes. He had merely pointed out again that if the enemy suspected she had special knowledge, she would immediately be taken, and once taken, they would find out what she knew soon enough. Even if she managed to die before capture, the knowledge could be forever lost to her own countrymen.

"They won't be looking for me just yet," she had said.

"And what makes you so sure?"

He had been driving her home through the almost empty streets. Taxis were not bound by the curfew law, nor were civilians with special passes, but there were police patrols, and Martha had felt unpleasantly exposed. The Empire State Building blazed with red lights. Not just the tower, but the whole building had now been covered with strings of bulbs. Their glow lit up the parties of street workers, who were piling up the debris left by the evacuees. One of the men, on his hands and knees as he gathered up litter, looked up as the taxi swept past. He had a look of Greg Maynard. She had hardly thought of her friends, Martha remembered with a pang. What had happened to the Maynards?

"It's the computers," she told Daniel. "The way they're set up; the way they work. I've seen it in my office. Now all the data is in the bank of the appropriate region. They don't use states. Martha Adams is in the data bank of Region II, that's New York. New York address, New York job. Of course, it's possible to make cross checks, but it means special retrieval of the necessary items and that's time consuming. Right now they're much too busy."

"What's all this about regions?" he said, deflected for a moment.

She had told him, and explained further that even special travel passes were limited to the local region unless otherwise specified. He pulled into the dark of a loading bay on a side street and examined her documents carefully with a flashlight. She was surprised to see him using a jeweler's loop. "Hmph," he muttered at last.

"Didn't the Israeli consul let you know?" she asked.

"We're not exactly in touch," he said. "The Consulate people are under house arrest."

She guessed his mind was humming away like a computer itself. "There's something odd there." She told him about the arrangements, so obviously made before the strike.

"Natural enough," he said, with a shrug. "The Russians had to have their takeover plans in place. What easier spot to ready them in security? The Soviet Embassy was always under surveillance, but in the massive UN bureaucracy you could bury a plan to run the world. And Virinsky, one of the Under-Secretaries, is the KGB's top man in this country."

Martha was shocked. "Virinsky?"

"Yes. You might not have noticed, but when the information was given to the newsmen today about the Committee of Three, the third man wasn't mentioned. My guess is that it's Virinsky himself, it would figure."

Virinsky had been merely one of those functionaries, she had always thought, whose position was a UN political plum. There were many such. What was he Under-Secretary of—Political and Security Council Affairs? Ustinov's old job. Virinsky was familiar from the restaurant, where he would order special sweet dishes, the bar, where he drank little, unlike most of the Russians, and the corridors, where he moved with ponderous deliberation. He looked unwholesome, her grandmother would have said. Lardy, heavy-jowled, almost bald; monkish, perhaps, but no jolly friar, he. His eyes were pale and had a downward slope and there came from him a perceptible chill.

In the end she had told Daniel almost nothing, and he had said little more. She had agreed to meet him again; he had to leave the city for a day, but he would meet her outside the UN the night after next. Now she rose and saw Madame Paul seated not too far off, sipping a cup of black coffee and nibbling on a croissant. She looked unusually relaxed and pleased. As Martha went down the steps to cross the Delegate's Lounge, she saw the stout, pale figure of Virinsky looming in the entrance. Accompanying him was a girl whose lovely face and form were familiar. Her former assistant, Thu Thuy.

* * *

Virinsky had spent the morning checking on the lists that had come in as a result of a worldwide sweep of enemy agents, ordered from Moscow. One name he had hoped to find was absent: Bar-Lev, the name, or code name, of an Israeli agent who had long been the bane of the KGB. He had penetrated the Soviet Union itself to assassinate Lavrentin, Chebrikov's successor, and worse still he had managed to melt away. The incident had been hushed up but his name was on every KGB list. There was always the possibility that the surrender had caught him in the United States. Virinsky decided to find out, despite his preoccupation with Magna.

That afternoon the guards were removed from the Israeli Consulate in Manhattan. Diplomatic relations were still in force between the Soviet Union and Israel. The Consul had been penned up in the building on Second Avenue since the week of the surrender. Now he ventured out, hoping to get home to his wife. On the corner of Forty-Third Street he was stopped and whisked into a police van. It was announced later that the Consul had been taken in for questioning and was held on a charge of spying.

His interrogation was long and professional. The Consul was a man of high courage and of a fortitude grudgingly respected by the KGB men who worked on him. He denied any knowledge of intelligence agents, Israeli or foreign. When given specific names, he again denied knowledge, except for what he read in the newspapers.

At the same time, the Israeli ambassador and key members of his staff had been arrested in Washington, and consular officers were picked up across the country. The results were generally poor. Mossad, it seemed, had screened its activities from its own government's representatives. And the US representatives pointed out that there had been no need of secret activities in such friendly territory. That was certainly, to a great extent, true.

The results of the interrogations were brought together, studied, and compared. A general pattern emerged, indicating that the officials involved believed there might have been Israeli agents in the United States on the day of the surrender, but that they knew little more. In answer to the question on the notorious Bar-Lev, no one knew where he was. The interrogators believed these replies to be the truth. Bar-Lev had always been chary of official connections. The evaluator concluded that the possibility of Bar-Lev's presence in the US could not be ruled out. It was eleven o'clock the next morning before Virinsky received the preliminary report and it did not please him.

At the same time that Virinsky was receiving his report, Martha's intercom was ringing. It was the main-floor receptionist. A man was asking to see Mrs. Adams; he gave his name as Gregory Maynard. Martha went down at once. How odd, when only yesterday she had been thinking of the Maynards. She walked towards the reception desk but she didn't see him. The woman at the desk, a sleek young Indian, nodded her head with an air of faint distaste to a workman who came forward from the corner where he had been waiting. This was not a UN workman, his overalls were ill-fitting and filthy, and he was covered in dirt. Only his light blue eyes made her recognize him as Greg Maynard, and at the same moment she realized that he was the man she had seen two nights before.

A guard approached quickly.

"Do you have a permit to come here?" he asked Greg. Greg's face blanched under its dirt and stubble of beard.

"Mr. Maynard is here to see me by appointment," Martha said, and taking Greg's hand, led him through the building. It was warm enough still in mid-September to stand outside on the deck over the highway, though even there they were not alone. Men were working: a wire fence was being added to the balustrade not, presumably, to keep employees in, but to keep others out, though how they could get up there was hard to imagine. For a moment Greg stared across the river to Queens, as though it were a far country.

"Sorry to bother you, Martha," he said. "But I saw you in that taxi the other night and I thought . . ."

"I'm sorry I didn't stop to say hello," Martha said. "I had been thinking about you and Birdie. But we were going quickly and I didn't . . ."

"You didn't think the street cleaner was Greg Maynard." He laughed, without mirth. "Birdie arranged that. She's O.K. it seems. Her program is closed for lack of funds, but she's still working for the city. Labor relocation. There's no ration card for people without jobs and no permit for city living space either. As it is, there are three women from Birdie's office moved in with us. Martha, I think Birdie wants me out. And when I saw you I wondered if there was anything . . ."

Suddenly he couldn't face her, and turned away. His hands, cut and bruised, still were brown with a sportsman's summer tan. Last year when they had won the cup at a tennis tournament he had insisted at the celebration that their party all drink champagne from it and he had held the cup for their bobbing heads. Greg had always been to her the husband of an old school friend, a clever financial man who had helped with investments. The Adamses, he once told Martha, seemed to have had some of the worst investment managers in history. She suspected that Josh had not entirely approved of Greg, but he and Birdie had been fun. "You mean here," Martha said. "I can try, Greg. I don't think I have any influence, but I will ask."

There were plenty of jobs that Greg could do, with his quick brain and grasp of money matters, but she had seen few Americans left in the building. "Surely, though, Birdie won't . . ."

"I heard her talking about divorce. Not to me, but to one of the lodgers. She's just covering her flank. A survivor, Birdie." He spoke without rancor.

Martha thought of Daniel; of Buzz, living in the woods and fields; of Colonel Fairfield, gone underground. Could she suggest to Greg that he join them? Hardly, without risking their betrayal.

She stared hard at the fence. It was being electrified; the cable was being looped on now. "Some of the youngsters, I hear, have taken to the streets and the fields," she said.

He laughed again, and it was a harsh sound she had not heard from him before. "The fields! Yes, until November, maybe. But how long can they last? We're not in the days of Robin Hood. As soon as the leaves are off the trees, not even the forests can hide them from the 'copters. I'm no guerilla, Martha. I'm a broker. An underwriter, and as damned good at calculating odds in this game as Birdie. I guess I'll hang on in the apartment for a few more days. If you have any luck, you can reach me there."

"I'll do my best," she said and meant it, though as she took his hand, she could see Buzz's face, stern and unforgiving. To Buzz, those who were not with him were against him.

"Martha . . ." She had already turned to go inside the doors, when Greg held her back for a moment. He was grasping her shoulder and her hair brushed his wrist. There was a light, fresh fragrance about Martha's hair, and it came to him with a teasing hint of an embrace, long desired, so painful here, now.

"I wasn't going to say this," he said. "It's not going to help me, but I've got to say it. You'd better look after yourself. Anyway you can. I got back after my shift last night and Birdie was just getting up. I was in a hurry because I'd been switched to the day shift, but I noticed a form she'd brought home from the office. She'd started to fill it out. I didn't get a chance to see it all; she snatched it up soon enough, but I did see Josh's name . . ."

He walked back with her to the bank of elevators with a firmer step and when they said good-bye he blew her a kiss in a jaunty, not quite broken gallantry. Martha went straight to the office of Madame Paul and made her request for Greg Maynard at once.

"I'll look into it," Madame Paul said. Martha noticed she was looking much smarter than usual. She had always dressed in rather drab, narrow, tubular garments of grey, dull purple or dark green, of a cloth that looked much the same, summer or winter. Only her shoes had been fine. Now, although in outline she looked much the same, her clothes were of a stuff and cut so excellent that her dowdiness had turned to elegance.

Martha was soon dismissed. Madame Paul did not bother to write down the name of Gregory Maynard. Few Americans were being hired, and those were only people of great political reliability. The gangs of street workers would be needed a little longer, and then most of them would be deported. Oil wells were to be drilled in the new Soviet State of Bering and there would be a vast need for labor of all kinds.

But not much of her attention was on that small

problem. The sight of Virinsky walking with Thu Thuy
yesterday had left her with most disagreeable sensa-
tions and disturbed her night's rest. Thu Thuy's level in
the Organization was extremely low; she held the rank
of a senior typist. It was most unusual, in the hierarchy,
for an Under-Secretary to accompany such a one into
the Delegate's Lounge, even if her party record was of
long standing. And Thu Thuy could not be more than
twenty-four. Madame Paul was sure that a week or two
ago Virinsky would not have done such a thing. Her
pleasure in her office, and her new wardrobe, was
lessened considerably and she thought no more of Mrs.
Adams that day.

Martha, at her desk, had to realize that her time for
lingering was shorter than she had believed. She had
been worried about informing on others. Stupidly, she
had not thought that some of her own friends might
inform on her. Birdie, she realized painfully, would, of
course, be a collaborator. Birdie had always liked to feel
herself secure in the regions of power. She had toler-
ated Greg's infidelity for the sake of his wealth; she had
pursued her career in government, believing it would
give her a political base in the popular party. It seemed
odd to Martha now that she had never seen her old
friend in that light before. Suddenly, for no reason, she
remembered that Birdie had been caught, in their senior year, cheating in an exam. Not that any of that
mattered, but Martha knew she must soon disappear.
She would meet Daniel that night as arranged, but she
would not become a refugee, and she would not go to
Canada.

Outside the UN building, Greg was picked up by the
patrol car which had been summoned by the guard. He
was arrested for visiting an international body without
the proper permit.

—— XVIII ——

A thousand feet below sea level men were laboring in the Valley of the Moon. Strange shapes loomed monstrously in the haze as the smoke from the great stacks was transformed to a dirty, yellow glare between sun and sand. Kafavi, laboring and sweating with his men, knew himself to be a fearless man. Yet he felt a prickling, elemental fear, fear of this place, where the earth seemed to have been ripped by the hand of Allah.

With discipline he turned his mind to his work, guiding the great crane that dug the ore, watching the trucks being loaded that would go later into Dimona, and his men with them. They were to direct the forces that were assembling from the Jordan range to the East and from Egypt in the West, flooding through the borders that were already weakened now that the soldiers of Israel must be everywhere at once with no place safe and no friend in all the world.

When the shift ended, the men went to the trucks, tense and eager for the kill. The plan had been to wait for dark and then to dispose of the regular drivers quietly, making off with their papers. Already such precautions seemed tame, and waiting was out of the question.

"Remember," Kafavi cautioned, "the target is Dimona."

One by one the trucks moved up, heavily loaded, on the road leading to Beersheba. The drivers stopped when flagged down by their fellow workers, and in each case it was the work of a moment to cut the throat of an unsuspecting man and to toss the body into the pile of ore in the back. The men were jubilant as they left behind the desolation of Sodom and the Dead Sea, blood-colored in the afterglow.

It was almost dark when they reached the target, the nuclear plant at Dimona on the Sodom-Beersheba road. Already there was pandemonium. The attack, which had been scheduled to begin after their arrival under Kafavi's direction, was already under way. The roads, the buildings, the gates, the roofs, were swarming with Arabs, not troops or trained guerrillas but civilians, not in hundreds but in thousands.

Kafavi stopped, aghast. Some carried flares; all were armed, and they were slaughtering everyone in sight, often each other. The only Israelis to be seen now were dead Israelis, and a cry went up when a live one was discovered in a hiding place, a cry taken up by a thousand tongues. Buildings were looted, burned; the confusion was incredible, but at least the few trained troops had flung a cordon round the place and secured it.

Kafavi estimated the numbers of men and weapons and calmed down. The Israelis would not retake this area soon. But there was no order. If the installation was to be secured, there was no sense in burning it. And something was wrong. There was little sign of any Israeli defense: no weapons, and the bodies were those of old men, civilians.

He heard the man at his side cursing at the stupidity, and he had to agree. This young man had joined them to take the place of the cowardly Ferooz, and was proving to have a good, cool head. But most of his men were caught in the general blood lust. The cry sounded as another old man was dragged from a ditch. He looked like a gatekeeper or watchman, but they joined the rest in setting on him.

"The plant's closed down; the place is empty," the old man adjured them. "Go home, you maniacs . . ." But his blood soon ran over the dust of the road.

Kafavi was splattered by the gore and felt a cold disgust. It was as well the plant was closed down. These people were a danger to themselves and everybody else. Already spurts of flame were shooting to the sky. If the Israelis were to counterattack they would not be long. A shriek of expectation rang out as one more find was made. Yet another old man was crawling from the rooftop, trying to escape the leaping flames. "Let's try and get him," the new man said. "He might have information which could be important to us."

The crowds dragged him down. Kafavi and his new partner made their way through the mob. The quiet use of knives cut their way through the press of bodies until they could almost touch the fallen man, burned, battered, the bones of his right leg broken and piercing the thin stuff of his pants.

Kafavi flung his arm up, pointing to the flaming roof. "Over there," he shouted. "More, coming down on the other side," and the crowd surged off in one great flow, screaming in anticipation.

"In that truck," Kafavi said, and the young man, by the light of the fire, helped him drag the moaning prisoner to lie in the back of the truck beside the stiffening body of the driver.

The escape was more difficult than he had expected, not because of the Israeli opposition, but because of the flow of Arabs, mindlessly seeking Jihad, still pouring across the borders. The armies had followed orders and remained at their posts; these were merely a rabble.

Kafavi was already aware that he had blundered. He would gain no credit for this action. But he had a prisoner, and in time the prisoner was delivered to an interested party of interrogators in Akaba.

* * *

The thought of Canada was worrying Marshal Borunukov even more than it had troubled Mrs. Martha Adams. After the triumphal procession, he had expected to stay for a time in New York, a city he much preferred to the capital. Instead, within two days he had had to return because of some disquieting events.

Already he had checked the elementary security of the People's House. Machine guns were emplaced on the East and West terraces. A twenty-four hour military guard of picked men from his own troops also covered the grounds and patrolled the house, and a special barracks was thrown up behind the State building next door. A wall was being built around the periphery and the outside of the house was being painted black to make it less of a night target.

His aides had set up a photographic session in the Oval Office, guaranteed, they thought, to put the Marshal in a good mood. At sixty, he was still handsome in the style of a European Russian; in the old days his appearance would have been called noble, and it was whispered that he was a descendent of high-ranking "former people." He liked to see himself pictured in the magazines and daily papers, so much so that while he was in New York he had ordered that the *New York Times*, which had been taken over by the *Morning Star*, be returned to its old format so that his image could be seen in full splendor under that prestigious name. But he brusquely ordered the photographers out and dressed down his aides for unbecoming attention to frivolous matters. He quoted Lenin: "What we need is

furious energy and more energy," and they knew they
were in for a bad day.

Everyone was cleared out except his chief aide and
Borunukov sat at the Presidential desk which was covered in a litter of papers topped off by a dirty coffee cup
and a mess of crumbs.

"What the devil . . ." he ejaculated. The Marshal was
used to military order and the style due to his rank.

The aide snatched up the offending coffee cup and
swept the crumbs away. He cleared his throat. "Señor
Perez was in earlier. Perhaps I should remove his papers." The Marshal swore, using a racial epithet com-
monly applied by Russians to black diplomats or students
at Patrice Lumumba University. To him, all Cubans
were blacks.

Another thing not yet decided was the use of the Oval
Office. The sharing of the White House facilities was
impossible in Borunukov's view and should never have
been considered. There was space enough in official
Washington, where half of the offices were now empty.
It was true that he had the use of the private accommodation and he had taken for himself the Lincoln bedroom. But when his signals men had gone to the
communication rooms in the basement, there had been
arguments with Perez's people who were already setting up their lines with Cuba.

The aide tidied the papers and a soldier-servant
brought the Marshal a tray with one glass and a bottle
of vodka. The Marshal tossed off a glassful and regarded
him moodily. "Well, it's not what we expected, Andrei."

It certainly wasn't. The aide was well aware that the
Marshal had expected the United States to become his
province. He had planned that Washington would become Borunukov City—the new Alexandria. Doubtless
he had expected in due course to be hailed by the
populace: Glory to Great Borunukov, Glory, Glory,
Glory, as the Muscovites used to chant *Slava Velikomu
Stalinu, Slava, Slava, Slava*.

"No, Marshal," he said discreetly, and poured him another glass.

Perez had spoiled that, demanding that the city be named for himself, and General-Secretary Ulyanov had taken over the decision and declared for the colorless, almost forgotten American. The aide had also been furious; the army to a man was with the Marshal. The ground forces and the strategic rocket forces in their separate organizations were often rivals, but in this they were united. They had no intention of allowing the guerilla groups to survive and all their energies were devoted to the bringing down of Perez.

Discreetly, he mentioned a few of these murmurings to the Marshal, and succeeded in soothing him slightly. The Marshal permitted one photograph, taken with him holding the Great Seal of the United States cupped in his palm. Odd Masonic flummery, he thought, glancing down. But the eagle on the reverse was handsome. A pity that the double-headed eagle was no longer used as a state symbol in Russia. The Red Star looked like a decoration for a Christmas tree. Lenin, after all, had used the eagle-decorated, Romanov china in the Kremlin. It was time for a change.

Then he got down to business and went through the troubling reports on his desk. The Chinese armies massing on the Russian border were ominous. This was something different from the Chinese penetration army that was never very far from the border, two or three million men, carefully scattered, ready for guerrilla operations against Siberia. These latest forces were regular troops. A hint had already come from Ulyanov himself that he might be expected to return in person to command the Russian armies on the China front. He countered by suggesting General Gvishiani, with much experience in that area. Old Marshal Stapshyn, Minister of Defense, would support him, but Ulyanov's maneuvering was a threat. Ulyanov, who bore the famous name, and wanted the position once held by the man with whom he claimed kinship. Ulyanov, already General-Secretary of the Party, who planned to take over the chairmanship of the Council of Ministers as well. He would then be absolute dictator like Lenin, like Stalin, but it was a move he had not yet dared to make. Ulyanov, that ally of Perez.

Borunukov had reported to the Politburo long in advance of the American strike that they should have knocked out China at the same time. Their atomic installations were in easy reach, and the Russian capacity was great enough to take out the two enemies at one stroke. He had been convinced that the Americans would not launch on warning and he had been right.

But the State Committee for Science and Technology, backed by Ulyanov, had made a five-year plan and were not inclined to budge, though he had shown how he could put the new, great SS-18's, with the 25 megaton warheads, or an even more deadly load of MIRV'd warheads, to good use. There would be no question of "clean" missiles in China. Stapshyn had agreed, but Ulyanov had only smiled. "While you are on the way to the Americas? Very brave, Marshal."

That had been all the other Politburo members needed to hear. Those great heroes. The Marshal pushed aside the reports impatiently, and reached for a cigar. His aide was at once at his side, snipping the end and providing a light. The Marshal smelt the fragrance, but was not soothed. The Politburo could live and run the country for years in the deep, comfortable shelters they had so carefully prepared but they were afraid the Chinese might surprise them, an absurdity, considering the limited range of the Chinese missiles. Now, here, was a real danger. All the evidence showed that Canada was a nest of Chinese agents and they were infiltrating over the US border. Borunukov could not close the border completely without more troops, and with the big scare at home he would not get any. The American troops under his command could not yet be considered reliable for border work.

One of his first orders had been the rounding up of all Chinese Americans, and in this Virinsky had been helpful. The Marshal had not objected to Virinsky being added to the interim government, for Stapshyn had pointed out that he was there merely to give the Russians, that is Borunukov himself, the majority vote. So it had proved. Virinsky, that deformed sexual cripple, was hardly of the governing class, but such men had been traditionally useful, as the shrewd Kharkev had noted. Yet only a KGB oaf would give his daughter to a man with the tastes of Beria before him.

The Chinese were being sent to Seattle and from there by sea to Anchorage. The journey was slow and a land route would have to be established. Canada must therefore cede a strip of territory. Alaska was full of oil that the army needed and the prisoners could make themselves useful at the oil drillings. How considerate of the Americans to have saved the oil for them! Yet this thought brought no pleasure either for, doubtless, some of the oil would go to Perez.

The feasting and celebrating last night in New York had been enjoyable, but his sixty-year-old stomach was sour and the hurried journey to the capital had exacerbated his malaise. New reports of huge numbers of Chinese agents and saboteurs at large in the Canadian population now infuriated him, especially since up until recent years it would have been impossible for this to have happened. Any Oriental in British or French Canada had been conspicuous. Then that fool of a Prime Minister had filled the nation with so many Orientals that it was beyond the resources of any intelligence service to check each and every one.

The Marshal was careful to note it as a black mark against Virinsky in case he should ever need one, but in his heart he believed it was Perez who had encouraged and nurtured this Third World passion, which had led to China's gain. Who knew, the Marshal brooded, with that kind of man, what deviationist ideas lurked under the guise of the brilliant Party leader?

If a Chinese terrorist aimed an atomic weapon at the American continent, Borunukov would have little protection. Already he had put in orders for more deep shelters to be constructed, though these would still be far from adequate in the event of a surprise attack. Moreover it would be safer for the Chinese to attack the Red Army here than in Russia. Here the Americans themselves would be suspected and Ulyanov would not order massive retaliation against China on such dubious grounds.

The Marshal's head ached; a dull throbbing in the temples that spread to a tight band across the forehead. No one in the GRU had found the slightest whisper about the Magna mystery. The new Soyuz satellite, his pride, had shown up nothing of significance except the massing on the China border. The secret deployment of troops he had feared: could it have been Chinese? Chinese troops armed by the Americans, perhaps with some new super-weapons, made with a technology those dolts at the design bureaus had not yet discovered? Korolev, Yangel, Glushko, bloated with praise, had become lethargic. Reagan might certainly have consummated the love affair begun by Nixon, and Carmody perhaps was not as stupid as he seemed. Certainly nothing of magnitude could have been hidden in the United States, but it could well have been hidden in China. Had Carmody, like the wily Nixon, come to a rapprochement with the Chinese and then proceeded to mastermind a secret joint endeavor? No, surely, he thought, if that were so something would have leaked, especially given the American passion for record-keeping. But the thought did not relieve him.

Carmody was presently under house arrest. He had been questioned, but not with the full questioning techniques of the GRU. Borunukov sent a detachment of

men to pick him up, and to take him to the new special
unit at Walter Reed Army Hospital, now manned by
personnel from the Pokrovskoe-Streshnevo prison for
military offenders. After all, Carmody had been Commander-in-Chief. Then he picked up the telephone and
had a short, decisive talk with Virinsky in New York.
The Magna case was to be given absolute priority with
the KGB as well as the GRU. The two intelligence
agencies would give full cooperation to each other on
every level.

Virinsky said nothing of his similar arrangement with
Perez. But undoubtedly with three great intelligence
services working together (with some reservations, no
doubt), the Magna secret, he concluded, must soon be
discovered.

It was dark when Martha left the building that night,
and she did not see Daniel. Concerned, she walked
slowly, looking for the light of the radio cab. Probably
for safety's sake he was cruising around. Despite the
hour, a lot of Secretariat people were leaving at the
same time, and the guards were checking the passes
somewhat mechanically.

A boy in jeans and a windbreaker walked by quickly
and the guard called "Halt!" Glancing back, she saw
that the call came from a soldier, one of the party who
had been added to the regular UN guard. He carried a
repeater rifle, and she saw he was watching the boy
who had a heart-stopping, familiar look. The boy broke
into a run; the guard fired, but the boy was zig-zagging
and the shots hit the passers-by. Whistles blew, more
guards were running towards them, but they were partly
blocked by pedestrians who crouched on the sidewalk
or were fleeing in terror from the sound of gunfire.

Martha, still ahead of the guards, followed the boy as
he dodged through the thin traffic and then rounded
the corner of Forty-Third Street. Two guards came
rushing behind her, jostling her as they passed, and ran

down the avenue in hot pursuit of a youth of the same height as the fugitive, in similar dress, who had taken flight in the general panic.

"Walk!" she commanded. The boy slowed to a walk. On Second Avenue a cab, southward bound, slowed up beside them. Daniel peered out and Martha grabbed her son and bundled him in, speedily, not gently.

The taxi bounded off and Buzz caught his breath.

"They looking for you, kid?" Daniel asked.

"Not specially for me," he said. "It was the pass. They must have spotted it for a fake. It wasn't so hot but I took a chance when they were busy."

"Why didn't you come to my office?" Martha asked. "I would have got you out. You could have gone straight to the apartment; Rose is there."

She looked at her son in the near darkness, trying to see if he was hurt.

"I wasn't coming to you," Buzz explained. "It was someone else I wanted to see. I might have dropped by the apartment later if it looked cool."

The arm of the windbreaker was damp and sticky.

"You've been hit," Martha said.

Daniel was already driving west at a good pace.

"I'll look at it when we hit the garage. The further we get the better. That area will be locked up tight until they find a kid that looks like you, poor devil. He yours, lady?"

It was hardly a question. The expression on the two faces was a better match than the two red heads.

"Bruce Joshua Adams," Martha said primly.

Daniel pushed the butt of a good-sized, black pistol through the partition. "Take this," he instructed her. "If they get on our tail, shoot."

Martha was more used to a shotgun than a pistol but she took it. She had practiced firing one when Josh had urged her to apply for a permit; he had never liked her being in the city apartment alone. Now her pistol was gone: a city inspector had come to the apartment to collect it. He had warned her that the penalty for keeping a gun was death. There was no pursuit; the guards were probably still questioning their suspect, and the taxi traveled down Eleventh Avenue to pull in at a gas station on Twenty-Seventh Street.

"Get on the floor," Daniel said.

They followed his orders, crouching down in the small space.

"Christ, Mike, didn't you just fill her up?" a voice complained.

"Don't get your balls in an uproar," Daniel retorted. "I just pulled in to check the ignition. She's been starting like an old cow."

"Come on, Mac, get going," another voice said. "I'm meeting a fare at Grand Central, and some hungry slob will pirate him if I'm late."

The voices faded as the cab passed the pumps and pulled into the dimly lit garage.

"Stay here," Daniel muttered to Martha, as he opened the passenger door and eased Buzz out, pushing him ahead. "Over there. In the john."

The two of them disappeared while Martha waited, cramped, sweating, jumpy. It seemed a long time before they returned, though by her watch only nine minutes had gone by before Buzz crawled in quietly beside her.

"It's O.K.," Daniel said softly. "Only a nick."

The arm smelled of antiseptic, which was some comfort.

"Hey, Mikey," the voice followed them as they rolled out again. "You sure it's the cab's ignition acting up? Looks like you're the one who's slow as an old cow."

"Like your old lady says about you, lover?" Mike-Daniel sounded as irate as a constipated cab-driver might be expected to be. When he reached the road that once had been covered by the West Side Highway he stopped.

"Where do you want this sprig delivered, do you know?" Daniel said.

"I'm not a package," Buzz said sharply. "I don't have to be delivered."

He reached for the door.

"Don't be silly," Martha said. "Let me think."

"I have business," Buzz retorted.

"Perhaps I can help you, Bruce," Daniel said with a change of tone. "Whatever you have to do, you can't wander around showing evidence of a gunshot wound."

"Call me Buzz," Martha heard her son mutter.

"I can find you a place for tonight. I'll get you out of town in the morning."

If Daniel took Buzz into hiding, she would be in his hands. This was Martha's first thought. The second was that she was ashamed of her suspicion, and the third was that, ashamed or not, she would keep on being suspicious.

"I'm meeting a friend, the one I went to see," Buzz said. "He's got a place for me. On West End Avenue."

Daniel was driving north slowly.

"Did anyone see you talk to this friend at the UN?" Martha asked.

"No, I was careful. I got in the building on the delivery truck with the produce this morning. I knew where to find my friend, no sweat. But he didn't want to talk there. He gave me the sign: ears all over the place. Electronic ears," he explained. "He let me see his home address and he gave me a visitor's pass to get out. But they put names on them now and it didn't match the one on my papers, so we had to alter it, and I guess it wasn't such a good job."

Martha hadn't known that Buzz had a friend at the UN. He had hardly ever been there. Once, twice? Like his father, he had hated New York.

"Meet him but don't stay there," Martha ordered. "You can't be sure. Someone might have seen you together and there'll be questions asked tomorrow."

Daniel took him to the rendezvous, protesting. "I might as well be a real hackie," he said. "Make more money. Sleep in my own bed."

A short way up West End Avenue Buzz stopped the cab, and stepped out.

A young man appeared from a dark doorway, and the two had a hurried conversation. The light from a street lamp caught the young man's face, and Martha was surprised to recognize him: Armand Lesseps, an effervescent young Frenchman, a favorite at staff social gatherings. He had even charmed the dour Madame Paul. She believed he was an interpreter, but she had had no idea that he and Buzz had ever met.

While the youngsters were talking, Daniel slid the partition aside and poked his head towards her. "So?" he said. "Have you decided?"

"Some things," Martha replied. "A friend is giving information about me, right here in the city. So the powers newly arrived will connect me with Josh much sooner than I had expected. I won't become a refugee, I don't intend to go to Canada, but I will have to disappear. In any event, it's time I started on my business."

To Daniel's ear she sounded very much like Buzz. He might have been with a group of amateur guerrillas.

—— XIX ——

After some discussion, they decided the apartment would be safe enough for Martha that night. It would take time for Birdie's information to be processed, a day or two at least. Buzz went with her: "We've got to talk," Martha said.

When they arrived at the building, Buzz looked round warily. His air was oddly familiar. So he had looked, Martha remembered, when he stalked the woods, hunting for deer.

"Where does the super live?" Daniel asked.

Martha indicated the semi-basement apartment that showed no light at the moment.

"You'd better watch out, Buzz," Daniel said. "All the supers are official spies now. Each one is an *upravdom*, a sort of director of the building. They have to report anyone going in after curfew, and anyone there other than residents, to the street patrols."

"I'll go up the back," Buzz said. "No one will notice

me. When I get up, if everything's all right, I'll flip the light switch off and on twice.

He slipped through the shadows to the old service entrance, not much used since the building lost its doorman several years ago. For a very little while it seemed to Martha that Buzz was a child again, playing some game of cops and robbers with a grave, important air, but the illusion faded as she saw Daniel with his hand on a gun as they waited for the signal.

"I'll need a team of expert missileers," she said. She had thought it all out carefully the night before. "I may need some troops if the area is defended. Transportation I can probably manage myself, but if you can help with communications to New York . . ."

Daniel laughed, a sound of real amusement. *"You'll need?"* Who do you think you are? Joan of Arc? On a computer instead of a horse, maybe? Perhaps you've been listening to voices?"

"I have my voices," Martha said. Her countrymen had all heard their voices since childhood, but perhaps they had forgotten to listen.

"Look, Mrs. Adams," Daniel said. "All you have to do is to tell me what and where. Then you forget all about it. *All* about it. You'll be much better off. You're a nice lady," he said, in his taxi-driver voice. "It's one thing for the kid to go underground, but it's another for you to do the same. You could get a job in Toronto, a decent apartment . . ."

"I'm going to make my way to the West," Martha said. "Do you have the men and the means to help, or do I have to go on looking?"

The front of the cab was almost dark, and she couldn't read his expression.

"You can join the mission if you insist," he said in a different tone, "but only on these terms. You will do anything that's required for the mission, and to evade capture. If captured, you must commit suicide. I'll give you what's necessary. But you cannot be permitted to delay me."

"I'm not much older than you are," Martha said with asperity, "And I'm in top physical condition."

"Leave the house before daylight," he said, watching the lamp flicker at the window. "I'll get a truck and park it down the block as soon as I possibly can. Walk as if you're going somewhere, don't appear to loiter. Be ready to travel light."

"I'll be ready," she said.

To her surprise, when she got upstairs Buzz was lying down, fully dressed, fast asleep on her bed.

"He drank some water; we're out of milk," Rose said. "And ate some of that corned beef, and then he fell down like he was pole-axed. I guess he's been livin' rough."

The jacket he had thrown beside him was in reasonably good condition, but it was not his own. Nor were the jeans he wore, his mother noticed. His shirt and underwear were the same in which he had left the house in Bantam, and much in need of a wash. Rose pulled them off him, and gasped at seeing the wound. But Daniel had made a neat job of it, and she made no further remarks. Rose had seen many wounds in her time, Martha guessed, and had learned to ask no questions. Rose's husband, long dead, had had a child by a previous relationship, a wild, unmanageable teenager, who had refused to stay in his stepmother's home. Through the years he had visited Rose only for succor after a fight, or when he was hiding from the police. "He got into dope," Rose had told her once. "Pushing it among the kids. Then I heard he was dead. I was glad his father wasn't alive to know it. But he was a lesson to my Luther. Luther . . ." Martha knew that Rose must be thinking of Luther now.

Rose gathered up the clothes, remarking that although there was no hot water, the electric dryer was

still working, and disappeared. Rose. She could not stay
in the apartment alone. She had no papers, no ration
card, and the kitchen shelves would soon be empty.
Frowning, Martha considered what Greg had told her
about Birdie. The thought of Birdie left an emotional
bad taste but she had to be practical. Birdie's usual
household helper had probably been swept up in the
first evacuation wave. With four working women in the
house she would want a housekeeper, and in her position she might be allowed to have one. Martha sat at
her desk to write a note. It seemed the best she could
do.

   In the event it wasn't needed. The doorbell rang and
she froze. Rose crept back, silent, grey-faced, but Martha knew that the lights could be seen downstairs;
anyone who wanted her would not easily be put off.

   She took the gun that Daniel had given her from her
bag.

   "See who it is, Rose," she said.

   It could be Daniel, but his knock surely would have
been more discreet, not the impatient rapping that still
continued.

   There was a one-way viewer in the door. Rose looked
back at her, relieved. "It's only Mrs. Maynard," she
said.

   Martha concealed the gun as Rose opened the door.

   Birdie was poised on the threshold, looking uncertain
of her reception. She was as smartly dressed as ever,
though her hair, under her little brown hat, was not as
soignée as usual. It had been clumsily cut. The hair-
dressers, of course, had probably been sent away, except those with special protections. Fleetingly she
wondered what had happened to her own nice young
man at Bergdorf's.

   "Come in, Birdie," she said.

   Rose had already closed the door to her room. There
was no need for Birdie to see Buzz. Birdie had a defensive look.

"I had to come," she said. "Luckily, I'm not bound by the curfew, but it's not good in the streets at night just the same. Too many people hiding out; they'll jump you for anything. Martha, I had to warn you. We're such old friends. They gave me a form at the office; I had to complete it. It was no good lying." She talked rapidly. "They're checking everything, and they have all the records. The census, tax data . . . I have to try to survive," she said. "It's bad enough with Greg . . . I don't suppose you know what's happening to people like us. Not just the men but their wives. After all, I was never a broker. I've always been in useful public service. I'm sorry, but you can still get away. You're English born, you could go there. Or perhaps they'll take you in Canada. The Canadians don't want any more of us. They're sending Americans back."

"Don't worry about it," Martha said. The ugly wisps of Birdie's botched haircut seemed to her oddly pathetic. The soreness of betrayal had lessened. "What about Greg?"

There was no need to say that he had come to her. He could tell his wife that if he wished.

Birdie's face clouded. "I think he's gone. When I got up he came in for a moment and left. When I came back from the office he wasn't home. I checked at the armory which is where the street workers are sent out from, and they said he was missing. I hope that doesn't make more trouble. It was only temporary in any case; all those people will be sent off as soon as the debris is collected to work as labor crews somewhere else. I'm filing for divorce, Martha. It's the only way."

Martha could say nothing.

"It's all very well for you," Birdie said, flushing. "You and Josh, well, that was something special. But Greg was never a good husband to me," she went on hurriedly. "I knew all about his other women, but I had to put up with it. I wasn't going to give up everything and be another almost-forty divorcée in New York. I'd had enough of being good-family poor. And for what? So that Greg could make a fool of himself and marry his secretary? She's nineteen. Anyway, if I did want to be a long-suffering wife and a heroine now, it wouldn't do any good. I would be sent out with a labor gang myself."

There was no point in discussing it. Instead, Martha took the opportunity to talk about Rose. Birdie's face cleared.

"I would love to have her," she said. "Rose, could you stand taking care of four of us?" Her brow wrinkled. "I don't know where you'll sleep, but there's Greg's bed in my room. Cora can have that and you can have the living-room sofa. I can get you a permit," she said brightly. "Women in government employment over a certain grade are allowed to have a household worker, but we might have to share you with another group. You'll have a ration card. I might have kept my Pilar, but it all came together too late. I don't know if she was evacuated, or if she just ran off. We can't pay you much Rose, our salaries have been cut to nearly nothing but . . ."

It worked out. Rose, rather reluctantly, took her things and went with Birdie. Birdie looked back from the front door, her face alight again for a moment with what Martha thought of as her "gossip" look. "Martha, do you believe it? Greg told me he had seen *Jason Purfleet* on a street-cleaning gang. Surely they could use him, if television gets back to normal. And he thought he saw Tom Lewis, looking very scraggy."

Rose pressed Martha's hand as they parted. They both knew that they would not see each other for some time to come, if ever, and they were both saddened by the knowledge. Birdie had been Martha's friend since their early schooldays, yet it was not as difficult to part from her as it was from the woman who had come in by the day to clean and dust the often empty apartment.

Tom Lewis. Martha remembered the day on the

train to Bridgeport when the executives had been talking of the difficulties of the publisher in getting a travel permit. Thomas Lewis had been president of one of the largest publishing houses in the United States. She had seen him arrive for a great UN dinner; some celebration for UNESCO. But a publisher, it seemed, was the wrong thing to have been.

She got her things ready and wished she had something for Buzz. But Buzz had hardly been in the apartment since he had gone away to school. Then she reminded herself she was not a mother getting her son ready for summer camp. She tried to sleep until it was time to leave, but every sound in the street was startling. Were they coming? Had her calculations been wrong? A car pulled up outside the building and stopped. She jumped up, grabbing the pistol. She should never have let Buzz stay here; she had put him in further danger . . .

The car moved off. She sank back on the bed, listening to the ticking of the bedside clock, her mind crowding with images of Rose, of Luther, of Greg in the labor gang, even of Tom Lewis, as she had seen him holding a glass of brandy, making a speech that was irresistibly comic, even as it was politically naïve. The new masters were destroying the good and the bright.

* * *

Virinsky was the first of the troika to learn the stunning truth of Magna. He was already in his office at four a.m. for he had worked through the night. His only concession to the hour was the removal of his coat and tie and the donning of a long robe made of a vicuna cloth so fine that it felt like silk. So dressed, he resembled a monk more than ever, if a somewhat luxurious monk.

For days he had been working with the best Russian and UN financial experts on the Reagan Treasury figures and the all-too compendious budgets. They had done what they could but a sharp young accountant from West Germany had told him bluntly, "You would have been much better off to have consulted some of the big money men here in New York and the budget people in Washington. This was their game, after all."

The man who was now one of the three rulers of the United States and destined, it seemed, to be one of the greatest members of the Politburo like his father-in-law, Kharkev, gazed at him with a frightening chill. The position of West Germans now was anomalous, despite the moves towards unification with the East. Remembering this the accountant withdrew, subdued.

Yet Virinsky agreed with him, though the young man could not know it. The Russian was sitting, absently polishing the nail of his forked thumb with the mound of his right hand. It was stupid to have removed all those people so quickly but it had to be done. The orders, the plan, had been part of a pattern that had always been successful in the past. The United States, Virinsky believed, was a different case, but it would not have done to argue with the policy-makers. Certainly he would have had no support there from Perez, and Borunukov, though agreeing, would have backed down at the last. The military had never really stood up to the Politburo. Not yet.

He concluded that he had better comb the labor camps to see if anyone useful had survived. Fortunately, last night, the figures had started to come clear. It was the newspapers that had helped; the glaring headlines of that irresponsible press, shrieking of the millions that they accused Reagan of having stolen. They had had a field day, hounding his widow before the tears of mourning were dry, writing screeds about her love of luxury. Even the responsible newspapers had taken a more-in-sorrow-than-in-anger tone.

An investigative reporter had found that some of this money had been buried in an item for water projects. A consumer advocate had discovered that few of these

projects had ever begun. Much of the money could
never be accounted for, and the scandal had died. It
was another Watergate, but with the victim already
sacrificed. Talk of prosecuting the former first lady,
then living quietly in California, had been stifled by
Carmody who had his own, bourgeois sense of honor.

The KGB had been happy to keep the pot boiling
though no one in Moscow had paid much attention to
"Reagangate" at the time, satisfied as they were with
the events, and believing it was mostly a ploy by Department A disinformation. Virinsky, however, had long
realized that the late American president had been far
more subtle than anyone in Moscow had supposed. In
fact, it was the very image the Russians had tried to
project of Reagan, that of the swashbuckling, foolish,
actor-cowboy, which had clouded their own minds.

If there was a key to Magna it might therefore be in
those water projects. There, monies had changed hands
even though the records had been destroyed long ago.
Decisively, he pushed the buzzer for Thu Thuy, who
was still working quietly in the outer room. She came
in as fresh, neat and beautiful as if she had just emerged
from her bed and bath.

"I want a search made through the government pay-
rolls for the years of the Reagan presidency of any and
all persons working on Federal government construction. We already have Region Two computers here, the
others you will have to check through Hall City. Then I
want all these people found and brought to New York
for questioning. Another special camp can be set up in
Central Park to receive them. I'll give orders for the
questioning teams later. Also go to the Labor Directory files. I want the information collated on all high-
level experts in the fields of finance and budget. Those
still alive will probably be widely dispersed; I want
them also brought in to a separate section of the special
camp."

"The first group may be very large," Thu Thuy offered.

"It doesn't matter. They will be screened through quickly."

She nodded and turned to go. Her sheath-like dress clung to her narrow hips and her legs were long for her height and slender.

"Better still, reach Madame Paul and get her to work on it," Virinsky said. "She is excellent at these procedures. Then return here."

She went with a murmur of acquiescence. He was gratified with the result of his labors; soon, he believed, the solution to the Magna problem would be in his hands. He would use the newly-arrived contingent of Border troops to guard the prisoners and keep Borunukov and Perez to wait at his will. These thoughts gave him pleasure. He also felt an unaccustomed stirring in his loins.

Virinsky knew what people whispered: that he had the tastes of Beria. Beria, who had kidnapped very young girls off the streets and raped them. The whispers did not disturb him. In truth, he was a man of small sexual appetite. He had no desire for his buxom wife, who in turn treated him with an ill-disguised contempt. She had never wanted to marry him but Kharkev had been eager for the alliance with the rising KGB officer who would, in the years to come, protect his own flank. Elizaveta had done what she was told. No doubt she had feared that her children might be born with his deformity.

There was no shortage of women and girls for men of his rank and infidelity without open scandal was accepted. The Borunukovs of the regime kept harems, consorting openly with their women outside of the Soviet Union. Virinsky as Kharkev's son-in-law was more cautious. Thu Thuy was a good, disciplined Party member. She would be no problem. Unconsciously, he began a long, slow stroking of his thumb.

Thu Thuy returned, and Virinsky told the two guards by the inner door that he was not to be disturbed until further notice. It was still dark outside and the only light came from his desk lamp. Thu Thuy had slipped off her dress and undergarments and took her place on the bench. Her slim form, pale against the black leather, was all grace and youth, small-breasted, child-like. That and her docility were pleasing to the man.

He was aroused beyond his usual limit when the mood was shattered by the ringing of the telephone. All the other systems were turned off, so it had to be Kharkev on the special line that was always open. With an ill-tempered wave of his hand, he sent Thu Thuy away, telling her to wait in the outer room.

If he was in an ill mood, Kharkev sounded close to terror. Normally a cool head, he was spluttering. Ulyanov had had to be informed. There was to be a special meeting of the Politburo. That chicken-hearted Shushkin was already calling for them to take to the shelters. Virinsky soon gleaned the first essential fact. A small PLO group had led a rabble against the atomic research center in Israel.

"The head of the Eighth Department had already informed me that this Dimona, in the Negev, had been closed down," Kharkev went on. "What was left was merely a *pokazukha*, to deceive us that their main plant was still there, while doubtless they were building another. However only the Arabs were deceived."

He went on to tell of the young KGB officer's brilliant saving of the old Israeli from the mob. "A senile old fool, but our local people got enough out of him to patch him up and put him on a jet to be received by a crack group of scientific interrogators in Tripoli."

"If he's senile, is his story reliable?" Virinsky asked, frowning.

"The Israelis thought him sane enough to do his job. He was there to sort out any important papers that might have been overlooked in the hasty move. They wanted to leave just some rubbish that might convince the commanders of an invading army that this was all the research they had. They sent this Fogel, who was retired, because he had known about the work of Shlomo Darin."

Virinsky didn't have to know Department Eight's work to recognize the name of Darin. In Israel's early days he had been their brightest atomic scientist.

"Our local people couldn't understand what Fogel was saying. No one there knew an isotope from a neutron, which was why they gave him up to Tripoli. He was a madman, that Darin." Kharkev's voice was quavering. "The mad scientist we've always been afraid of."

That was true. The KGB's job was to control, not just the Soviets, but eventually the world. Almost to a man they hated and feared all atomic weapons, even as they assiduously stole everything possible to aid Soviet scientists. Atomic weaponry was too big, too all-destructive for the control of any police force, until the world was made one. And even then . . .

"His own government got angry with him, and would no longer fund his research. They actually forbade his going on with it. But the stubborn old swine went on, under cover of other projects. It wasn't until we and the Americans turned to laser-satellite weapons that he was heard from again. The Israelis knew they couldn't finance a war of satellites from space. But their enemies could. It was then that they remembered Darin. Our people in Tripoli got it all from old Fogel. The great excitement in the highest circles of Israel's government. And then the letdown. Because Darin *was* crazy. Kostya," he said, and then choked. "Kostya, *he went on with the cobalt bomb*."

Thu Thuy returned, but Virinsky had no more thoughts of pleasure. Dawn had not yet broken, but Thu Thuy was ordered to locate and produce any scientific members of the UN AEC in the area.

"If they're not English or Russian speaking, bring

interpreters. You'd better get Madame Paul to help you."

Thu Thuy went off to Madame Paul's office. Madame already had teams working on the finance and construction projects, but she turned her attention to the new demand without protest. What she thought of receiving instructions from the younger woman no one could have known: her face was impassive. No doubt, she told herself, it was easier for the Under-Secretary to use a messenger than to take time on the telephone. Thu Thuy was a good messenger.

An hour produced three men who needed no interpreters, a Frenchman who had worked with the successor of Joliot-Curie, somewhat disheveled and disgruntled at being torn from his bed; an Englishman, part of the team from Windscale, fresh, clean-shaven and clear-eyed. The third man was a Russian scientist that Madame Paul had found, who had come to address the UN group in New York. Virinsky had already heard what the Central Directory had to say, but he allowed him in with the others.

When the men were seated, Thu Thuy brought in tea for the Russians and the Englishman and coffee for the Frenchman. Fruit jelly, lemon, sugar, milk and cream were provided for each taste. *Ponchiki* were also served, but only the Russians ate them. Virinsky allowed the men to swallow the refreshment to clear their minds and then asked bluntly:

"What do you know of Shlomo Darin?"

"He's dead," the Englishman replied at once, his large blue eyes bulging slightly. "He died, let's see . . ." he hesitated. "It wasn't widely reported. He had been retired for years."

"Pensioned off. The old man was ga-ga," the Frenchman said. "After the middle fifties, to the young men he was just another 'encore la'."

"He died in August of '81," the Russian said. "Kidney

failure. But he had been of no official interest for the last thirty years."

"Unreliable," the Englishman added. "Met him once at a dinner. He wasn't asked to speak, but he mumbled all evening. A lot of rot about hemoglobin, chlorophyll, and vitamin B." Obviously, he was wondering why he had been torn from his lodging at such an hour to answer questions about a dead Israeli; just as obviously, he was shrewd enough not to ask.

"How do you mean, unreliable?" Virinsky asked.

The Englishman lit a foul pipe that annoyed the KGB man but he let it pass.

"He wasn't a team man. In atomic physics, the team is everything. Old Darin was a loner. A crank. There used to be a lot of men like that in England," he said meditatively, as though there were all the time in the world for a cozy chat. "They would work on some mechanical project by themselves, in a shed in the back of a garden, all their lives. Sometimes they came up with a useful invention, most often they didn't. But they were secretive, solitary workers. Darin was a brilliant physicist, but he had that nature."

"But he could have done nothing, alone," the Frenchman interjected.

"He had a small group who were devoted to him. They worked for him personally, not the main project. The Israelis would have got rid of him sooner, I think, but they still have a reverence of a sort for the founders."

Virinsky waited until they finished and then asked: "What do you know of the cobalt bomb?"

All three men, very different in appearance, now wore the same expression, surprise, perhaps a little amusement.

He had no trouble in reading their thoughts. The cobalt bomb—what bogies were frightening the scientifically stupid KGB? The Frenchman spoke first. "But, there is no cobalt bomb except for medical use, you understand. A little device like a football, used in the treatment of cancer. Is that what you mean?"

The Russian was certain that that was *not* what Virinsky meant, but he remained silent.

"No," Virinsky said. "There was talk at one time of a cobalt bomb as an atomic weapon, was there not?"

The Englishman knocked out his pipe on the saucer that Thu Thuy had provided for his glass of tea.

"Only talk." He pointed the stem of his pipe at Virinsky like a schoolmaster making a point. "A piece of research never followed up. No bombs were built. Though there was a lot of hysteria, I remember. People called it a Doomsday weapon. Properly placed, a group of them could poison the winds of the world. Some researchers said they might knock the earth off its axis. No one was interested."

"No," the Frenchman said, and then pursed his lips. "The Anglo-Americans could well take a moral stand because a shell of ordinary uranium on the big, new, dirty hydrogen weapons causes as much radioactivity—or more."

"That is true," the Russian said. Nobody ever harmed himself by exposing the duplicity of the Anglo-Saxons.

"The Israelis," the Frenchman went on, "certainly had no interest. Most of their current research, like that of many of the advanced nations, has been in laser technology."

The Frenchman in the past had worked with the Israelis and had reasonably good relations with their scientists. KGB reports, Virinsky knew, confirmed what he had said.

"Laser-satellite weaponry," the Englishman said, not happily. The atomic scientists had not liked having to share the glories of destruction with the laser-satellite men. And England could not afford satellite warfare. Like Israel, it had found itself out of the game.

Shlomo Darin had not accepted that, it seemed. "That crazy old bastard just plodded on," Kharkev had said.

"By the time the government went to him, he had all the theory for a new weapon, a cobalt-dipped missile. This projected weapon was of such a horrifying capacity that one, just one, Kostya, with MIRV'd warheads, could turn a land mass stretching five thousand miles into a death valley. The blast and fire alone . . ." He could not go on for a moment. A terrible silence fell.

"But from such a weapon the radiation would sweep the world," Virinsky had said at last. "That's why it was known to be useless."

"Old Fogel was asked that. He was very weak at that point and unreliable, babbling about the monster's breath. He had never been a top-ranking researcher himself, of course, and only knew from hearsay. Shlomo Darin had claimed that using his theory, adjusting for prevailing winds, if Moscow were a target the wind would clear by the time it reached the Kolyma range."

Virinsky had been left speechless.

"Of course," Kharkev said at last, "It hasn't been tested." He sounded very weary. "By its nature, of course, it couldn't be. But then neither was the Hiroshima bomb. And it worked."

"But was such a weapon ever made?" Virinsky asked. The Middle East was not his territory, but there was nothing wrong with Department Eight. Surely such a thing could not have gone unobserved.

"It was of no use to Israel, that's obvious. Darin was really insane. Israel is such a tiny state—in killing its enemies it would destroy itself. No, we didn't need this old Fogel to tell us that."

"Then?"

"They gave the research to their protector in return for present and future service," Kharkev said. "What else could they have done?"

"But the Americans never built such a weapon," Virinsky said. They were talking now of his own Department; his reputation was at stake. "It *could not have happened* without my knowing it. Impossible."

"Fogel, before he died, spoke of it as a functioning weapon. He called the missile Aharit-Ha-Yamim," Kharkev said. "The Doomsday weapon. The interrogators said he laughed, or made a noise that could have been a laugh. It's in the United States, Virinsky. It's certainly somewhere. I always thought those cursed Jews should have been done away with. Hitler had the right idea."

Virinsky was rarely taken aback, but there were few men in the Soviet Union even at this date who dared to praise Germany, the one-time arch enemy, and Kharkev had not been one of them. For him to have expressed such a thought meant that he was really frightened.

Kharkev had been one of those who had opposed the strike, believing that in a very few years it would not have been necessary. He had felt sure the United States would crumble without the need of atomic weaponry. The risk, admittedly small, had not been worth taking. Borunukov had disagreed, he and his Politburo supporters had won the argument and then gone on to win the victory. But Kharkev was still afraid. Now his orders—Ulyanov's orders—were clear enough. The weapon or weapons, if they existed, must be located; they must be shipped to the Soviet Union; and anyone who had any knowledge, or was suspected of having any knowledge of the existence of Aharit-Ha-Yamim must be eliminated. At once. The knowledge of the technology must pass only into the hands of Ulyanov himself who would bring in trusted Soviet scientists under his personal direction, completely bypassing Tikhonov and the Council of Ministers. Further, all this was to be done with the maximum discretion and speed.

"If this discovery falls to our enemies," Kharkev had rasped, "it will be they who are giving us the ultimatums."

Before he hung up, Virinsky had the satisfaction of telling him that the matter was already in hand. He had heard rumors and had begun a search. The project was coded "Magna." Kharkev's relief at hearing this had been shortlived. "I should have been informed," he said. "This matter will be laid squarely at the door of the First Department. It seems impossible, Virinsky, that you should not have discovered it sooner." With anger replacing fear, intimacy was left behind.

Kharkev always liked to have the last word. Virinsky was not much troubled by physical fear; he was neither nervous nor emotional. "A dry man," his enemies called him. He had no friends, only allies. But now he did feel frightened, not of the Doomsday weapon, but of the criticism of his department. His work was such that he had never been vulnerable. Now he felt his bare scalp crawling as he faced the scientists on the other side of his desk.

He came to the point. "The small group you mentioned," he addressed the Englishman. "Could you identify them?"

The Englishman looked nonplussed. "That was so long ago . . ."

"It was Ari Kenan's group," the Frenchman said. "Brilliant physicists. Wasted themselves with that *vieux fou.*"

"Dead. All dead," the Russian said, with a sigh. "A dinner at the Weizmann Institute, not so long ago. '82. A Palestinian bomb."

It was the end of that line. The Russian who had kept his eyes open and his recollection sharp was a good man. It was a pity, but Kharkev had been specific. Virinsky pressed a button for the special guard. None of these men could now return to their normal lives.

As they were led away he turned to his first task, mere routine. The orders for mass arrests of Jews, as Jews, was not scheduled for at least six months. His men were busy with arrest teams, supervising city evacuations, and the special operation on Chinese Americans ordered by Borunukov. But now that Israel was known to be involved with Magna, it must be done.

Probably the only resistance would come from the Jewish Defense League, and most of their leaders had already been picked up by the primary arrest squads.

Outside the sun was rising, bright and clear. He had wanted to know the secret of Project Magna; now he knew. It was impossible that the missile had been built in his Department and he not know about it. But it could have been built in many places in the world. His orders were to find Magna, so he had the world to search and its population to sift through. He might as well start counting all the sands of the sea. Frowning for a moment, he opened one of his secret files. Then he put through a call to a man in Boulder, Colorado.

BOOK THREE

THE GREAT FEAR

Who then holds the helm of Necessity?
The Fates triform, and the unforgetting Furies

— XX —

"China," Borunukov said positively. "Almost certainly China. Where else could such a thing have been built in secrecy?"

Virinsky had called Borunukov with the news. He would have been informed anyway and in this case Virinsky had no wish to keep the whole matter in his own hands. His first thought had been to set up a meeting of the troika, but Perez had gone on a state visit to Cuba and would not return for two days.

Of course, Borunukov was right about the secrecy. But the technical problems of building the missile in China would have been great, and trusting them with it, Virinsky was sure, would have been contrary to anything he knew about the Reagan people. He had lived in the United States and Borunukov had not. Naturally, Borunukov's mind would go to China; China was now the chief enemy, and he had long wanted to destroy it. "General Patton," Kharkev dubbed him, with some justice. Borunukov had been known to say, among his intimates after too much vodka, that from a military point of view Patton had been right.

But wherever it had been built, the Americans must have intended to bring it home, to slip it in their missile system—its special nature unknown to all but a necessary few—without having to cope with the fury of enraged pacifists, environmentalists, and the counterforce of his own organized groups.

Had they done it, before Reagan was killed? He looked again at his notes on the Cunningham tape. The words were so few.

"Magna . . . sleeping giant . . . will destroy you . . ."

Borunukov had pointed out that Napoleon (whose life he had studied in great detail) had referred to China as a sleeping giant. He had thought that of immense significance.

"Magna." It was possibly an incomplete word or phrase.

Between "sleeping giant" and "will destroy you" a gap with a combination of sounds that might be "perhaps."

He sent for Madame Paul. She had worked late, and then been torn from her bed long before daybreak. Now, in the light of day, the heavy make-up she had applied to cover the damage did her no service. She was far from lovely, but very useful.

"I want you to listen to the Magna tape again," he said. "Listen very carefully, to see if any of the sounds might have been a reference to China."

Madame Paul nodded. She took the reel again. She spent an hour listening closely, and then returned to his desk.

"There is nothing that sounds even remotely like China, any province of China, or any name usually connected with it. There are many sounds that cannot be fitted into word patterns at all, of course. But from any practical point of view, I would eliminate the possibility of the word China, or Chinese, from a transcript of that tape. Of course, I could have a Chinese interpreter listen to see if there might be a Chinese word that I didn't recognize . . ."

Cunningham had spoken no Chinese. Virinsky rejected that possibility.

He dismissed her, but she hesitated at the door. "The work we began last night is far from complete. Would you like copies of the lists prepared so far?"

"Leave them with Thu Thuy outside," he said. "She will deal with them as necessary."

Madame Paul withdrew. She regretted that she had ever put in Nguyen Thu Thuy as a temporary replacement for Mrs. Adams, in a position to catch the Under-Secretary's eye. She should have stayed where she belonged, in the Personnel department.

It was not the probable sexual relationship that Madame Paul resented; she knew how little that meant to the man. In a place like the UN the stories about Virinsky and his black bench could not be entirely suppressed. Mr. No-Frills, the girls called him. Vulgar sluts. They did not understand his dedication to work, and they thought more of a man's virility than the scope of his brain, his abilities, his power.

No. It was the placing of Thu Thuy in a position of authority, giving her the right to transmit orders and to monitor their communication that caused two little red patches to mount on the elder woman's cheeks. But the special relationship between herself and the Under-Secretary was of long standing and it was hardly possible that it should be lessened by the attractions of a competent but inexperienced newcomer, whatever political work she might have done elsewhere.

In the computer room, a dozen girls and young men were at work on the special projects, retrieving information and performing the complicated cross-checks. Another group of girls were busily transcribing the computer records into an easily-read, typed form. Leafing through a pile of papers on the Western States water projects, the name of the Columbia Construction Company caught her eye. She slipped it out for special attention. The Columbia company had been one of those involved in what came to be called Reagangate. The president of the company, she remembered, had died conveniently. Some people had suspected it had been suicide. It had made headlines at the time. Certainly *he* could not be brought in. As her pencil marked out the name, another caught her glance. Job Superintendent, Joshua Adams, of Bantam, Connecticut. This country was full of Adamses.

At nine-thirty that morning, word had come to her that Mrs. Martha Adams had not appeared at her desk. And yet Mrs. Adams had been one of those summoned on the emergency roster last night. She sent in another worker to take charge of the unit and thought no more of it for a time. Transportation was difficult and many of the UN staff were uneasy about walking through the streets where some predators still lurked, though they would not survive for long. But when by noon Mrs. Adams had not arrived, her name was sent in to the Security Office, under the new rules. It was mostly a waste of time. Mrs. Adams probably had received no call, and if she was ill she could not telephone in. Madame's request for the restoration of telephone service to her people so far had been complied with very sporadically. State security again took precedence over the smooth functioning of her offices. She was irritated by the reminder and the uncomfortable thought that the start of the new regime was not as entirely satisfying as she had expected.

* * *

Ramon Perez, still in Havana, also had his pleasure dimmed that day. He had publicly taken possession of the Palacio de los Capitanes Generales, once a Presidential Palace. Now it would be a Presidential Palace again. His guerilla days were over. He enjoyed the quiet elegance of this place. The statue of Columbus could remain in the courtyard, he decided, but his own portrait would take the place of honor at the bottom of the wide staircase.

On that morning his people had taken control in Haiti and the Dominican Republican. It had been one more satisfaction, coming after his great moment. It was from Cuba that the great SS18's had rained down on the United States; it was Cuban technicians who had launched the tactical missiles from Panama; it was from Cuban waters that the *Kiev* and her sister ship had sailed with their eight twin launchers that had destroyed the Pearl Harbor fleet. From Cuba he could rule all the Americas and, he thought, a lot more besides. His organization was worldwide and larger than anyone knew, except for himself alone.

He had already learned, with some interest, of the mob attack on Dimona, repulsed at last by the Israelis. The Israelis still seemed prepared to fight, though by now they must surely know that their best course would be mass suicide, like that of the zealots at Masada. Perhaps they would stand at Masada again.

He had also received reports of the capture of old Fogel, and his subsequent journey to Tripoli for questioning. But of his connection with the Magna mystery, he had as yet heard nothing. The only real interest Perez had in Israel, a state ready to pass into history, was the man known as Bar-Lev. Mossad itself was almost overwhelmed but Bar-Lev, their most deadly yet almost unknown agent, would remain a threat until his death. A more feared assassin than his own Carlos, he was also a Zionist fanatic. He would not quietly submerge himself in the New Order. Bar-Lev was the only single human being that Perez feared.

His first known act had been the killing of Meir Pavan, an Israeli turned Soviet agent, like the notorious

Israel Ber before him. Pavan was the Philby of Israel.
He had escaped the country, but not Bar-Lev. It was
he who had tracked down the last of the Nazi leaders,
long thought to be dead and buried, leading a comfortable old age in a suburb of Buenos Aires. It was Bar-
Lev who was believed to have killed Quaddafi; and it
was Bar-Lev who had assassinated Lavrentin, when he
had proposed a systematic extermination of the unassimil-
able Jews. The assassination had never been made public, but the plan had not been adopted.

Yet very little was known about Bar-Lev personally
except that he was said to be a man very attractive to
women, all sorts and kinds of women. Perez knew
exactly what danger that represented. A man favored
by more than half of the human race found it easy to
disappear. He came and went like the wind.

Then the call came in from Ulyanov. Even before he
took in the significance of what was being told he heard
the raw fear in the voice of the Chairman of the Politburo and the General Secretary of the CPSU. His inner
reaction, though his words were suitably correct, was
not at all what his caller might have expected. Perez's
first thought was that the time had come for Ulyanov,
as the world's leading communist, to be replaced. As
Ulyanov went on with the story of Aharit-Ha-Yamim,
his second thought was that that position did not have
to rest in the CPSU, although it always had. There
were other communist groups in the world. The third
thought was that a little pasting on their own soil might
take the Russians down a little. All this was while he
was expressing shock.

"And it is our considered opinion that this weapon is
in North America, in the United States. Although there
are only two submarines unaccounted for; believed scut-
tled, our experts say it is extremely unlikely such a
missile would be launched by submarine. The accuracy
is not as great . . ."

"With such a thing would it matter?" Perez asked.

"It is also the nature of the former President," Ulyanov said. "It would be in keeping with his character to have wanted to store that missile, wherever it was built, on American shores." Old Ulyanov had always been a good judge of men. Better than the revered Lenin whom he claimed as kin. That was how he had reached his present eminence and stayed there.

"But Comrade Chairman," Perez continued, "even if this tale is true, and a group of guerrillas were holding such a weapon, it couldn't be fired without our knowing it. And the new beam weapons could shoot it down anywhere. Even the old ABM's . . ."

"We dare not take that chance. Besides," Ulyanov cleared his throat, "this is for your ears only, my friend. In truth the ISR, the whole Academy of Sciences, is behind schedule on the laser and particle beams. Since Korolev died, things have never been as they were. After October 26th, Petrov will have to answer for that. It was against policy, of course, for this lagging behind to be made known."

A *pokazukha*. It was too bad for Petrov that the Americans had given up on research as well as production. The good, reliable Communist scientists of the ISR weren't moving so fast now that Department S could not hurry things along with gleanings from their Western counterparts. The last important piece of technology they had filched was the inertial guidance systems that had ensured the SS18's ability to wipe out the US land-based missiles.

Perez, averting his mind from the truly terrible destructive power they were facing, was almost amused. It had been his efforts, and that of Virinsky's Department A, that had whipped the anti-war feeling to a frenzy, thus destroying the United States' research and development. One hand had strangled the other. Fratricide, as the missile men would call it. He pointed out the KGB's blunder to Ulyanov. Perhaps he would manage to get rid of Kharkev, which would be pleasing to himself.

"Kharkev tells me that the KGB already has a search in hand," Ulyanov said, without making a direct reply to his last remark. "Virinsky . . ."

"We had all heard rumors, nothing more," Perez said sharply. "The troika as a whole has been looking into it. Project Magna." Most certainly, this had been what Cunningham had babbled about. Just as certainly as the GRU had bungled the investigation. The army people were fools. Just that morning he had been delivered a copy of the *New York Times*, showing a picture of Borunukov posturing with the Great Seal of the United States. All vanity. *The Times* had been merged with the *Morning Star*, and Perez's people there were not going to be happy about the paper returning to its old banner.

"So," Ulyanov was saying. "You will give this Project Magna 'A' priority. Kharkev has been combing the world for former U.S. and allied agents, bringing them to Moscow for questioning. Between us, this weapon—if it exists whatever and wherever it is—must be found and shipped to the Soviet Union."

"Then we must find someone with knowledge of it," Perez said instantly. "If there is anyone left alive . . . Kharkev must share all information immediately. After all, Comrade Chairman, the weapon could be a bomb or a missile. It could be on the ground, under the sea, perhaps even hidden in some artificial libration area in space. Of course you are right," he said, remembering himself, "that Reagan would have wanted it in the United States. But he has been dead for years now, and whoever controlled it might have had other ideas. The world is large and space . . ."

"You are right, Ramon," Ulyanov said. The old man sounded depressed, but he soon recovered. "I will order searches . . ."

He detailed his plans, which were what might have been expected.

Perez made the right responses, but he was no longer really listening. He was looking out of the window to *el Templete*, built like a Doric temple, on the other side of the Plaza de Armas. A handsome building once, but long neglected, it stood dismally in the slanting rain. Like so much of Havana, it looked shabby and poor. In fact it looked like what it was, the capital of a Soviet satellite state. Even the great park that served the city was Lenin Park.

The land mass of North, Central and South America was far greater than that of the USSR. The leader of what was truly the Western world should be the greater master of the world. Just for once, he thought, Ulyanov had misjudged a man, because Perez had not labored all his life to make the Russians masters of the globe. And now it seemed that opportunity had come to his hand, for whoever first found this weapon Magna would control the world.

His aide-de-camp entered and with a more discreet air than usual murmured, "The *muchachas*, Commander? Do I bring them here?"

Perez frowned. "No. Not here." It seemed unfitting. "Take the girls to the Hemingway place. I will take that also, as a little pleasure house.

Looking out at the plaza, he decided to replace the statue of Carlos Manuel with one of himself, in battle fatigues, brandishing a rifle in one hand, and guiding a small peasant child with the other. That would be effective.

In the meantime there was this Magna business. If the Israelis were involved, Bar-Lev *must* be found. Perez had a short conversation with Virinsky, that left him partly satisfied. "We have already begun," Virinsky said. "The rounding up of the Jews was on the list. I have merely set it ahead of schedule. The teams are already working."

The probability of catching Bar-Lev in any general sweep was very remote. But they could pick up people who might turn out to be friends, relatives, allies. All the usual bolt-holes would be closed down one by one. Then he had some talk with his most trusted aide about putting into action a long-cherished plan. Outside the rain still beat down on the Templete.

— XXI —

A small truck bearing the legend "Isaacs Brass" was parked by the loading platform on Greene Street, behind a long black car. Daniel sat in the driver's seat with Martha beside him. Dressed in khaki pants, a plaid shirt and moccasins, her hair pulled back from her face and tied with a narrow cotton scarf, she did not look out of place. She had brought no more than she could pack in a soft bag that she carried on her shoulder and a hand grip.

"I sent Buzz up to collect a few things because I wanted to talk to you," he said. "First I think it's a bad idea for you two to travel together. When the alarm goes out, the patrols will very likely be looking for a woman and a boy. And soon your photographs will be in every police station in the country."

Buzz had woken early: the telephone had rung. It had been connected at last. Of course, it was Madame Paul's office: an emergency, would she please report to work as soon as possible.

223

Mother and son had talked. To her surprise, Buzz accepted Daniel easily. The boy who had had to learn quickly how to survive outside the law was already more sure in his judgement of whom to trust, whom to avoid, than his mother. There were groups of young outlaws around the countryside, he had told her, some merely predators, others were fighters, determined never to give in to the occupying power.

"Last word we had from the West was there are some army and marine units hiding out in the Rockies. In New York, West Point was taken over but some cadets got away. They're trying to organize a corps. Robbie and I were trying to catch up with Colonel Fairfield. There's word he's been trying to get a group of retired officers together, before the Russkies find 'em. They move fast," he had said.

The boys' ambitions had been as gallant as they were suicidal. Postponing their atomic scheme, Robbie and Buzz had thought of a plan to assassinate some prominent Russians at a General Assembly meeting.

"That's why I had to see Armand. He would know who was coming and when. And he'd help us smuggle the guns inside."

"Armand? The interpreter?"

"He hates interpreting. Couldn't take his job, except he likes fooling with the sound equipment. He's a great guy, another ham, and a nut about electronics. And he really hates the Russians. I knew he'd want to be in it with us. He told me in the street that there's some big deal coming up on October 26th . . ."

"You would get yourselves killed," Martha had protested.

"We're not idiots," Buzz countered patiently.

It had not been difficult, though, to persuade Buzz to leave this for a while to accompany her on her mission. "Dad left a cuckoo in a nest somewhere, didn't he?" he said. She had been jolted. But it was natural enough that Buzz had guessed the truth. He had known about his father's work, and the two of them had always been close, despite the long physical absences. Buzz had been far closer to his father than he had been to her, although she had been the one who raised him. He already knew enough not to ask too much.

But in the moments while she thrust a few things into a bag, knowing she might never see this place again, Buzz had to speak. "Is it going to be just a spit in the eye or can it really make any difference?"

Martha knew of just one Magnanimity missile. She knew the general area where she could look for it, praying that no one else got there first. Daniel hadn't told her much more than she'd told him. Yet—our only hope, he had said. And Josh had made certain that she would get his message from the grave. From the night she had found the package of plans in the old pump room she had felt a certain inner conviction that here was the means to raise the United States from its prostration. Knowledge, instinct, whatever it might be. The sun was high now on the little, cobbled street. Other trucks were rumbling up from Canal Street. A horn sounded as they passed.

"Yes, it will make a difference," she had said. Buzz had nodded, satisfied.

Daniel roused her from her reverie. "I spent last night doing some checking." And the morning she thought, for he had come hours late to their rendezvous. While he spoke to her she noticed his gaze on the empty car in front. It was a heavy Cadillac, with a long radio antenna. He was frowning. "The roads are tough. Regional borders are guarded like national barriers or the old border between East and West Berlin. And so what I've done . . ."

At that moment Buzz bounded out of the building, carrying two violin cases and a shopping bag. "Move," he said.

Daniel slammed into first gear and pushed the accelerator down to the floor board.

Buzz's voice was low but calm. "A butcher's shop. Looks like they had a small war up there. Special police, three of them, and some little guys, two of them in skull caps. A couple of them could have been Puerto Ricans, and there was a big guy with a curly, grey beard. All dead. The bodies are still warm. But I got the guns."

They were already rumbling down Canal Street. Martha saw Daniel flinch when Buzz mentioned the old man. Near the Manhattan Bridge, Daniel pulled into a private garage next to a small house.

"We'll have to dump this truck," he said. "They'll be sending out a patrol to check on the men who didn't report back. An arrest team that ran into trouble."

His expression was dour.

"Were they your people?" Martha asked.

"The old man was my father's friend. Not one of us. My father worked for old Isaacs, years ago. He was also a taxi-driver, before he made his Aliyah to Israel. Old Isaacs was a good man. I just left these guns with him for a night; I'll have to find out what happened. You and Buzz can stay here for a few hours while I arrange for different transport.

There was nothing in him now of the sardonic New Yorker. His face was set and hard and a chill came from him that made her aware he was very much a stranger. Noticing her glance, he gave her a quick smile.

"You'll be all right here. Buzz, stay with your mother. I'll leave you the guns." He nodded towards a side door leading into the house. "There's food inside. I might not be back until dark."

"Can't we get away today?" Martha said, impatiently.

"You're going to be waiting around a good deal," Daniel said. "Get used to it. "When the cat is hunting the mouse, a smart mouse stays in the hole. You're a mouse now, Mrs. Martha Adams."

He saw the indignation on her patrician face, and laughed quietly as he let himself out.

* * *

The next morning a small van rolled over the Williamsburg bridge in the tide of commercial traffic. The congestion at the approach was no worse than usual, though every car was stopped for the checking of identity cards and permits. There was much less traffic since the surrender.

The unmarked van, with its load of ball bearings and invoices to a factory in Astoria, Queens, with its driver and helper, passed the check point with no difficulty.

"See? You pass easily enough for a laborer, Mrs. Adams. All you need is confidence."

Daniel was grinning as they bumped over the old bridge. Martha's reply was drowned by the noise of the subway train thundering past, with its load of identified workers. Below them the East River, blue and choppy, was still alive with river traffic. It might have been a normal September scene, except for the Red Flag flying on the new naval patrol boats that circled the island now as the old tourist boats used to do.

When Daniel had returned with the van and the new papers, he also brought a man's leather jacket and a brown wig for Martha. There was a rumpled, dark blond wig for Buzz which he had accepted with resignation.

Buzz had gone earlier alone with a load of restaurant supplies.

"Deliver the stuff and then leave the truck with the papers inside at the hotel parking lot by La Guardia. Someone else will take it back."

Buzz had bounded off, only pausing to give his worried mother a quick hug. Now, on the Brooklyn side, Martha was impatient as the van poked along through the small streets. "Can't we move along a little faster?"

"No hurry," Daniel said lazily, as though they were out for a pleasant ride. "Nothing worth drawing attention to ourselves. You might notice that no one else is pushing."

It was true. The usual impatient thrust of traffic was noticeably absent. Even people on the sidewalks were moving at a slower pace.

"Labor and commerce are no longer as rewarding as they previously were."

As they rolled on Martha could feel the lethargy born of defeat and submission and it gave a bitter taste to the bright day. The pigeons still fluttered over the rooftops, cooing and calling, though not as many were stalking impudently on the roads. Were people trapping and eating the birds, Martha wondered?

Suddenly, among the noises from the traffic and the cooing of the pigeons, another noise rang out, loud, sharp. A gunshot? Martha sat up and Daniel's hands on the wheel tensed.

They were at an intersection. The narrow street that lay across their path was almost filled on the right by three army trucks. Another evacuation. Women, children, black and white, were being herded into the first two trucks, carrying a few possessions. A few old men were being pushed along with them. One bearded elder, wearing the flat, black hat of the Hasids, was clinging to a post, refusing to go. Martha could not see if the old man was wounded, or if it had been a warning shot.

As she stared, a small squad of darker-clad troops jumped from the third truck with automatic weapons at the ready. The pigeons fluttered from a roof across the street; a shot rang out and a soldier fell. Martha caught a glimpse of a head of a boy in a skull cap behind the snout of a rifle that was firing down and another soldier screamed. Shots rang out from up and down the street. Two soldiers jumped on the fire escape to check the roofs but strong, young, black arms reached out from the windows, pinned them back and slashed their throats. The spurting blood dripped onto the old Hasids below and they chanted louder.

"They'll have radioed for reinforcements," Daniel muttered. "The kids won't have a chance . . ."

The soldiers, panicking, fired their automatic rifles, slicing through the women, children and praying old men. Running youths, Hasids and blacks, converged on the soldiers from doorways and windows, a few falling in the fire, but overwhelming the small squad. But the third truck had been maneuvered round and now a burst of machine-gun fire roared from the tailgate, cutting down the youths.

Daniel swore.

"Get on the floor," he ordered Martha, and then jumped out of the car, a pistol in hand, and ran like a cat through the melée, swinging up to the front door of the truck and disappearing inside. The soldier slumped over his gun; toppled sideways and fell from the tailgate to lie on the cracked city road. Martha was staring at the corpse when she saw a flash of metal; a bloody soldier, almost concealed behind a low brick fence, had raised his weapon and trained it on Daniel, who was leaping down from the truck. Her gun was already in her hand. She heard the crack and felt the kick of the .45 and smelled the cordite, while the man she had shot was flung backward to lie on a dusty stretch of grass beside the garbage cans.

For a moment the street was quiet, except for the moaning of the wounded and the muted sobbing of a child. The youths stood, looking at the tumbled bodies of the soldiers.

Daniel gave them his sketchy salute. "You've won the first battle of Williamsburg," he said. "But you'd better scram."

A tall, Hasidic boy nodded, and began calling quiet instructions. Daniel leaned towards him, whispered something and then jumped back into the van. He had left the motor running and now he shoved it in gear and accelerated up the street. The van screeched round the turns, with Daniel handling it as deftly as a racing driver.

"They'll be throwing up barricades round this area

within five minutes," he said. "I guess I have to say thanks. But you should have stayed down."

"The same way you shouldn't have stopped," Martha said.

He grimaced. "Touché, Mrs. Adams. But those kids . . ."

"What did you tell the leader?" Martha said.

"About a place where he can meet someone," Daniel replied. "At least get organized. All those brave kids, fighting in scattered groups without direction. They'll be wiped out, to no purpose."

"There *is* a purpose," Martha said. The old Hasid clinging to the lamp-post . . . She remembered from long ago Solzhenitsyn's injunction not to go quietly. *"You ought to cry out,"* he had said. Fight back, so that no arresting team could feel secure, when it left to do its work, that all its members would return alive.

They were already more than a mile away, moving into the streets of Queens. Daniel slowed down to a less conspicuous pace.

"Well," he said, "this is what it took." His voice was meditative.

"Took?"

"Didn't you notice? The black kids and the Hasids, fighting together. Brothers in arms."

"One good thing from all this, then," Martha said. "I just hope it lasts."

Daniel grunted. "We're not in Disneyland. In some parts of the country there have been pogroms already. People will take out their frustrations where they can. Bloodbaths, some racial and some for no reason anyone can see. And the Russians have already started to round up Jews, systematically. That's probably what happened to old Isaacs. Caught in the first wave."

Martha's mind had gone to Buzz, wondering if he would get caught up with the struggling, city youth. She was anxious for their meeting.

Three police cars, their sirens screaming, roared past

them in the direction of Williamsburg. The cars were marked NYPD. Daniel's expression reminded her of Buzz, when he had left the juvenile camp. "New York cops."

Martha shared his feelings. But she remembered the anxious patrolman outside Grand Central Station, with a large family and no food in the house but cornflakes. It was no easy thing for a family man to become an outlaw.

She stared at the street in Woodhaven that she had never seen before, not seeing it then. Today she had killed a man. When the Soviets had taken her country, they had made every citizen a soldier. As a soldier, she would do her duty. What she had seen didn't strengthen her resolve, for it needed no strengthening, yet it did make it easier. Without Magnanimity it would not only be Soviet troops destroying the United States. It would be every man against his brother; a holocaust not only of bodies but of the spirit. As each man or woman collaborated with the enemy, there would be those who saw the treachery. And those who surrendered body and soul would become afraid of those who struggled to be free. No respect for human life could balance against that spiritual genocide.

When Mrs. Adams failed to appear for work on the second day, two Security Officers were sent to her apartment as a routine procedure. When there was no answer to their knock, the house-warden was ordered to let them in. They reported back to their headquarters that the apartment was empty; the beds did not appear to have been slept in, and the house-warden informed them that he had seen Mrs. Adams leave very early the previous morning, from the window of his street floor apartment. She had walked down the avenue, carrying a light grip. The house-warden was severely reprimanded for not reporting this at the time, and not checking the apartment later.

The name of Mrs. Martha Adams, a citizen of the British Republics and a UN employee, was put on police lists as an absentee from official employment to be stopped for questioning. It was, however, merely a Class C priority.

At One Police Plaza, the senior security officer for Manhattan (Section A of Region II) received the notification that a party of three of his men had been murdered while attempting to arrest a factory owner and two Jewish workmen. The Jews had themselves been killed. Two Hispanic workmen were dead also, possibly merely caught in the cross-fire. Questioning in the street indicated that two or three accomplices had escaped.

The officer sent out orders for the families of the dead owner and his workmen to be brought in for questioning. He also wrote a memo on the increased difficulties of the KGB working in a population that was armed and dangerous, and requested an increase in his force. He knew that this action would not be seen favorably by his superiors, but he had lost too many men in clearing Harlem and Spanish Harlem, although his troops had only been backups for the Americans.

Moodily, he walked into the NYPD office next door, where a uniformed captain was drawing up a work schedule. In his rather stilted English, the Russian complained to his American colleague. "This city of yours is badly policed. It seems to be in the hands of bandits." His colleague smelled of drink. His complexion suggested that this indulgence was habitual. Drunkenness was sabotage in the KGB, punishable by death. But the offense was too common for the rule to be applied rigidly, and was only invoked when a man became a nuisance or a senior officer wished to be rid of him for other reasons.

"This was the Big Apple," the captain said, and gave a belch. "No one ever said it was Shangri-La."

The KGB officer had studied English, but American,

he decided, was really another language. He went to the communications room and ordered a special alert on roads, train stations and airports.

When the van rumbled into Astoria, Daniel made his delivery and collected a receipt. He grumbled loud and long at the receiving door about being given a helper afflicted with low back pain.

"I would have helped," Martha said indignantly as they rolled away from the loading platform.

"Hands," Daniel said. "More women have been betrayed by their hands—and you haven't even taken your wedding ring off."

Startled, Martha looked down, prepared to remove it. That ring had been on her finger since Josh had placed it there eighteen years ago, in the old church in Litchfield. It was so familiar that she hardly remembered it was there, yet now she felt a flood of sadness. The plain gold band slipped off easily enough; she had got thinner.

"Keep it on," Daniel said. "You've got to change back into a respectable married woman. But keep the wig."

In the back of the van Martha changed into a dress, shoes with heels, a buttoned-up sweater and eye-glasses, according to instructions. She was booked in at the airport hotel as Mrs. Mary Blunt, a member of a Commission on Women's Rights, a citizen of the B.R. The night before she had had to give Daniel an indication of where they were going. She wasn't sorry, for after Williamsburg her ability to trust him had grown. But she had not been quite truthful. "Moab," she had said. Moab was a long way off even from Blanding, but that was as much as she was willing to give away. Yet.

"Utah?" he had said and she nodded. It had been difficult to make out his expression. Now he took Mary Blunt's papers from under the back seat. The photograph of Mrs. Blunt might have been Martha in the brown wig.

"The British Consul was obliging," Daniel remarked.

"Mr. Aspey?" she asked, remembering the man with the pink face and silver hair, the bright, intelligent eyes, who had tried to be helpful.

Daniel didn't answer directly. But then, he rarely did.

"The British were free for a long time. Some of them never got out of the habit. Remember to ask me about the Nelson fleet. Mrs. Blunt was going to this hen-party in Detroit, but she changed her mind after the fireworks and stayed at home. That's the longest hop I could arrange this bout."

Martha registered at the hotel alone. They seemed glad to see her; the usually busy place was very quiet. Among the few travelers there was a large sprinkling of Russian and East European army officers. And always there were the police. Daniel promised he and Buzz would meet in her room later.

"Call this number," he said, "and ask for a delivery. Pizza, any style you like. Don't forget to give your room number."

"Pizza?" she said, bemused. She had seen very few eating places open in the city since the week after the surrender, and they were not open to the public.

"There are still places that cater to foreign travelers, especially round the airports," he said. "But eat a meal in the hotel dining room anyway. You'll be expected to. And Buzz might want your pizza."

He grinned, and she smiled back, as though he had been a member of her family for years. They had adopted each other, she thought.

Later that night her room had a very family air. She had followed orders, and eaten in the half-empty dining room. The food had been adequate, if hardly up to its former standard, and she thought of the minimal ration for the average citizen, the starvation for those without papers. She had no appetite, but she did have a longing for a drink. There was bar service, but she told herself that she'd better keep a clear head.

Two hours after dinner she had telephoned the number Daniel had given her, and put in her order for a large pizza, with sausage. Buzz was very fond of sausage. In ten minutes, Daniel in a white apron and white cap came up bearing the large, fragrant box.

"Still hot," he said, grinning. "I made good time from Woodhaven Boulevard."

A tap came at the door soon after. Buzz slipped in, very quietly.

"Fire exit," he explained to Daniel, briefly. "Easy. This place is a morgue."

He had settled down to eat with pleasure, taking the other chair. Daniel pulled a flat bottle of whisky from his capacious pocket and brought in the tooth glasses from the bathroom. "I hope you can drink it straight, Mrs. Adams, or with tap water, maybe? We'd better not bother room service right now."

Mrs. Adams could and did. She felt surprisingly relaxed for a fugitive from justice, or injustice, as it happened to be. Buzz, who preferred Coke, refused, but was in high good humor anyway. He had made his delivery, and he had not seen any shooting in the streets.

While Daniel had been busy, delivering the Greene Street weapons to some unnamed person, Buzz had stayed out of sight in a small house nearby. A local housewife, seeing him pass by, had invited him in to help with some small chore. Her husband was away, she did not know where, and she was lonely. She was also nervous, not knowing when she might be moved, or if some predator would attack her in the house. Apparently she had found Buzz's presence soothing.

Daniel listened, smiling. "All the makings of a good underground man," he said, from the floor where he sat in a familiar pose with his hands lightly grasping his ankles.

Buzz and Daniel were to leave on a plane an hour earlier than her own. To her amusement they were traveling as a bio-chemist in a wheelchair, and his young attendant. "A study on radiation effects. We're in luck. That meeting was transferred from Chicago. Enough priority to get us there."

"As long as no one asks you about biochemistry," Martha said.

"Believe it or not, I studied it once," Daniel said, "though I gave it up, to be an artist. I can get by. I am, Mrs. Adams, though a Sabra, not a stalwart son of the soil. My father, after he emigrated to Israel, married an Israeli girl. But he lived in Tel Aviv and I am a Sabra of another sort."

He and Buzz made their arrangements for the morning, and then Daniel gave Buzz the cap and apron. "That'll get you out. Take the service exit."

"Where will you stay?" his mother asked.

"Don't worry, Mom," he said in his patient-with-parent voice, and Martha let him go, wondering if he would return to the lonely lady.

When he had gone Daniel refilled her glass. The curtains were drawn and only the bedside lamps were lit. The room had a cozy air. With Daniel sitting at her feet, and them both in a circle of lamplight, it seemed more homelike than the apartment had been, filled as it had been with her loss, frustration and despair.

"And what about you, Mrs. Adams?" he said. "What were you doing in an office at the UN? It doesn't seem a job for a woman of your sort."

Her sort? Suddenly she remembered the drunken harridan who had screamed at her in the street just after the surrender. "It's all your fault, you and your kind."

"What's my sort?" she asked.

"Upper class," Daniel said. "Old American."

"Old American, yes. Not upper class any more, even before the surrender, I mean. If we ever were. No great fortune in the family, and not much land left. Just part of the great, American middle class, really. Yet I know what you mean. My husband never liked my job very much. But there weren't many jobs for a thirty-three year old woman who'd majored in English and never worked before. They give a lot of leave and it's flexible, ideal for a woman with a family. Of course, the first glow soon vanished, I think when I found that nearly half of the budget of the 'great moral force' went on administrative overheads."

He had been looking up at her, the lamplight reflected in his dark eyes. His hand rested on the arm of her chair, close to her own. Without thinking, she moved her hand and he laughed.

"Always brisk, Mrs. Adams."

He jumped lightly to his feet, and was already at the door when Martha asked, "And where will you go?"

He paused with his hand on the door knob.

"Next door," he said. "The room's empty, I checked. No one will be around the floor until seven. If you get lonely, Mrs. Adams, like Buzz's friend . . ."

She gave him a cold look; he laughed again, waved and was gone.

Her grandmother would have said she deserved that for having a man in her room for drinks . . . It meant nothing. No doubt just his way of talking to women. And he was certainly efficient. By this time tomorrow she would be in Detroit. Then there would be the rest of the journey to arrange. And what would she find when she got there? She fell asleep and dreamed of herself lost in a forest of missiles, while Daniel, walking with the silence of an Indian, led her through.

But the next day everything was changed.

—— XXII ——

Borunukov, in the Pentagon, was in his own kingdom. Russian soldiers guarded the doors of the Joint Chiefs of Staff theater where the Marines used to stand. This huge, interior room, lined with heavy curtains, furnished in leather and decorated with flags, gave the Marshal a comfortable, familiar feeling as he gazed at a projection screen, set up near the lighted map of the world.

He was studying some data from satellite photographs, taken very recently. There were indications of gatherings of men scattered through the Rocky Mountains, though the numbers were not significant. The Americans had not practiced guerilla warfare since their Revolution. Vietnam had proved they had forgotten those lessons from long ago. Doubtless, these were merely the usual outlaws that were to be expected after any surrender, and a few groups of military men who refused to obey the order of their Commander-in-Chief.

Borunukov had wanted to keep six battalions in readiness to drop into the Rockies shortly after the strike. With control of the Rockies, he could effectively have divided the country in two, and easily put down any attempt at rebellion. It was for this he had supported the attempt on Afghanistan, where the men had learned such valuable lessons in mountain warfare. But Ulyanov, always cautious of military power, had rejected the scheme. It had not been needed, for the Americans were not fighters.

It wouldn't be too difficult to send in a small force of well-trained men and clear them out now. He was considering the action when he received a top priority signal from Moscow. It had been sent by Stapshyn himself. The Politburo wished him to return at once to give his opinion on a most urgent matter. Ulyanov's call had followed at once.

"The majority opinion here," Ulyanov said, with hardly a pause for greeting, "is that the Magna weapon is in the hands of the Chinese. If the Americans had it under their control, it is believed they would have used it. A decision is being taken on the value of a preemptive strike, to dispose of this weapon on the ground. Stapshyn has informed us that all the new sites have been targeted as well as the Manchurian sites and . . ."

The Politburo, the Marshal realized, had worked themselves up into a fine fit of collective hysteria. For the first time, they themselves were truly threatened. They knew that none of their deep shelters, fitted with all the comforts they had provided for themselves, would be enough to protect them from the ravages of Magna. And even if they should disperse and survive, they would find they were the government over nothing but a radioactive wilderness.

That was always the trouble with a civilian government, he thought. From Alexander to Napoleon, all the great rulers had been military men. Civilians, on the other hand, were generally chickenhearted, unable to move when move they must, screaming for action when it was clearly time to hold the line. His own GRU had confirmed the story which Virinsky had told him about the Dimona raid. Borunukov had agreed with the KGB man that the search should concentrate on persons rather than on places.

Although he believed that the Magna weapon must have been built in China, the work would have been carried out under American direction and tightly controlled. Certainly the Joint Chiefs would never have left it in the hands of the Chinese. Ulyanov himself could not believe such an absurdity was possible, but even Ulyanov could not entirely control the panic-stricken Politburo. Those grandsons of peasants would be digging up the earth all over the planet, while the Americans could have hidden a weapon system on the moon, or even further out in space.

Perhaps only Reagan had known its whereabouts and the knowledge had died with him. It could be lying unknown, unarmed, harmless, moldering away on land or sea. Carmody's policy about the aging US missile system had followed the popular cry: "Let them rot." The last president of the United States most certainly had known nothing of Magna. The interrogators had been careful not to kill him, but he had lapsed into more than his usual state of befuddlement from the narcoleptic drugs. He knew so little he could well be released, but his extreme simple-mindedness might draw notice.

Borunukov had to consent to go to Moscow. Much as he had wanted a China strike, this was not the moment. At this point he needed more reliable Soviet and East European troops here. They could assist in the Magna search and the pacification; guard the laborers building the fortifications on the Canadian border, clean up the stragglers and, more importantly, counterbalance the Latin-American influence of Perez. This was no time for the Red Army to be tied up in a guerilla war in Siberia and he well knew that as the first missile flew the Chinese would be over the border in strength. And here in the former US his men were thin on the ground. The West and South-West were sparsely guarded, for his main orders had been to secure the industrial East.

His gaze went back to the photographs. Nothing there of urgency, he decided. Better, in fact, to let the malcontents collect, and then sweep down. That would be a good time to use the poison gases which had proved so effective in Afghanistan, though here the prevailing winds would be a nuisance, blowing them back east. Maybe, he thought sourly, he could persuade Ulyanov to let him use Perez's guerila forces and they could die to some purpose. He called for a supersonic transport to be made ready. He could be back, after all, in a few days. And he would get a hero's welcome in Moscow.

Virinsky's habit of working through the night had always annoyed his staff, though they were not in a position to say so. He never seemed to need the ordinary things of life, and he often did not bother to return to his modest quarters in the Riverdale complex. He would nap, when he felt like it, on the black bench. A small store of his clothes were kept in a closet in the file room adjacent to his office, and a small bathroom had been built in what had previously been a utility room on the other side. There was both a shower and a bath tub, but his girls noticed that "Mr. No-Frills" was not especially interested in either. He shaved his small growth of beard punctiliously, however, and spent some time combing and greasing his fringe of hair.

A week had gone since Borunukov's departure for Moscow, and the Under-Secretary had been working harder than ever. He was not concerning himself with the possibility of the China strike, though he had been duly warned by Kharkev. That was out of his hands, and Virinsky did not waste time in brooding over events beyond his control. Besides, Kharkev, Ulyanov and

Stapshyn together could defeat the motion. Virinsky had in fact been working steadily on the one truly important matter, the tracking down of the man or men with knowledge of the Magna weapon.

Perez had stopped sulking in Cuba, since Borunukov had left, and returned to Hall City—formerly Washington, D.C. He was taking women to the second floor of the People's House and had installed a mistress in what was still referred to as the Queen's Room. Trouble ahead there. But that was no problem to Virinsky. The more Perez and Borunukov quarreled, the better for his own plans. In the meantime, Perez had been useful. He had pointed out the likelihood of the Mossad agent, Bar-Lev, having knowledge of Aharit-Ha-Yamim and he was using his considerable forces to help track him down.

Virinsky had been certain that his own method would bear fruit more quickly, but so far he had been disappointed. Of course, it had taken time to locate all the names on Madame Paul's lists. Such men were all over the country and many abroad. Some had been tracked down on installations in Saudi Arabia; some were working in South America; some were among the deportees and had to be returned from as far as the Antarctic; some were still to be found and a good many could well be dead.

All of the first batch to arrive in the Special Camp had received preliminary processing with no positive result. A few of the men had actually worked on the Reagangate water projects, but their information had been peculiarly disappointing. Those water projects had indeed been water projects, completed as planned. The truth was easily ascertained; the dams and waterways were located exactly where they were planned to be, visible to the naked eyes of the inspectorate that he had sent.

He had checked over and over the interrogations and come up with nothing of interest. Only one female employee had mentioned that she had suspected something not right, the possibility of corruption, but the interrogators had thought little of her remarks. She had been a government inspector, not an engineer, merely a low-grade technician who had drawn wages above her grade level. This was not unusual, he knew, as the Federal government at the time had found itself obliged to promote women, whether there were suitable candidates for promotion or not. The interrogators had reported that her present complaints might well stem from her having later been demoted in the national economy drive. Nevertheless, Virinsky had ordered her to be brought up this morning to see him personally.

Thu Thuy brought her in. Her name was Cheryl Huck. She was short, squat, bespectacled, with lank hair, wearing what looked like a mechanic's denim coverall. Virinsky recalled that she had been in a branch of the army, but had returned to civilian life. Next to Thu Thuy she looked like a monster, but in fact she was in reasonably good health. These interrogations had been purely verbal with no use of force of any kind unless the detainees proved recalcitrant. Dead men can tell no tales, but willing men make rich informers.

The only promising thing about the willing Huck was that she had been assigned for a one-month period to inspect one of the Columbia water projects. After that the project Superintendent had managed to ease her out. Thu Thuy left and he motioned Huck to a chair. She did not seem nervous or intimidated, and was looking round with interest. Huck, he realized, was enjoying her sudden prominence. He had seen this before, though never in the Eastern bloc.

"You told the official at the Park center that you had observed irregularities while you were inspector at a Columbia Company project," he said.

"Irregularities," Huck said scornfully. "That wasn't the half."

"And where was this project?"

"East of Grand Gulch. On the border of southern Utah and Arizona. The original plan was to take water from a Colorado tributary and run it south-east into the desert. They were beginning work on some of the digging when I got there. The biggest mess you ever saw. Nothing ever got going. They'd taken over an old trading post and spent their time making themselves comfortable. They'd even built themselves a pool. Laziest bunch of men I ever came across. Worse than a bunch of Indians, and that place was crawling with Indians. Dirty, lazy bunch. The men were still putting up site fencing when I got there, and they were using the wrong wire. The specs were quite clear. They just said it made no difference and there would have been a six-week wait from the factory before they could have got the wire specified. Construction men always say that. Then I found air bubbles in their solder joints on the posts. So I stopped the job," she said, and smiled.

Virinsky's eyes were half-closed. It had been a long night, after all. He should have left this Huck to the interrogation team; he was wasting his time. The woman was merely a spiteful fool. She understood almost nothing of engineering and construction, but she had been sent out as a government inspector. An ugly woman who resented men, she had used her power to the limit and stopped their work, at enormous cost to the company, probably passed on to the State. Such females were known and dreaded in the Soviet Union. They could not easily be tried for the sabotage they committed with every act, because they always followed the written instructions. To the letter.

"And that was the end of your work on that site? And with the Columbia company?"

"Almost. Shortly afterwards I was sent to inspect a new plant construction near Minneapolis, Minnesota. But they did get started because the Chief Superintendent came out and he got them back on track. Mr. Josh Adams—he was a wonderful man."

She smiled again, a sweeter smile. "He got the specs changed himself, so that they could go ahead. And he told me he was glad there was someone like me looking out sharply to see everything went right. He bought me the most beautiful heavy bracelet of turquoise and silver; I felt quite like a slave girl when I wore it." She batted her sparse eyelashes and sighed. "But it was all for nothing, because the conservation people had made such a fuss that the project was stopped right after."

While she was burbling on, Virinsky had checked automatically the list of superintendents employed by the Columbia company. Joshua Adams was there. This idiot woman was truthful, if useless. He dismissed her, and put in an inquiry to Madame Paul as to the whereabouts of this Adams, who had not as yet arrived at the camp.

Madame, with dark circles under her eyes which could no longer be hidden by make-up, came in person to inform him that Joshua Adams had last been employed at Grand Forks, where he had been during the attack. There had, of course, been no survivors. He nodded and dismissed her, suggesting that she take a few hours' sleep.

Nothing, nothing, and nothing. Virinsky stood by his bank of files, and his private computer terminal like a priest before his altar, but no help was forthcoming. It was possible that there had been nothing in the water projects scandal after all. The usual corruption and no more. The tales of the missing millions had come from the press and there had been no real proof, only tortured financial calculation. Nor had there been a word or a whisper during Reagan's life time. This Adams, of course, was dead. All those missile sites destroyed utterly. If the Magna weapon had been a missile, it could have been in any one of them. In appearance it might have been no different from the other ICBM's, with its crews having no knowledge of just what they held. In that case, now it would be gone, and forever, unless there was someone with the knowledge to build another. Yet very likely any such man was dead, like Shlomo Darin and his team.

The indicator on his special line from the People's House in Hall City blinked red. He picked up the telephone to hear Perez, exploding with indignation.

"Comrade Under-Secretary, can you tell me how my men can get about their work when they are stopped everywhere by your agents?"

It took some time for Virinsky to realize what had happened. Several calls had to be made, first to One Police Plaza in Manhattan, and then round the different Regional Headquarters. He found, to his satisfaction, it was the new technology that was curbing the Perez organization.

After the murder of three KGB men in Manhattan, the senior officer had, very properly, put out a special alert in an effort to catch any possible suspects. A special alert now included the use of the new computer terminals installed at airports and railway stations and which, when sufficient were available, would be used at all check points on the roads. Travelers were finger-printed before they boarded and the prints were submitted to a central bureau. Any set of matching prints on the police or political files triggered the warning to the terminal and no matter how good false papers might be, the miscreant was caught fast. As Perez's people were so often on police files, many of them had already been arrested. Virinsky had to hide his amusement, while calming the fuming Perez. "It is merely a matter of adjusting the police files to the New Order," he said. "The prints of your people must be expunged. Of course, you will have to give us their names."

Perez was trapped. He by no means wished the KGB to know each and every man he had under his command. He ended the conversation greatly displeased. If Perez could have caught the developer of this new tool,

Virinsky thought, he would have chopped off his finger-tips and made him eat them.

Virinsky felt much less tired. Buzzing for Thu Thuy, he asked her to bring in tea and his favorite honey cake. There was no room, he reflected, in the New Order for Perez's rabble. The KGB man had understood Ulyanov's use of such people, but not what he and Kharkev saw as a certain softness to Perez himself. In his view it was that softness alone that proved Ulyanov would not be one of hisory's great dictators.

Virinsky cared little for recreation, but one of his few amusements was reading the lives of the great dictators, and evaluating them. Stalin could, perhaps be awarded the laurel, yet Stalin had inherited greatly from Lenin. Amin had been merely a petty tyrant, despite the gruesomeness of his regime. Hitler had had no real opposition. Mao-Tse-Tung was a close contender, despite a certain looseness in his organization. He had had to fight an entrenched power, though with the help of the Japanese. Virinsky gave a certain honor to England's Cromwell, who had fought powerful forces, and then managed to keep control when the fighting stopped and imposed an entirely new rule on a mostly unwilling country. And he suffered no nonsense from any rabble. No, there would be no peasant power, the government must win.

He went on with his day's work, refreshed. Neatly, he marked down that nothing to date was proved against the Columbia Construction Company, and that one of its Chief Superintendents, Joshua Adams, was undoubtedly dead. The usual check on his family should be made forthwith.

—— XXIII ——

Mrs. Joshua Adams opened her eyes, to see a patch of blue sky between rotten slats. For a moment she could not remember where she was. She lay on a blanket under a light cover, her head resting on a hard cushion. Plenty of light came through the boards of the small wooden shack and she could clearly see the legend embroidered in petit point on her cushion; "If there is righteousness in the heart there is beauty in the character." She remembered. And for the first time since the surrender, she woke up wanting to laugh.

The shack looked as though it might have been a henhouse, though there were no hens in it now. But then, at the Corbett place, nothing was where one might expect it to be. Somewhere a rooster was crowing; the sound had awakened her.

A hand came round the doorway, holding a mug that smelled invitingly of coffee. Agnes Corbett, in a long denim skirt, a man's scuffed, brown leather boots, and a sparkingly clean white blouse bustled in. "Thought you might like this," she said. "Breakfast in half an hour. Father says it's sinful," she said, looking at the coffee wistfully, "but I say if the Lord provides, it's not for us to question. At least when father is away."

Agnes might have been anywhere in her fifties or sixties, a plump, quite good-looking farm woman, friendly, hard-working, quite overborne by her patriarchal and decidedly eccentric parent. "Sure sorry we couldn't put you up in the house," she said, fretting. "But never in all my days did we have so much family and folks about, and the house is fit to bust. And the big barn is all full of my Myra's kids, and her little Dan's. He's a good boy, one of the best, but he was real young to get married, only seventeen. And his Dulcie has seven kids already. But the Lord said to go forth and multiply, and so it must be His Will."

Martha assured her that the shed had been most comfortable, and thanked her for the use of the pillow.

"Did that myself," Agnes said with pride. "Mother Liza taught me years back. Used to be great with a needle herself, but her eyes is gone bad now."

Martha drank the coffee with pleasure. It was the first she'd had in a week, or was it longer? Here, towards the end of September, she could feel a touch of the crispness of fall. It made her hungry. She stood in the doorway and gazed out over what might have been farmland, but instead looked like nothing more than a great old car lot. The return of her appetite was due not merely to the privations of her days on the run. Her recovery came from being in motion, however twisted, getting towards her goal. She also now had in Daniel an ally she could trust.

"Is there somewhere I can get washed?" she said. From what she'd seen of the old farmhouse last night, it didn't promise much in the way of bathrooms. The moon had made it clear that it didn't even have a whole roof.

"There's the backhouse," Agnes said, nodding, to a

small structure. "It's a two-holer, but it's full of kids right now. And there's a pump you can use right here. Used to be for the chickens, but we haven't kept none in quite a while. Quite a while."

Water actually came up out of the rusty old pipe in the ground after Martha had tugged hard at the spigot. She washed as much as seemed decent to her and rather more, by Agnes's expression, than that lady thought proper.

"You might go and call your man," she said. "Tell him to come and eat. He's gone over by Cindy's house. She's married to my son Luke, but Luke went off to California some time back and Cindy moved in here with the kids." She looked at Martha placidly. "They all move back here with their kids. Always have. All this farm grows now is kids and we have quite a crop."

She walked along with Martha in the direction of the house, past the heap of old Fords, Chevrolets, Datsuns, small cars, large cars, station wagons. There was an old jeep, rusted clean through, like many of the others. This was not an old car lot, she realized, it was a car graveyard. Generations must have brought their old cars here and abandoned them, as, apparently, they had abandoned farming. Nowhere around, beyond the car graveyard and over the fields, was there any sign of any crop having been sown or harvested, though this was some of the richest farmland in the country, and far superior to the Connecticut soil where rock and stone were never far away.

Agnes turned into the farmhouse through the crooked door over the sagging porch. A hearty smell wafted out through the cracks. The windows of the house were all closed, though many of the panes were broken.

"I'll finish off the breakfast while you get him," she said. "I daresay Cindy and the kids will be along too. Unless she managed to get some of that cereal they like, but they tell me that's all gone now. There's no ham left so it's rabbit for breakfast. Real useful critters,

rabbits. Folks can get by if they put their hands on a
good rabbit. Some of these foolish young girls have
never learned one useful thing, but now they're learning about rabbits all right. Now those food stamps are
gone, they're learning the ways of the Lord."

She paused with her hand on the door. "Many's the
time I've told them the Lord will strike down those
who sin, and with the whole state so full of sinners I
expected the end to come before this. When we heard
years ago about Three Mile Island I thought that was
the vengeance of the Lord, but it turned out no such
thing. Just a false prophecy. Now the wrath is upon us,
and the good Christian will come into his own."

Agnes was still talking as she vanished into the house.

Smiling, Martha cut across the fields to the house
indicated as Cindy's. She smoothed her hair (she had
lost her wig at a windy railroad crossing) and thought
about getting a good splash down at the pump after
dark, if they hadn't moved on. Daniel didn't say much
about where they were going. To protect his friends,
she had thought at first. Then she had suspected that
he had no plan and just improvised, day by day, since
the disaster at La Guardia. But how he had ever got to
know about the Corbetts, she could not imagine. There
was no doubt he was very resourceful.

It had been pure luck that Daniel and Buzz had been
booked on a plane to Detroit an hour before her own.
Buzz had told her he'd noticed nothing wrong, and
Martha feared she herself would have checked through
before being asked to step into the seating area by the
boarding gate. These areas were now partitioned off,
she was told. Buzz and Daniel had been waiting to
enter, when they had seen a woman come out, wiping
her fingertips.

"They might at least use the clean grey ink instead of
this stuff," she had said.

Daniel had looked convincingly ill, and his worried
attendant had taken him to the hotel, where he got a
room for this important traveler.

"They'll be looking for Mary Blunt when she doesn't board that plane," Daniel told Martha. "We can't use any airports—we don't know how many of those things they've got in operation."

He looked sour. "They've fouled up the distribution of food all over the country," he said. "It hasn't all gone overseas. A lot of it is moldering in warehouses and at sidings. But they can get this hellish contrivance installed with no trouble at all. I wonder which American firm helped out with the technology."

They had left the hotel by the service entrance.

In his workingman's pants and shirt, Daniel looked inconspicuous as he unlocked a battered old Impala. When he threw Martha's things in the trunk she saw his bulging canvas bag already there. "Belongs to the pizza parlor; I have the papers," he said, sighing. "They need it; I'll leave it not too far off."

Once away from the vicinity of the airport, he had abandoned the car. To Martha's dismay, he had sent Buzz on a route of his own, with no definite meeting place closer than Boulder, Colorado.

"We might run into each other," Daniel had said, "but this way it's safer."

Buzz had gone off, as though he were going over to Robbie's house.

"Watch out for the Regional borders," Daniel had warned him. "It's like getting into a different country now. Trains stop and roads are checked. And papers for one Region are no good for another. Don't forget that."

He had turned to Martha. "He's going to friends. He'll be OK. You stick with me, kid." He had given her his smile that had changed his face from plain to attractive, though she didn't notice his plainness anymore, nor did he strike her as monkey-like. He must have been an old movie buff, she thought, for he loved to talk in the slang of the thirties and forties. Humphrey Bogart, George Raft lines could pop out at any moment. That had made her laugh, and she had needed the laugh, because she soon came to realize that when he had said it would be hard for a woman like her to go underground, he had spoken the simple truth.

Getting back through Manhattan into New Jersey had not been a great problem, though it had been uncomfortable enough. They were still in Region Two. Daniel had found a large truck carrying a shipment of rugs for deliveries in Newark and Trenton. What arrangement he had made with the driver, whether the man was an ally or had been bribed, Martha did not know, but he looked the other way when they scrambled over the tailboard and concealed themselves among the rolls of rugs. There seemed to be no air to breathe in the tight-packed truck, and rolled rugs were hard on the human form. Martha soon felt waves of nausea coming over her and and was not a little irritated with Daniel who arranged himself like a cat and went straight to sleep. His eyes opened when they were stopped at a bridge and at a tunnel entrance, but the papers of the truck and the driver were in order and they went on through.

In Newark, however, they had a disagreeable surprise. It had taken several hours to find a suitable means of transport, and by the time the driver had made his delivery it was six o'clock.

"All right, I leave her here till the morning, Al?" they had heard him shout.

Soon after he had poked his head inside. "All clear if you want to get out. You'd better not stay in the truck overnight. The garage security might check the back to see if there's something small enough to steal easy. No sense my going down to Trenton now, everything's closed, so I'll meet you at the corner tomorrow morning, seven-thirty sharp."

They had reluctantly rolled out, wishing it were dark. Martha had left her hand grip hidden in the driver's cab. "You don't want to look like a traveler. They're always the first to be stopped," Daniel said, and she left with only her shoulder bag.

Desperate for a cup of strong coffee, Martha began to look about for some coffee shop that might be open, but Daniel soon persuaded her to forget that idea. "You're still in Region II. Even if you're not on a primary arrest list, the police will be looking for you all over the Region. They probably won't have connected Martha Adams with Mary Blunt, but you can't use her papers. She'll be down as missing from selected transport. And any public eating places left open are constantly patrolled. Often their main use is as fugitive traps."

They had hidden in the cellar of an abandoned building until dusk. Daniel had left for an hour after checking her gun, and hiding it behind the crate where she sat. Her flat poison capsule she carried on her person, under a layer of something that matched her skin. "I expect you'll be O.K. here," he said, "but watch out for prowlers."

She had listened to his warning, but her fear had been of the enemy and she had given little thought to any risk among her own people. When she heard the rattle of the lock of the cellar door, the scrape as the door was pushed open, she had expected only Daniel. The very last rays of grey light struggled through the grating high in the wall and as the door opened she blinked, for Daniel had brought a flashlight. The beam of light bounced down the steps. Daniel's figure behind it looked distorted, too tall, moving with a tread too heavy . . . It was not Daniel, but a stranger.

The light had flashed round the cellar, sweeping past her. In the second before it returned, she caught a glimpse of a youth, wary, hostile, brutish. Fear rose in her belly and every nerve end in her skin was alert. Then the light was dazzling. Suddenly she felt the tug as he bent down and snatched at her shoulder bag. It had Mary Blunt's papers, the Consul . . . She pulled back and hung on in a silent struggle. Her friend must not be exposed. . . .

A great blow to her head had knocked her flat to the concrete floor. Half-stunned, in sickening pain, she reached back behind the wooden crate for the gun. Nothing there, it was pushed aside in the struggle. She was afraid he would notice her groping hand but the light traveled up and down her supine body. The cellar was very quiet. The light fell to the floor and she felt him beside her, leaning over her, fumbling at her shirt. Her hand closed on the butt of the gun. His breath was in her nostrils when she jammed the gun against his temple.

In the bright, warm sunshine of the Corbett farm, she shivered, remembering. The youth, she judged, was not a refugee from the new rulers, but a street criminal from the old days. Street smart, he understood the threat of a gun at his head and realized that she would use it if she had to. Yet it seemed as though she sat on that floor guarding her prisoner for hours before Daniel returned, though in fact it was only twenty minutes.

Daniel had needed no explanation. "Go outside," he said at once. "Be careful. It's after curfew."

"Can you tie him up with something?" she asked.

"Go." It was a command and she went. She was half way up the stairs when she heard the shot. She was suddenly very angry.

"You didn't need to do *that*."

"Be quiet."

He appeared, carrying the boy's dark jacket. As she shrank away, he impatiently thrust it over her torn shirt. Moving in the shadows along the street, he found an apartment building with an unlocked door, and gestured to her to follow.

Once inside, he took a piece of wire from his pocket and fastened the door. "The police patrol will think it's locked, and the building warden won't be likely to look

around before dawn." He knocked the light bulb out
and pushed her, not too gently, to the darkest corner.

"Goodnight, Mrs. Adams."

"You didn't . . ."

She couldn't see his face, just the outline of his head
as he turned towards her. "Mrs. Adams," his voice was
low but very cold. "You insisted on joining the mission.
Against my expressed wish. I now must make it clear
that whereas you personally have no more importance
than any other citizen, at this moment only you can find
Magnanimity. I can get you there, but I can only do it if
you don't leave behind a trail, a criminal who can
identify you, and who is certain to fall into police hands.
You weren't even wearing your wig."

"It must have fallen off in the van," she replied,
wretchedly.

They shared a couple of chocolate bars that he had
scrounged from somewhere. Then Daniel had gone to
sleep. She had lain on the cold tiled floor with her bag
under her head. Her head still hurt badly; soon she
ached all over. She was thirsty. And she was dirty. The
stolen jacket smelled of the stranger's body. Mrs. Martha Adams, a shopping bag lady. Her mind was sorer
than her flesh. Daniel had been right, though it went
against the grain to admit it. She had to learn to think
like a soldier in enemy territory.

The next morning she had been subdued and followed orders. She had even found her wig inside the
van and was combing it before they had reached Trenton. They were stopped twice at the toll booths, getting
on and leaving the Jersey Turnpike and both times she
had the gun in her hand.

They had spent the day in a closed school building
where there was still running water. Next they had to
cross into Pennsylvania, but that was Region Three,
and the back of a truck would not be good enough. At
Regional check points, Daniel said, it was bound to be
inspected. And there might well be a fingerprint ma-

chine. Daniel had gone out and come back with some
fruit and sliced bread, in a modest glow of triumph.

"The fingerprint check seems to be only at the major
entry points like the Turnpike," he told her. "It's a
heavy check all up and down the river, but on the
smaller roads it's a paper check."

"We seem to be having more trouble crossing the
Delaware than George Washington," Martha said,
despondently.

"Papers I can handle," Daniel said. He nodded towards
his heavy bag. "Pandora's box . . . Cheer up, he won,
didn't he? Your George?"

The next morning they had to separate. Martha had
the papers of a farmwife, returning with a load of tools
to Lancaster in a small station wagon. Farm workers
now received an allocation of gas. Martha had looked
questioningly, but Daniel smiled. "A friendly transac-
tion, with a little money to sweeten it. I wanted to get
my girl across state lines. Everybody loves a lover.
You'll leave the car with the papers at her home. Her
son will get them back to her. I will meet you at . . ."

Daniel had a way with women. They had spent that
night in a cow-shed on a farm near Lancaster. Daniel
had brought sausages and she had cooked them over a
fire of twigs. "Campfire Girl," she had told Daniel.
"You're not so bad, Mrs. Adams. For one of your kind,"
he said, and they had both laughed. That night was
memorable for what he had told her about Magnanimity. "A strange name for a weapon," she had said.

"It was the choice of your President, from what I've
heard." Daniel had regarded his split, charred sausage
with resignation. "When he talked about it with my
people, they urged him to have it built outside of
America, or the opposition would have had it before the
Americans. No insult to the FBI. A secret like that is
almost impossible in an open democracy. He talked
of the terrible power of the weapon. It could be used to
blackmail the whole world, by a dictator. And he de-

cided to call the project Magnanimity, because the US would build the power, but never use it. It would be held for no other purpose than to let freedom live."

His tone was casual, but Martha had not been able to speak for a time. Then they had talked of other things. It had taken three more days and nights by car, freight trucks and bicycle to reach the Corbett place, somewhere between Sayre and Lawrenceville. She had protested about the northward journey, which was out of their way, and Daniel had looked at her patiently.

"For a mouse, Mrs. Adams, the long way, roundabout, is the shortest way in avoiding the cat."

He had not explained why he had wanted to go there, except that there might be a chance of meeting somebody, not identified. When they had arrived last night, she supposed it was as good a place as any. In the sprawling mess of humanity there, odd guests would hardly be noticed. It was mostly women and children. Husbands, she gathered, were occasional visitors. As farm people, they had not yet attracted the notice of the conscription agents.

As she walked across the path, an ancient van, bearing a faded inscription, *The Guiding Light Mission*, stopped with a screech of brakes. A man in overalls with a patriarchal beard and rheumy eyes regarded her. "Greetings, sister. God be with you."

There was a loudspeaker fixed to the top of the van. Doubtless this was the father of whom Agnes had spoken: Amos, the family founder, who had given up farming to pursue an evangelical mission.

"Greetings, brother," she said, hoping this was the correct reply. "May God be with you also this day."

"The devil is among us," he said in gloom. "I was refused gas because I was about my calling. No energy for the Lord. Nor am I allowed to go to Elmira or Binghamton. They are now in a foreign country. The brothers and sisters there will await me in vain. I had recorded two grand new sermons," he said wistfully, "and my son John had put in a new amplifier of glorious resonance, fitting to the purpose."

She had been too tired last night to listen when Mother Liza had talked (as well as she could with no teeth) of her errant husband. "Always a bad farmer," she said. "My mother warned me, but I would have him. Then Washington gave him money not to plant, and that was the end of him. Took to religion and the whole tribe of Corbetts went to the bad. Except Agnes, but she's too good for this world. It was the money for my teeth that he used to buy that van," she had said crossly. "Don't seem to me the good Lord needed my false teeth." Now Amos regarded Martha thoughtfully. "There's a lot of the devil in redheaded women," he pronounced.

While the prophet went on his way, Martha resumed her walk. Along the path was the foundation of a house, dug into the field, covered by a tarpaulin. Through an open flap Martha saw all the signs of long habitation. A woman was asleep on a bed with a handsome headboard and a lamp and radio beside her. Three sturdy children were playing just outside.

They stared at her as she approached. "Is it time for breakfast?" they asked. "Yes," she said, thinking of the rabbits. "Yes, it is." They scampered off to the main building.

Martha had heard of places like this, though she had never seen them, in the South, in Appalachia perhaps, though she had always believed that they were things of the past. To find Tobacco Road in the Eighties, up here on the border of New York State, was so absurd, the incredible variety of her own country so striking, that an odd, unseemly bubble of laughter caught her up. In the bright, warm sunshine on the Corbett farm the strange, often frightening, events of the past days now seemed far behind.

The place pointed out as Cindy's house was before her. It was more a shack than a house, carelessly thrown up

on the family land. Four more children, closely resembling the others, were marching out and looking to be
fed. No one who resembled a Cindy was to be seen,
nor was Daniel. Martha looked inside. The rickety
kitchen was empty; a sitting room looked unused. Upstairs, four bunk beds with a heap of untidy bedding
showed where the children had slept.

In the next room a buxom, fair young woman had
thrown back the bedclothes for the sake of coolness or
exercise, and on her bosom rested the dark head of
Daniel. His eyes opened.

"Mrs. Corbett asked me to bring you both to breakfast," Martha said tartly.

"Ah." He gently nudged his partner, "Allow me to
present my wife," for so he had described Martha the
night before on their arrival.

Cindy was not perturbed in any way. "I think I'll
have my sleep out," she said. "I've got no fancy for no
more rabbit. Nice to meet you, ma'am."

Daniel jumped up, quite naked, and Martha turned
away and went down the stairs. She was soon followed
by Daniel, dressed and smiling. "I don't think my wife
should be so prudish," he remarked, as they walked in
the bright sunlight. "You must be a better actress, Mrs.
Adams."

Martha felt unaccountably irritated. "Your wife must
have a lot to bear," she said.

"No, I was faithful to my wife," he said. "But she was
killed in the Yom Kippur war."

His voice was matter-of-fact, but Martha was instantly
ashamed.

"You're blushing, Mrs. Adams," he said. "I have very
rarely seen that."

"It's a problem for redheads," she said. Josh had
teased her about it. Josh. *The lilies there that wave and
weep above a nameless grave.* She was seized once
more by a sense of desolation, and the antics of the
Corbetts, with Amos preaching over the rabbit stew,

could no longer distract her from the terrible burden of her mission. Even the Corbetts were already touched by the new regime.

Agnes introduced her to child after child. "And he's our Mark's, but I'm afraid his father might have gone to the Lord, because Mark ran off to the Navy after some rumpus on New Year's Eve. He was out at sea when the doom and destruction came. Not one word have I heard from him."

"Never heard anyway," a girl, presumably Mark's wife, or widow, said.

"Now all the boys have registered," Agnes went on. "They will all be taken in their prime. . . ."

"Peace, woman," Amos said, and she subsided.

After breakfast she found Daniel rummaging among the old cars. "I found this place when I came down from New York State after I hopped the Canadian border," he said, smiling. "I thought it might be useful, some time."

He took out old bits of CB equipment, maps from glove compartments, removed a set of old license plates, and then made once more for Cindy's house. "Come on, Mrs. Adams. I can use you." He saw her expresion, and grinned. "Not all pleasure at Cindy's. Her husband left an almost working CB."

In the kitchen Daniel already had spread the component parts of the small unit on a table, and he had found and cleaned some tools. He substituted transistors, boosted the power and fixed a larger antenna. Fortunately, she had seen Buzz do the same sort of thing enough times to make her a fair helper, and Daniel gave her a grunt of approval.

"You could make the signal stronger," she volunteered.

"Um," Daniel said. "But we'll be taking a chance as it is. If this gets picked up by state or town police, they'll institute a search. You can be sure there are radio detection vans about. Death penalty now for illegal use of transmitting and receiving equipment."

He had a quick mental image of Eli Cohen, executed before television cameras in the main square of Damascus. The body had hung for six hours draped in a white sheet as thousands of Syrians passed by, staring. Cohen had been a Mossad hero and he had been trapped by a detection van.

Briskly, he spoke into the transceiver. "This is Rose Red, Rose Red. Meet me as arranged, Snow White. Papa's waiting."

He switched off quickly.

"Don't you wait for an answer?"

"The shorter the signal the better, they can't get a fix. No sense making it easy for them. This is a big property. I'll use different spots to repeat at intervals. Our party will be listening, if he made it here. This was the backup plan, you might say. I managed to get a message off at La Guardia through a friend in the control tower. You can amuse yourself, Mrs. Adams. We might be here a few days."

"We have the whole country to cross," she said. "We can't just wait for somebody to show up."

"We'll wait for this guy," Daniel said. "I'll give him a week; longer, if we have to."

"Who the devil is he?" Martha said.

"You're catching the prevalent religious mania," Daniel remarked. "He is what you might call our insurance, Mrs. Adams."

His expression, as he gazed at some interior vision, was strange, unreadable except for a grim wariness. It was as smothering as a shovel of earth, and her sparking impatience subsided. But not for long.

— XXIV —

Perez, in the continuing absence of Borunukov in Moscow, had made himself master of the People's House. It was pointless, now, to keep his house in the slums. The population of the inner city had been removed. Hall City was to become a complete administrative center. Non-workers had been found work on the regional wiring projects. Bourgeois troublemakers were put on the clean-up gangs in the areas still paralyzed from the initial Russian strike. Workers were being moved closer to their jobs. The faces of some of the workers when they saw their new quarters had been amusing, but they need not have been disturbed. Most of them would go in their turn.

Already he had dismantled much of the old bureaucracy. Congress had been prorogued and would be dissolved formally on the 26th of October. The former departments of Health, Welfare and Education had been turned over to the new Department of Hispanic and Indian affairs. The State Department had been abolished, its functions handled from New York. Policing, for the time being, was being run from New York also, and Borunukov's men were running the military.

It pleased him that the People's House staff, accustomed to swift changes in the occupancy of the house, had already assembled a suite on the second floor quite to his satisfaction. It comprised all of the seven rooms of the private quarters. If Borunukov returned he could be given Blair House, for after the 26th of October, President Bristow, that bourgeois democrat, would no longer be useful. In fact, Perez decided, he would have him moved now into the apartment complex with other minor officials, another step in the degradation of the office of the United States' head of state. Besides, the historical connotation amused him: the Presidency would end at the Watergate.

Perez had fond hopes that the Marshal would be kept in the Soviet Union and was using his considerable influence upon the Politburo in trying to prolong Borunukov's stay. The Marshal simply was not needed here; the generals installed in the Pentagon could manage perfectly well without him. There were no great battles to be fought in the United States. What was left of the American forces, leaderless, had followed the order given by their former Commander-in-Chief to submit to the conquerors.

Yet all these things, good in themselves, brought him no ease of spirit, for he had found no trace, no hint of the whereabouts of the all-destructive Magna. He shivered slightly. He wasn't used to the airconditioning he told himself. Still Magna was an awesome thought. Never before had Perez felt awe: it was an emotion he had believed for illiterate peasants, who filled the vacuity of their ignorance with religious drama. But the power of Magna was not the imaginary might of a gentle Christ or a wrathful Jehovah. It was real; it was present.

An image flashed before his mind; something forgotten from years before, now clear and bright. A young people's rally in a Washington park. They had slept there, on a few summer nights, making love and talking revolution, and they had disturbed an old man who slept each night on a bench. He would wake, every so often, shaking his fists, a strange figure before the light of the campfires. His half-blind eyes would bat hopefully at the dark heavens, yelling, "Behold, the Kingdom of Heaven is at hand."

The Kingdom of Heaven; the Kingdom of Hell. Perhaps it was all one. Heaven for the ruler; hell for the rest. And where, in the name of Hell itself, was Bar-Lev? Perez's people suspected that Bar-Lev had been in Canada not long before the surrender. Had he been there because of Magna? The Canadian government would never have allowed Reagan the use of Canadian soil—but could it have been done *sub rosa*? No, it was too unlikely. Perez dismissed the idea.

Most probably Bar-Lev had crossed the border. This business with the fingerprints would actually be helpful here. Unluckily, they had no set of Bar-Lev's prints, nor even a photograph, but the new technique almost compensated for that, for every long distance traveler now had to file prints at the central registry.

Perez was getting on very well with Virinsky, who seemed content with a subservient, inglorious, bureaucratic role. The man had found his niche and knew himself well-placed as he was. It would be as well to give him a tidbit and appear to be keeping their bargain. Using his line to the UN office, he passed on all his speculations about the Israeli agent to the KGB man.

Virinsky, in turn, was cordial, and took note. Perez and his people were still good for something, though it was a pity they had nothing definite. Bar-Lev was already on the primary arrest list. Soon some information should be coming from the Jewish camps and there must be people, however few, who had some knowledge of him. Eventually they would talk. Virinsky or-

dered an especially stringent watch in areas close to the
Canadian border, and found to his irritation that
Borunukov had ordered great numbers of men to be
used in hunting down Chinese. Some good party members among the Vietnamese population had been swept
up in error by Czech troops who couldn't tell a Japanese businessman from a Filipino houseboy.

The arrest and prisoner lists were growing. He had
had a new computer room installed next to his file
room. Two Under-Secretaries had had to be moved, but
that was of no account. Virinsky had been one of the
first in the KGB to realize the incredible powers of the
United States computer technology. He had learned
from the Eighth Department of the Second Chief Directorate that ran the surveillance in the Soviet Union
itself, but he had gone beyond his masters and had kept
up with every advance in Western technology. With
this computer it was a matter of seconds only to find
who was in each prison or camp. This was a boon, for
many people picked up in general arrests were also on
special lists and the computers saved a wearisome amount
of record searching. Also, the workless and the elderly
sent to labor on the wiring or in Bering could be
sorted if one was wanted for interrogation, and the
check against the death lists was the work of a moment.
Virinsky truly loved the silent efficiency of the machines, perfected to the point where they were never
"down." Neither Beria nor Himmler had had at his
disposal what Virinsky had under his hand—terror plus
technology. The proper use of both made a man
invincible.

Despite Perez's seeming cooperation, however, he
signed the arrest list before him. It was for members of
the former Black Liberation Army. Perez had put a
protective order on them, claiming they could still be
useful. Virinsky found, as always with such types, that
they were a nuisance and did not fit in with the general
pattern. They had appeared on worldwide television,

appropriate speeches had been made, but now was a good time for their liquidation. He would have them shot by American servicemen. The servicemen could be tried later, and Virinsky would not be involved. He himself would declare the BLA members heroes of the nation. The FALN would follow, but that would have to wait for a time.

Perez, who usually called himself a Cuban, sometimes also claimed a Puerto Rican side to his heritage. Only Kharkev and Virinsky knew that actually he was the son of a female Spanish comrade who had visited Moscow and an unknown Russian father. Not even Kharkev nor Virinsky had ever discovered who the father was. Perez had been well-trained and sent to the Caribbean to take over from the Castros, who had once been those "dangerous little brothers."

But whatever Perez thought (and it was amazing how his judgement was decaying now that he had come to power) Borunukov was going to be back for the 26th of October. Ulyanov was coming to address the meeting at this great circus and nothing would change the date, his name day, which he had managed to connect with Lenin's revolution. Ulyanov, with his family claims, had true Lenin fever. He used Lenin's office, kept like the museum it had been, down to the statuette on the desk: the bronze of a crouching ape staring at a human skull. Ulyanov would be in New York, and not even the possibility of the China strike would postpone his coming. Naturally Borunukov, with his victorious forces behind him, would not let Ulyanov preside alone over the legal dismemberment of the USA. And so, with Perez, it would be a three-ring circus.

Virinsky had been staring ahead, unseeing. Now his gaze took in the obligatory portrait on the wall opposite his desk, too familiar to be often observed. Lenin. Not one of those three was a Lenin, nor a Stalin, any more than Khrushchev or Brezhnev had been. The next follower in the ranks of the great dictators would be a

Chekist. Beria should have followed Stalin. Beria, who had made the NKVD the greatest police power the world had ever known, and yet had allowed himself to be destroyed by lesser men in the Presidium helped by the army. He, Virinsky, would not make that mistake. To hold the Magna weapon, whatever it was, had become his one great aim.

Once again he pulled out the list that had disappointed him. The water projects. So many of the men on the list were now marked as dead. He buzzed for Thu Thuy, and told her to check with Madame Paul on the families of the dead men who had already been placed on the arrest list.

Madame Paul brought the lists herself. "The names checked in green are already in the Special Camps. Blue means they are in transport. Black is for those in areas where they are almost certainly deceased. Red is for those not yet located."

As his gaze scanned the red list one name leapt to his eye.

"Bruce Joshua Adams?"

"Son of the Joshua Adams, deceased, Chief Superintendent of the Columbia Construction Company."

Everything he had found about the work of that company had been innocent enough. Joshua Adams had bribed the government inspector with a silver bracelet but that meant nothing. Government inspectors were bribed all over the world.

"We had bad luck there," Madame Paul went on. "This boy had been in the Juvenile Detention Camp II in Region I. Vagabondage and trespassing in a restricted area—the Haddam atomic plant. He was released on some trumped-up plea by his mother. The camp commander, an American, was relieved of his duty, and is now administering a labor gang in Bering. Another arrest order was signed for the boy, but he had disappeared. It is believed he is now part of the juvenile hooligan movement styling itself as some kind of *Maquis*."

"The mother?" Virinsky said.

"Also not yet located," Madame Paul said. "Her name is here, on the female list. As you see, Mrs. Drummond, the widow of the owner of the Columbia company is in the camp and is being interrogated now. If you would like a running report, I have a sheet here where she lists her husband's associates, business and personal . . ."

As she talked, Virinsky looked at the page where the wife of Joshua Adams was listed. Martha Adams. His mind wandered back to an afternoon when he had been standing in the outer office with his hand on Thu Thuy's shoulder—so slim, so childish—while she typed a list. He had paid little attention then, but he saw it quite clearly now, in his mind's eye. It had been a Missing Personnel report. The 'A' report: people located after investigation, usually ill. The 'B': those still not found after preliminary search. Most of those were dead, some of natural causes, others from the attacks of violence still prevalent in the streets. And one of the names on the 'B' list had been a Martha Adams.

Martha Adams. He suddenly remembered the great day, the day of the fall of the United States. He had gone down to the entrance himself to see the arrival of the first contingent of KGB troops that he had ordered to be brought up the river from the troopship *Leonid*, already waiting in New York Bay. By his personal order the doors had been closed to anyone except the troops and he had gone down there, only to find an arrogant, redheaded woman marching past the guard like the Tsaritsa Alexandra at the Winter Palace. As the column entered, a guard had drawn her aside, with apologies, as though to protect her light dress from the splashing soldiers' boots, as sycophantic as the Romanov's serfs.

Of course, it meant nothing. There were as many Adamses in this country as fleas on a dog. Yet he could not resist saying, "The Martha Adams on the missing list of the Organization, who is she?"

Madame Paul, cut off in mid-sentence, floundered for a moment.

"Martha . . . oh, I see. No, no connection there. Our Martha Adams is in charge of a typing section dealing most recently with WHO reports, and she is a British citizen. She lives here, in Region II. The daughter of a George and Abigail Adams, deceased. I checked the file for the investigation squad. She called herself 'Mrs'. Some women find this useful."

Virinsky remembered that she herself was also a mademoiselle. He nodded. "Very well. Continue."

But nothing she had to report was of immediate interest. After she had gone he frowned and sat irritably tapping the computer terminal. Almost always he found a mental flash, linking seemingly disparate items, was fruitful. But an English Miss Adams could have no connection with Joshua Adams, the Columbia Construction Company, the water projects or any of the detested late President's schemes. Yet that woman had stayed like a burr in his mind.

He turned to his reports from the West. That plan at least was going well. The reports were hearteningly positive.

In half an hour, Madame Paul was back. "Under-Secretary, the interrogators of Mrs. Drummond decided, because of certain hesitations and obvious falsehoods, to use more intensive questioning. She has revealed the one word, 'Magnanimity'."

Virinsky, usually impassive, started visibly.

"Tell them to continue, and to send reports at once. Did this come over the open wire?"

"By messenger," Madame Paul said serenely. "For my eyes only."

He nodded, satisfied. It had been a good decision to give Madame Paul a KGB rank. But for the rest of the day he had found it hard to put his attention on other matters. By ten o'clock that night, the interrogators reported that the woman most certainly had no more information to give. It had been little enough, after all. Her husband, at the time of the Reagan killing, had been involved with an Alaskan oil project but had not been able to continue because of the problem of the caribou. Virinsky, impatient, had the interrogators brought to his office, and they sat at his desk, uncomfortable enough to be in the interrogation chairs themselves, before the man they knew to be in charge of the whole First Department. These men who had been torturing the sixty-five-year-old woman on the dusty grass of Central park, gazed in some awe about the Under-Secretary's room, and at the East River, sparkling far below them, as though this glassy eyrie were indeed the nest of an eagle, an eagle of such power that he could snatch them up and fling them anywhere he would.

Virinsky well knew the effect this place would have on them, but he had not brought them to be impressed. "Where, in the new Soviet Republic of Bering, was this project?"

They made a point on a map. It was in a rich oil area, but that could have been a deception. The labor camp was already set up there; a thorough search should be made.

"And there was nothing else, nothing at all, on the subject of Magnanimity?"

"Nothing. It was merely a phrase."

"A stupid remark," the second man said, somewhat anxiously, "supposedly made by the former President Reagan, whom the husband, apparently, knew. "We call it Magnanimity, because we have it, but will never use it.""

It wasn't much. A stupid remark, the usual American cant. But just the sort of thing an American man, usually discreet, might feel moved to confide to his wife. For so little it was a pity to lose two highly-trained interrogators. They had been put through a long, intensive course in English language, Western customs and interrogation technique and these men could be trusted. But in such matters it was imperative to obey Ulyanov's orders to the letter. And so the men were, after all, given to the river, whose bright surface received their corpses with scarcely a ripple.

Daniel had been gone three days before Martha got the call from Snow White. She had repeated Daniel's message, according to his instructions, at intervals during the day from different parts of the farm and the fields beyond. The expected visitor did not arrive and she heard nothing but signals from state troopers and police calls from the small township of Wappasening Falls a few miles to the east.

Late on the third day the transmission came. A man's voice said simply, "Snow White, Maple Lane," and that was the end of the signal. Martha wished desperately that Daniel had returned. He had said nothing about meeting anyone. Her own signal might have been picked up and this could be a trap.

She went up to the main house where Agnes was skinning rabbits and woodchucks, helped by three, hungry-looking children. Agnes, like old Liza sitting in her rocking chair, or even Amos himself, showed no surprise that their visitor was still with them. She seemed to expect women, with their children if any, to come and stay while their men went off on ploys of their own. Often, she looked absently for Martha's children who should be beside her at the table. Already, Martha thought, she was established as kith if not kin, the exact relationship forgotten but still honored. Martha asked if she knew of Maple Lane.

"A terrible, sinful place," Agnes said. "That's where my poor Hannah got pregnant from the Wabey boy and the child was a judgement with a crooked shoulder but a sweet thing just the same."

"All the Wabeys was crooked and simple besides,"

Mother Liza said. "And your Hannah was simple to go down Maple Lane with him for all his sweet blue eyes."

"She should have been cast out," Amos grumbled. Now that his preaching van was confined to an old stable, his ardor was subdued. He looked round at the company of women, many pregnant, and no doubt wished that most of them could be cast out.

Maple Lane was a lovers' lane on public land between the Corbett farm and Wappasening Falls. Far from the highway, it had been a favorite spot for illicit love. A good place for Snow White to pick, for if his message was caught it might be dismissed as an attempt at a lovers' tryst. But did Snow White realize that possession of a transmitter meant death?

Martha had to go. Daniel had made it clear that Snow White was of the first importance. He could not be lost. Why he had not come as arranged to the farm she didn't know. She would have to find out.

She borrowed papers fom Dan's Dulcie, the widow with seven children, whose description was not too far from her own and was not yet much known in the surrounding country. The Corbett women were free with their belongings, few as they had, and the new papers meant no more to them than the food stamps had done. Here they had only seen the familiar local police and the new regime was marked for them only by the loss of their familiar perquisites, and the lack of things to be bought even for those with some remaining funds. Cigarettes were mourned as much as supermarket foods. The conscription of young males was as yet merely a peacetime draft to them. Martha hoped fervently that her visit would not cause the terrible realities to burst upon them sooner than they must.

She set off at a brisk pace shortly after sunset. The curfew law was in force up here, but was not as strictly applied by local police, for gas was hard to come by and long journeys were taken on foot or in some cases by horse-drawn carts. Amos had been trying to buy a team of horses, but his resources would not stretch to the price, and besides, he had found he could no longer buy the power pack for his loudspeaker system. Preaching without power had no joys for him.

She approached the avenue with caution. In the dusk, under the interlacing branches of the trees, the figure of a man close against the trunk of a tree could have been anyone, but as she cautiously drew closer, she saw a mane of white hair, smiling eyes, a lined and friendly face. Surely not a police spy, yet she wondered. "Our insurance," Daniel had said, but what insurance could this grandfatherly-looking man be to them on their arduous mission?

"I've come on behalf of 'Rose Red'," she said. "He had to go away for a couple of days. If you'll come with me I'll find you a bed, though I'm afraid it might not be very comfortable."

The man laughed, a spontaneous chuckle, at the formal words of a hostess coming from this female with distinguished features and goddess-like walk, (dressed in ill-fitting dungarees and a man's plaid jacket) as though the world had not changed, and they were not in mortal danger. But he admired gallantry.

"Johann Meister," he said formally. "At your service. Shall we take my car?" He gestured towards a clump of bushes. "Back there; I am here legally, and I have papers. A citizen of Canada. They are being quite polite to us just now."

"We'd better go separately," she said. "We'll attract less attention if we're stopped. You know where the Corbett place is? I'll meet you there."

He bowed over her hand, and in a moment his car was roaring off down the road, outlined by the lingering afterglow. When the motorbike patrol roared down the lane a moment later, her first thought was thank the Lord that Meister had driven out of sight. Quickly she made for the bushes but it was too late. The last sunlight caught her hair and then a heavy hand fell on her shoulder.

"Let's see your I.D., lady."

His expression changed when he read the card with the aid of his flashlight. "Hey, this is Dulcie Corbett, young Dan's wife. The widow-woman with the kids." The other man looked at her and laughed. "A nice young seventeen-year old's not enough eh? How long's Dan been gone? Who is this Snow-White?"

Martha kept her eyes down and pulled her earlobe, trying to look naive, awkward. A bashful Corbett.

He strolled round behind the bushes. She heard him kicking the twigs. "Took off, did he? Or ain't he here yet? Keepin' the little lady waitin'."

"Aw, come on, Pete." The younger man sounded uncomfortable. "Lady, where'd you get that CB? Don't you know it's a felony? There's a death penalty on that, ain't you heard?"

"CB?" Martha's voice came out in a squeak. She looked up, vacantly.

"We'll have to take her in." Pete strolled back, disappointed at failing to see signs of a scuffle in the soft earth. "The captain can ask her questions. I'll call for a car."

For a moment Martha considered making a run for it. But the young man looked friendly.

"Hell, Pete, she ain't got no CB on her. You can see that. How d'you know she's Rose Red? Half the county's been down here, sometime or other."

"Looks red enough to me. If she ain't, what happened to Rose Red then?"

"Well, you don't see no Snow White, do you? Who you waitin, for, lady?"

"Nobody." Martha tried to emulate Dulcie's slightly Southern voice. "I was just out for a walk, trying to get away from all those kids. Place is three kids to an inch."

"That's the truth," the concupiscent officer said. "And one of them I'll swear is young Billy's here."

"Oh, come on." Billy's face reddened. "Suppose we call in Mrs. Corbett, see if she's wanted. Those two singing love-birds probably changed their minds."

"Yeah. Not enough good red meat these days to keep the heart up." He laughed, pleased with himself and called in to the station.

Although it was late September the weather was still mild, yet Martha could not restrain a shiver. Suppose the unknown Dulcie was wanted; suppose they called back at the farm for further proof, suppose . . .

Wappasening Falls had nothing against Dulcie Corbett, "Except child-molesting," the captain said, amused, thinking of young Dan, who had run off, though his family didn't know it, to join the army. Doubtless he was sorry now. Dutifully, the captain checked Philadelphia, the Region headquarters, with the woman's description, but found no complaint of any kind. His men had reported illegal CB use in the area. God knows, it would be years before they got them all out of the country, and most of the kids meant no harm.

"Think you like that gadget," his lieutenant remarked, as the captain waited for a reply on the computer terminal.

"Orders are orders," the captain replied. There was no more to be said.

Philadelphia had nothing against Mrs. Corbett either. A woman like that wasn't the type to be fooling with CB equipment. Just another Corbett out looking for a piece of tail away from the eyes of old Amos.

"You can let her go," he told the motorcycle team. "Tell her if she doesn't get home before curfew, she can be pulled in for sure."

Martha walked away, not too fast, hoping that the shaking of her body, from head to toe, wasn't visible. Her feet, in borrowed boots, seemed to thunder on the path and it might have been forever before the motorcycles rumbled off.

Meister, waiting by the farmhouse door, saw her

white face, with the few freckles protruding like signals of fear. "I'm sorry I drew you out," he said humbly. "I saw those men after I'd turned off the road. It was stupid of me, but when I heard a woman's voice as Rose Red, I thought it might have been a trap."

"I hope you can eat rabbit stew," Martha said, and then both laughed, though her voice was still shaky.

The captain at Wappasening Falls was thinking and shook his head. Orders *were* orders. He thought of the Corbett place. A junk yard. Amos's farm machinery, good expensive equipment, left to rust and molder in the fields. And the cars, wrecked and abandoned by a score or more of feckless male Corbetts. They must be full of old CB stuff, probably none of it working. He would have to send some men over one of these days to hunt it out. But it was ninety acres. The regular work took so much time now with all this pass and paper business. Here it was, seven-thirty, and he had been on duty since eight in the morning. And some of his men had been co-opted for city and border work. It would have to wait a couple of days, that was all.

At ten-thirty that night in New York, Thu Thuy heard Virinsky's buzzer. She was too well-trained to sigh, but the corners of her lovely mouth turned down, very slightly. She had been pleased to get the post of personal assistant to the Under-Secretary, very aware of his real position. As his assistant, she had the rank and pay of the head of a large section. She was also amused at the chagrin of Madame Paul. Thu Thuy was not much more fond of the French than she was of the Americans. Yes, it had been very amusing to put that long nose out of joint. But even Thu Thuy, trained to work long and hard, did like to have some unbroken rest. Virinsky's catnapping, a few hours at a time, was not enough for a young woman, and besides, he often left her work when he napped. And she could not use an assistant because all the work was confidential. She had good food and pretty clothes, but she was tired. Even the sense of great power was dimmed by sheer physical weariness.

And there were her other duties. She had been performing them, quietly and well, for important party members for over ten years but never had they been as difficult as they were with the Under-Secretary. The old *liet duong*. The appellation she used in her mind was far more to the point than Mr. No-Frills. She had been taught, in her early classes, of the pride of the women of North Vietnam, who had fought by the sides of their men as equals, and who had never abused their beauty and their bodies by becoming bar-girls for the Americans in Ho Chi Min City, in the days when it was Saigon. She had thought then how fortunate she was to be a Party woman, devoted to her cause. Now the unbidden thought came, that those men at least must have been young, healthy. Not a feeble creature whose ejaculation could only be induced with much labor and stupid, childish games.

What did he want now? Weary as she was, she would rather work past midnight than spend another hour on the black bench. Viciously, she wished Madame Paul could take her place, but what could *she* do? Nothing. When Thu Thuy went inside, she could have groaned. Virinsky was not writing, or looking through his files. Instead he was stroking his thumb, in a gesture that now seemed to her obscene, knowing what it presaged.

He nodded toward the bench. She prepared herself and waited. It was not unusual for her to be kept waiting like that; she fancied it gave him some special satisfaction to see her there, awaiting his pleasure. Sometimes he suggested she change her position or perform some gesture, while he calmly went on working. Soon he did so. He had already put on his silky robe which meant he was, as it were, prepared for the night. The day staff had left, the night staff was working in offices all over the building, but no one would disturb the Under-Secretary, unless it was Hall City or Moscow.

He rose, went to the door, and spoke to the guard that stood outside, fully armed, night and day. As he gave an order, he left the door ajar enough so that the man's gaze fell upon her, as she was. Worse, when Virinsky's voice ceased, Madame Paul's voice came from close by. Could she, too—Thu Thuy's face showed no expression, but she felt humiliated through to her bones. The Russians were pigs, she thought. She remembered tales she had heard of the Russian monk Rasputin, who lived in a time long ago.

The Under-Secretary closed the door and he came towards her. He touched her as a curious child might have done, using only his deformed thumb, and then spoke, as if ignoring his own gesture. "I had sent for Madame Paul, but she can wait outside. The reports from the Special Camp."

Lucky Madame Paul. Thu Thuy's anger against the powerful Under-Secretary veered to the elder woman. She should be humiliated, as Thu Thuy was. "Disappointing," he added, fondling her absently. "The one promising lead was useless. You remember, the Columbia Construction Company, Joshua Adams. Even his wife, Martha Adams, disappeared."

"Mrs. Adams from the typing pool?" If she prolonged the conversation, he might forget his purpose, as he had done before, to return to his labors, which Thu Thuy knew gave him far deeper satisfaction.

"No. Madame Paul tells me *she* was English, and unmarried."

Thu Thuy gave a small, rare smile. So, she thought. Madame had blundered. "But I heard Mrs. Adams tried to call her son in Region I from the office. Later she tried to get the switchboard operator to make the call."

"Do you have the number?" he asked abruptly, his flicker of passion completely forgotten.

"I can get it," she said and dressed swiftly. After all, it had been her job to watch and keep such records. She brought the number to him, and he ordered the telephone operator to find out to whom that number belonged. The telephone company's records were somewhat in disarray. Earlier investigation teams had lost some records and erased others in error. It was broad daylight when Virinsky had his answer, and Madame Paul had reason to regret it. Worse, a computer cross check showed that information had been filed against the wanted woman, but it had been programed into the banks of Region I and forgotten. Before another ten minutes had passed Madame Paul was in Virinsky's office being accused of sabotage, before the impassive stare of Thu Thuy. And an all-region alert was put out, with accompanying photographs, for Mrs. Martha Adams.

—— XXV ——

Daniel returned on the night of Meister's arrival. The Corbetts had received Martha's friend, the old man from overseas, as casually as they accepted any chance visitor. Though the young women cast no sheep's eyes at his person, they were pleased with his gifts, because he had brought chocolate, that the children hadn't tasted for a month. The mothers had a bite also (it was a good change from stew) and old Amos announced that those who served the Lord deserved sustenance.

After the meal, Martha, Daniel and Johann Meister, who liked to be called Hans, found privacy in an old barn, at a good distance from the house, to sit in the smoky illumination of a paraffin lamp. Daniel had laughed and joked with the girls at the table, causing squeals of giggles. Mother Liza had cackled, and Agnes had allowed that the Lord loveth a cheerful doer. But now he was serious enough. "Obviously," he said, "we can't travel across country as we came here. I couldn't ask Hans to do that."

"I'm in quite good condition," he protested, but Daniel shook his head. "As you know, I had meant to use air transport. But commercial flying is too risky. I don't know if they use the fingerprint check all over but we can't take the chance. So that leaves just one thing."

The light flickered over the countenances of the two men. Hans had his usual air of faint amusement, perhaps at their condition. He was an urbane man, very out of place on the dirt floor of a tumbled-down barn, but taking it all calmly. Daniel was just Daniel, sprawling on the ground. Casual. In charge.

"Military transport," he said. "That's the only way. I've looked about, made a few connections. At a military air field there's no time for fingerprint checks. They know who is on the base, anyway."

"But difficult to arrange?" Hans asked.

"Something might be done."

"Well, I don't suggest Plattsburg," Hans said resignedly, "though I might know somebody there. I passed by when I crossed the border. They are wiring the border, you know. Essential points first and then the rest. Wire mesh as fine as a woman's crochet-work and as sharp as a razor. It goes three feet into the ground to prevent burrowing; I saw them working at it. Anti-personnel mines at head, waist and knee level, triggered by trip wires. They have to put a separate strand of wire along the top or the birds blow it up when they perch on it. All the ground beyond the fence is ploughed under and finished off with anti-vehicle ditches and strong barricades. And then there are watchtowers. It looks like the old border between East and West Germany. I couldn't believe it, Daniel."

"Call me Daniel," that nameless man had warned him earlier.

"And then at the state border—when I got to the Pennsylvania line—I had already seen many things. Romulus is swarming with Soviet troops. It was a storage place for nuclear weapons, I think. It's all happened in a month, the labor gangs, the wire. I had my papers and I had to go through a regional checkpoint not far from Elmira. On either side was a deadly stretch of sand, seeded with trip flares, fenced with electrified wire, more watchtowers. You couldn't believe it."

Martha thought of the Juvenile Camp at Greenfield Hill.

"I can believe it," she said.

Daniel gave her a glance, but Hans went on. "I can understand the Canadian line, but these internal barriers . . ."

"The new masters intend to break the American habit of free travel rather quickly," Daniel said. "But if we can get to Pittsburgh, and we avoid the main airport . . ."

"We can take my car and travel in comfort," Hans suggested. "I'm here legally, a Canadian citizen, with proper identification. No Region checks, so you two could get there. You can 'borrow' some documents, surely."

"It's tempting, but I think you have to disappear, Hans," Daniel said slowly. "What business were you here on, officially?"

"Representing the Vancouver Mining Company. I am still working for them, selling strategic metals, you see. Carmody, Bristow, Borunukov, it's all the same to my sort. It was easy for me to come, though tourists, of course, are not welcome as yet." His smile seemed more amused than cynical.

"It's not safe." Daniel frowned. "You've always used your own name. You might be on some record; they could discover who you are."

"An old has-been. Ask this lady, she is wondering why you have brought this old crock to delay your mission." His smile was kindly but Martha blushed, for his guess was, in the main, correct.

"We can't take the chance. They're not fools. Not about things like that. After all, Andrei Tupolov headed the Tupolev Design Bureau until he died in '72 and by then he was eighty-four years old. No. Above all, you can't be connected with Mrs. Adams here."

"Hm, a pity. Still, if we can get as far as Pennsylvania Dutch country, I can pick up a change of identity. A cousin, who has lived in the United States for thirty years, but still a German citizen. An agreeable fellow and very handsome, similar to me in appearance. Annoying about the fingerprints . . . Of course, they might be dead down there. Or scattered."

"I'll have to think about it," Daniel said. "It's time we left."

He had heard of Martha's episode with the police.

"Well," Meister said, "I must be off, then, to my rest. I am invited to Mrs. Cindy's tonight. I still have some chocolate left, you see."

He strode off, smiling, and Daniel grinned. He and Martha left the barn, heavy with dust and paraffin fumes, to breathe the fresh air gladly.

"And who or what, exactly, is our insurance?" Martha asked, rather impatiently.

"Curiosity killed the cat, and the mouse too, Mrs. Adams," he said. He lifted his arm in mock fear. "No, don't pounce."

He sat down beside a gnarled old maple and Martha joined him on the grass. A fat, full moon shone through the branches still heavy with leaves.

"We have some useful allies," he said.

"You mean the British? You spoke of the Nelson fleet."

Daniel smiled. "Oh, yes. The insurgents. There are people in Britain who don't care for the one-party state, especially in the navy. They're hiding out, many believe in Australian waters, with some newly designed subs, each carrying two missiles, waiting for the right moment to paste the Soviets. And some say the royal Charles is with them. But I was speaking of your own people, in this country, out West. Including, you will be pleased to know, your Colonel Fairfield. However, in case anything should go wrong—for I am a man who is used to things going wrong—I brought the insurance."

She was pleased to hear Colonel Fairfield's name. So there *was* a real, organized underground. But, insurance?

"You must have wondered," Daniel said slowly, "where the Magnanimity missile was built. It had to be in a society where the details could be hidden, where controls could be applied. A country with sufficient technological and trained staff. There aren't many in the Western world. The Russians must be pondering that at this very moment. They know the secret of Magnanimity, by the way. By now that is certain."

Martha's heart beat so fast and hard she felt the pain against her bones. "The secret . . ."

"What it is," he said. "The ultimate death weapon. Doomsday. Aharit Ha Yamim. And they must know that at least one was built by the United States. There was a raid on a certain facility in Israel and by gross stupidity on someone's part," Daniel was very grim, "an old man had been left there to be captured, and to talk. But he couldn't tell them the theory, because he never knew it."

Her heartbeat subsided, but she was still sweating with anxiety. "Oh, my God. They will be tearing the country apart. This is a real disaster, Daniel."

"No, perhaps not." With one of his sudden changes in mood, he grinned. His face was half-devil, half-impudent boy. "I had been thinking of how we could let them know."

"Let them know?"

"Think, woman," he said. "We find the missile, occupy the site. We deliver our ultimatum. If they don't know what it is, and fear it in their brains, bellies and balls more than anything in existence, then what would they do? Temporize. Look for us. We would have to use it," he said simply. "We must be prepared to use it. But Jahveh himself, as fierce a god as the Bible shows Him, would surely prefer that we hold back if we can.

Smite them at hip and thigh only if they refuse to surrender. And if they know what it is, they *will* surrender. They will give up half the world to save their continent."

He watched her. "You have a fierce look, Mrs. Adams. I think you are like Jael after all. I think she had small compunction in smashing the head of Sisera."

Taking a match book from his pocket, he doodled on the inside with a pencil stub. Martha paid no attention and hardly heard his teasing. What he said made sense. But he had not answered her question. "And our 'insurance'?" she asked.

"Nothing deflects you, implacable woman," he said.

He showed her the tiny sketch recognizably herself though in Biblical dress, wearing a bellicose expression and purposefully hammering into the figure of a supine warrior.

"Why, that's very clever," she said in surprise. "You are an artist."

He raised an eyebrow and gave a grunt. "Just a fool, lady. Your fool." He tore the cover off the matchbook, struck the match and burned it. "So. Wernher von Braun, you've heard of him?"

"Of course," she said. "He was Hitler's rocket man. He came and worked for us, after the war. He helped begin the missile program."

"He *was* the missile program," Daniel said. "He brought some of his team with him. Including Johann Meister."

She understood. "But that was thirty years ago. I know,just from the talk I've heard from people like the Fairfields, that missile construction is as different now from the early days as night from day. The reliability, accuracy . . ."

"And an old fogy like Hans Meister wouldn't know about that. He worked, for what is now NASA, for a few years. Then he met a Canadian girl and fell in love. His German wife was dead long since. He married the

girl, moved to Canada, and appeared to have retired
from the world of missiles, except that he became a
business representative for a strategic metals group.
When the Magnanimity missile was in the planning
stage, the President had to look for a brilliant designer
who could also direct the project at Valindaba and the
St. Lucia range."

"Valindaba?"

"In the Republic of South Africa. It had to be a man
not only with the necessary expertise, but someone
who could get along with the Afrikaaners. Meister was
the obvious choice. And it made the project seem less
American."

He was lying on his back at her feet, as though he
were a casual companion, or a lover. She caught her
breath as she comprehended. Daniel was perhaps the
only man in the world who had known about both
Aharit-Ha-Yamim and the missile built in Valindaba.
And the man who had built it: Hans Meister, a charming, good-looking man with a pleasant laugh and a light
sense of humor. Hans, who had designed and built the
monstrous weapon, the death-bringing engine that could
end the world. In the pleasantly cool Pennsylvania night
Martha gazed up through the maple branches to the
moonwashed sky, caught in this strange and awesome
thought.

Suddenly Daniel's arms were about her, pulling her
downwards to the grass, his head hard on her face. His
hands pressed on her wrists; and his mouth was a vice
over hers, a muzzle more than an embrace. She heard
the footfall almost simultaneously.

"Well, what d'you know." A flashlight shone on their
struggling bodies, and moved off. "The Corbetts, at it
like it's going out of style."

"Told you it was nothing," another voice grumbled.
"Let's get to the house, serve this warrant and go
home. Don't know why it couldn't have waited till the

morning anyhow. Wake up old Amos and get preached at, most like."

"Orders says warrants are served at night. Not that Joey Corbett will be there. He went to California with a rock group and he ain't never coming back. These two are out after curfew; we could take them in."

"They ain't out. This is the Corbett place. Ain't no law against doing it out of doors, yet, is there? Some squirm that gal's got."

"Stop flappin' your lips. Come on, let's get it over with."

For the third time that day, Martha was covered with the sweat of fear. She lay rigid as the steps moved off.

"You can let go now, Mrs. Adams," Daniel said, laughing in her ear. "Emergency is over."

The next morning Martha was very distant with Daniel. Her rest had been broken by dreams, dreams of the Magnanimity missile, flaming with terror across the globe. Dreams of Josh, his thoughtful face concerned, and she had woken with heartache and tears. She had not even raised a memorial to him in the Litchfield churchyard.

And there had been other dreams. Martha flushed at the memory. The pressure of Daniel's body on her own had roused sensation, a tingling in the breasts, a stirring of sexual desire unseemly, unwanted. It was natural enough she told herself. She and Josh had not been together for . . . how long? So many months since she had seen him. He had only been able to take short leaves. Best to get this job finished, he had told her. God knows, it's urgent. And even before then. . . She had to admit that with Josh so much away, busy, and usually a worried man, their love, after so many years, had become a companionable love. Still deep and true, but flaring less often into ardor. And so she was cool to Daniel as they sat early in the morning in her chicken run, planning their route.

"A plane," he reiterated. "The only way of crossing the Regions without the checks. And for Hans, seventy is seventy. He couldn't make a cross-continent underground hop. And we don't have the time. We have to get to Pittsburgh."

"But that's a commercial airport," Martha said.

"You'll see," Daniel evaded an answer in his usual way. "Be ready to move out after breakfast. I'll have to collect Hans from his no doubt exhausted slumber."

They were walking out from the shack and she gave him an irritated glance. "You didn't need to be quite so emphatic last night. After all, I'm not Cindy."

"Right," he said easily. "You're not so gorgeous. Skinny. Getting long in the tooth. Red hair yet. Freckles. Think yourself lucky."

He grinned and Martha had to laugh. She couldn't imagine why she felt complimented.

Colonel Fairfield shivered. There was a brisk wind sweeping down from the peaks of the Rockies that made the season seem more advanced than the last week of September. He stood fumbling at the door of the tourist cabin, one of many deserted now. There would be no tourists this fall. If people could have traveled they would not have come here. The early rumors of atomic weapons raining on Denver would have scared them off, though in fact the missile complex, mostly closed down through the Carmody years, had been spared and was now occupied by Soviet troops.

It was fortunate in a way that the troops were locked up there; it meant few on patrol. But he was glad when the door opened, and the man he had taken some risk to meet admitted him.

"Forty-three degrees," Clayton Rance remarked, rubbing his hands. "And it feels colder. I've got this kerosene heater going. Didn't want to take a chance on building a fire. I don't think there's anyone about to spot the smoke, but there could always be a helicopter."

Fairfield nodded. It was good to work with a man like Rance, who used his head without being reminded. Not like some of the young hotheads he had to control. A real professional, making no unreasonable demands.

"I thought some of the others might have come with you," Rance said.

"There was no need. They all take orders from me. And our men are stretched thin, now."

Rance looked impressed. He wore Rangers' dress. He would pass well enough, Fairfield thought, tall, tanned, in good health, just a little thick about the waist, though his hands might have given him away. Rance was an indoor man, an administrator. How high he had really been only he could tell, but now he was almost all that was left of the once great Central Intelligence Agency. And very useful he was.

"So, where do we stand?" Rance asked.

"We've already located three sites. Two operational, one might be salvaged—a matter of parts for the GSE. But unluckily, only one contained a missile. The big question, and it's a heated question I've been thrashing out with the others, is how much more time we should spend on the search for the Reagan missiles. There was a great deal of luck in our finding the ones we did, and we had some idea of where to look."

He paused. From above came the unmistakable droning of a helicopter. As always, it gave a sickish sensation in the pit of his stomach. But it passed over. "For the rest—almost none of the original Carter plan was used, you see. No 'racecourse' system, no underground shuttle, and if the transport was supposed to have been above ground, no special roads were built. It looks as though the missiles were meant to have been moved on ordinary public roads and highways, unless an air shuttle had been planned, but no one knows."

"But you think there were more?" Rance asked.

"There would have been no sense in planning such a limited installation. But with Reagan's sudden death, the whole project could have been stopped abruptly. The condition of the silos we found spoke of just such neglect. There seemed to have been no maintenance. They were abandoned, in fact."

"What is the type of missile in the operating silo?" Rance asked, frowning. He had heated water on the stove and made instant coffee. It smelled slightly of kerosene, but Fairfield hadn't tasted coffee of any sort for weeks, and he was grateful for it. He wondered how Rance managed to get hold of it, but he wouldn't ask.

"A Titan II. Pretty old but still serviceable. Like me," he said, grinning.

"If it wasn't for you and your group," Rance said wryly, "we wouldn't have a prayer. You're the best chance we have, John."

Fairfield gazed at the warm stove. When he had first gone on the run, it had been just that. He had warned other retired officers, who began to collect around him. No persuasion had been necessary; they all realized it was just a matter of time, and not much time, before they were caught up in the ever-tightening dragnet. Before long he had become the center of a formidable underground, formidable because these were men with authority and knowledge.

He had been going into Chicago, looking for an old friend, not realizing that it was still tainted by radiation. Rance had recognized him from an old photograph and stopped him, just in time. It had been Rance who put him in touch with the young Minute Men collecting in the Rockies; Rance who had warned him of the different enclaves of Soviet troops; Rance who had brought up the possibility of the hidden missiles, the bee that had been buzzing in Walt's bonnet. And it had been Rance who suggested the Nevada sites.

"I had heard," Rance had told him, "that Reagan first approached the governor of Arizona. But at the time there was such an uproar going on about—what was it?—the Sonoran pronghorn antelope, that it couldn't even be discussed."

Rance had been a station chief in Moscow and he, alone it seemed, had managed to slip back, via Canada, to try to help his stricken country.

"Unfortunately, there was no plan to use after a surrender," he had told Fairfield dryly. "It was unthinkable—so nobody thought it."

"One Titan missile won't give us much edge," he said now, thoughtfully.

"They won't know how many we've got," Fairfield answered. "They'll have to bargain."

Rance sighed. "Once we threaten, they'll be warned. They'll know what we have, soon enough."

"No, it's too well hidden," Fairfield said. "It's targeted for Moscow now and could do some nasty damage. It won't reverse the surrender, but we can get some decent concessions. Rations for all US citizens, an end to the conscription and the evacuations. Perhaps a free zone west of the Rockies."

Fairfield's head lifted as the buzzing sound returned.

"Don't worry," Rance said absently, "they're over here all the time." His face was somber. "If we only had more. Trouble is, they might decide to rely on the ABM's. Worse, they might soon install ABM's here and they could bring it down over American soil. If we even had a little more information. What about the woman your brother spoke of? You thought she was coming out here?"

"Martha Adams? I don't know that she had anything to tell. That was one of Walt's notions. Her husband had worked on a lot of silo construction. But he most likely told her nothing about it. She's the sort of woman you'd expect to see at a country club, though she played at some job at the UN—cooked up for her by an old school friend, I think. I'm sure if she knew anything, she would have told me."

There certainly were a lot of helicopters about. Rance got up restlessly and was looking out of the small window of the cabin. "But you said Walt sent someone after her, to New York?"

"Yes. I don't know who it was. Some would-be Minute Man, perhaps. Walt thought they might join us, but nothing came of it. Martha could have come easily. With her UN papers she could travel anywhere."

"Perhaps not," Rance said. "With the new Regional barriers, she might find herself limited."

"Well, then, it looks as though we'll have to make do with what we've got."

"We will," Rance said. "We have a deadline."

"A deadline?"

Fairfield looked blank.

"About three weeks. I got it from one of my people, still in the GRU. October 26th is the cutoff date. Ulyanov is coming to preside over the official end of the United States. It's being carved up, parceled out and soon will be part of the United Socialist Regions of the Americas. Perez wants Florida directly for Cuba, but in any event it will be part of his sphere. Mexico, Texas and California will probably be merged in one Region. It's to be televised all over the world with great parade. It's a full dress affair with blacks, Indians, Eskimos brought in to thank the great Soviet Union for their freedom. They're making sure they save enough from the labor gangs. Once they've done that, I don't think they'll budge. They'll just go ahead and shoot down our tired old bird. After Ulyanov's speech, just for extra kicks, the Siberian complex is sending up their newest Soyuz maneuverable spaceship and orbital weapon system. Then we'll have as much chance as a snowball on an SS18."

John Fairfield suddenly looked old.

"So you see, John, whatever we do, it will have to be before then. But in those three weeks, your men should make a last sweep at any other possibilities. Even if we have to risk lives. I'll do what I can. I still have a few communication lines; a few contacts. Did you bring the lists I needed?"

"Yes." Fairfield took out the neat handwritten list from the pocket of his plaid shirt. Rance had to have these, though they worked strictly on a need-to-know system. "Most of the SAMSO men are probably dead, or if not in interrogation camps. Their names were filed where anyone could get at them."

Rance pulled a face. "So there's hardly a space or missile man left."

"These names are from Aerojet Solid Propulsion, Boeing, Chrysler Space, Pratt and Whitney, GE, Grumman, McDonnel Douglas, Rocketdyne and Rockwell, TRW, United Aircraft Research and Xerox. I've ticked off the ones I found and spoke to, but that's only a few. It's a forlorn hope, Clay, especially in three weeks."

"I'll do everything possible," Rance promised. "And I'll stay in touch. It's a nuisance, having to keep moving. I'm not used to it. It's a long time since I was in the field.

He shook hands with the elder man. "Keep your spirits up, John. And be careful. There's a lot of our people working for them, now. And by the way!" Rance was walking with him to the cabin door, "If you *should* hear anything from the Adams woman, I'd like to talk to her." He smiled. "Trained interrogator, you see. I might find out from your featherhead more than she knows she knows."

"Oh, she's not a featherhead," Fairfield said, without much attention. A helicopter was buzzing right overhead, it seemed. "Just a lady of the manor born out of her time. But I'll let you know—"

The noise grew louder. He had already opened the door, but he stopped instinctively. The helicopter was landing in a clearing not two hundred yards away. The pilot looked across at the cabin and gazed right at him.

Fairfield broke into a sweat and a fit of trembling. *I'm getting too old for this*, he thought quite distinctly.

"I'll cope," Rance said at once. He strode towards the helicopter with the air of a commanding officer, and barked at the pilot and a soldier who looked taken aback. They hardly put up much of an argument, and when Rance stepped back they took off meekly and flew away.

"What on earth . . ." Fairfield muttered as Rance returned. "What did you say?"

"Told them they weren't allowed here. Borunukov's private game preserve."

"Clay!" Fairfield gave a sudden whoop of laughter. "However did you think . . ."

"Easy," Rance said. "So happens the Great Borunukov does want to have a game and fishing preserve in the area. I have my ways of knowing . . . Just waiting for us to get out."

As Fairfield departed, he thought with admiration of his quick-witted colleague, with his sturdy courage and decisive manner. If only he himself—Then he remembered Rance's words. "You're the best chance we have, John." And in spite of his disquiet, he felt a certain glow.

—— XXVI ——

Sitting on the terrace of this gracious house, looking out over the softly rolling land of the Amish country, Martha, bathed, cleanly dressed, refreshed by a sleep that had lasted through a night and a morning, felt for a moment that she had dropped back into a lost world. She had been furious at having to come here and had argued hotly with Daniel. His caution and circuitous delays were unreasonable and maddening, driven as she was by a flailing sense of urgency.

He had been unmoved. "You're a very bad mouse, Mrs. Adams," he had said reproachfully and gone on with his plans.

Hans had looked at her sympathetically, but afterwards he said, "He's right, you know. He's the expert; he'll get us there. You and I," he smiled and shrugged. "We are merely parcels. Intelligent parcels, but parcels."

Martha remembered Buzz's angry words in New York. "I'm no package!" And she shared his feelings.

Her host appeared in the doorway. He did, indeed,

resemble Hans closely. They were first cousins. Fortunately, it was his mother who was a Meister; he was merely a Mr. Hoffman, a long time resident of the United States but still a German national and likely to remain, as yet, unmolested. It was this that had decided Daniel on making the detour.

"Dinner is ready, Mrs. Adams," Hoffman said.

The dining room was large, high-ceilinged, with portraits of Hoffman ancestors over the sideboards and the chimney piece. The china was set on the gleaming mahogany, and candles were lit. Martha thought for a moment of her old home in Litchfield, and wondered how the evacuee women and children were managing there—if they were still there. She had seen families of them on the road, being marched to some unknown destination.

The meal was delicious, well cooked and well served by the Hoffman housekeeper, a quiet, still handsome woman in her early fifties whose touch of African heritage was most noticeable in the richness of her voice. Hans was already at the table, and Daniel came in while their host was pouring sherry.

The housekeeper had brought Martha a long, silk skirt and a lace blouse that she could fit into with the help of a tuck at the waist. The clothes had belonged to the late Mrs. Hoffman, she had said, and the host would be honored if Mrs. Adams wore them. Martha's hair had grown too long to manage and she piled it on top of her head with the help of Mrs. Hoffman's hairpins, still sitting in a crystal box. Martha smiled: it was a long time since she had seen hairpins on a dressing table, not since her grandmother died. Even Daniel had taken some trouble with his appearance; from somewhere he had found a clean shirt and a dark jacket, not too well fitting, though he had not gone so far as to wear a tie.

"Sorry to be late," he said to his host. "Couldn't get the ink off." And he displayed his hands that were indeed still slightly stained.

While the housekeeper was serving, they spoke in generalities. Hans complimented Martha on her looks. She looked very striking with her well-coiffed hair and a string of borrowed Hoffman pearls around her neck. Mrs. Hoffman's slippers were pinching Martha's long feet but she decided that the pain was worth it for the courtly remarks.

Daniel was not courtly. He looked but said nothing. Probably he had no taste for make-believe. Hoffman mentioned that candles were growing scarce with the electricity cut off and the moments in another world ended.

The cousins chatted; Daniel looked preoccupied. He had been hard at work all day and his eyes were tired. Earlier he had taken Hans's car to a remote part of the Hoffman land and used the transmitter. He only did that in an emergency, she knew. He hadn't wanted to bring it at all.

Martha had been ready to leave the Corbett farm on the morning after their encounter with the police, as Daniel had ordered. Then he had disappeared. She had changed into her own jeans and a shirt, and had collected what was left of the things she had taken on the road. Already it seemed like months ago. Impatient, she had had to wait until Daniel returned, and they did not leave until the late afternoon.

"Trouble," he had said, briefly. "A good thing I took time to check. We can't get straight to Pittsburgh. Soviet troops have been moved in along the Western reaches of the Susquehanna."

He had looked at her. "Rumor has it that a group of men had collected there—women, too. Miners, National Guardsmen, nobody's quite sure who or what. The Citizen's Liberation Group, they called themselves. But they are, or were, armed. Poor devils. The Soviets moved in very fast. They used tactical atomic weapons to blast them out. So we have radioactivity in Pennsylvania after all. Though not from Three Mile Island." He had laughed, but it was a grim laugh and she hadn't cared to hear it.

"We'll take Hans's suggestion," he had said. "And go to his cousin." He produced papers for them all. A dairy farmer's for Hans—"You were trying to buy winter feed." He and Martha were a farm manager and his wife, returning home after being stranded in Northern Pennsylvania until they could get gas. "We were visiting your family."

She had wondered, then, how he got the papers, and looking at his harsh face, she had been reluctant to ask. But, as he so often did, he read her thoughts.

"No, I didn't take them by force from a helpless family. Live victims would report their loss; dead ones would cause a hue and cry. I have other methods." His mood switched, he looked amused. "It might ease your tender conscience to know that your companion is a well-trained forger. I was taught by Shalom Dani himself." He patted the heavy case he carried in his canvas bag. "Pandora's box. Cards, paper, inks. Pens, brushes. A great nuisance, except when I can travel as an artist. Which I used to do."

The name Shalom Dani had meant nothing to her then. Later she learned the pseudonym was that of Mossad's greatest forger, who had traveled himself with the Eichmann mission to provide them on the spot with any cover they might need.

Hans had used his own car, after they changed the plates and registration. "You should get the transmitter out," Daniel had said. "It's too dangerous."

"Not unless we use it," Hans protested. "They won't be looking for that. It was built into the dash by a genius. Me."

Daniel and Martha had used another car, an abandoned jalopy from Corbetts' graveyard, after cannibalizing a few other cars for parts. Martha had looked at it doubtfully but Daniel pronounced it serviceable.

"It can do anything except a New York pothole, lady," he had grinned, a taxi-driver once more.

The journey had been reasonably uneventful, for themselves. On the way they had seen labor gangs, mostly women, working on the roads. Some were pregnant, some were old. A white-haired woman dragged from her home, perhaps, before she had finished dressing, had only one shoe. The stocking on the shoeless foot had worn through; the toes were filthy, the heel streaked with blood.

Daniel had stayed off the main highway and they looped around Scranton to stay clear of the nuclear zone. As they rounded a bend they glimpsed, back from the road, a high wire fence topped with gun turrets. Another detention center. Martha imagined the inmates and thought of Buzz. Where was he? When would she see him again?

When they had arrived at the Amish country, Daniel remarked that there they would be reasonably safe. "The Amish are organized. Peaceful but fighters when necessary, I hear. So at first they will leave them alone. After a time, if we don't succeed, they will be wiped out, of course," he said.

"But we will succeed," Martha's voice was cold and her chin tilted upwards.

"Yes, Mrs. Strongjaw," he had said, amused. "We will."

The meal set out in the Hoffman dining room was adequate for all, though there was no meat. The small fish, caught in a local stream by Hoffman himself, were augmented by fresh vegetables and the housekeeper had made a shoo-fly pie. When dinner was over, Hoffman led the party to a drawing-room, served them brandy and then sat down at the grand piano. He played a group of Chopin nocturnes. He played well, Martha thought, and his interpretation was sensitive. The only candles in the room were on the piano, and melancholy came with the music.

The little concert was lightened when he turned to

Lieder, and to the surprise of the guests the house-keeper, who had joined them, began singing with the ease and confidence of a professional. When it was over she accepted their applause and praise, and retired.

"I must go too," Hoffman said. "I will leave you to your talk. Help yourselves to the brandy." Martha thanked him for his hospitality and the music. "Mrs. Johnson is remarkable, isn't she?" he said. "She was with my wife for many years. My wife recognized her talent and found her a good teacher. If she had been younger, she might have made a career of it. I've been a lucky man," he added, quietly. He looked up at the portrait of his wife. "If it was all over for me tomorrow, I couldn't complain. This country has been kind to a former enemy. I wish I could do more."

"You're doing enough," Daniel said. Hoffman had gone into town that day and bought supplies from a list that Daniel had given him; he had presented them with hundreds of dollars in the new red currency, and he had given his cousin his papers, keeping the forged copies for himself. "I shan't be going anywhere for a time," he had said. "And the real thing will be the safest for you."

Martha sat at Mrs. Hoffman's dressing table, trying to undo the clasp of the pearls. A tapping sound came from her door, and she paused, startled. She had heard no one approach. Of course. . . she smiled a little. Only Daniel walked as lightly as an Indian.

"Give me a hand," she said, her head bowed.

As he dealt with the clasp she was very aware of his touch on the nape of her neck. She was afraid she might blush, and hoped desperately that he wouldn't notice her confusion. "Do you like my hair this way?" she asked hurriedly, trying to sound normal.

His eyes met hers in the glass. His lips were pursed. "You look like a stranger, Mrs. A." His manner was somber. "Anyway, it has to come off. Give yourself a boyish cut. Military style. I'll do it if you can't manage. And rinse it with this."

He reached inside his jacket for a small package and placed it on the dressing table. "You'll need warm water. The housekeeper will bring you some first thing in the morning. We'll make an early start."

He turned and left. She felt oddly deflated. Getting to work at once, she snipped at her hair until it was a little shorter than Buzz's. Observing the result she was surprised to see how much she resembled Buzz—he had always looked like Josh. Family resemblances were so strange, though they were hardly a family any more. Depressed, she turned to Mrs. Hoffman's bed, and then started. Lying across the white counterpane was a long spray of flowers. She picked it up, puzzled. Daniel? Daniel must have left it. Could it be some amorous, courting gesture? A tribute, a consolation—a joke? The tiny lavender flower clusters on the long stems were fuzzy and rough, a roadside weed. Of course, jopey-weed they called it at home. How like Daniel, to give a fond token of jopey-weed. She was smiling when she went to bed but she dreamed of weeds in gloomy churchyards, thrusting themselves up between dank bones.

In the morning she sat in the car, her damp hair wrapped in an old scarf, as Daniel laughed and joked on the steps with the housekeeper. She had brought out a beautifully-packed lunch basket. "There's a thermos of hot coffee," she said with a smile.

"Thanks, Ophie," Daniel said, patting her hand.

Hans, just about to step into his car, raised his eyebrows. "Ophie! But nobody is allowed to call her that."

Daniel apparently was; the woman was still smiling.

"Ophelia," Hans explained. "She hates her name. But our friend has all the women eating out of his hand. Lucky fellow. What use was it," he grumbled, "when we all followed the advertisements and had a bright toothpaste smile and wore a dashing eau-de-cologne, when what the ladies like is that little monkey of a man?

My bed was comfortable, but I wonder where he spent the night."

He went on joking, but Martha listened no more. She was glad when they pulled away, not only because of her sense of urgency, never stilled, but because the peace and graciousness of her temporary haven struck her now with a false note, as though it were a mockery of calm against the background of detention camps and roads where pregnant women and old people labored. She felt relief at riding into decent danger once again.

Virinsky, who had been early at work in his office, was coldly furious. He was expecting Perez, who had come to New York the night before for the meeting, but he would not be there for hours. Perez was not habitually an early riser. The hero of the Caribbean, Borunukov joked, must have directed his battles from his bed. Ulyanov, learning of the remark, had retorted that he didn't care if Perez fought from the lavatory—at least he won.

Perez's lateness was not the cause of Virinsky's wrath. Although so much of the day-to-day running of the country had devolved upon his organization, it was not much more than Virinsky had expected, and he had prepared long ago. From the day of the surrender, he had begun to change what had been the UN Secretariat building into a government headquarters. The military were handled by Borunukov's men in Hall City. Perez had been dismantling the old government structures there. Dismantling. Even Virinsky's still features twitched into a grimace as he thought of the activities covered by that sober word. Perez's shooting parties that disposed of Congressmen and administrators had already earned him the name, "Amin of the Potomac."

Everything else however, all serious business of state, was being done here in the UN Secretariat building. Some of the Secretariat's former work was parceled out into various empty government buildings in Manhattan and the outer boroughs. The Trusteeship Council still met in the adjacent building and talked of Indian affairs, much televised. They had had to forget South Africa, for the Politburo had voted that that strategically-placed, rich nation should be left alone until its fate was settled in a Soviet, not an African takeover. Other councils and agencies were being ruthlessly cut down and needed little space. Much of the charade was therefore no longer necessary, and now there was no longer a compliant United States to pay an elephant's share of the cost.

Nor was it, precisely, the fear of Magnanimity that had brought him to this point of rage. The KGB investigation, (the extent of which he had kept secret, despite all agreements, from Perez and the still absent Borunukov) had the problem almost completely solved. "Not *Magna*," his informant had told him. "I had been certain that could not be. *I would have known. Mini*, rather," and he had laughed.

Virinsky was inclined to believe him. But they could not be certain. There was still a missing piece. For the hidden installations that had been discovered and seemed to comprise the misnamed Magnanimity project had no official existence. None of the men and women he had rounded up from all the Reagan construction projects had known of them. The woman Huff had never inspected one. Only the wife of the president of the Columbia Construction Company had ever heard the name. Therefore much data was unaccountably missing, and the existence of more secret installations could not be ruled out. The only possible lead was the Adams woman, and she had disappeared from the face of the earth. The Adams woman, that insolent redhead, whom he had had tight in his hand was still at large. *This* was what made him tense with fury.

Only two people in his organization knew that the Adams woman had been identified, Thu Thuy and Madame Paul. Neither of them could be suspected of alerting the woman. And so what had made her run? He thought for a moment, and then buzzed for Thu Thuy.

"Find out from Madame Paul if anyone informed on the Adams woman," he said. "And if there were any informers, have them brought in."

In his first rage at the Adams woman's escape, he had sent Madame Paul to a detention camp, where she got a taste of what she could expect if her work failed to please. True, she was a French national but that would be of little importance soon. On the latest map of the New Order in Europe, already prepared in Moscow, France had shrunk to a small place in the sun. Too unreliable, like the not entirely quiescent English, with that irritating little Nelson fleet.

However, he had come to forgive Madame Paul her lapse. No one else was so efficient; no one else could get as much useful work from her staff. Nor could he trust anyone else with the high-level security work she handled. Thu Thuy had made her look foolish, but in truth, a woman who was working so hard and long, and was responsible for as many different projects as Madame Paul, simply could not think of everything. Women's spite. Thu Thuy, who looked so much like a child, was a woman. Her body, now familiar territory, excited him no more; the wisps of pubic hair were repulsive. A woman after all, an unclean beast. Yesterday he had glimpsed by the bank of elevators a blonde girl; the daughter, he had discovered, of a Swedish delegate. An angelic creature, just nine-years-old . . .

Perez entered at last, half an hour late for his appointment, and unshaven. He had been tasting the delights of the city. A few pleasures remained for the right people. The theaters were closed, but some actresses were allowed to perform privately. Perez had taken over the top floors of a famous skyscraper for a party, and Virinsky already had a report of his activities.

"Sorry," he said, and to Virinsky's fury, tossed his cap on the computer terminal. "I had to come all the way from the foot of this island." He rubbed his head and winced.

Virinsky was unusual for a Russian in that he did not share the common desire for alcohol. But he used that desire. He needed all his wits to get through his business with Perez, who though momentarily sluggish, was no fool. They managed to get through the day's work well enough.

Perez, who in Borunukov's absence saw himself as virtual dictator of the United States, was bored with detail and willing to let Virinsky run the bureaucracy which was merging neatly with the police forces. Perez was interested in the military, and Virinsky was obliging as he overlooked that part of Perez's proposals which meant a usurpation of the powers of Marshal Borunukov. He did not have to sign any orders, he reflected, and whenever it suited him he could see that Borunukov was informed. And the two could quarrel as much as they liked.

Perez was inveighing against the stupidity of Borunukov's generals. They had used atomic weapons to handle that tiny group of men on the Susquehanna who were armed with nothing larger than machine-guns. "If they do that in every little outbreak, this country will be good for nothing."

Virinsky agreed. It had been just that kind of mindless destruction he had been intent on avoiding. But the army had its prerogatives.

"There are a lot of people to feed in the world," Perez said. It was one of his most repeated public remarks.

"Yes, you and me," Virinsky said. He wasn't given to humor and for a moment Perez stared in surprise. Then he laughed.

"Ah, you are realistic, *amigo*," he said. He looked more comfortable, demanded black coffee and stretched his legs, setting his boots on Virinsky's desk.

Virinsky ignored this second injury. "I think we should change this arrangement concerning the former National Guard," he said, getting back to business. The Guard had been turned into a national police force, with KGB officers. "It is not working well. These young men are not responding to the situation. I would suggest, after their present assignments are completed, we disband them and send them to work on the wire?"

Perez agreed at once. "Yes. They were untrained, undisciplined, spoiled civilians. As a group they couldn't be useful now. And there have been cases where, as they put it, they've been fragging the geeks."

Virinsky knew about the murder of the KGB officials and other Soviet officers. Borunukov had used public hangings. And he knew the term fragging from the Vietnam days. But geeks?

"A stupid sort of word play," Perez said. "On *Komitet Gosudarstvennoi Bezopasnosti.*"

Virinsky understood. In the Soviet Union, people— even some KGB men—ironically referred to the KGB as the "crude bandits."

"It is also," Perez added, rather enjoying himself, "a carnival term for entertainers of the lowest intellect. They bite the heads off chickens. My men can take over such installations and equipment as they have. It's not much," he concluded, casually.

The Under-Secretary paused. That was not at all what he had in mind. His own men were already in charge, and Kharkev was sending him five more battalions.

"They can work under your officers, *amigo.*"

Perez was being unusually agreeable, but Virinsky still didn't care for the idea.

"We will need all of your men, I'm afraid, in the West and in disaffected areas of the South. Borunukov would bungle it, as, in my opinion, he bungled Afghanistan."

"You mean a few hillbillies and the Minute Men in the Rockies? We could move in now and handle them."

Virinsky wondered whether he had got the information from his own people or from his spies in the Pentagon.

"Not just yet," Virinsky said. "We will draw up all the pus and then we'll drain the wound."

Perez was satisfied. His men were busy enough in the Florida land program; the growers had been recalcitrant about turning over the groves and fields, and had shown little appetite for laboring under the new owners. Kulaks. They should have been killed at once, but Ulyanov himself had wanted them spared for a time until their knowledge, methods and organization were understood.

"It is not good Marxist theory," he had told his protégé, "so I could not say it to Kautsky." Kautsky was the doctrinal purist on the Politburo. "But Kautsky has never produced much in the way of vegetables or fruit."

The items on the agenda had been completed. Perez looked over at Virinsky, a great white slug of a man, he thought, but very useful. "Any more on the Magna business?" he asked.

"Nothing very much," Virinsky said smoothly. "I begin to doubt all this Aharit-Ha-Yamim nonsense." That was true and both men felt an identical sense of relief and disappointment.

"*Adios.*" Perez took himself off. Virinsky wondered what pleasures he had in store. Well, anything he wished, as long as he failed to notice how little work of importance he had left to do in Hall City.

At once, the Under-Secretary pressed his buzzer and had the Chief of Region II KGB brought in from the waiting room and gave him an unpleasant twenty minutes. How was it possible that Mrs. Martha Adams had escaped from the city, let alone the Region, and if she was still in the Region, how was it that she had not been found?

The Chief's excuses, that the wiring was not complete, that fingerprint checks could not be installed on every country lane, that the woman might have escaped before the arrest order came down, did not save him from Virinsky's wrath.

"You have the photograph. You can check all transportation. You have the whole police forces of the country at your disposal. But you cannot find one redheaded woman."

"Redheads are trouble, *amigo*." To Virinsky's annoyance, Perez was back, once again walking in without a by-your-leave. He flicked up his cap. "I forgot it," he said with a smile meant perhaps to be ingratiating. Virinsky at once suspected that he knew of his appointment with his Region Chief and wished to spy. Now he was there, Virinsky could hardly order him out, and the Chief, too nervous and excited for good sense, was going on with his apologia.

"We did pick up one thing from Region III, but it might have no connection. A group of local police in a town called Wappasening Falls went out on a sweep and search for illegal transmitters, the small CB's, that are very prevalent there. On one of the premises they found a woman called Mrs. Dulcie Corbett. They were surprised because a Mrs. Dulcie Corbett had been stopped by police on an illegal radio charge just two days before, but that was a different woman, a redhead, who might fit our description."

Virinsky was instantly alert.

"There's more, but not much. On the night before the raid, two other men had been to the Corbett place, with an arrest warrant for a Corbett boy evading the conscription. On the way, they almost tripped over a couple making love in the grass. Again, the description of the woman fitted—as much of her as they could see."

"And your men passed her by," Virinsky said sourly.

"The special All-Region alert was not out then, the one with the photograph," the Chief said. "These men were Americans, local country policemen. A proper investigating team was sent, but by then the man and

woman had disappeared, with another man, it seems. A
foreigner, they were told. The people on the farm
seemed to know little about any of them. Apparently
they are simple-minded. Religious fanatics and useless
mouths. All they knew about either man was that the
younger one had been there before and he had made
love to at least one of the women. This redhead was
supposedly his wife. Oh, yes. They believe he is a
salesman and they called him Harry Daniel."

"What was the description of this man?" Perez asked,
with a quick interest.

"Well, it was hard for the police to say," the Chief said
uncomfortably. "In those circumstances. They said about
five ten and a half, a light build—agile—dark hair."

Perez turned to Virinsky. "It's an old Mossad trick,"
he said. "The couple making love. Surprising how many
otherwise good security men will pass them by. I wonder. We've never had much of a description of Bar-Lev.
He's believed to be an expert in disguise. But the
height . . . I think it *could be*."

He looked at Virinsky speculatively. "If this redheaded woman is someone of importance . . .?"

It was at that moment the call came through from
Kharkev. It took Virinsky by surprise, for it was now
one a.m. Moscow time and Kharkev would be expected
to be fast asleep at that hour. Perez did not offer to
leave him in privacy; he merely wandered over to the
window and stared down at the river.

Virinsky was obliged to report that he had not found
the missile corresponding to the description of a doomsday weapon. Kharkev already knew of the others. "But
it appears now that the Aharit-Ha-Yamim business was
merely a tall tale," he added.

"A tall tale?" The two men had always been on good
terms, and Kharkev had never used that tone to the
man who would be his successor. The cutting edge
reminded Virinsky that Kharkev was still the Politburo
member and active head of the KGB while Virinsky was

merely his appointed Department chief. "Are you mad? Let me tell you that information was elicited from one of old Begin's men that Aharit-Ha-Yamim was everything we believed it to be, though he knows nothing of the technology—ignorant old fool. And the missile was built and shipped to the United States. We have it from one of our informants in BOSS. It was built at Valindaba, and the missile technology alone was something completely new. The South Africans were trying to get it for themselves. The head of our Ninth Department is being replaced and is now under arrest for his previous gross laxity in this matter, although South Africa was never easy prey like the United States. A tall tale . . ." He sputtered as though his rage was boiling over. "I tell you, Virinsky, there is consternation here, about the weapon, and your failure. America seems to be having a strange effect on some of our best men."

Perez, who had ambled forward, peered surreptitiously at Virinsky's face. The expression was impassive, but he saw the sweat on the brow. Obviously, then, they had both been wrong about Magna. The monster was alive and unconfined. The two joint Chiefs of State of the Americas gazed at each other and for a moment both were caught up in a great wave of fear.

—— XXVII ——

It took all of ten hours, by Daniel's route, to get from the Hoffman place to Pittsburgh, and then Martha found that they were not in the town proper and certainly not at the Greater Pittsburgh International Airport. Instead, she was in a neighboring town called McKeesport, in a small frame house, where Daniel proposed to leave her with Hans.

Martha felt ready to explode with frustration. From the time they had crossed into Region III, Pennsylvania, they had done nothing but circle, chasing their own tails. Perhaps it had been necessary for Daniel to go north to meet Hans Meister, but certainly she could have gone on alone. Then the endless poking about on small roads, making detours round areas with the slightest possibility of a lingering taint of radiation . . . One might think there was no urgency in their mission; that the country was not every day more and more driven under the relentless lash. But Daniel merely said, "You'll be a terrible nuisance if you're sick, Mrs. A."

By now she was accustomed to the severities of traveling with Daniel. Even if they passed an eating place that still remained open, they could not enter. Nor could she avail herself of any ladies' room. His instructions on that point were brief and hardly polite.

"Every time you stop in a place like that, there will be a few people who remember you. Your height, weight, regional accent. Leaving a trail to be followed."

She accepted that as she must. In this escape she was like a rookie in the company of an experienced soldier. A parcel, just as Hans had said. But she had to hope that her postmaster really comprehended the need for haste.

"Is this a safe-house?" she had asked, with vague memories of spy tales, when they arrived at the suburban dwelling. Daniel had roared with laughter.

"No, it's a dentist's house," he said. "Mossad keeps no safe-houses in the United States, Mrs. Adams." He did not depress her spirits by telling her that it was already rare to find even an acquaintance or possible ally left at liberty. "In this case," he told her cheerfully, "We improvise."

"Then why are we here?"

"Because I've met this dentist, and he's a good man," Daniel said. "I stopped at his clinic once when I was passing through and he fixed a bad tooth. We talked. I know a good man when I see one. He'll put you up and not ask questions."

The dentist was there, shrunken and bowed with age, but his eyes were keen and clear. He greeted them with courtesy, offered them food and rooms to sleep in. "My family is all gone," he explained, "and so there is only me here." He had had to close his clinic; his young partner and his nurses had all been sent elsewhere, but he kept a small office in what had once been his wife's parlor.

Daniel had not paused after the first greeting, but

had vanished into the night. Martha vented some of her wrath against his cavalier behavior in an outpouring to the sympathetic Hans.

He smiled. "He's an amazing man. He always has a hatful of alternative plans. I was supposed to fly from Toronto straight to Boulder, Colorado, Denver being heavily populated by "the friendly ones" right now."

Martha remembered the Titan missile plant there. Not that it had had much business in recent years. Perhaps the Russians planned to get it going again.

"Then I got a message saying that would be unsafe. I was to go by road to New York State and wait in a town called Waverly on the Pennsylvania border to be radioed in." He began to laugh. "Who but Daniel could have found a family like the Corbetts? But he does, each knowing him with a different name, a different occupation. The Corbetts thought he was a salesman of ladies underwear. He uses almost no professional acquaintances. I think that's his strength. Just odd friends, fond ladies, even very decent dentists, as you see. Though I would take a guess that our present host suspects and approves his present line of business. Daniel knows how to survive. For himself, and for us, too."

Martha was silenced, but before she went to bed that night she learned a little more about Hans Meister. "Our friend will get us where we want to go, I think, and perhaps even get us out. Not that that's so important, to me."

She paused at the foot of the stairs, with her hand on the old newel post, in silence, waiting for the confidence that was to come.

"The time I spent at Peenemunde," he said at last. "It was my work. I could say, and did, that I had no choice but to work for Hitler. Now, I have a choice. I take it. Perhaps it will wipe my slate clean."

Martha reached out and pressed his shoulder gently. He had the look of a man who had thrown off a burden.

She lay on the bed, but she did not sleep. It was as well, because three hours later she heard the sound of a motor. Daniel was back and tapping at the door.

"We're in luck," he said. They sat in the small room that had been allotted to Martha alone, a boy's room at one time. A stereo set filled a stack of shelves; pictures of rock stars and ballplayers on yellowing paper lined the walls. "There are two transports going out to Boulder, the day after tomorrow. The National Guard are using the Air Reserve base."

From a canvas sack he pulled out two sets of fatigues, socks and shoes, as well as a few big commercial-size tins of frankfurters and baked beans and a bag of coffee beans. "Can't eat Dr. Weicker's food. He only has one civilian ration and it's not much. His patients bring him bits and pieces, I think."

Hans looked with interest. "And what did you give in exchange for these goods?"

"Some of your brother's money, and most of your cigarettes. Better for your lungs."

Although Daniel spoke jestingly, Martha thought he was not pleased by this good luck. He fidgeted about, not lighting anywhere as her mother-in-law would have phrased it, always a sign that he was disturbed.

"You think we'll have trouble getting out?" she said.

"Not after I've set it up. No, it's just that we're too lucky. I don't like it."

He was speaking more to Hans than to herself. "I didn't want to use this bit of a base, but there wasn't much choice. But we could have waited weeks, months, before they used it for Colorado at all. I thought we'd have to land somewhere and make two, possibly three hops. But no, they've been sending a steady stream of men out there. It looks like they might be onto our friends."

"Satellite pictures," Hans said with resignation. "They get better all the time. And the last one they sent up is nothing compared to the new Soyuz they have ready. With its photo-reconnaissance equipment, they'll be able to read a driver's licence, except on foggy days."

"Well, then," Martha said, "the sooner we get there the better."

Daniel nodded. "In the meantime we'll fit the uniforms, and dye Hans's hair. Younger than springtime you might be," he told him, "But with that hair you'd be hard to pass off as a junior officer, and I didn't see anyone over the rank of captain going out with the men. A real bit of luck is that the officers are Russians and assigned from a transit pool as the men come in, so that when they see you, transformed, they won't know the difference."

Hans, quickly understanding what was being proposed, expostulated with vehemence. "*Gott in Himmel!* My knowledge of Russian is guidebook and what I picked up on a sales trip to Moscow."

"We'll manage," Daniel said. "Don't worry. Get some sleep."

The next morning he recut the fatigues quite expertly and handed them to Martha to sew. As he ripped open the shoulder and added some padding she asked him, "And was your father a tailor, also?"

"No," he said, removing the pins from his mouth. "My grandfather."

"What's that for?" she asked, regarding a strip of flannel a yard and a half long and about six inches wide.

"You'll see before we go."

"What about the officer's uniform?" she said.

He held up a warning hand. "Don't worry, Mrs. Adams. My father, God rest his soul, spoke Yiddish. In Yiddish there are many wise sayings, also jokes. The Jews were often poor, but at Passover, which we call Pesach, they are required to eat matzos. I don't sup-

pose you know that, but it is important. Often there
was no money for matzos," he said, "but the good Jew
would say, in faith and hope, 'Pesach will come and
matzos will come.'"

He grinned at some private joke, looked at the waist-
band of the trousers and added another pin.

"I get the idea," Martha said. "We have a saying too.
'Take no thought of the morrow, What ye shall eat
and what ye shall drink. Consider the lilies of the
field . . .'"

"Who would say that? A Jewish boy," Daniel was
placid. "But no lilies today. Work, work."

He left her to work and was gone all that day, much
of the night and most of the next day. When he returned he told them they must be at the field at four
o'clock the following morning.

"There'll be plenty of electric light there so I have to
turn you into a military man," he told Martha.

He was also an expert with makeup, she saw. With
a few tiny touches he subtly altered the look of
her face. "That jaw helps," he said. "The neck is the
problem."

When she was ready to dress, he told her to take off
her bra and brought out the strip of flannel. Her eyes
widened and she flushed when she saw his purpose.
"Start it yourself," he said resignedly and turned his
face away. "But it has to be firm and tight. I'll pin the
back. You're going to be jammed in a plane with a
group of men and if any of them bump up against you,
you don't want to be betrayed because of a silly fit of
modesty. You're very out of date, Mrs. A."

Hans was in the dentist's chair. Martha had to help as
nurse while his mouth was well packed and his cheek
protruded nicely. No speech could be expected now of
this Russian officer. He was groaning, for Dr. Weicker
had made a convincing cut in his gum.

"A nasty abcess, that was," he said, giving it a profes-

sional scrutiny. His photograph on the wall showed a
tall man, solidly built, smiling amid his nurses in his
clinic. Now the man in this small parlor had lost not
only much of his flesh, but his very bones had shrunk
away. All that was left was the intelligence to know his
danger in aiding these odd strangers and the will to go
on. Martha's eyes stung.

She had been bitter about the men she had heard in
the train to Bridgeport, eager to serve the new masters.
She had lost respect for those like Greg Maynard who
would not fight; she had nearly despaired when Senator
Webster did not rush off to form an opposition. Now
she knew of the boys of Williamsburg, the heroes of the
Susquehanna, the brotherhood of youths like Buzz linked
in rebellion across the country, the Minute Men in the
Rockies' fastness. And men like this. Dr. Weicker was
almost too frail to strike a barking dog, but he was
strong enough to do his part in driving the enemy from
his country. Courage still lived in this land.

Then she was groaning as she had to put stuffing
round her feet in the army issue shoes; the smallest size
had been too big. She doubted that she appeared a very
credible soldier. On the other hand, Hans, she thought,
apart from his swollen cheek, made a most imposing
captain.

"KGB," he said, looking down at the uniform that
Daniel had brought back with him that night.

"That's who they send out with the Guard," Daniel
told him. "These are your papers."

"How did you know who was going on what flight?"
Martha said curiously, after Hans had gone to collect
his kit.

"A glance at the manifest while I was talking to the
clerk-sergeant," he said.

"And they just let a stranger wander about, peeking
here and there and . . ."

"Who's a stranger?" Daniel said. "He knows me like

a brother. I'm the guy who steals a little here, trades a little there. The army knows guys like that the way a housewife knows the man who comes to read the meter. Not always the same one, but there always is one. I sold him a bottle of Canadian rye that our Hans was hogging for a few of those nearly worthless redbacks."

"And the papers and the uniform?"

"You ask too many questions, Mrs. Adams."

There was a remoteness about him now that she had seen before, the night he had killed the youth in the cellar in Newark. He looked past her, to Hans Meister coming down the stairs into the light of the hall lamp.

"I'd better touch up your eyebrows," he told him, and Daniel and Martha spoke no more until they were getting into the long, black limousine.

"You drive," he told Martha. "I'll direct you. Officer in the back."

With a flourish, he opened the car door for Hans.

"I'll show the papers when we're stopped," he said, "and I'll do all the talking. If anyone speaks to you, look stupid."

After a time he added quietly, for Martha's ears. "The fatigues you're wearing really did come from stores."

Martha felt a relief that she knew, sadly, was out of place in this war. What will we become before we've finished? she wondered. And yet, without Magnanimity, Americans were without hope. And when men are hopeless, they can be enslaved.

It was a nerve-racking ride. Martha had papers in the pocket of her fatigues, but she remembered what Daniel had said about hands. "Surely there might be some women in the Guard?" she had said.

"A woman draws too much attention," he answered and that had been that. She had square-cut her nails and hoped for the best. But she still sweated a little at each traffic light.

Once they were on the highway, she breathed easier for a while. Traffic was light, mostly military convoys, the lines of heavy trucks rolling steadily. As they came into town, she saw tugs chugging away on the river. An old ferry was tied up peacefully at its mooring. They passed several bridges but Daniel kept her in the main traffic lane. Then they arrived at a major junction. As she turned onto a broad bridge they were pulled up for a paper check. Daniel showed all their papers, with the officer's prominently displayed, and jerked his thumb towards the back of the car. They were waved on at once, with the convoy held up to let them pass. The same treatment was accorded them at the tunnel and Martha breathed more easily as they wound up the hill on the expressway.

Following Daniel's directions, Martha turned off at the exit for the airport, looping round the expressway, and stopping at the light as they came to the crossing. A sentry was at the side of the road and there was another check; this time Daniel just waved the papers as the light was changing. But the sentry motioned them to stay where they were and stepped towards them. Martha's mouth went dry.

"Take a left," he directed, "then the entrance is to the right. You can follow the trucks moving in there. You'll see the hangars and the runway."

Daniel nodded and they went off before the light changed again.

"Usually two officers go out with each plane load," he informed Hans. "But the pilots are American and they won't ask questions. They've learned not to. They'll just check your papers. Most of them hang out in the shed and they just join the men as they board. Hold the handkerchief to your jaw."

The part of the airport they came to had nothing of the familiar bustle of peacetime aviation. There were a few hangars and sheds; convoys of National Guardsmen lounged by the tarmac, with instructions coming from loudspeakers. In the floodlights were a couple of DC 3's, sitting on their tails; a huge transport, crammed with men, already taxiing onto the runway, and a small cargo plane, an old turbo-prop at which Daniel was looking with displeasure. Men were already boarding, and at the appearance of the officer one of the men gave a shout to the pilot, who began warming the engines.

"My officer's not going up in this dying duck," Daniel told the traffic manager. "This flight's for Boulder, you guys must be nuts."

"Well, if it's Marshal Borunukov, he can't get craft we haven't got. This is a Reserve field, it ain't Andrews. We've been shipping guys out to Boulder for days, and half our maintenance crews are working over in the main airport. They're ripping the guts out of passenger planes to make more troop carriers. So there ain't no executive class, sergeant. If the Captain don't like it, he can wait until 16.00 hours and . . ."

"Orders," Daniel said, gloomily.

"Well, then, get your ass in there. You're late for takeoff already."

Daniel's face was longer than ever. "Christ. The Captain's been tearing my liver out as it is. By the time his butt gets mashed up there he'll put us on dog biscuit."

"Don't tell me your troubles," the other man said wearily. "He can take it or leave it. Where's his sidekick, anyway?"

"Are you asking me?" Daniel said, walking away. "Borunukov forgot to write. Maybe they're running short of big, shiny officers. Maybe some guys have been fragging their geeks. I'll tell him you're not satisfied."

The manager told him where he would like him to go and they joined the men on the plane. Hans made a convincing pantomime of disgust as he strode up to take his place by the pilot. It served to distract the men from Martha and her clumsy gait. They easily accepted the Captain's total lack of interest in them or anything about them as normal. Martha guessed that the work of officers was actually done now by non-coms; the KGB men were merely police. Hans, she noticed now, was carrying a nasty-looking weapon like the KG9—a machine-gun type of pistol. The Guardsmen were not armed, as yet.

She looked round the dimly-lit cabin for Daniel, but he had taken a place near "his officer." She strapped herself into a seat on the side of the plane against the bare ribs. No one was taking notice of her; their attention was on their own concerns. She pulled her cap down over her face and pretended to sleep, but she could hear the excited, young voices.

"It's Boulder, I tell you. I heard it from the pilot. He was talking to the tower. Most of it's been taken over for the military. I bet there ain't much left of Colorado Springs."

"Just like I said, Charlie. We're goin' in there. And it's still as hot as a fried egg."

"Nah, we're not goin' anywhere hot. We've got the geek with us, right?" They glanced at Hans, remote and stiff.

"They won't send us into Springs." A confident voice. At the Last Trump there would always be one young man who knew all about it. "They're using civilians for clean-up work now. They want us fightin' men to fight."

"Hell. I'm a shoe salesman. All I can fight is feet. I had exactly six weeks training in total. Who are we supposed to be fighting in Colorado? Indians?"

The soldier who knew it all bent a little closer. "Word is some units didn't surrender. Holed up . . ."

"Shut your face, Charlie. The geek can hear us."

"The hell he can. They don't understand much anyway. But those guys out west must be crazy. Did you hear what happened to those dummies on the Susquehanna? They nuked 'em, by God. I talked to a guy from B company and he'd met someone from the burial detail and he said they burned out the place."

"Not half as hot as the Springs'll be. If we get sent in there . . ."

"Say, Footsie, I wonder why there's only one geek. They always go in pairs."

"Maybe they're runnin' short. Or maybe we're such a great, trustworthy group. Ready for promotion to full geek rank like that monkey up there, holding his face."

"I'll believe it when I see my pay come in more than ration stamps."

"I tell you though," Footsie's voice was a whisper. "If they try and send us into the Springs I think I might . . ."

"All right, enough." The soldier with a stripe had an anxious look. "Get some sleep now, all of you. It might be the last you get for a while."

When the plane lifted off Martha felt a great sense of relief. As the hours passed, flying in the darkness, surrounded by unknown men, it seemed she was moving into another world. But overriding any other sensation was a surging sense of joy that at last she was moving towards Magnanimity. It was the beginning of the end.

Sometime in the night Daniel moved through the rows of sleeping men and paused, giving her a cigarette. Charlie and Footsie were snoring, and under the cover of their snorts and whines Martha asked softly, "Did they really take out Colorado Springs?"

Daniel shook his head. "Didn't have to. Just took out their sensors and left them blind. It's occupied already. Even if they'd wanted to drop a few big ones there, they wouldn't have done it. It would have poisoned all of Kansas and the wheat crop with it."

When he took his place again near Hans, Martha closed her eyes, sure that she would never sleep. But it was two hours later when she was awakened by sounds coming from the men at the controls. Even in her sleep Martha had picked up the voices almost blanketed by the engines' throb. The radio operator was talking to Hans.

"A message from base, sir. We've been rerouted to Region IX, South. The men's orders are changed for New Camp."

Daniel leaned over Hans and murmured in something that might have been Russian. Hans made a barking noise. "The Captain wants to know what kind of transport will be waiting for him," Daniel reported.

The operator murmured for a time and then reported, "Two trucks will be made ready to take the men into camp, sir. There'll be another officer waiting to take over these men. Captain Boychenko will return to Pittsburgh with us."

Hans and Daniel murmured together.

"Radio for a car to stand by for the Captain. He will take his own driver. You will inform me of takeoff time as soon as possible after landing."

The men had woken also, with a swift awareness of pending disaster. While Martha was puzzling out Region IX South—that would be Arizona—she heard the news flowing from seat to seat in a wave reaching the tail of the aircraft.

"New Camp? Where the hell's that?"

"They're taking the geek off. It don't look good."

"Aw, Footsie, you didn't want to go into Springs. We ain't goin' into Springs and you're still crabbin'."

"Maybe Footsie's got a right to be crabbin'. It don't sound so hot to me, either."

"Maybe it's hot all right," Footsie sounded gloomier than ever. "Too hot for the geek. If we see one of our non-coms take over, you can bet we're goin' in to get fried."

It was eight in the morning when they landed. Blinking, tired and cramped, the men were ordered to wait by the tarmac. Two trucks were standing in readiness, but the acting officer had not yet arrived. A car was waiting for Captain Boychenko, and Martha marched over to the driver's seat, feeling the envious eyes on her back. Her mind was whirling. This was Williams AFB—Chandler, Southern Arizona. She had yet to cross the border into Utah. And Buzz Fairfield and his men were still waiting for her in Boulder, Colorado. Her physical discomfort was pressing. On the plane the door of the toilet had been insecure and she had not dared to use it. Yet she was in a sweat to leave, before someone suspected Hans, or a check was made why only one KGB officer was returning.

Daniel was at the car door, speaking to Hans in Russian. Then he turned to Martha, with a voice loud enough to be heard at a distance. "I have to make a call for the Captain. Back in a minute."

He disappeared into the communication shack. On the way out he stopped by the soldier called Footsie. Martha couldn't see Daniel's face as he spoke, but she saw Footsie's. The young face had looked drawn in the bright sunlight, now it turned white. He nodded and spoke to the corporal. Martha watched the men piling into the back of the trucks, while Footsie and the corporal took the wheels. No one else seemed to be paying attention as they rolled off to the gates.

Captain Boychenko's car moved up behind them.

The guard looked at the corporal's orders. "Rerouted to New Camp," he said.

Hans, with an imperious gesture, waved them on.

The guard stepped back and let them pass. They drove out at a good pace, but as soon as they were out of sight they slowed down. Daniel jumped out and spoke rapidly to the corporal. The trucks then took an eastward fork in the road and Daniel gave the men his usual salute of farewell.

"Where are they going?" Martha demanded.

Daniel shrugged. "To steal some other transport, I don't doubt, and clothes. To try to get lost somewhere. That New Camp was near Tucson—whatever's left of Tucson with Davis-Monthan gone. These men were diverted here for clean-up duty. First time I've heard of the Guard being used to clean up a place while it's still hot. Usually that's work for prisoners. Well, it's a nuisance for us. I've managed to let our people know, but I had to use an 'emergency only' connection."

They watched the trucks disappear in a cloud of dust towards the Verde River. Daniel's face was clouded also, with a concern that he did not explain. Then he looked at the fidgeting Martha and his gloom changed swiftly to a wide, amused grin. "So, I got you here. Welcome to the West, Mrs. A."

BOOK FOUR

THE SECOND DECLARATION

*. . . the roar of thunders
Reverberates, gleams the red levin,
And whirlwinds lick up the dust.*

—— XXVIII ——

Ramon Perez sat at his desk in the Treaty Room of the People's House, under the huge, ornate, crystal chandelier. He had chosen this room as his private office, finding its Victorian solemnity reassuring, soothing. A sheaf of documents was under his hand. On top was a memorandum, a mere scrap of paper, simple enough, but it brought him to his moment of decision. So this was it.

He already knew that Moscow was planning the China strike. That decision had been taken and he had not been consulted. The Chinese Department of the KGB in Khabarovsk on the border had warned of increased activity, and this had convinced the frightened men in the Politburo that the Magnanimity weapon was somewhere in the stockpiles of Manchuria. Borunukov was not so stupid, but he could not hold out long against the delights of a pre-emptive China strike. He believed that the United States was subdued, and if it had ever had the Doomsday weapon it was moldering somewhere in the ground, forgotten, unknown.

And in that he was right. Almost. Perez knew, for the luck of the game had gone his way. He had been a brilliant revolutionary, and the greatest of the guerillas. He was also a most devious and successful politician. But he knew in his heart how great a factor luck was in success. And it had come to him. Not without preparation and care, but it had come.

The Russians had always been convinced that the blacks were the group they could most profitably aim to detach from allegiance to the United States. The blacks and the Hispanics. It was he who had seen the possibilities in the New Indian movement; it was he who had sent in his own men, making friends, arousing hopes. Not that it had come to much, he had believed. But now this.

Such a small piece of information, from a not very reliable source. He had not believed it to be important, but he had sent in men who would know. And they had reported, those reliable and knowledgeable men. Very carefully, he had placed a few men there as safeguards, a few experts . . . not enough to excite suspicion. But now the time had come: would he go forward, or make a cautious retreat? Would he report his discovery to Ulyanov, as befitted the good Communist, the American satrap of the great Soviet Union? Or dare he claim the power for his own?

He thought of all the might of the Soviet forces, and he thought of Magnanimity. He had atomic scientists of his own. With the weapon under his control, surely they could fathom the secret, build further weapons. It would take time, but the Soviet Union would be caught up in the struggle with China, while they held on to their conquests around the world and kept their grip on the neutralized countries of Europe.

Or he could take what they were prepared to give

him, after October 26th, just three weeks away . . .
Control of Central America, but he already had that.
He looked at the portrait of Theodore Roosevelt which
Reagan had placed on this wall; Roosevelt, who had
taken his big stick and announced that the Anglos would
forever hold sway in the Caribbean. Now he, Perez,
had the big stick.

In the lives of all great conquerors such a moment
came. Win all, lose all, on one throw of the dice.
Alexander at the Hellespont; Caesar at the Rubicon.
But not to grasp greatness when it came one's way was
the most pitiful failure of them all. This hemisphere had
been claimed and conquered by the men of Spain. In
his own veins there ran the purest Spanish blood. It
was his fate.

The clock above the fireplace chimed the strokes of
midnight, but he heard nothing. Yes, he would take his
birthright, and much more besides. He grasped the
memo with its query on copies to New York and Moscow and scribbled on it in his bold and characteristic
hand. No copy. Most secret. All references to be
destroyed.

There would be no report. *Nada*. This was his hour
and he would not let it pass.

Virinsky, full of his new sense of power, had simply
ordered the Swedish child kidnapped. She was being
held by two KGB men in a small room in a sleazy hotel
off Times Square. It was not the sort of place where an
outcry drew much attention, but the men carefully kept
her tied and her mouth sealed except when she had to
eat or drink. Their chief would not allow her to be
drugged; he preferred her senses to be sharp. At first
she was blindfolded, but in her frantic fear she kept
struggling in her bonds, bruising her fine skin, until at
last they turned on the television set, uncovered her
eyes and allowed her to watch. But she must be a

stupid child, they decided, as she did not seem to
follow the entertainment, and after a while just stared
ahead vacantly.

But Virinsky had no time for her after all. The woman
who had informed on Martha Adams, a Mrs. Bertha
Maynard, (wife of a prisoner who had been sent to work
as a cleaner on the atomic submarines) had been brought
into the detention camp and had provided proof of
much he had suspected. And it was this wretched female who, having informed, had then warned the wanted
woman who had at once escaped. She had had good
reason to escape.

Maynard had told her interrogators that the Adamses
were close; that any knowledge Joshua Adams may have
had on hidden weapons might well have been passed
on to his wife. Virinsky looked, frowning, at the map
marked with the hidden Reagan weapons that had already been discovered. He checked again all the records that had been compiled by his staff on the Columbia
Company, its owner and the late President Reagan.
The two men had been friends for many years in California before Reagan's ascension to the Presidency. Yes,
this Drummond was the man the President would have
trusted. And Joshua Adams was known as the man most
trusted by Drummond.

Despite the treachery of the female prisoner Maynard, his problem was almost solved. If the Adams
woman had not yet been captured, he knew where she
was heading. He had set the trap and baited it himself.
And when she arrived, if she got that far, the game was
his. He should have been enjoying the tea and *ponchiki*
he was taking at his desk, but the *ponchiki* seemed
greasy and the tea surely had come from the wrong case
. . . Nothing sat quite right. It was because, he thought
suddenly, that wretched Adams creature was a woman.
A hateful sex, not only unclean but emotional, irratio-
nal. In matters of this kind, women were an unknown

quantity, precisely what was *not* wanted. The very thought of her made a troubling nerve in his head throb painfully. He would not be easy until he had her under his hand again. His gaze was fixed unseeing on his computer banks. They could bring him no comfort.

His personal assistant entered, carrying a file, and he shivered at his master's grim look. It had not been entirely a pleasure, he reflected, to get his former post back. He had expected it; they had been through the female phase before. Now Nguyen Thu Thuy had been sent back to Hanoi, he would be the one to work day and night. At least he didn't have to contend with the black bench. He knew about the Swedish child but she would not be brought here. Even Virinsky would not go that far. She was the child of a delegate, with diplomatic status, and neither the Politburo nor the stodgy Kharkev family would care for such scandal.

A pity, in a way . . . A new affair might take his mind from this Adams obsession. An obsession was what it appeared to the assistant to be, and he had been with Virinsky for many years and knew him as well as anyone, more than Kharkev himself, and certainly more than Virinsky's wife Elizaveta. In the month since the surrender, half a million Americans had been killed, and millions more sent to the armies, the camps and the labor squads. Yet Virinsky was brooding over one simple, redheaded American woman, and with his surveillance precautions on her behalf he was stopping the functions of the entire nation. And turning his stomach sour, the man thought, notic-ing the uneaten delicacies.

"I don't know whether I should bother you," he said, hesitating. If Virinsky wasn't interested he would be in for a bad half hour. "But Major Pilowski thought it curious enough to be brought in. Early this morning, a KGB officer, a senior lieutenant Shushkin, was missing from a scheduled transport in Region III. He has not been seen since."

Virinsky looked coldly impatient. The man stumbled on, "Of course, it would be handled locally. But when the flight arrived at its destination . . ." he fumbled with the papers in the file, dropped one on the floor, and picked it up red-faced, "the destination was changed en route, because of the new orders, to a base in Arizona—that is, Region IX South. The senior officer, Captain Boychenko, disappeared along with the contingent of about sixty men. This has never happened before and . . ."

"Get me someone at the base in Region III who saw Captain Boychenko board," Virinsky said, cutting him off.

In five minutes Virinsky was speaking to a frightened traffic manager.

"I want a description of Captain Boychenko from you and anyone else who saw him," he said.

It didn't take long to get a description of the officer, whose face had been badly swollen. It took even less time to ascertain from Captain Boychenko's fellow officers from the Pittsburgh pool that nothing had been wrong with the Captain's face or jaw when he had eaten dinner the previous night.

Virinsky grasped his telephone in sudden excitement. "Did anyone arrive with him at the airport?"

A corporal and a private who acted as chauffeur, the answer came back, with a description of both. The corporal had been very talkative; he had argued and been troublesome. The driver had been silent.

Virinsky frowned and tried to get more details about the three men, but nothing more was forthcoming. "Except that the driver seemed to have bad feet. Limped a bit."

A driver with bad feet. Not unusual. And yet . . . he had a feeling about this.

"Make up the orders and I'll sign them at once," he told his assistant. "I want every man in Region

IX South. And send in men from the surrounding area."

"For Captain Boychenko and . . ."

"Captain Boychenko, with Senior Lieutenant Shushkin, is probably at the bottom of the Ohio river. Doubtless they are dead. These men are dangerous spies and saboteurs. And I want the photograph of Mrs. Martha Adams displayed everywhere in Region III. Anyone who harbors her will face the death penalty."

It could be, he thought. Instinct told him that it was. No fingerprint check at military airfields—what a fool he'd been! And he had been looking too far away, too fast. Now that woman had sent off her confederates—carrying orders.

An idea struck him. He had his secretary call the base again. "You said the flight was diverted—where had it been heading?"

"It had been going into Boulder. But Boulder radioed us that they had reached their full complement. We had just received new orders and . . ."

Virinsky had stopped listening. Boulder. The woman *had* done it. Martha Adams. And yet she had now evaded his grasp. Ironically, it was his own orders that were partly responsible for the diversion of that plane from the place where he wished her and her confederates to go. But he would find her, in Region Three or wherever the men had left her. Once he had them they would talk. They could not escape again. General-Colonel Suskov down in the Pentagon would not like it, but fingerprint checks would be installed in military airfields also. Yet . . . suppose she was somewhere in the West already? And these men merely a diversion? He ordered that Mrs. Adams' photograph and description should be in the hands of every military and police officer throughout every Region. He would tie each Region up so tight that not even a mouse could escape. She would be captured, and she would put Magnanimity in his hands. And that imperious redhead would be brought low. *Low*.

Traveling with Daniel in the west, so much nearer to their goal, was no simpler than it had been in the east. Sometimes it seemed they spent more time moving away from their destination than towards it. And the roads they used were much worse. But she supposed she was lucky they could travel by car, remembering the weary walking she had done through parts of Pensylvania.

At least he wasn't much concerned about the Regional border here, she found. "This country isn't Berlin, or even Eastern Europe," he said. "It'll take them years before they wire all the west, even with the slave labor gangs."

It had taken two days just to get near Prescott. Martha had been changed back to a woman. She and Daniel were again husband and wife, owners of a trading post on the Navaho reservation, returning to close up for the winter. That had been her idea. She had learned from Josh about the traders, and Daniel had applauded the suggestion.

"Thank God for bureaucrats," he had said cheerfully, after he had wandered off to observe a road check. Region IX had the same yellow books as the Regions they had passed through; perhaps they were nationwide. "Their passion for conformity does help."

"You're going to run out of those," she had said. "And how do you know the right signature for the area?"

"That's easy," he had told her. They had still been in sight of Camelback mountain, uncomfortably close to the air field, and she had been nervous. But Daniel had looked relaxed. He worked on their papers in the back of the car, not the car that had come for Captain Boychenko, but a four-wheel drive that had been aban-

doned, like so many cars on the road now, for lack of
gas. With the dirt roads Daniel took, she was to be glad
of that four-wheel drive. He had siphoned off the Captain's gas with a rubber pipe in his mouth like a delin-
quent boy—he often looked just like one, she thought,
slight as he was, in his plaid shirt and jeans. "When I
stole the ration tickets I took the wallet and papers as
well and had a look."

Martha had regretted that Daniel's victim would have
to go hungry, but they had little choice. Some restaurants were open, but Daniel still forbade her to enter.
"We'll be tracked here fast enough. There might be a
bit of confusion with the guardsmen disappearing too,
but we can't rely on that."

Hans, his hair restored to its own color, was using
his cousin's papers and traveling separately. A German
national who had been touring in the west and was
returning, by slow stages, eastward, he was in a safe
condition. He stayed in motels, and had hired a car
legally, even getting an allocation of gas. When he
could, he brought Martha a container of coffee. She
didn't mind eating little, or care much what she ate,
but her craving for coffee was unabated. Daniel deplored it.

"Such a habit. There was a time when I had to
smoke," he said, "but in my line of work, compulsions
aren't healthy. Anyway," he said, as Josh had done.
"It's bad for you."

Josh. The thought of him had been with her since
they had left the airbase. He had spoken so much of
the west. She had seen little of it, an occasional, hurried trip. They had always planned to take a long,
leisurely drive, lasting several months, going at their
own speed, seeing what they liked, staying where they
wished. "When I retire you will leave that talking shop,
Martha, and we'll spend our time traveling and going
home to Connecticut. Maybe we'll build Buzz a house

on the lot in back of the barns for when he gets
married."

Well, she was seeing the west. Not Phoenix, but
the country. It had been warm on the base and round
Phoenix, but as they traveled it had grown cooler.
Cows had been grazing under the shade of giant cotton-
wood trees, then there was rolling brushland with far-
reaching views of a pigmy forest and now they were
sheltering in pine woods. The scent of the trees made
her think of home. As Josh had thought of it, when he
was here, his homesickness implicit in his practical
letters . . . "I heard from the Swensons about the storm.
You might take a look at the roof of the big barn. I
had been meaning to go over it . . . You had better
call in the Morells, they do a decent job." Or "Will
there be anyone this year to pick the apples? It seems a
shame to let them go. When Buzz gets back for the
weekend . . ."

The roadsides here were full of slender plants with
flowers like white forget-me-nots nodding in the October breeze. *The lilies there that wave* . . . She had not
buried her dead. For the first time, she looked beyond
what she must do. If she succeeded, if Magnanimity
brought freedom, that would be her first task. She
would raise the tombstone and arrange the memorial
service. It would be fitting, for the victory if it came
would be Josh's victory.

Daniel had been sitting back in his seat, a Western
hat over his eyes, sleeping. He could sleep anywhere,
at any time. They were waiting for dusk before moving
on and the sky was already the color of lavender over
the darkening pines.

"The curfew isn't used out here, except in the bigger
towns," Daniel had said. "Safer to travel by night."

Now he pushed up his hat and glanced at her. "You
have a sad and solemn look about you, Mrs. A."

Impulsively she asked, "What do *you* see at the end
of this, Daniel?"

He shrugged. "I've long since stopped looking further than the next move. I do what has to be done, a day at a time. The future? Perhaps there is no future. Who knows?"

"Oh, yes. There is a future," she said strongly. Her mouth took on the stubborn line that amused him.

"You should have been Mrs. Horatio Alger, Mrs. Adams," he said.

"Well, you should know. Your people had no future and they made a new nation. My people left everything behind, landed on a rock at Plymouth and began a society that has amazed the world. And we're still here. There will be a future."

"Not Mrs. Alger. A prophet, crying in the wilderness. There is something Old Testament about you, Mrs. A. Uncomfortable," he said thoughtfully.

"Why uncomfortable?"

"Here we are, romantic setting, an attractive guy like me, and you . . .not bad for your age and disposition, Mrs. A." He flipped up the short hair that was curling over her ear and tweaked the lobe. "Nothing to do for an hour. Why not make the most of our opportunities?"

His touch lingered for a moment on her throat. There was a tremor of response shooting through her body, a pulse of ardor, muted, ghostly.

"Opportunity!" She sounded half-amused, half-censorious. "We're not young lovers, Daniel, we're comrades in arms."

His embrace settled about her shoulders.

"Perhaps not so young," he said. "But who's counting? So, we're comrades. But male and female. It's a cold world, Mrs. A. A wise man once told me, if you see a fire, warm yourself."

His head was close to her own. She drew back, and stepped from the car. "The air is good and clean here," she said. "But I've been warned against camp fires."

"I might have known," he said gloomily. "I think I
find a fire and what is it? An angel with a flaming
sword. The worst kind."

She laughed. "You're incorrigible, Daniel, but it's
getting dark. Where do we meet Hans?"

He bent his head over the map and they soon moved
onward. They crossed the Verde river and wandered
through the ponderosa pine country. In the night Martha had heard the howling of coyotes and felt like a
stranger in this land. Then they turned east to loop
around by Walnut Canyon and drove along the rim. As
they wound about, they glimpsed the cliff dwellings set
deep into the recesses of the limestone walls, a haven,
perhaps, for another beleaguered people, long ago.

Hans was at the meeting place outside of Flagstaff
before them. Daniel would not take Martha into the
town. His plan had been to strike northeast through the
Hopi and Navaho reservation, still largely untouched
by the invaders. But it was not to be so simple; no
longer a matter of avoiding the main roads with their
paper checks.

"On the way out here I was stopped by State police
and questioned thoroughly," Hans told them, frowning.
"And I got a look at a book they were checking. They
had a photograph, black and white, it looked like a
satellite print. The hair was more elaborate but it closely
resembled you, Martha."

Daniel cursed technology with the passion of a
Luddite. "That means they'll all have it."

"There's more," Hans said, handing Martha a container of coffee for solace and a doughnut topped with
jam and filled with something that was definitely not
cream. It was the kind of thing she had never eaten but
she gobbled it up hungrily. She and Daniel had been
subsisting on the canned vegetables he had got with the
stolen ration stamps. "There was an announcement posted
in the motel office, *and* the manager told the guests

personally. Curfew is now statewide, and journeys must be planned to keep off the road at night."

Daniel, still muttering, was groping around in Pandora's box.

"Can you manage contact lenses? Eyes are very convincing."

Her hair had been given a second brown wash, back in McKeesport. She managed to fit in the lenses, and blinked at the early sunlight.

"A little shadow on the upper lip," Daniel said, stroking her face with makeup, "And let's see if we can get any of these on you."

He pulled out an assortment of tooth caps. "Try them for fit."

But Martha's teeth were evenly spaced and there was no room for the bulky plastic.

"Let me fiddle with it," he said. "Just this little sideways job here."

He pushed the caps over both the laterals and grinned. Then he took the scissors and snipped off more of Martha's hair. "Short back and sides. A real hick."

He giggled. "Not bad. What a beast, eh, Hans?"

In the car mirror Martha could see that the small changes had made her look unprepossessing to say the least.

Daniel was humming. "Brown eyes, why are you blue?"

"Your green eyes are too striking," Hans said tactfully, fearing perhaps that her feelings might be hurt. But she was well aware that Daniel was afraid for her. The danger of Mrs. Joshua Adams must be greater than his. He was not suspected and alone he could move like a fish in the ocean. Daniel had proved to be a faithful comrade.

Hans gave them a bag of food he had smuggled from the motel, and left after arranging to meet on the border of the Navaho reservation. They moved on in

their usual crabwise fashion, but even then they were
stopped once by State police who caught them on a
rutted road. But a quick check of their papers, a swift
glance, left them to go on their way with a perfunctory
wave. At sunset they drove off the road onto some
brownish scrub behind the very poor cover of a Joshua
tree.

"We'll say it's engine trouble if we're spotted," Daniel said. "Better to take that chance than to be caught
indoors. And policemen being what they are, with the
curfew they'll probably do less checking out here, not
more."

Martha pointed eastward.

"That's the Painted Desert."

Beyond the miles of sandy stony soil the horizon was
jagged with broken ridges of rock, from deep blues to
purples and a rich rust color in the setting sun.

Daniel peered at it. "Glorious technicolor. Doesn't
look real at all. Like Masada, jutting out of the Negev.
You should see it some time," he said, with the manner
of a tour guide, and they laughed.

That night she told Daniel everything she knew of
the whereabouts of the Magnanimity missile. He listened intently, and without surprise, as though he had
always known he would gain her complete confidence.
His mind at once grappled with the problems.

"Near this lodge, that's not marked on any map. Six
hundred square feet. The launch pad can be camouflaged, but the service structure has to have an entry
point. Hans will know what to look for. By the way, you
told me Moab."

"I couldn't be sure," Martha said simply. "Not quite
sure."

"And now you're sure."

She nodded, and he smiled, taking her hand.

"Never thought I'd be so pleased at a vote of confidence from such a homely woman. Those teeth. Elsa
Lanchester, maybe, or the bride of Dracula."

Cross, she snatched her hand away, and Daniel closed
his eyes and seemed to fall asleep still laughing.

They were woken by the blazing sunlight, and made for
the point where Hans was to meet them. The previous
night was to be the last he would spend in comfort.
Daniel had decided that they were getting too close to
their objective and no trail, however innocuous, should
point the way.

But the sun rose high and Hans still had not come.
They had eaten their food, rolls and cheese, and drunk
from their thermos of water. Finally, at nine o'clock,
Hans arrived with more bad news.

"I was kept at the motel for a special check on travelers. Not just State police; there were special Soviet
troops. When they left, the rumor in the motel was
that a special contingent had been landed at Luke, and
now they are fanning out across Route 40. Thank God
for the CB's. The troops have been spotted on 93, north
and south."

"They could be covering the State," Daniel said.
"Probably they cottoned on to our little game from
Pittsburgh. Or else they have a clue where we're going.
I don't know which is worse. We'll have to strike out
northwest and then swing back. If we get separated,
we'll meet just south of Kayenta."

"I don't like it," Martha said lowly. "If it's now too
dangerous for Hans to rely on his cousin's papers in a
motel, then perhaps we should travel in one car."

If Hans were suspected, it must be easier for the
three of them to fight their way out together than for a
seventy-year old man to struggle alone. While they
were discussing the pros and cons, two large military
trucks roared up the road and stopped. Martha's mouth
went dry, as a staff sergeant and a corporal jumped out,
demanding to see their papers.

"What are you doing here?"

Daniel pushed his hat off his forehead. "The old guy was having trouble with his starter. I gave him a hand."

He no longer sounded like a New Yorker. His voice had a slight western twang.

All their papers were studied, and Martha saw again the large black book against which the names were checked. How can they stop the whole country from moving like this? she wondered. She remembered the empty food stores of New York City. Even if the food was not being shipped out at the ports, they would have got damned little.

She didn't move from where she was sitting and just looked vacantly ahead, so this time she couldn't see whether or not her photograph was in the black book. But she passed the scrutiny, and the men were walking away. "O.K. You can go. Don't forget there's no night driving. Curfew ten o'clock tonight."

One truck had pulled up in front of them and blocked the narrow road and the other was behind them. Before they pulled away a man came down from where he had been seated beside the driver. As if on a pre-arranged signal, two others joined him from the backs of the two trucks. These men wore a dark khaki uniform piped in green that she had seen before on the men arriving from the first river transport at the UN building.

Now she felt another kind of fear and the sweat started on her forehead in the bright Arizona sun. The first of the men looked at her, at Daniel and back at Hans. All three were ordered out of their ears, lined up before the truck and subjected to further scrutiny. The Russians spoke together, and then the leader said something to the Americans. In her nightmares she had often thought of capture. But not like this . . .

The staff sergeant grunted, and pointed to Hans's papers, indicating his German nationality, no doubt. Hans made indignant remarks and some attention was paid to him. He was allowed to take his bag with him into the truck, and he was not handcuffed. Martha, seeing the men grasp Daniel's wrists, could not believe he was going quietly. They could at least make a run for it.

A man came towards her, the steel links shimmering in his hands. As he grabbed her, she gave him a swift kick and turned and ran off the road onto sand and stone, until her breath was sobbing and catching in her chest. She stumbled; a hand clutched her shoulder; a great pain smashed into her head; it was night, and she knew no more.

— XXIX —

The pain remained with her as consciousness returned. Her eyes had opened once or twice, but she had seen little in the dark interior of the truck. Bodies were sprawled about her, snoring, groaning. Bumping along poor roads made the pain worse; the smooth stretches were a relief. The stops were frequent, and a shaft of sunlight would pierce the interior as the back flap of the truck opened to admit yet more captives, noisily indignant, or silent with fear.

Something childlike held her back from complete wakefulness, but the thought of Magnanimity came and she was once again Martha Adams, with a bad pain in her head. At the next stop she watched the guards carefully; the American soldier jumped down, but the Russian stayed by the opening, his hand on his weapon, his gaze stolidly on his prisoners. *She had to get out of here.*

She could not imagine where they were or where they were going. They seemed to be stationary far more than they were moving, but the Russian never budged. The truck rumbled on, endlessly.

"We're goin' in circles," a woman's voice complained. "Not goin' anywhere. They're just lookin' for anyone, anyone at all. Been back to Flagstaff, twice."

"Guess they have a quota, like State police with traffic tickets. They're just fillin' up the truck."

"But what do they want us for?" A woman's voice, fearful.

A body had been inching closer to her own. Under cover of the talk a familiar voice whispered in her ear.

"I've got to get you out. Listen. They don't know who you are. It's some general arrest, trucks circling all over, picking up everyone in sight. Hans is out. He yelled a lot when we passed back through Flagstaff—indignant citizen of a friendly power. I saw him go—he even got a car. Will you be able to walk?"

She cautiously tested her limbs. They seemed to be in good order. The pain in her head was just a pain. "Yes," she whispered. The pain was worse when she spoke and her mouth felt as if it was full of ash.

"Sleep now."

Much later some water was put to her lips and she drank it thankfully, wondering how Daniel managed with his manacled wrists. Then she dozed again. After a while she was aware that when the truck flap opened, the light outside had dimmed. Night was coming and the other prisoners grew more fearful. There was a constant murmur now, despite the presence of the guards.

"What are you in for?"

"Hell, I don't know. Ma and me and Sonny were drivin' on 89. We were lookin' to see if we could trade for some sheep with the Navahos, not that we've got much to trade with. Then we were turning off for Grey Mountain and these guys stopped us. Just hauled us out of the car and shoved us in here and Sonny in the truck at the back. One of them soldiers, he's just a kid, comes from New Mexico. I asked him what the hell was goin' on and he said it would be all sorted out at the depot."

"They snatched three of us too. And we've been running our lodge for military personnel. I told the sergeant but he said—"

"Fresh young punks," a woman's voice was fretful. "They came and pulled me out of the bar while I was cleaning up. Special today on redheads, they said."

"What depot?" Another man's voice, rough with fear. "I figure we're going to Grand Canyon National Park. I head they've built a big camp there. Like the only way out is over the big drop, if you can get out. We're not stopping any more. I've been figuring the turns and I tell you . . ."

"If the kid from New Mexico said the depot," the trader was more hopeful, "there's no reason for him to lie. Always someone with a scare tale. How would you know about what's goin' on in the National Park?"

"The Indians know. They have their ways, and I heard . . ."

"He's right," another voice joined in. "They don't say much but . . ."

"Shut up you mugs." A soldier cut across the talk. "No gabbing till you hit the depot. You can all shoot your mouths off there."

A bright beam from his flashlight probed around the truck. It was painful to Martha's eyes but she got a look at the back of the truck. There was a machine gun mounted near the flap. The silent soldier looked like the Russian who had struck her down. Both of them were smoking, and the young American moved the flap to clear the smoke. It was quite dark out. The truck had been wandering round all day. Where could they be now? Were they in Grand Canyon Park? *She must get out*. Flexing her body cautiously, she judged that she could move now without great pain.

The barmaid had clutched the hand holding the flashlight.

"Got a cigarette for a lonely girl, fella?" She was trying to strike up a friendship. If only the soldier would move towards her, away from the flap. The other might be caught off guard. Martha tried to judge the speed at which they were going. It seemed they had slowed down, but still too fast to make a jump for it.

They stopped with a jerk that tumbled the prisoners. Martha could hear voices from the front of the truck raised in argument. The argument continued and the Russian jumped out and presumably went forward.

Daniel eased his way back towards her. "Think they've taken the wrong road," he whispered. "This is called Cameron; they're on the reservation. Someone wants them to go back the way they came."

Cameron. Martha remembered. On the Little Colorado. Suddenly her head cleared. It was time for her to stop being a parcel, intelligent or not. This was her country, not Daniel's. A little lamplight came from the open flap, turning the dozing figures about her to dim shapes. A man with a bloody forehead groaned, a young boy was examining an arm that looked broken. She sat up and gave Daniel a quick, signaling, glance.

The American soldier had his head outside of the flap. Then Daniel was behind him. The soldier, silent, slid quite slowly to the road. No one seemed to notice. If they did, they didn't speak. It was quite a drop to the road in the darkness and Martha was still manacled, but she made it almost without a sound. While the men at the head of the truck were arguing, the two figures ran on cat feet into the night.

Cameron was a very small place. In the starlight, it appeared to be mainly comprised of one large building, where the soldiers were arguing with three Indian men.

There were some shacks and a gas station. By the gas station, a party of young Indians were having a raucous get together. Uninterested in the problems of their elders, they were crowded round a car with a tape deck that was blaring away with the inevitable rock sound; they were drinking, smoking and cat-calling—a teenagers' night out.

Another car was parked at the pump. Martha and Daniel stepped into it quietly, but it didn't matter. The young people were oblivious to everything except themselves. There was no outcry as yet from the truck, but Martha was stiff with expectation.

A youth came running from the shack with his arms full of cigarette cartons, and a bottle under his arm. The doors of the front car were open and he jumped in and started up the ignition. A roar came from the echo-cans attached to the exhaust pipe and the youngsters piled in around him, their voices high with laughter over the din of the car. Daniel swiftly crossed the wires and as the others moved down the road, he took off along a small jeep trail. The trucks were still parked by the main building. "They couldn't have heard us go," Daniel said with satisfaction, but Martha knew they would not have much time.

"Follow the river west," she said.

He followed her instruction, but remarked, "I hope you know what you're doing. Pandora's box is gone, I didn't dare hold onto it. I dumped it in a gully while you distracted our friends. We can't get far with this much gas either."

"If they have any idea where we're heading, they'll look for us north-east of here," Martha said. "And they won't expect us to be going towards the camp."

Daniel smiled. "You've learned," he said.

When they were well outside the hamlet, Daniel stopped long enough to take the handcuffs off Martha's wrists, using a small, steel object not unlike a tooth-pick.

"How did you manage for yourself?" she asked.

"The same way as Houdini," he said, shrugging. "How's your head?"

When she thought of it, it was still painful. But there was no time to attend to aches and pains. She was trying to remember what Josh had written to her once about a boating trip. "You can still rent boats, not those damned rubber rafts," he had said. "It's good exercise and a break for the men who can't get home."

There were probably several places that rented boats along the river, though the sport here was not like that on the Colorado itself. They would be closed now, she supposed. The car had come a fair distance, purring along by the river bank, and she felt a little calmer. Then the moon swung out from behind a cloud, turning the muddy river bright between its banks, and doubtless showed the car up bright and clear to any onlooker.

Lodging places here were not as common as she had hoped, and the two small ones they passed were closed, shuttered, with no signs of boats. Josh had been writing, she presumed, about some other river, some other place. The two of them had left the car to search, but Daniel, wary as a wild creature, rushed her back and drove on. A narrow track led down to the river bank. They took a gamble, followed it, and there ahead was River Lodge, dark, empty, shuttered—and the boats in the yard covered with canvas.

Martha poked about and found a dory that looked as though it were river-worthy. "Come on, Daniel," she said to her somewhat reluctant companion, "We'll take the water route."

The KGB men, who spoke little English and certainly no Navaho, were somewhat flustered by their first encounter with the Indians, whom they had been ordered for the time being to treat with courtesy and respect.

The Navahos merely reiterated that Peter MacDonald himself had received a solemn promise that no foreign soldier would step on tribal land. The American driver pointed out that to return the way they had come would be a time-consuming detour and they would be just as long on tribal lands as if they took the western route. In the end, after apologies had been made and accepted, the trucks were given permission to proceed.

Unfortunately, the soldier with the knife-wound in his heart was discovered a moment later. A count was made of the prisoners, search parties were requested by radio. The Indians were furious and showed no desire to cooperate, but army and air force cars soon arrived at Cameron. The prisoners were sent on under a new guard, while the KGB officers joined in the search parties.

The river journey did not work out as Martha had expected. They had spent too long following the river by car, and she had been misled by its twists and turns, which seemed so simple on a map and yet were highly confusing in the fleeting moonlight that revealed and then hid the landscape. Daniel had hidden the car, covered by tarpaulins, in the boatyard behind the lodge. She had thought to make their way downstream, to land on the north side at some spot where they might appropriate a vehicle and then turn back, striking northeast to Kayenta. From the argument at Cameron she gathered that the promise of the inviolability of Indian land was being taken seriously, which should be a help. The promise should last at least as long as it took for her to arrive at her destination.

The river at first had been little problem. In fact, it proved her friend. They dipped silently through the water hugging the south bank, invisible, she hoped, from the road above. When the sound of cars came, reverberating between the high banks, she held her breath, but the cars rushed on, unheeding of the quiet ripples down below.

They rowed hard and long. Daniel caught her glance and pulled a face. She felt a certain pride that she had kept her muscles strong and her limbs supple and she laughed silently at his discomfiture. Somehow the danger and the exercise made the pain in her head subside. She felt even a certain well-being, a confident control as they slipped through the night, dark again now except for starlight.

But soon, ominously, dark clouds massed to cover half the sky. Martha could no longer see the familiar stars or almost anything else. She grew afraid, peering about the river. The water now was carrying them along. Had they been swept into the Colorado? The water was flowing fast, too fast. She searched for a spot to land, but there were only the steep rock walls. And then the rain came.

It fell with a hiss as it pounded the river. She was soaked at once. The boat was flying, flying downstream on the swelling waters and Martha saw nothing but the river and the rain. Swiftly as they were moving, they were suddenly jerked forward like fish on a line. Martha clung to her oars with a wild desperation as they were tossed helplessly into a foaming rapid. Daniel yelled something she could not hear; the growling sound of the river filled the night. The boat reared up, perched high on a cliff of water and plunged deep. Down in the trough, foam slapped over her knees. Martha glimpsed Daniel bailing, but she could do nothing; almost at once they were shot into another rapid and she was clutching frantically to save one set of oars.

When the water calmed slightly they tried to pull the boat over to the bank but soon they were in another rapid and water filled the boat. They were almost through the white water, heavy as they were, when they were pulled irresistibly into a counter-current. Daniel was trying to hold the head of the boat downstream, but it was flung up, right out of the water, and the boat capsized.

Martha was hurled into the river, caught by the whirlpool, and dragged down head first as though she were going straight to the bottom. She kicked with all her strength and struggled to turn. Her breath was gone; she felt she was finished, but she refused to surrender to the current and gave another, mighty kick. Then the river vomited her up; she was flung high. Grabbing at anything, she found herself clinging to the keel of the overturned boat. As she looked up, Daniel was tossed over the gunwhale. She had no breath but she managed a grin.

The short cloudburst was over. They managed to right the boat and rowed into an eddy, where they bailed out and landed on the southeast side of the river, just at the head of another monstrous rapid. They lay upon the shore on a sandy stretch.

She glanced at Daniel, dashing the water from her eyes.

"The Devil won't take you," she said, choking and laughing.

"He looks after his own," he groaned. "Mrs. Amazon."

Only God knew where they were, she thought. But for now she could go no further.

It was the next day before the stolen car was found at River Lodge, discovered by State police. The police had not been informed at once about the escape of the KGB prisoners and it was a few hours before the stolen car was connected with the murder of a soldier at Cameron. There was some confusion and the facts were not fully established until the rest of the prisoners were questioned at Adult Camp Number One in Grand Canyon.

It took another two hours for someone to remember the boats at River Lodge, and the hunt for the boat did not start until Daniel and Martha were already making their slow, agonizing way on foot to Tuba City. Daniel had stopped long enough to break up the boat, which had been hard work despite the action of the rapids. It was partly luck that some of the spars went down into the whirlpool and other bits dispersed themselves in the white water. It gave the patrol a long, miserable search along the rumbling waters of the Colorado in the Canyon, and their report was that any boatman who had traversed those waters in the night was surely drowned. A man's body, in fact, had been washed ashore near Granite Gorge. Spars which they had come across upriver gave weight to that opinion. The report was believed by everyone until it reached Virinsky in New York who received it when he was deeply engrossed in other matters.

The Swedish diplomat had been making a most obnoxious outcry on the disappearance of his child. The kidnappers had been careless, and had been identified as KGB troops by children of other delegates with whom the child had been playing. Virinsky's propensities, in an organization like the UN, could not be kept secret. But everyone there now understood his new position—and most of them understood their own. There was no great outcry, but there was a persistent buzz. Many of the delegates, and much of the Secretariat for that matter, did not care for the New Order, though it was far too late for them to do anything about it. No one was going to put up a battle. There were no Solzhenitsyns here.

Ulyanov, however, had wanted the preservation of at least outward harmony until the 26th. After the New Order became international law by acclamation, then the delegates could go, and they would not be recalled. They had talked too long for any good they could do, Virinsky thought, remembering the admired Cromwell. In the name of Ulyanov, they would go.

In the meantime, the buzzing was uncomfortable.

There were muttered references to Beria, that unacknowledged genius. The black bench remained unused except for Virinsky's solitary naps. He could not have the child here. She was still in the small hotel apartment, under heavy guard, but he had no time to visit. Events were moving too fast. Yet the child could not be released for she would talk too much. Perhaps she should be killed, for it would be better now that he not be distracted.

He was about to order the killing when the reports came in from Arizona. The description of the missing woman caught his attention at once. The teeth, the eyes, the brown hair; none of those were meaningful, they could be altered in minutes. But the height, the weight, the carriage . . . One of the soldiers who had seen the woman first had described her as "an ugly old broad who sat in that heap like the queen of a dunghill." Or an empress. He felt a sudden certainty that it was Martha Adams.

But in Arizona? She had been arrested with two men, whose descriptions *might* match those of "Captain Boychenko" and his sergeant. Then he remembered the "private." The private who hadn't spoken, perhaps to hide a woman's voice? The limping feet . . . it all became clear now. Of course. A woman who could disguise herself to look like "an ugly old broad" would have had no trouble. Except in having to wear men's shoes . . .

Another report was brought in swiftly. One of the men who had been arrested had been released, the possible "Boychenko." He carried the papers of a citizen of the German Republic. Virinsky thought carefully. Should he have him found and re-arrested? No. He had a better idea. He knew what to do.

But, sitting at his desk, gazing at his banks of data, he was forced to consider something else. Martha Adams, untrained, unequipped for undercover work, could hardly have got so far without trained and expert help. The knife wound on the American soldier had been made by a professional killer, a man who knew how to kill quickly and quietly.

Perez had always believed that the infamous Bar-Lev was behind all this. Possibly he was right. Perez would understand the workings of such a man better than anyone, after all. The KGB themselves, though they had underground operatives, were always part of a tight organization. It was Perez's people who were used to submerging themselves in a population. An agent could work quite alone, with only one person knowing his actual employer. Even that wasn't certain, for such a man could change loyalties as it suited him. It was at once a strength and a weakness.

But whether this man was Bar-Lev or not, he was a dangerous man and the protector of the Adams woman. He must be found and stopped. Virinsky now turned his attention to the other important matter which had been chiefly occupying his mind before the report from the west came in. He looked again at a copy of a memo, with a report, that lay on his desk. It had been flown in by special messenger, at dead of night, from Washington. It was to be his means of bringing down Perez who, like most guerilla leaders, would have to be destroyed at last. He had gone too far, and he had been discovered.

Virinsky wondered. Should he send this on to Moscow at once; or should he save Perez until he had helped him find this killer? No, he did not need Perez, he thought. For he, Virinsky, alone in all the world, knew whom this Adams woman had to meet. The killer could aid her all he wished, he would only deliver her into Virinsky's hands.

He looked at the memo again, before he locked it in his special file. Just for a day or two. Let Perez's continuing silence be the rope to hang him by, and then Ulyanov must be the hangman. Virinsky sent out orders

that the search for the Adams woman be continued; and
he spoke for a moment to his man in the west. He
smiled, satisfied. The world was heating up, he reflected. Borunukov was readying for the China strike.
Perhaps he should take an hour or two to visit the hotel.
He stroked his thumb absently. In times of war, after
all, men always found time to go to their women.

—— XXX ——

A weary night was followed by an exhausting day. Martha had wanted to rest by the river bank, but Daniel had driven her on. "You'd better keep moving," he said, "or you'll tighten up by morning." They followed the bed of a creek that seemed to lead up to the plateau, but the going was hard. The moonlight was fitful, the rocks were wet, and each step treacherous. Her knees were skinned, her nose was bruised and even her toes were bloody. Then she stumbled and fell several feet, and Daniel had given up. He found a boulder where they could shelter, but she was cold, very cold. By morning, however, she was hot. At least the stream had clear water which refreshed them both.

The sky was high and pale blue, dazzling in its purity and freshness. It was the sky that the first Adam saw, Martha thought, and hoped she wasn't delirious. The tumbling river had brought them miles out of their way; even when they reached the plateau, it would be a long journey on foot. Her little backward loop had turned out to be a major setback. "Come on, nature guide," Daniel urged. As a guide, Martha thought, she was as good as Wrong-Way Corrigan. She couldn't even move. Daniel massaged her aching limbs and she accepted it as she would have from any comrade, too bone weary for any sexual thought of lust or modesty.

They continued the arduous upward climb and it was blazing noon before they reached the top. The sun had dried their clothing. They collapsed under the shade of a scrubby pine and regarded the Painted Desert that once again stretched before them. She had planned on making for Tuba City where some form of transport might be found. But here they must be about fifty miles away, and they were hardly in condition for a long, desert hike.

Daniel looked at her and laughed. She had lost one contact lens, the loose caps had been washed away from her teeth in the pounding river waters and her hair shone up fiercely red in the sun. "You'd better take out your right eye," he said in resignation. "One blue and one green—it's too striking to be true."

Even her disguise was gone. As she sat, perched, it seemed, on the edge of nowhere, she felt as conspicuous as an idol on a mountain top. Daniel was feeling cautiously in his pocket. He took out a little package that Hans had given him just before they were arrested.

"Would you believe it," he said, with a broad smile. "The miracle of plastic wrap."

Martha gazed, unbelieving. The wrapping had survived, almost intact, and the crumbled, only slightly damp remains of six Graham crackers nestled snugly inside. It was only a scrap of food but it gave her heart. She needed it, for when they started walking on the desert trail, she had a fear that they might die there. "Something will turn up," Daniel said, cheerfully, and something did, though not that day. Weakness and hunger did not trouble her as much as her thirst, or perhaps it was her fear of greater thirst, and she rested uneasily at night by the roadside.

She woke in terror in the early morning at the sound of screeching tires. But it was not the soldiers, merely a young Indian in a jeep, looking at the two bodies curiously. When they stirred, he offered them water from a flask. While Martha was brushing off the dust and dirt as well she could, Daniel was talking to the driver.

She saw him offer the youth some of the red dollars, still soggy, but he was not interested. Then Daniel offered him his watch, and it seemed they struck a bargain.

"Our friend here is going into a Hopi village," Daniel said. "It's a bit out of our way, but he'll take us so far today, and tomorrow he'll go as far as Moenkopi, that's near enough to Tuba City."

The young man seemed well-disposed and offered them sticks of sweet chewing-gum, which they readily accepted. The journey by car now seemed incredibly swift after their laborious plodding of the last two days. Before noon they were driving through sandy cornfields and then they came to a village where the stone, pueblo houses, perched high on the Mesa top, were almost indistinguishable from the surrounding rock.

The driver let them out, waved as he drove off and said that he would meet them in the morning. Martha's shoes were cut and ripped, the sole of the right shoe flapping now so that she could hardly walk. Daniel himself, holding her arm, was near to complete exhaustion.

A Hopi woman, standing in the doorway of her house, looked at them and without a word, drew back and allowed them to enter. She gave them a bowl of water to wash themselves, and a dish of parched corn with a little dried meat. They had some liquid to drink that Martha did not recognize, and then the woman showed them where they could rest, and covered them with a blanket. Martha slept through the day and the night, and when she woke, despite some aches and pains, she felt whole again.

Daniel was already up and out. Her hostess, seeing her revive, smiled and offered food. Martha ate sparingly, knowing that food must be a problem here, as it was everywhere, for all the Hopis could grow themselves and the Russians' present "hands-off" policy.

Daniel returned, with his driver in tow, and they readied themselves for the journey. As they had nothing to carry, it took little time. Martha wanted to give the woman something for her kindness. She had taken them in, although whites were not now welcome in the area, and she had given the best she had. But Martha had nothing to give. Then she saw her wedding ring gleaming on her finger. Gently, with a thought for Josh who would have wanted her to repay this hospitality, she took the ring and put it in the woman's hand.

The woman's eyes widened for a moment at the sight of the broad, gold band, and then she exclaimed and left the room. When she came back she was holding a pair of soft leather boots that wrapped around the instep. She held them against Martha's feet, and then took her ripped, sad shoes away and tried the boots on her.

"My daughter's," she said, smiling. The soft leather clung to Martha's feet perfectly, as the woman tugged and worked the straps. "My daughter is away," she said. "She worked in Flagstaff. But I haven't seen her, not this week, not last week, not the week before."

Martha could only hope that the girl hadn't been swept up, like other young people, into the work gangs. An Indian girl in American dress might have gone with the rest.

The driver was much quieter that morning than he had been the previous day. They drove well away from the paved roads, through a red-walled canyon, past cornfields fenced with crooked posts. Then they climbed a steep hill to the small, stone village of Moenkopi. Just before entering the village, the driver stopped, let them out and showed them the way to Tuba City. His manner was not hostile, but it was no longer friendly. Their journey together was over.

"I didn't see many men in the last village," Daniel remarked. "I wonder where they've gone. One friendly soul I found seemed to be trying to put me off from going into the Navaho part of the reservation."

"Well, it is sort of off limits," Martha said, "in the present phase of the New Order. But we have no choice."

Tuba City was more than a trading post. It had a gas station, a shopping center, a hospital and was really a small town. But the shopping center was closed and there were few people about. No white men were to be seen, but there were some Navahos around the trading post, and Daniel disappeared with them and talked long.

Martha, curious, looked in to see what they were trading. Apparently they were accepting some of the red dollars, which Daniel had laid on the counter against which they had put down two flannel shirts, a bag of foodstuffs, and a flask. Then they all wandered out to the gas station where some cars still stood, abandoned by the owners who had run dry and were not entitled to an allocation.

Daniel pointed to a jeep in good condition. The men murmured. He checked the first pump, pulled a face, and checked all the rest. They were bone dry. There was more talk with the Indians. Eventually they were persuaded, and they showed Daniel a line of metal cans, secreted in a doorway, into which any drops had been drawn off. They measured up to a good tankful and some to spare,

Now the hard bargaining started. Daniel offered more money. It was eyed, but not accepted. Sighing, he reached into a zippered compartment inside his shirt and removed a cigarette case from a sturdy cover. Flipping the lid before the curious gaze of the Indians, he removed a tray with what looked like the heads of a dozen cigarettes. The remainder of the bits and pieces that he slid out fitted together into a tiny pistol.

"It's an electric pistol," he explained, "and it fires without noise."

He gave a demonstration. To Martha's relief, it actually worked. The matter was settled at once. They got the car and the gas and were soon on their way to Kayenta.

"They told me that thing was waterproof," Daniel said reflectively. Martha wondered who "they" were, but she didn't ask. "I never knew just how waterproof it was."

"You must be sorry to lose it," Martha said.

"Well, I couldn't have got away with it with the geeks," Daniel said. He had picked the word up from the Americans and seemed to like it. "Actually, it's one of their jobs." He grinned at her. "Find a use for anything if you keep it long enough. But I hope those guys don't damage themselves with it. It's a mean weapon."

Martha regretted its loss. Her own pistol was still in the glove compartment of the car from which she had been so rudely dragged. Daniel had nothing left but his knife.

"Well," he went on cheerfully, "we'll see who we meet in Kayenta. I told Hans, if he could, to get in touch with some of our friends."

But the first face she was to recognize in Kayenta was not one that she expected to meet there at all.

—— XXXI ——

And so it had begun. Borunukov had unleashed his volley of missiles on the Manchurian silos. The Chinese had responded with attacks on Soviet installations that had caused much dismay. The range had been far greater than the Russians had expected, well over the 1750 miles confidently expected to be their limit. Petropavlovsk had gone and Vladivostok with it, and an attempt on Sverdlovsk, even though it had failed, had made it clear that the Russian heartland itself could not be sure of immunity.

The counterstrike had ceased, but a furious enquiry was taking place in Moscow. The Politburo was sour indeed. The new ABM 10 system, in which they had placed so much confidence, had failed dismally, at least at Petropavlovsk. The Chinese had tried a new technique of exploding their missiles above the atmosphere which destroyed electrical and electronic systems. The result was that some generals in their deep subterranean redoubts, despite metal walls, circuit-breakers on the cables, and with vacuum tubes replacing transistors in their equipment, found themselves as ignorant and powerless as the civilian population fleeing from the holocaust.

Even the MIG 22's, with their look-down, shoot-down radar had not performed as well as had been hoped. Borunukov was blaming the Commander-in-Chief of the Strategic Rocket Force for all the problems; the Commander was blaming the Marshal's GPU. Borunukov asked for permission for a second strike; the Politburo was unenthusiastic. Moscow's defenses were being hurriedly augmented, even though military areas were stripped. Even more prudent, some Politburo members were leaving early for the United Nations meeting on the 26th, in New York City, which some sycophant proposed should now be called Ulyanovgrad.

This was the way the world could end. Virinsky, in his office high above the East River, understood, but he felt no fear. He feared the end of the world no more than he did his own death, which must come in time. If he died, the world could go with him. Rather, with the Soviet Union embattled, it was borne in on him more strongly than ever that the man who held Magnanimity would control the world. But he still did not have the woman . . .

This was the time, he thought, to take the pawn that was Perez. He sent a copy of the secret memorandum to Kharkev, and one directly to Ulyanov himself. His own operatives would pick up Perez's men. They would have plenty of help from Department Two. The KGB Department for Latin America would be very glad to see the end of the hero of the Caribbean. Virinsky would get all their data very quickly. If Perez *had* learned anything important about Magnanimity, that knowledge would be his. And Ulyanov would be forced to sacrifice his favorite at last.

But the woman. He found he had troubled himself with the Swedish girl to no purpose. The clumsy child could not rouse him. He was consumed with all the intensity of passion to capture that woman, and have the Magnanimity weapon in his hand.

Yes, he would take Perez, now, with Borunukov fallen from favor. The old United States was his alone. Even Kharkev did not know how far he, Virinsky, had come. He stared down at his area map of the hidden missiles. Utah, Nevada and now perhaps Arizona. If he told Moscow even that much, in their fear and panic they might send a strike of SS18's over the likely areas, a strike of such terrible ferocity that if Magna was not destroyed in its silo, the destruction above and around it would give a living death. Better for them not to know, as yet.

In Moscow they laughingly referred to him as Under-Secretary Virinsky. Kharkev's son-in-law and sometime whipping boy. There were other names too. He knew them all. He had always been a bureaucrat like Himmler, a man he admired almost more than Beria himself. A man who kept his place like a spider at the center of a web. Never a field operative, he was a man of records, of computers, of silent deductions made after hours of study in a quiet place, like this room where he sat with his back against the sky. He took the raw stuff provided by others and distilled it into precious knowledge, and had others translate that into action.

But this time it was different. His men were too slow. The language training given to the Border troops had not proved sufficient. And they had never seen the woman. Mahomet, he thought, would have to go to the mountain. He would have to eliminate her personally. Perhaps he had known that from the time he had first seen her, in the blaze of the September sun, full of confident life, sweeping like an empress into his own halls. Yes, he would go. And he would take control of the weapon in its silo under his own hand. Aharit-Ha-Yamim. He would have it for himself, to use or not to use, as he deemed best. He would be the last, the final broker of the great death to come.

* * *

Kayenta was about seventy miles away. On a good road, not more than an hour. But despite the argument between the soldiers and the Indians at Cameron, Daniel was still cautious and they took a long, meandering way across small paths and side routes while Martha got into a high state of the fidgets. At another time she might have paused to gaze upon the strange shapes of the erosion-formed Blue Canyon, which was actually blue-grey in the full daylight, or at the graceful antelopes, appearing so unexpectedly, and all the wild beauty of the desert. But she had little attention for that now. Soon the buzz of a helicopter drove Daniel deep into a canyon, where they hid in the shadows of the rock until dusk.

The way had become too dim for them to drive, and they slept for a time until the moon swung high. Finding a graded dirt road they made good progress through a valley until the sound of circling helicopters was heard again. They pulled into a hollow by the roadside, thankful when the moon was obscured by a large cloud.

"We'll have to take a chance and move on," Martha said. "Better now than in daylight."

"Especially if we're not going in circles," Daniel said. "You don't happen to have a compass in your pocket, Campfire Girl? In daylight there will be other cars to attract notice."

But when the helicopters flew off, Daniel started up the motor. It purred for a moment, sputtered and stopped.

"Damn," he said, after repeated efforts. "We'll have to wait for daylight. Look, about a mile back I spotted a few hogans. Do you want to take a chance on finding them? We might get a meal and some sleep."

It was not a long walk before they saw dimly the shapes of a small cluster of hogans not far off the road. An Indian, wrapped in a blanket, came out and looked at them in surprise. He was soon joined by his wife, who looked at Daniel and then at Martha and motioned

her to come inside. Evidently she thought the desert
at night was no place for a woman to be. Martha
stepped inside, immediately falling as the inside floor
was more than a foot lower than the outside ground
level. This caused much amusement to the family, as
Daniel caught and steadied her. She was to become
friendly with them before she left but that night she
merely noticed that the hogan was bigger inside than it
had seemed to be; that there were boys as well as girls,
and that the woman was starting to boil coffee on a fire
of pine chips. After drinking it gratefully, she rested on
a sheepskin on the north side of the hogan where the
women slept.

As soon as light came she was ready to be off. Daniel
was already up and came in, wiping his hands on a rag.

"I've cleaned out the air filter," he said. "Our friends
kindly gave me some kerosene. Martha, are you up to
riding?"

She gazed at him for a moment.

"They have some horses here . . . I might be able to
make an arrangement. We're only a few miles from
Kayenta, and we'll be a lot less conspicuous on horse-
back. What do you say? We can send back for the car
later."

She went out and examined the horses tied to the
hitch rail. None of them were candidates for the Triple
Crown, but they looked like serviceable mounts. Martha saw that the Navaho had little interest in the
redbacks, which was all Daniel had left to trade, but he
pointed to the car. It was their deposit, as it were, and
their hosts seemed satisfied, and after they found two
battered saddles, Martha was hoisted up.

Daniel looked at her, not pleased, and before they
left he acquired two rather ill-fitting but broad-brimmed
hats. "Not so bad," he said, critically. "At least you're
not flaming."

It wasn't like riding along the bridle paths of Central
Park or the lanes of Connecticut, but at least she stayed

up. Daniel, she was amused to see, didn't cut too fine a figure on a horse. "For a taxi driver I'm doing well," he said, groaning.

He wouldn't allow her to enter Kayenta itself, and left her in a deserted shack a half mile off while he went to reconnoiter. "Those helicopters were looking for someone," he said. "Whatever the Russians have promised about keeping out of the Reservation, if they know you are here all that will be over."

It seemed to her that she had sat in the dusty, lonely hut on the edge of nothing for half a day, but it probably wasn't more than an hour or so when she heard a car outside. To her delight, it was John Fairfield, accompanied by a man whom she had never seen before. The Colonel looked fit and tanned, better than she had seen him look for a long time. He seemed at peace with himself, and an air of command sat well on him.

"How wonderful to see you, Martha." His handshake was a warm welcome. "What you must have been through. I gather that you've come the hard way. We could have done better for you, but all the same you're here. We were waiting for you up in Boulder, when we got a message to meet you in Moab. Then I heard from Hoffman that you were coming into Kayenta and I had to see you. Your Archie said you were here."

It was wonderful to see him, Martha decided. To hear the voice of home. For a moment she felt like Martha Adams of Connecticut again. He introduced her to his companion, a large, fair, blue-eyed man, with broad shoulders, a slight thickening at the waist, fifty-ish, with a charming smile.

"Clayton Rance, Martha. Our C-in-C, really."

Rance shook his head deprecatingly. "You're the C-in-C, John. I thought we'd settled that. National Security Advisor, you might say."

Fairfield nodded to the sky. "No buzzards up today. I hear that two of them crashed in the desert last night. Good luck for us. So we'll drive you into Kayenta. My

man will take your horses." As they drove, Fairfield
told her of the extent of the resistance, of the troops
now under his command, and some other things that
surprised her, and were soon to disturb her. At that
moment however she was still in a glow with the sense
of coming home.

"It was a lucky day for me when I met Clay here,"
Fairfield went on. "I was on the road, not in too good
condition, just a few miles out of Chicago. He recognized
me from a JANNAF meeting—Joint Army, Navy, NASA,
Air Force."

"Don't ask me *how* I recognized you," Rance said,
grinning. "A bearded old reprobate."

Fairfield laughed. "He grabbed me, and I thought I
was finished. I took a swing at him. Lucky he doesn't
hold a grudge."

"Thought I was going to lose a tooth. And I tell you,
Mrs. Adams, for a man on the run, there's nothing
worse than needing a dentist. Who can you trust?"

Martha thought of Daniel and his man in McKeesport. But this was a time to listen, not to talk. Clayton
Rance was CIA. He had been a high-ranking officer, at
one time a station chief in Moscow. On the day of the
strike and the surrender he had been in Germany. He
had at once made his way to Canada, and slipped over
the border to see what could be done.

"Nothing with my shop," Rance said, heavily. "They
had us pegged, every one. A slaughter. The one thing
we had never planned for was surrender. There are
plenty of brave kids and good men, and women, in the
country but there was no organization, no leadership."

"It was Clay who told me about the men pouring into
the mountains," Fairfield said. "I'd seen the bands of
kids myself, hiding out when and where they could, but
I didn't think they had a prayer. I was just running,
Martha. I'd had no thought of fighting back. It seemed
impossible. You remember, when we talked. It was
Clay here who persuaded me that I, and the friends I'd

found and warned, owed the fighting men something.
They had nothing but a few guns and a lot of courage.
We could join him in providing leadership."

They were traveling through a land of big and little
mesas, sand dunes and oddly shaped rocks and butts.
Perhaps it was the strange look of the country that
started up in her a small sensation of uneasiness. Fairfield was regarding Rance with an affectionate respect.
"Martha, Clay knew something I didn't. He was sure
there were some missiles hidden round the country,
stashed away from the days of the Reagan administration. There had been talk, you might remember, of a
limited Mobile MX scheme, but it got snarled up in
long arguments about the basing mode. Clay thought
that if we could get men all over the country searching
we might come up with something, and then we could
really bargain."

Had her journey been for nothing? Martha wondered. Had they found it? She was aware of Rance's
eyes on her. He was a competent-looking man, but she
wished she could have had this first talk with John
Fairfield alone.

Fairfield was unaware of her slight discomfort.
"Carmody wasn't a bad man . . ."

"Wasn't?"

"Perhaps I should say isn't. But he hasn't been seen
in public for some time. Anyway, he never intended, I
am sure, to make such an unconditional surrender,
where the terms would be so harsh, but that was, of
course, what happened. We want to turn that back, to
make an arrangement we can live with . . ."

"Did you find anything?" Martha asked. Her voice
was cool.

"We had some luck. Some disappointment. Many of
the silos were empty; that was the plan. And the missiles were only the old Titans, after all. Two silos have
been restored to functioning order. Anyway, when we
make our demands, they won't be sure of exactly what
we have."

"Of course," Rance said, "if we had more, it would be better." He smiled at her. "We rather wondered if you might have some information for us. It was your husband, I think, who built some of these silos."

They were coming into Kayenta and Fairfield slowed up beside a small roadside lodge. Daniel was standing by the door, grinning.

"Did he?" Martha said. "How extraordinary!"

Perhaps she imagined the glances of disappointment between the two men as she stepped briskly from the car. But she didn't think so. *They had not discovered Magnanimity.*

"There's a surprise for you," Daniel said.

"See you later, Martha," Fairfield called as he drove on, talking intently to his companion.

Now why did I do that, Martha wondered. They would have to know. She had just grown into the habit of silence. Josh's message: it was a trust. But certainly it was to have been given to a man like Rance who was now in charge of the resistance. But something Fairfield had said had made her hold back. What was it?

She looked round, expecting to see Hans. That was the first face she had expected to see, here in Kayenta. The shades were drawn against the bright sun of early afternoon. On a camp bed in the corner of the room there was a figure, or could it be two figures? She drew close in the dim room and saw first two long pairs of legs, quite naked, a girl's and a boy's, intertwined in a confiding sort of innocence. Two pairs of jeans lay in an untidy heap beside them. A short, plaid coat lay across their torsos. The boy's tanned and grubby hand held that of the girl, and her long blonde hair lay like a fan over Buzz's red bristles.

Martha had found her son, and in the same moment realized that never again would he be her son in the old, familiar way. Mrs. Adams, who had lost her husband, looked down at the boy who had grown up. He would love her, she thought, but he would not belong to her ever again.

"Buzz," she said, and her hand was gentle on his head.

He gave a shout, was at once upright and she was folded into a bear hug. For a moment they were a family. She was introduced to Karen. "A great girl, Mom. We've been together since Ohio." Karen smiled, a little shy, a girl of the eighties but a pleasant one, Martha thought.

She and Daniel left the youngsters to tidy themselves, and in a back room she found Hans. He had come into town as Leo Hoffman, and he had continued in that role.

"I recognized Fairfield easily enough; I've seen him in photographs, gazing out over the border into East Germany. But Rance I didn't know, so I kept quiet until I saw Daniel here. They think I'm just your messenger, a sort of friendly 'useful idiot.' "

"Just as well," Daniel said. "They've done quite a job so far. They brought Buzz and Karen, by the way. The kids had got as far as Boulder, bless them. Rance and Fairfield between them don't have much idea of Magnanimity. And their plan is to make a deal."

"A deal?" Martha asked. Her spirits plummeted. It was the hint of a deal in Fairfield's words that had troubled her.

"Well," Daniel said, "of course, with what they've got, they haven't much bargaining power. What they're after is better conditions. Full rations for every US citizen. An end to the forced labor and conscription. Return of evacuees. Maybe a free zone west of the Rockies."

"With Magnanimity they could get that," Hans said. "Without a fight."

"Trust the Russians," Martha said. It wasn't a question. "A free zone? The United States is a free zone, nothing less. One nation," she said grimly, "indivisible. From sea to shining sea."

Daniel's face cleared. "My thoughts precisely, Mrs. A.," he said. "And, a small matter perhaps to Mr. Rance and Colonel Fairfield, but then my country, too, will be able to survive."

"What's the matter with our military men?" Martha asked. "Aren't there any left with real fight in them?"

Daniel shrugged. "They were too visible. A lot went in the first arrest waves. For the rest, it was a sudden, tough decision. Their Commander-in-Chief had surrendered. It was their duty to follow his orders."

"Would you have followed such orders?" she demanded.

Daniel shrugged. "For us, it's different. We cannot surrender. Dachau taught us that. So, Mrs. A.," he smiled, with a change of mood, "let's get our supplies and push on. Give them the slip until we are, you might say, in possession."

"In Dad's little nest?"

The sound of water being vigorously splashed in the next room had been slightly misleading. Buzz, his sketchy toilet made, was already standing in the doorway, yawning, his hand running through the bristles of his hair.

"You won't shrug off Rance so easy, Mom. He's already asked me a lot of questions. He had an idea there's more, all right, and that you know it. He's going to watch you as closely as the geeks would if they could grab you."

The room was warm. From chinks in the shades, beams of light stretched into the room, fingers pointing up the dancing motes of dust. The empty lodge was quiet and Martha felt an odd sense of conspiracy. She was conspiring with two foreigners and a boy against all that was left of the military power of her country. Yet her sense of uneasiness came only from the idea that they might be overheard. Somewhere an ear might be pressed by the wall; an eye might be watching at the ill-fitting shade. Paranoia, a classic case. Natural enough she supposed, under the circumstances. She caught Daniel's gaze, and saw that he understood.

"Do you know what happened to Robbie, Buzz?" she asked quietly.

His face was dark. "He was caught. We couldn't find him, they shipped the group out too fast. But he might have been shot; anyone they know was on the road gets shot at once. But I've good news of . . ."

Daniel's face warned him to silence, and the awkward moment was broken when Karen came in with fresh looks and a bright smile asking, "Is there anything I can do to help?" It might have been a charity tea, and Martha, liking the girl who kept her manners in a world turned upside down, smiled with the others. But she thought she heard the sound of a foot falling quietly on the gravel bed outside.

A short afternoon stroll, well away from the curious, was enough to make their plans. Buzz and Karen would ride back to the Navaho village and collect the jeep. The five of them would meet well after dark, when the Kayenta group should be sleeping.

"And so who are you supposed to be?" Martha asked Daniel, when the young people went back to collect their things. Colonel Fairfield had called him Archie, she remembered.

"Archie Bloom, a taxi driver. Very helpful for carrying messages for people like his brother Walt, for money, of course. A useful sort of fellow, whom you persuaded to become your right arm. A Jew who had to get away in any case, and was glad of the resources of a well-to-do woman." He grinned. "Your son, by the way, has a good, close mouth. I like him."

"But how did you get in touch with Fairfield?" Martha wondered. "You knew he was in Boulder . . ."

"Not many of my people about, as you can imagine," Daniel said. "But one or two. Here and there. The flight into the Rockies started before Fairfield ever got there. But when he did, I heard. When I got in touch with him, I used his brother's name."

"But you really knew from someone in Mossad?" she persisted, curious, though aware of how much he disliked the question. In the weeks she had known him she had learned that well enough. Yet in other ways she had learned so little of him.

"No, not Mossad. If you must know, from a curio dealer on Madison Avenue." He looked at her puzzled face. "No spy. But a man who had passed messages for certain people for a long time. You'd be surprised what can be hidden in pieces of old junk. But I daresay he's out of business now."

His face took on what she thought of as his other look, a grim coldness that she had once found frightening. But now, she supposed, she looked rather grim herself. Not much softness left after killing, traveling underground knowing that she endangered everyone who gave her aid, holding back, lying, deceiving her friends and bearing the burden of knowledge that no mortal being should ever have.

"Then we'll see you later, Mrs. Adams," Karen said as she rode off, her young body sitting lightly and well on the horse. Her manners were as courtly in her generation, Martha thought, as those of the young French aristocrats were in theirs when they went off in the tumbrils to face the guillotine. But Karen and Buzz would *not* face any guillotine. She would save her young.

Her young lovers. She smiled. The usually silent Buzz had been loquacious. "She's the greatest. As brave as—as the guys at the Alamo. And steady, as steady as Dad. Nothing fazes her, nothing—except maybe getting locked up. She goes a bit crazy when she's shut up. She was picked up once near Columbus and she'd nearly gone ape by the time I sprang her from the cell. But really great . . ."

Martha dined with Fairfield and Rance simply but

well in the small house they were using. John was so warm, friendly, so much his old self that she reproached herself for thinking he could have sent someone to eavesdrop on her. It must have been her imagination.

The little town had been empty save for the Indians when they arrived, the men told her. Once the supplies of gasoline and food had stopped coming the inhabitants had dispersed, first the whites, going to the cities where they expected life to be better and where no doubt they had found it worse. Then most of the Indians had wandered off, no one knew where.

"We arranged our own supply system early on," Rance told her. "We have parties raiding factories and bringing out equipment so we have plenty of trade goods. And we do some shooting. Here we get vegetables from Navaho farms."

Before Rance arrived for the meal, Fairfield had been praising the CIA man. "You must appreciate his courage, Martha. He could have stayed in Europe, well hidden. Instead he returned, knowing what was in store if he were captured. And his brilliance, his organizing capacity has given us a nationwide network now. Some Russian-held installations have been penetrated."

He had certainly inspired Fairfield, Martha saw. The two hosts had invited "Leo Hoffman" to join them. Hans, in his role of a wealthy property owner of German background, had managed to present himself as a sympathizer with their cause, and a helper of the refugee Martha Adams. Martha felt, rather than observed, Fairfield's slight hesitation in asking the taxi driver to join them. Daniel was being very much the New York taxi driver, proclaiming his dislike of the sticks, but swearing that the Arizona arroyos were no worse than the potholes of his home city.

Martha caught his eye once or twice, afraid that he was overdoing it. When Clayton Rance asked if he would like to join their force, he complained long and bitterly of the state of his kidneys from long years of driving, and of his low back pain. She was certain that the other two men must see through this heavy caricature, but they did not.

"An odd little monkey," Fairfield said later, over a cigarette, after Daniel had left them, saying that an Indian girl was waiting for him. Hans had also excused himself, pleading weariness. "Not the type to join us. So few city people are. I wonder that he wasn't more of a nuisance to you than he was worth, Martha."

Fairfield had the idea that her UN papers had helped her travel, at least much of the way. She let him think so. Rance, she gathered, had more understanding of the realities of the situation.

"Well, John, it's always useful for a woman to have a man with her. I don't suppose Mrs. Adams had all the choice in the world, and he was sent to her by Walt. That Hoffman is a decent type. You joined forces in Chandler, he told me. He's offered to do anything he can, and we might be able to use him. But that taxi driver is something else. We have to keep him under our control if he likes it or not. If he ran into the wrong hands he could do us incalculable damage. We're pretty secure here, but it's not like the Rockies. The Sovs haven't shown much stomach for challenging us there as yet."

"Martha," Fairfield said. "We've got some news out of the old NORAD complex—a few of our people are in there—and I think the story is reliable. There's been an exchange of atomic weapons between the USSR and China. A terrible thing, of course, but it must be, sad though it is, to our advantage. Under these circumstances they will be more likely to want to come to terms with us. They will need their troops for the border."

"Then we tell them to clear out," Martha said. "Shall I draft the message for you, John?"

The two men laughed. "It won't be as clear cut as that, I'm afraid," Rance told her, as though he were addressing a child. "They are very much in command

here. They have every military base, and I am afraid
that they have almost all of our submarine nuclear
force. According to the terms of the surrender, the
vessels and the ports were handed over; only a few of
them had been taken out. By now most of the crews
will be Soviet or allied men. But we will be able to deal
with them from a position of *some* strength."

The men went on discussing the details but Martha
stopped listening. I suppose you're behaving oddly,
Martha Adams, she thought. But she was in no hurry to
tell Colonel Fairfield, the new C-in-C, about Magnanimity. Much as she liked him, she wished that some
more traditional type of officer had survived to take
charge; one more forceful, less inclined to endless,
thoughtful deliberation. The country did not need a
Hamlet now, it needed a MacArthur, a Patton—a
Washington.

Then her mind went to the difficulties of finding
Barkham's trading post that was unmarked on any map.
She had been so blithe back east. Although she had
known the distances in Arizona, the huge sweep of the
land with its inhospitable terrain, it was blurred in her
mind by her years in the tidier spaces of New England
and the confines of city life. Now it seemed she had
taken on a labor of Hercules. But she had changed
from the woman who liked to take decisions and make
detailed plans. She would go on as best she could and
trust to the Fates.

After she said goodnight, she returned to the house
where Buzz had been staying. Daniel and Hans had
checked the posting of the Colonel's men about the
place. His sentries were watching for people coming,
not going. As long as they didn't use the road, the three
of them would be able to slip away quietly enough.

"Walking," Hans groaned. "*Not* my favorite sport."

"Only a mile or so," Daniel said. "At least now I've
got a decent compass. Some decent guns as well."

Before they left, Daniel provided both of them with

heavy pistols. He himself still carried his knife, and Martha saw that he carried a gun in a leg holster. They were also to be burdened with a large can of gasoline and one of water: "You never know," Daniel said. Martha was handed a third package; food, for the journey, and, it was hoped, for the destination.

Just before they left, Martha hesitated. "Perhaps I should leave Fairfield a note? I could say we went down near Shonto to meet Buzz and Karen who are collecting the car. It might keep them from looking for us, for a bit."

"They know we wouldn't walk so far," Daniel said. "I'll have to take another car and dump it, out of sight. Not a bad idea, though it means getting rid of a sentry. Hans, I think you can get one drunk. The Colonel is rather sparing with his men's comforts, I hear."

When they finally made their way by moonlight on a small dirt track, Daniel was talking about their chance of disappearing, mainly, she thought, to keep Hans's mind off the difficulties of the walk, laden as they were.

"I don't think Fairfield and his group can stay round here much longer. I can see the Russians rolling in here in strength and they will have to make a quick retreat. It puzzles me a bit," he added, "that they aren't here already. Martha, they must suspect you were on that aircraft to Chandler. That roundup was to catch us. And disguise or no disguise, surely someone has worked out that you were the woman who jumped the truck at Cameron. The New Order in Indian Affairs won't hold them back on anything that matters."

They plodded on for a time, and Martha thought crossly that they might have taken the stolen car in *this* direction. But for Daniel that would never do.

"It's surprising in a way," he went on, "that they haven't sent in men to take on the group in the Rockies. They know they're there, why wait?"

"You think like a foot soldier, not a missile man," Hans told him. "It's a long job, and it takes a lot of men to comb those mountains. Better to let the troublemakers collect, fortify themselves, dig themselves into the rocks and then blast them out. A couple of SS 18's, no problem."

"And perhaps they don't have a lot of Russian troops to spare," Martha said. She told them of the strike against Manchuria, and the counterstrike.

"And so it has come," Hans said softly. "I wonder how much, how long? Where it will spread, now it has started. 'The roar of thunders reverberates, gleams the red levin, and whirlwinds lick up the dust.'" His face was somber.

"It has gleamed already," said the more prosaic Daniel, "when they hurled their lightning bolts over here. They will be more wary of reprisals from the United States now. When they hear from us, Martha, I think they will pay heed. They will be ready to give up conquest, to keep their own homeland."

But the quiet of the night, the vast expanse of sky, afflicted Hans with a certain sense of doom. When they came to the meeting place at the foot of Black Rock Standing, Martha was relieved to see Buzz and Karen waiting beside the car, young, confident, single-minded.

"How far are we going, Mom?"

"All the way," she said.

—— XXXII ——

Ulyanov sat in his study in the Kremlin, bowed over his desk by a piercing, crushing grief. The room had once been Lenin's and long kept as a museum. He had taken it for his own, keeping everything from the photograph of Karl Marx to the bearskin rug, and the cast iron statuette of the ape regarding a human skull. It had been a matter of pride, to show himself the true successor of the man he claimed as kin. For a time he had thought he had achieved this goal. With the death of Tikhonov, and his own gaining control of the Council of Ministers, he was without doubt the greatest of the Soviet leaders since Stalin, and, with the fall of the United States, the one great leader of the world.

Then the blows had fallen. First there had been the discovery of the Doomsday weapon, or weapons, lurking somewhere on earth or in the heavens, to be flung at the Soviet heartland in one wild passion of revenge. Then had come his first defeat in the Politburo where the hawks had urged the pre-emptive strike on China.

383

And third had been the surprising, confounding strength
of China herself, using technology previously unknown.

That had set the cat among the pigeons. Some Politburo members had already fled to the safety of the
underground shelters, earning themselves, he hoped,
the title in time to come of the new heroes of the
October days. And some were already off to New York
City. He himself had not worried for his own safety.
The Chinese were not yet ready to strike at Moscow
itself. Hers was the war of the cat's paw. A blow, a
withdrawal, perhaps another blow, much later, or perhaps a long and wearing struggle waged by the guerillas, already infiltrated into the Asian Soviets.

These were heavy blows, but it was none of them
that had turned him from a man approaching seventy
but still vigorous, to a man old and weary with all his
joy in life pulled up by the root. Looking down, he
stared at the papers before him that had brought him to
this pass. He had gone through the agony of trying to
believe that they did not mean what, obviously, they
did; that they were misinterpretations sent to him by a
jealous rival, distortions of the facts, outright forgeries.

But the signature was too well-known to him for
doubt; the trustworthiness of the men who had pro-
cured and forwarded the papers was above suspicion.
Ulyanov had not become who he was without being
able to face the truth, but this was the bitterest truth of
all. Perez had discovered, or thought he had discovered, the Doomsday weapon, and Perez had decided to
betray him. Perez, after all, had decided that he, and
not the Soviets, should rule the world. Like Castro, a
"dangerous little brother." He looked down again at the
words in the bold hand, the familiar script. "No copy
. . . *nada.*" But Perez was not, like Castro, a fraternal
comrade. Perez was his son and his joy.

The Spanish Civil War, World War II, were history,
history in the books, history to Ulyanov, except for the
memory of the Spanish comrade, that lovely woman,

who had taken refuge in Moscow after Franco's victory.
Ulyanov, already married to a conventional Russian
wife and father of a child, had fallen in love, for the first
time—and the last. In the shadow of Stalin, he was not
yet a man of much importance, and he had kept his
affair away from the notice of Beria and his thugs. After
the war was over, and the mother left to resume her
struggle in Spain, he had had their son placed in a
special school. He was sixteen when Castro had taken
over in Cuba, and the boy with his fluent Spanish had
been trained to become a "Cuban" hero, ready to wrest
control from the Castro brothers if they became too
difficult.

Ulyanov's three children by his marriage had been
disappointing, spoiled with an appetite for Western
luxury and Western vice. His pride in the youth called
Perez had to be secret, but it grew all the stronger for
that. If he could have made him his successor he would
have done it, but Ulyanov knew the limit of his power.
Perez might have guessed the secret of his parentage;
Ulyanov had stood his friend so long. But it had meant
nothing to him. In fact the father had been for the son
merely a step on the road to power. Like father, like
son. Ulyanov himself had stepped on every living being
in his path to arrive at the place where he now sat. The
pinnacle of power, a wretched, ugly and uncomfortable
room that was not even his own choice, merely the
reflection of a dead dreamer of a mad dream.

Ulyanov had always feared Kharkev. The present
master of the KGB was a formidable man. But this time
Virinsky, that clerk, had outdone him. Virinsky had
pointed out to him, with a cold inevitability, what now
must be done. And Ulyanov knew he must do it. His
love for the most brilliant of sons could not come before
his plain duty.

On his desk the lamplight gleamed on the figure of
the brute, staring at the sightless skull. Ulyanov's task
was simple. Perez would suspect nothing. Even he had

not realized that among the men closest to him, one
worked for Virinsky and one for Kharkev. Perez was
now at the People's House in Hall City, planning for
the celebration at the United Nations on the 26th. It
was to have been their great day. Perez was to have
been behind him in the cortège in the parade.

Now the cortège would be his funeral procession.
After his death he must be given suitable rites. It would
please the people of the Third World. As Ulyanov
signed the order that was his son's death warrant, it
seemed to him that he himself was a dead man. *Nada,
nada*.

* * *

"Utah is Region VIII," Martha said.

"Don't worry," Buzz told her. "We came this route,
didn't we, Karen? And there were no barriers up, or
ditches. They haven't got to it yet, I guess. Besides, it
would mean cutting across the reservation, though Rance
says after a few months that won't make any difference.
I dunno. Mom, all the tribal leaders have been invited
to your old talk shop for the big pow-wow on the 26th.
Old Ulyanov is supposed to be there and a lot of others."

Martha remembered. She also recalled Buzz's visit to
Armand Lesseps, interpreter, radio buff, that had nearly
caused Buzz's capture. That would have been the second capture. And the final one.

"Most of them won't go," Buzz went on. "They're
suspicious. Except a few—the young guys call them the
Uncle Tomahawks. They have their own ideas."

Her son, Martha noted, had become quite fluent in
his speech.

Hans's mind was on other things. "Do you think
we're in any danger from the tribes?"

The sun had not yet risen, but Martha could see
Buzz's face clearly enough in the first pale light. He had
an odd expression. "It seems to be the *military* they

don't want about. They don't like uniforms just now.
Normally they don't mind travelers. In fact, they do a
lot of trading. Especially the Navahos. But since the
strike, well, truth is, they've started doing the Ghost
Dance. They seem to be collecting near here. I don't
know if it's just the Navahos, or any of the other tribes,
but Karen and I saw it. It's real weird, but I guess you
can understand it."

Daniel looked up from his map. They had crossed
Laguna Creek and had to strike northeast or north-
west. As they still hadn't learned the whereabouts of
Barkham's Trading Post, it was a tossup.

"Ghost Dance?" Hans asked. The worldly European
didn't like the sound of it.

"It began with a Paiute, an Indian prophet, Wovoka.
It was a religion, Messianic, hopeful, with its own ceremonies and rites," Martha explained. "But it changed
. . . by the time it came to the Sioux they were at the
end of their resistance. If I remember correctly, their
rituals were supposed to hasten the day when a great
calamity would come to the whites, a huge landslide
that would swallow them up and leave the Indians in
possession of the continent again."

"Oh, I see," Hans answered. "I suppose if I were an
Indian I might be doing the Ghost Dance myself." He
pulled a face. "But do you think we're all right?"

Buzz shrugged. "OK for now. The women were great
to Karen."

Martha found that she had gone beyond such normal
fears. Now she had other, more dreadful thoughts crowding in. With the sunlight, the helicopters returned to
the sky and their small party hid until nightfall. Next
day, they traded the car once more with money and
goods for horses and two Navaho skirts for the women,
and rested before they set out again. While Martha
slept, or tried to sleep, the questions she had refused to
ask herself in the past days and weeks came to haunt
her mind. Suppose the Soviets called her bluff? Or the

silo was inoperable? The missile itself might be useless. Perhaps they would be spotted—especially if Fairfield brought up a division of troops—and bombed out of existence. It would take no great missile to do that.

She sweated, turned, tried to settle herself, and her mind went round again. If she delivered the ultimatum and the Russians were unafraid . . . Virinsky of the cold, monk-like aspect would not frighten easily, she knew that. The Russians might rely on their undoubtedly efficient ABM systems to bring down Magnanimity, perhaps over the United States. They could do that. They had taken over the Norad system. She jumped up in a sweat of apprehension, pulled on her clothes, walked outside the ramada where she had been sheltering into the bright sun, trying to restore her calm.

When she heard a step behind her she hoped it was Daniel, but Daniel always slept like a child, only wakened by some mysterious sense when danger came. She was not pleased at that moment to see Hans, Hans whose European fears at the spreading of the war, most natural, could not ease her. But she was wrong. Still half in the grip of her nightmare-filled mind, she blurted out her worries and he was as composed as he had been on their first meeting, in the lovers' lane in northern Pennsylvania, surely a year away.

Now he spoke from his professional knowledge. "Don't worry, I heard a lot from Fairfield. The Russians miscalculated. They ruined NAVSTAR which was the last thing they wanted to do. And they meant to knock out NORAD's sensors only, but they did a lot more damage than that. They have men working on it, but they couldn't bring in all Sov men and our people in there are managing to hold up sensitive parts of the work. And no matter what ABM's they have," he said, pride taking over, "they would need a miracle to hone in on the Magnanimity missile. Israel had its geniuses working on the cobalt theory, not only old Shlomo Darin but he had David Bohm on his team. Bohm had been here in the States, by the way, but he was declared a security risk and went to Israel. But the missile itself is something quite new. It was designed, if not by a genius, then by a *very* talented man."

He smiled. "We have some tricks that the boys at Glushko's Rocket Engine Design Bureau have never heard of. And they couldn't steal them from the Americans, because the Americans didn't know what they were. Heat sensors won't react to this bird and lasers can't knock it out. And besides, it has some other new tricks. The silo requirements had to be changed slightly," he said. "So your husband was probably the first to guess it was something very special. Magnanimity. If I had been working for Krupp it might have been the Big Johann. Oh, well. No fame for a design engineer."

They were to set off soon, but Martha felt refreshed and needed no more sleep. She had got this far by taking the obstacles one at a time, and that was the way she must go on. Sufficient unto the day . . .

The young missileer sat before the console in the firing capsule. He was trained, an expert, and had spent much time in similar capsules in the mountains of the Pinar del Rio, usually bored, as a missileer spends his life in boredom. But he was alone now, and he was afraid.

He had brought a tapeplayer with him, although it was forbidden. But the mournful singer was crying of love and death and the melancholy, plaintive note of the guitar struck him with chill though he sweated with foreboding. It had all started out so well. He had been honored to be among the chosen for this special mission. He could not believe it when he had met the commander Perez himself and been clasped to his bosom. The missileer had sworn to do his duty and uphold the honor of his native land.

The sight of this strange country, this vast and rocky

space, had sobered him. The Indians were hostile. The console itself was different from those he was accustomed to and that worried him. Senior officers and some men he didn't know had come with engineers and technicians and checked the big *pajaro*, the range equipment, the launch support. Some repairs had been made and they had left for the guardhouse on the surface in an old abandoned shack, half a kilometer distant. He was here alone, except for his connection to the support facility, also buried underground. There was only one firing capsule here. Two missileers could turn their keys and launch the *pajaro*, but he had been told not to concern himself. He and the other men were merely holding the big bird. The keys were still snug in the safe. Soon more missileers would come and there would be a regular rotation schedule. There was a state of peace and he need have no fear of dying by enemy fire. But he had not been afraid of enemy fire; that was always a chance in a missileer's life. He was afraid of the door.

He had hated and feared the door when he had first seen it, and he hated and feared it more now. For there was no way out of the capsule on this level except through that door, and it was a door of a kind he had never seen though he had worked on many sites. It was a door of death.

The door was set in the tunnel leading to the elevator shaft. It was really two doors, an inner and an outer, both made of half-inch armour steel with a steel-lined, five-by-seven foot cubicle between them. There was a small one-way peephole on the inner door. Once the outer door was closed, the inner door would not open until a man inside the chamber triggered it by pressing a small button. It was designed for a twenty-four hour guard system. No unauthorized personnel could enter, but the last man to leave had to pray that the electric mechanism did not stick. Otherwise he would be locked inside the door until his distress signal was heard; he was acknowledged as identified, and a team of electricians came to restore the failed circuit. Once he had been trapped in the airless space for three hours when the electricians had left the site for some enjoyment of their own and he had feared himself a dead man.

He buzzed the signal once more to the upper level but there was no reply. Up there, the men were just below the surface with an emergency exit allowing them to slip out into the sun and air, while leaving him here trapped in case of fire. His imagination pictured the Indians, angered by the intruders, slaughtering the handful of troops and himself moldering in this dungeon until his bones were dust. The singer went on, with a song of a soldier, some woman's sweetheart, lying cold and dead. The missileer was a brave young man but as the hours wore on he longed for his home and cried at the thought of his mother.

Virinsky was still in his office and in as savage a humor as any his staff had seen. He disliked air travel but he had made arrangements for a special plane to wait for him on standby. He expected a message from the west at any moment. But he could not leave; he was bombarded by urgent calls from Kharkev, messages and instructions relayed from Ulyanov, and sometimes by Ulyanov himself.

Perez was dead, and with Borunukov in the Asian Soviets, the responsibility for the entire country was now openly in Virinsky's hands. Although he had his administration in order, criticism was directed at him personally for anything that displeased a member of the Politburo, or the Central Committee. Susskin, with his responsibility for production and economic planning, had complained that Virinsky's Class A security measures in the comparatively docile United States were tying up the country and that production had slipped far below the expected levels. He should look to his own production levels, Virinsky thought angrily, now that the Soviet Union had a taste of atomic warfare and the Eastern Soviets were searching for Chinese under every bed.

The Perez assassination had been easy enough to arrange. He and his bodyguard had been shot by KGB officers of the People's House garrison. A group of four American youths had been brought in and gunned down by the same officers and denounced as assassins. But Ulyanov had given Virinsky the job of arranging the funeral himself, to be the exact equivalent of the Lincoln and Kennedy funerals. Ulyanov was coming over and Virinsky was expected to meet him in Washington. Bristow must be brought out from the Watergate apartments, where he had been living under guard, and dusted off for the occasion. Until the 26th, he was at least the leading official of the former United States.

The 26th was only a few days off. There had been little time for the extraction of information from Perez's men. As always with a guerilla group, its very lack of organization made it time-consuming to penetrate. Even the KGB men who had been among Perez's most trusted cronies did not know the location of the silo he had discovered, nor did they know much about Magnanimity. Perez had been cunning and wary. No intelligence organization had worked more on a need-to-know basis than his. It was believed that he had taken a few, very few but excellent missile men from Cuba. Recently he himself had disappeared for a few days. Possibly he had left a small force wherever he had been but no one knew.

Virinsky himself had a definite idea of the general area where the missile must be. He had ordered intense interrogation of all of Perez's known men in the area. But he had only to find the woman who was heading there. Once more, at a place called Kayenta, she had almost been in his hands but again she had slipped away. And now he had to go to Washington.

His manners to his department chiefs were brutal. To Madame Paul, his indefatigable assistant, he was demanding to the point where that woman of steel nearly broke down. Madame Paul was not the woman she had been. Practical, worldly, she had survived her demotion in favor of Thu Thuy; she had even managed to swallow the humiliation of the verbal scourging she had endured in front of one who to her was little more than a common prostitute, but her three days and nights in the detention camp had all but broken her. Her own clothes had been taken away; her long hair cut. Madame Paul had been given scraps to eat that she would not have given a dog. She had been physically mauled, abused and when she complained, she had been beaten, and she had been derided by both male and female guards.

The humiliation of the collaborators' child after the Allied victory had given birth to the hatred of the Americans that had turned to a love of their enemies. The days and nights in the female camp, though not purging the hatred, ended the love. When she was returned, to be greeted by Virinsky's cold stare, her fire was gone.

Bathed, with a new coiffure, in her new and elegant garments, she felt like an old woman. For the first time in thirty years, she felt a longing for home, for France. Virinsky would never let her leave, not while he needed her. But she was still practical enough to know that as the time of crisis passed, and enough efficient new workers were trained, his need of her would diminish. And then what? Thu Thuy had been returned to Hanoi, but she knew more than Thu Thuy. She knew that information had been kept from Ulyanov himself. Would she be returned to France? Or might it be the female camp or its equivalent? She shivered as she worked. And there was one more twist of the knife.

In the course of her work she had caught sight of Virinsky's secret map of the New Order in Europe that was to be effected when the United Socialist Regions of the Americas were solidly established. France itself was to be dismembered to the benefit of the United Soviets of Germany. The hated German Soviets would include not only much of Western Poland but also Alsace, Lorraine and much of Franche Comté.

She worked as she must, but the once brilliant Madame Paul was now close to an automaton. Virinsky's personal assistant saw it, but it was not his business. At one time, his master, the most cunning man perhaps in the KGB, would have seen this change. He would not have so humiliated the woman in the first place, for Virinsky knew well enough the deepest drives of the human heart. But his obsession had changed all that.

"I will make the final arrangements," Virinsky said at last. "Send me Madame Paul. I must go to Washington. The funeral will have to be the day after tomorrow. I will stay with Ulyanov in the People's House, and all important matters can be relayed to me directly there. I have seen that our people alone control the Communication Room. Most especially I want any news that comes in from the interrogation of Perez's men. The Chief here knows what I want particularly. The Secretary-General can go to Washington and make speeches. But three days from now I leave for the West."

His secretary's face was impassive, but if he had dared show an expression it would have been a combination of fear and irony as he watched the new master of the Western world who cared for nothing except his frantic search for one American woman.

It was a difficult journey. Trails came to an abrupt end and had to be retraced. Often rocks would block the end of a path. Stony ground had to be cleared for the horses, and then the horses needed rest. At the whir of a helicopter, Daniel would look for cover. Worse still, when they met a lone Indian and inquired cautiously for Barkham's Trading Post they were met with a blank stare.

Buzz and Karen were still cheerful.

"What I started to tell you in Kayenta, Mom," he said, "was that my friend Armand—you remember him—is still O.K. He's still ready to help us if we can use him."

It seemed like years since Buzz had parted from Armand on West End Avenue. The two of them had been planning to assassinate the Russians. And the debonair young Armand was still willing to risk his life. There had been many good people at the UN, once. She wondered how many of them were still there. What had happened to Bob Postern, his assistant, her own girls?

But even Hans, who was protesting ruefully about his ancient bones, stopped at times as they crept through the awesome sweep of Monument Valley. The European born, seventy-year old man stared at the huge, sandstone butts glowing in the sunrise, and the columns of rocks like giant fingers poking from the desert into the immensity of sky, with the eyes of a wondering child.

"*Fabelhaft*," he said. "You can see, here, why the native peoples could believe in spirits of good and evil and the power of something like ghost dances."

Daniel grunted. "A lot of Indian men have fought in everything from the World Wars to Vietnam and there are probably some stuck in Europe in whatever's left of the old NATO force. I think the tribes have become pretty shrewd about their oil and mineral rights. You won't find Hiawatha round here."

"But Buzz says he's seen it," Hans pointed out.

Daniel was watching the sky and not for natural phenomena.

"Do you hear anything?"

But it was nothing more than the sound of a jeep on a dirt road not far off. They had passed through Cane Valley and had kept in sight of Comb Ridge. According to their best reckoning, they were now near, or on the Utah border. Martha's mind now was only on finding Barkham's. They had at one point been directed to an abandoned trading post, and had made a westward trek to find it, but before they had got there Martha had been sure it was not the place. They were definitely still on the Arizona side, between the East and West Mitten Rocks. It didn't take too long for Hans to confirm that this post was nothing more than what it seemed to be.

Martha had heard back in Kayenta of a trading post even further west, and the Paiute Farms Post, but both were far more than fifty miles from Blanding. The Paiute Farms certainly didn't sound like the "poor excuse for a trading post" that Josh had described.

Hans, who seemed content to be a parcel, was chatting away. "Your good friend, the Colonel, must be anxious about you, Martha. He probably thinks we've got ourselves lost in the desert and has search parties out for us. He and Rance seem to have quite an organization. Rance seemed very confident that government troops wouldn't come marching in on them."

Martha winced at hearing the Soviet-led forces described as government troops. But, of course, they were.

"Plenty of geeks about," Buzz said. "I heard they keep a big force at the Yuma Proving Grounds and at Kirtland."

But the next drone they heard was a helicopter. Fortunately, the light was fading. Daniel headed into a dip of land surrounded by boulders and they kept close to the rocks but Martha felt anxiously that five humans and horses must be noticed from above, and she was sorry she had urged Daniel to risk a faster, daylight ride. The drone passed, but Daniel was looking for a hogan in which they might spend a few hours.

"They might come back looking when the moon is up. And Hans needs a rest."

Hans protested courageously, but his discomfort and weariness were plain to see. They were lucky again in their reception by the Navahos, who occupied two hogans huddling together in the middle of the stretching empty space. It was the presence of women, perhaps, and an old man. They hardly looked like a military group. And though their hosts spoke English, they were pleased when Karen gave them a Navaho greeting, "Hah La Tse Kis." The wife beamed and Martha remembered that it was the women here who decided who should or should not be guests. The travelers brought food as well as gifts: Daniel had raided the supplies at Kayenta and had useful knives, and cans of meat, coffee and some chocolate bars which made their welcome warmer. Karen and Buzz were taken into one hogan, Martha, Daniel and Hans into another.

Martha's hostess served her own corncakes with the canned goods from the visitors and the meal was pleasant until Martha asked her if she knew the whereabouts of Barkham's trading post. The husband rose from the table and walked outside. The two little boys ran and hid behind the loom where a rug was half-completed. Martha looked at the woman who busied herself making coffee but did not reply, as a hostess with an ill-mannered guest might try to soothe over a moment of awkwardness. Martha said no more about it. The women went to rest on the sheep pelts. Daniel walked out after their host. Martha heard them return later, apparently on amiable terms.

At first light the women were awake and when the Navaho woman brought Martha coffee and hot panbread she gave her directions to Barkham's quite matter-of-factly, as though the question had just been asked. It was close by, a short ride or a good walk, but there was no point in going as it had been closed down for years.

Martha went to find Daniel to tell him. He had already breakfasted; the women waited until the men left the hogan before they ate. "I wonder why she wouldn't tell me last night," she said, puzzled.

"It was the night," Daniel said. "I realized after dinner, they really do believe in some sort of evil night spirit. They are disturbed now. Frightened, of what Hans calls the red levin. Well, it could be the same in Williamsburg," he said with a shrug. "If the missiles were coming close, some Hasids would think it a judgement."

"But it was the mention of Barkham's that made them afraid," Martha said. "At least at night. Could they know?" She was frowning.

"You can bet your boots they know something, or suspect it. I've been wondering how Reagan got away with it. It's hard to imagine the Navahos agreeing to missile construction on their land."

"A water project," Martha said, sighing. "It could have been done. But the Indians who lived close by might suspect . . ."

Daniel made his hostess a further gift which she seemed to like, big, round silver dollars. He *had* been busy at Kayenta. Martha hoped that Colonel Fairfield would not discover the robbery quite yet.

The Navaho woman responded to Daniel much as the Corbett women had done. She smiled graciously and invited Martha to come back and stay when she wished and her daughter also. Martha thanked her warmly, but she determined that once she found the Magnanimity missile she would stay with it until the job was done. Even though Daniel, she knew, would like to leave her here out of the way of trouble. But Josh had given the responsibility to her and she would stay with it to the end.

─── **XXXIII** ───

Virinsky stayed in the basement communication room of the People's House while the solemn còrtege wound its way through Hall City. It had been two days of farce in his mind, beginning with the reception of Ulyanov who looked, suddenly, feeble. While Virinsky was collecting data from all over the western hemisphere trying to track down the men who were holding Magnanimity, and having to do without the presence of Madame Paul and his most trusted assistants, all of Hall City was rushing about under Ulyanov's command trying to learn whether the Kennedy còrtege had used a white rider on a black horse, or a black rider on a white horse, or whether it was a horse alone. Virinsky, who never swore, mouthed childhood phrases about which part of the horse might do.

Ulyanov, carried away by this propaganda display (quite unnecessary in Virinsky's eyes, the days for such things were over) had spent little time inquiring about the fate of the Doomsday weapon.

"You have secured the weapon?" he had asked.

"We are locating Perez's men. With the suddenness of his death, the communication lines in the organization were cut. But it is well in hand. Forty-eight hours will finish it."

And Ulyanov had been satisfied with that. Certainly he must be going senile, perhaps from the shock of the China strike. He had declared a national day of mourning and wept into the television cameras before the blacks lining the route of the parade. The organizers had had some trouble getting them back to the city in time, and showing them in presentable condition. Ulyanov had insisted on a headline in the newspaper now to be called *The Ulyanovgrad Times*. The men had not set up the new banner which was to have appeared on the 26th, and so it came out under its old name, a corpse of a newspaper trumpeting the death of a traitor, who could not even die under his own name, whatever it might have been.

RAMON PEREZ DIES IN HALL CITY.

Idiocy. And Ulyanov would have to go to New York without him. Virinsky had to trust his people to prepare for the big circus to come, just three days off.

A message was brought to Virinsky from the chattering tape. A helicopter had spotted a party of five people who might have been Anglos, in an Indian village on the reservation near to the Utah border. Five people. Five had escaped from Kayenta. And Perez's men had been seen in a little town called Blanding. Tonight Virinsky must be at the funeral feast, but tomorrow he would finally snare Mrs. Martha Adams.

It was as well for them that the Navaho woman's directions had been clear. It had seemed to Martha that they were traveling too far east, but when they inquired of any lone passerby, once again they met only a gaze of incomprehension. Karen, at nineteen, was already a student of anthropology and had visited the reservation the previous year. "The Diné, that's what they call themselves, really do still fear the Chindee. Evil spirits who work at night. And Ahson told me, while you were outside this morning, that they think Barkham's an evil place, full of Chindee."

Martha noticed that Karen had got on first-name terms with her hostess, but Hans's thoughts were darker. "German peasants used to believe in *kobolds*—evil spirits," he said. "*Kobold*, that's cobalt in English, Martha. Odd coincidence."

The smiling, urbane Hans was changing, as they all were. But Karen could go on chatting. "The Navahos have had the Hochonji Chant to chase the devils away, but they were too strong. She begged that we stay indoors at night."

"Very likely they have their reasons," Daniel said briskly. "If they're really doing their ghost dance, I don't suppose they want a lot of white people watching."

"If they are, it won't be at night," Karen observed. "I'm certain of that."

She stopped. They had arrived at the entrance to the valley which Ahson had described. Even in the morning light, this remote place, the narrow valley between soaring rocks, looked fearsome and inhospitable to man for all its strange, wild beauty. Martha, still sharp-eyed, could see no structure built by human hand and felt a sinking of the heart but Daniel, always practical, had already raised his binoculars (another "loan" from Kayenta) and was scanning the distance.

"It's there," he said simply.

"Well, let's get on," Martha replied. Suddenly she was seized with excitement. Her mouth was dry; her heart pounded and she felt a fierce elation.

"In good time," Daniel said. He frowned. "There are cars outside. Hard to make out how many. It's further off than it seems."

"We've seen cars everywhere we went," Martha pointed out. "Abandoned cars. On the roads, at the pumps . . ."

"I'll do the rec," Buzz said eagerly. He had been fidgeting for more action than their cautious ride. "I'll go on foot . . ."

"You take one side and I'll take the other."

Karen whipped off her Navaho skirt. She still wore her jeans underneath and she put on her gun belt.

Martha started to protest but Daniel waved her to silence.

"They're both armed and they know what they're doing. They're soldiers, Martha, and they can do their job."

He gave Buzz a case with a pair of binoculars and spoke to him softly. Buzz nodded and disappeared into the rocks. Karen was out of sight already.

"We'll tie up the horses," Daniel said. "The kids can pick them up later. We'll follow the others down the valley for about a mile, and then we'll wait for them there."

They hitched the horses to the rocks. "Unless you'd rather stay here, Hans?"

Hans, though moaning, would not stay. "Anything better than another minute on that animal."

They moved as cautiously as if the eyes of the KGB were on the road, though with less rapidity than Buzz and Karen who traveled the rocks like young goats. The three elder members of the party gained a cave-like clearing at the roadside and waited silently for the others to return. Daniel peered down the road and up at the sky over and over again.

"No helicopters this morning," he said, after a half-hour had passed. "I wonder why?"

"They're searching another area, I suppose," Martha said.

"Perhaps." He sounded unconvinced. It was not possible, he thought, that the Russians had lost the trail.

He knew the special strength of the new masters. Whatever else might crumble, the KGB had started functioning at once. He had not hoped to escape Virinsky's men, merely to stay ahead. Picking up his glasses, he stared down the road again. Did the absence of helicopters mean that Magnanimity was already taken? He said nothing to Martha, but she caught his anxiety and despite the warmth of the sun at the cave's mouth, she shivered.

The absence of the helicopters had nothing to do with Magnanimity. Although Virinsky had ordered the search to continue unabated, Ulyanov's demand for all officials to rush to Washington to attend the obsequies for Perez had denuded the area of transport. Army helicopters had been commandeered and quarrels between the military and the politicians had become tense. Virinsky himself was embroiled, though in another facet, because he had demanded the old Presidential "Kneecap" plane, only to learn that Ulyanov was keeping it for his own use, and that the old Air Force One and Air Force Two had been taken by Borunukov for himself and his staff.

Borunukov had torn himself away from his border war for the great day in New York—Ulyanovgrad, which he was determined not to miss. He was still in theory one of the two remaining dictators of the United States. Virinsky wished sourly that he had been disposed of at Petropavlovsk.

Then Ulyanov had demanded that Virinsky confer with him for at least a day on the American situation before the final arrangements were decided for the Peace Day of the 26th. He had wanted two days, but Virinsky had persuaded him that it might be another great propaganda stroke for the existence of the weapon to be announced that day, and that he must go beforehand and make sure that their own men were firmly in possession. Perez's people probably did not know what they had and it would be as well that they were eliminated before any announcement was made. And this matter was of such moment that it should have his personal direction.

Ulyanov had muttered something about Borunukov, but his protest was halfhearted. Borunukov had been humiliated by the Politburo for the Chinese fiasco and the thought of his having control of the Doomsday weapon was not inspiring. Virinsky, on the other hand, had no taste for glory. Ulyanov had looked at the pale, clerkly eunuch of a man. He was reliable. Consent was given. Virinsky could leave as soon as their conference was over. The two men, both weary, sat at their business in the West Hall of the People's House, hunched over the mahogany and satinwood octagonal desk where presidents of the United States had worked, while Martha Adams shivered in her cave.

The wait for Buzz and Karen stretched on. Hans, who had slept badly, leaned against the side of the cave and closed his eyes. But this time Daniel could not sleep. He gazed at the woman beside him, who was curled up with the stillness of an animal ready to spring. He remembered the lady in white that he had seen under the shade of the broad leaves in a Connecticut garden. He thought her rather lovely then, her eyes holding the color of the green land around her. He had mocked her once: "Joan of Arc," he had called her. Now it no longer seemed such mockery. He had seen those green eyes trained on Fairfield, compassionate but in judgement, to find him wanting. Martha, his comrade-in-arms. A good comrade. There was no romance in him, he thought, with a faint amusement, for it had to be here, on these rocks at the end of creation, in the shadow of a weapon that could destroy the planet, he found he loved this woman.

*   *   *

There was the sound of running feet. Buzz was at the entrance to the cave. Before he spoke they all knew something was very wrong.

"It's crawling with troops. Maybe missile guys. I don't know."

"Soviet troops?" Daniel asked sharply.

"No," Buzz said. "Hispanics. I could hear them talking. Bitching about the place. My Spanish isn't so hot, but I could make out they thought it was a lousy dump and they wanted to get the hell out. Something about orders not coming, but I couldn't get much more.

"Something about no word coming from El Presidente," Karen added. "I think one said he was dead."

"Bristow is dead?"

"Not Bristow. I couldn't hear clearly. Something about a radio report. El Presidente . . . *muerto* . . Senor Perez, I think, *muerto*."

"About how many of them?"

"I saw over forty," Buzz said. "But there might be more. It's a big, sprawling old place. A crazy swimming pool not far off. But they've got some heavy weapons. Not fixed weapons, but mean-looking stuff. Portable machine-guns; maybe a shoulder-fired rocket. I couldn't get close enough to see."

"And we have eight army pistols," Daniel said. "We'll have to get up closer and see what we can do."

"Wait for dark?" Hans said.

"No, we daren't. Some of the Russian troops could move in any time. We have to risk it. We'll go the way you went, Buzz. Stay here, Hans, if you'd rather.

"My father skied at Garmisch when he was eighty," Hans said. "I suppose I can manage a few rocks."

They spent an arduous hour, scrambling over boulders, bruised, skinned and bleeding. About a quarter mile away, Daniel called a halt and raked the post with his glasses.

"They're leaving," he said sharply. He signaled to

Buzz, who was in the lead, to look also. "How many do you count gone?"

"Couldn't spot exactly but they nearly filled two of the vehicles—light trucks, roomy. I would say about thirty."

"That leaves ten or less." Daniel looked more cheerful.

"You don't think it's a trap?" Martha asked.

"I'm sure we weren't seen," Buzz said. "They're probably scouting around looking for info. Something's gone wrong up there."

"Perez's private troops who've lost their boss, perhaps," Daniel said. "We don't know how much time we have. We have to move in."

As they moved cautiously closer Martha saw how Buzz could feel confident in his estimates. Most of the trading posts she had seen previously had been much like the flat, one-story shopping malls seen in many country towns or along a highway. Barkham's was in the old style, a large wooden building where the trader's family lived as well as worked. Beyond was an enormous barn. There were the usual gas pumps bearing the "no gas" sign and incongruously a large modern pool with concrete sides was shimmering in the sunlight.

She felt, rather than heard, Hans's startled, "So!"

"There was nobody in that main building that we could see," Karen offered. "They were in the barn, or whatever it is."

"No windows," Daniel said.

"No. We got a look through the doors; they were wide open."

"What's the layout, Hans?"

"It's not the first plan that was discussed," Hans answered. "Not the mobile launcher. I suppose at the last they couldn't arrange to move the missile about. But there was an alternative." Martha remembered Josh's trip for construction changes. "The launching platform is under that pool."

"The pool?"

For once Daniel was surprised.

Hans was using the glasses. "If you were closer you'd observe the sloped sides well waterproofed. Two feet below the surface a special plastic cover protects against visual and radar observation. I've seen these plans. There's a reinforced concrete ramp giving access to the pad on the lower level. The launch firing capsule is underground and well away from the pad, on the other side of the elevator shaft. The control blockhouse seems to be underground also but probably closer to the surface. Very likely the access is from that barn."

"And the access to the shaft that leads to the pad and the capsule?"

"I don't see it," Hans said. "And I didn't see that diagram."

"Great camouflage," Karen was saying admiringly, but Daniel's attention was fixed on the door of the barn.

"They don't seem to have any guards posted."

"Not expecting trouble," Hans said.

"Perhaps we can get them out." Daniel put his glasses down, considering.

"Not fire," Hans said soberly. "Not here."

"No," Daniel answered. "Lets work our way round until we have a clear shot."

They lay in the rock at the roadside, sheltered from the view of anything on the ground.

"Get your weapons ready, but don't shoot unless I signal. I'll shoot first."

He fitted a silencer on his own pistol.

"All right, Karen, laugh."

"Laugh?" She was startled.

"A nice lazy, sexy sort of laugh. A roll in the hay sort of laugh, or a roll in the rocks. Enticing, but loud enough for them to hear."

Buzz leaned over and gave her a hefty pinch on her seat. She shrieked and laughed, the laughter turning warmer, softer. In a moment two men's heads appeared round the barn door.

"Again," Daniel whispered.

Karen laughed. Her slight movement made a stone fall with a sound that to Martha seemed an explosion. The two men, grinning, curious, walked towards the rocks. Daniel's gun made two popping sounds and the men fell. It seemed like a game, except for the smell of cordite and the dark patches on the fallen men.

"Martha, come with me. You three cover us."

The two of them scrambled forward and dragged the bodies out of sight. Martha dragged about a hundred and fifty pounds of human flesh over the stones, glimpsing a still youthful, bearded face. Once behind the rocks, Daniel checked the bodies and took the weapons. "Both dead," he said briefly. "Again, Karen."

Karen looked sick. "You laugh, Martha."

The dragging had been worse than the shooting. Not knowing if the wounded man was still alive. Martha felt she couldn't laugh. A look from Daniel, and she laughed.

There wasn't much sex in it to her ears, but one after the other, three men ambled slowly from the barn, their heads lifted like those of dogs, scenting a bitch in heat.

"Drop your jeans," Daniel told Karen. "Martha, throw your skirt over that rock," and the torn Navaho skirt fell where he indicated.

He motioned for them all to get back. As the first man peered over the rock, Daniel's knife was waiting. His vocal cords went with his carotid artery and there was only a strange, creaking groan as Daniel and Buzz hauled him out of sight.

As the two others came within range they caught a glimpse of the long-legged Karen and stopped short. Before they recovered, Daniel's gun had pumped out two more shots. The head of one man shattered, and the second clutched his belly and sank moaning to the ground.

Daniel was already reloading swiftly. "Now," he said. "We don't have to be too quiet. They'll expect the others. Move fast and blast as soon as you can see round the door.

The inside of the barn was lit and Martha had a clear view of shelves filled with sheepskins and in front a large wireless transceiver around which a group of four men were huddled. She raised her weapon on command and took her shot; it took two to dispatch her victim. The men had been so startled that none of them had done more than reach for their weapons. She stared at the ruined bodies.

"And so we take possession," Daniel said.

—— XXXIV ——

Virinsky left the Communication Room still in a state of rage. He had finished Ulyanov's business, but his man who had so absurdly lost Martha Adams at Kayenta still had not tracked her down, despite all the assistance given to him in the search. Perez's missile team, cut off suddenly from the personal control of their leader, were as lost as the missile itself. Ulyanov himself was still drinking at the funeral feast but he, Virinsky, had excused himself on urgent matters.

"You must return with me to be at my side on the podium," Ulyanov had said in drunken amity. "Kharkev was too much engaged, but you should be there to represent the Committee of State Security. I rely on you, Kostya. We haven't settled the matter of the Caribbean. Without Perez, who will . . ." Tears actually started up from those eyes. "Surely the Guard can take care of the installation without you, after all."

Once again, Virinsky assured him that he would return in time for the great event. Was Ulyanov worried, perhaps, that he would follow in Perez's footsteps? The fool. If he, Virinsky, did so, he would not be so clumsy. But he must have the information. He could not go and take the time to search himself along the Utah-Arizona border, looking for a trading post that might hide a missile base. That was the location if anything the woman Huck had told him was the truth. Instinct told him it was so, but there was no time left for anything but certainty.

Borunukov was back, at least for a few days. If his men found the installation first . . . Nearly mad with frustration, Virinsky could neither sit, stand still or walk. He fidgeted with a nervous twitching that would have surprised his New York staff; the phlegm of the bureaucrat had vanished.

That idiot in Arizona deserved to be executed. And he would be, when this was over. The Second Department had moved in swiftly on Perez's men, but Virinsky had made certain his own men took the top ranking officers. A great deal of surprising information had been gained, but nothing on the missile base. It was nearly noon the next day before the message came.

For Martha, the inspection of the Magnanimity site was a time of wonder. She had seen a missile site before, but never where almost everything was hidden from view. Hans's engineer's eye had proved true: the access door leading to the concrete blockhouse was in the floor of the "barn," a genuine old barn, carefully reinforced and then camouflaged to deceive all but a most discerning gaze. Below the shelves of moldering sheepskins were the computer banks, communication systems, television screens as bright and shining as those of a NASA facility, winking before the cameras on the day of a great launch.

Buzz was taking the first stint of guard duty on top of the barn. Daniel had already drawn up a rota. Hans was inspecting, making notes, taking out of his breast pocket just such a notebook that Josh might have used.

"I'd like a day to check this," he said. "Everything seems to be functioning. Those men we slaughtered were good technicians. Didn't touch too much."

They had all helped in burying the bodies as best they could.

"But there's one thing," he added slowly.

Daniel looked up sharply at his tone.

"The main systems are switched through to the firing capsule. You'll probably find another team down there. We should be able to see them on the closed circuit, but the camera is placed so that you can only see the launch console. There's no one in sight, but that doesn't mean they're not playing pinochle or whatever they play now. It's a lonely, claustrophobic job down there. They should be in constant touch with the men on the upper level but those guys were the ones taking their leisure up in the barn. May God have mercy on them," he added, whether cynically or devoutly no one knew.

Daniel swore, tersely. "How many do you think?"

"Could be any number. Probably not less than two. One for each of the two keys. Two keys have to be turned, you understand, to make a launch."

"Only one way to find out."

Carrying the light machine guns, they traversed the underground artery to the square elevator block. The descent was ordinary enough, but when they left to take another passage to the firing capsule they were brought up short by a steel door that sealed it off completely. They stared.

"Is this it?" Martha said.

"No," Hans said. "Or not all of it. The wall is six feet thick. I've seen this job before, though not on a launch complex. There are two of these," he tapped the metal.

"Half-inch armor steel. And there's a steel-lined cubicle between the doors. Nobody is going to pop into the capsule and play who's got the keys. The inner door can only be opened by the guard in the inner room: he screens the arrivals through a one-way peephole. This door out here is opened by this button." He showed them the place on the wall, so smoothly set in that an observer without prior knowledge of its existence would never have found it. "There should be a guard out here. The Spanish contingent have been cutting corners. See?"

He pressed the button and the door slid up, giving access to the steel-lined chamber. But the second door remained firmly down.

"You mean we can't get in?" Martha's voice reflected her dismay and disbelief.

"Oh, I expect so," Hans said, as he closed the chamber. "There's been trouble with these things before. The men inside can't be trapped by the inner door because they control that button, but the second is another thing. If the guard outside has wandered off, they're stuck. And more than once a man has been caught inside the chamber by an electrical failure that keeps both doors down. Until someone turns up to repair the circuit, whoever is inside the chamber is trapped. Terrifying, for it has no air supply. We used to call it 'The Last Exit'. Just as a firing capsule was 'The Tomb Room'. So although no one is ever supposed to know about it, the senior officer on the post got a radio control. Top Secret, and he was supposed to keep it by him at all times. I daresay I'll find one back on the upper level."

Hans's voice, as always, was casual, but the rest were anxious and trying to hide their anxiety as they searched the upper levels and no such device was found. They had to wonder whether, in this case, one had ever existed. Martha went on searching steadily, though Daniel had picked the lock of every locked drawer and done everything but take out the electrical panels. Hans removed one or two of those.

The others flagged; everything had been searched and re-searched, but Martha had the image of Josh before her. Josh, who would not have left a man-trap behind him if he could have avoided it. And perhaps it was easier for a woman to find. In the first drawer they had opened and abandoned, filled as it was with blank report forms, time sheets and a yellowed, half-done crossword puzzle, there was a box of tissues. She plunged her hand into the box and felt a small, familiar object. It could have opened the door of a suburban garage.

Karen laughed, and Martha would have laughed with her, but laughter could wait until she found it worked.

"Our Spanish friends may not have known about that," Hans said. "That drawer had an undisturbed look."

Daniel gave her a smile. "There's some good in these country housewives," he said.

Since the night of her finding Josh's papers in the pump room of the Connecticut house, Martha had spent much time in visualizing her finding of Magnanimity, the entrance to the firing capsule, the moment of drama. The great door slid up; the second door was opened; the consoles were before her. But it was not, after all, the machines that first caught her gaze. It was the figure of a man sprawled across the metal of the chamber floor, supine, his face, still distorted with a look of terror, his eyes staring up at them but no longer seeing anything in the world of men.

Hans had taken a few hours sleep, and then went to work on his task of checking the equipment on all levels, even going down with Buzz to the lair of the beast itself.

He reported to Daniel in the morning, while the rest of them were looking for something to eat. The men in possession had apparently been living on canned goods. There was no functioning electricity in the trading post itself, but the barn had power from the installation's generator. Martha found coffee and a metal jug and Buzz connected an old hotplate. They drank the coffee and immediately Martha felt better. Perhaps the others did too. She relaxed a trifle, and then saw the trace of a splash of blood on the table before her. How many men did I kill yesterday? she thought. The image that persisted was of the man she had dragged, perhaps alive, perhaps dead, bumping across the rocks and stones like an unwanted mattress. She had done it. No sense to shut it out of her mind.

"I'll have some coffee, Mom," Buzz said, casually, and she rinsed another mug. Of course, Buzz had grown up. How many men had he killed?

They had all been sickened by what they had seen in the chamber door. The man's hands had been bruised and bloody. Panic, Hans had said. Heart failure, Daniel had added, pointing out the blue color of the man's lips. Both, most likely. The man had been young. The lone missileer had thought himself abandoned, entombed. A ghastly way to die. It was a pity that Karen had had to see it. The girl who had been afraid of nothing had turned a greenish white and shrank from the place as though its very touch was leprous.

"Hans says Magnanimity is all-systems go," Daniel told them. "He's running the last computer checks. We have to think now about the ultimatum, the wording, the delivery."

For an instant it seemed to Martha that she saw the end of a long nightmare, as at the moment when a dreamer drifts towards waking and the solid structure of the nightmare world starts to crumble and dissolve.

"Ulyanov," he went on, "and most of the Politburo

are in New York for the 26th and Borunukov I daresay is with them. The 26th is tomorrow. I suggest the ultimatum be delivered there."

Karen was on guard duty. Martha poured more coffee and nodded. Buzz listened.

Daniel, who claimed he didn't smoke, pulled on a cigarette in long, satisfying drafts. "Now as to the means of delivery. It might be wise, now we have Magnanimity, to contact Fairfield's organization. He has the connections to use military aircraft without challenge . . ."

"But one of *us* must deliver the ultimatum," Martha said at once. "The Colonel would water it down."

"Of course," Daniel was crisp.

The man who had seemed so natural in the role of a taxi driver, now played the battle commander and the role sat upon him just as easily.

"Fairfield was speaking of his people in the NORAD complex. They have all the communication equipment you can think of, and most of it is in working order. We really need only to get to Cheyenne Mountain and we could deliver the message from there, through telephone, telegraph. Like a happy-birthday message."

Looking at her son, Martha was struck with an idea. She must ask Buzz . . .

Hans came in, holding out a mug for coffee and smiling a rather odd smile.

"I've checked and re-checked the targeting. It seems that Señor Perez's men made no changes. I need make only the slightest adjustment to correct for prevailing winds. Of course, perhaps they just hadn't got to do it, but it does seem somewhat illuminating."

Hans could still be amused by the changing partners of political bedfellows, but Daniel could only think of the problem at hand.

"Where exactly?"

They bent over a map of the Soviet Union which Hans had brought up with him.

"Here, and here. Smolensk, Moscow. A series of in-air and on-the-ground explosions. Here . . ." Hans's finger swept along a path northeast, east to north then northeast to north. "It's plotted for the winds among other things. The radiation will be deadly up until the Kolyma range."

"But won't they figure they can bring it down over here?" Buzz said, scowling.

"They couldn't," Hans said. "And they won't dare take any risk, now they're embroiled with China."

"But what they don't know won't frighten them," Martha pointed out.

"That was thought of a long time ago," Daniel said. "Someone took a political gamble. Peace for Taiwan, and China got some of the new missile data. Not the atomic stuff, of course, but the mechanical. The Soviets have just had a few shocks from the power to their south. No, the game is in our hands now."

"One small thing," Hans said. "The two keys. They're in a booby-trapped safe in the firing capsule. I can take care of the booby traps, but the safe is something else."

"No problem," Daniel said, "I've already seen it."

Hans raised an eyebrow. "For such an amiable fellow," he said to Martha, "he has shocking habits."

The men went below and didn't return for two hours. When they came up, Hans explained that the firing mechanism had been made for two keys, at such a distance that one man, alone, could not start the final sequence, but he had adjusted it for a solo launch.

"We might not be able to spare two people," Daniel said.

Then he smiled. "Probably we'll have no trouble. It's just the winding up, now."

He was a little premature. While they sat at the table, arguing the terms of the ultimatum, Karen came running in. Two army vehicles were approaching.

"Looks like the ones that left yesterday," she said, panting.

"Go to your posts," Daniel told them. He himself took a light machine-gun and made for the roof. The previous day when they had assembled the weapons the men had left, they had found the heavy stuff was gone and assumed the main group must have made a final departure.

As Martha took her place by the barn door she was grim. Hans had said the technicians who had worked on the site had known their job. But these men were low-ranking, undisciplined troops. They would have little idea of what they were guarding. They would not have fear enough to respect the controllers of the Doomsday weapon. Neither Borunukov nor Colonel Fairfield would dare to try to take this place by force, yet in this stupid skirmish they could lose everything.

Daniel got in the first blow, raking the canvas of the second vehicle with machine-gun bullets and leaving most of the men out of action, while the retreat of the first was blocked. But they were trained fighters, and they quickly abandoned the light truck and disappeared into the rocks before the small party in the barn could pick them off. Martha had wounded a man, Buzz had brought one down, and Karen two, but there were still at least fifteen or sixteen men at large.

Hans cursed. "I've never been much with small arms," he said.

Daniel's voice came clearly from the roof.

"Martha. Your second station."

She obeyed instantly, though with dread. Slipping through the hidden door she made her way again through the labyrinth below. The plan had been, in case of serious attack, that one of the party must go to the firing capsule. "If enemy forces break in, you must fire the weapon," Daniel had said. They had all been instructed.

In the Tomb Room, she tried not to think of what

was going on upstairs, to think of anything else. This place looked like a dull utility room. The two bright, plush, posture-control chairs seemed incongruous. It was no use. The console was before her. Daniel's voice played in her mind like an insistent record. "You can see who is there through that one-way peephole. If it is the enemy, you know what to do."

She was seized by an uncontrollable fit of trembling. Time flashed on the console, second by second, minute by minute, hour by hour. Soon she was drenched in sweat. She thought of the man who had died there. She thought of Buzz, Daniel, Hans and Karen. Of the multitudes of millions who would die if she turned this key, die with no warning, no opportunity to withdraw from the battle, to make an honorable surrender.

Four hours had passed, and she might well have been entombed. There was no sound, not even the crackle of an open line to the upper level. Nothing. What if all her people were dead, and the enemy just stayed up there, on the face of the earth, waiting for her to emerge, as she must at last. Must she turn the key before she left? How long should she stay? Then she thought of the upper level. Could the enemy cut her firing connections from there? She knew so little, she thought in despair. And then she remembered some of Hans's words from the night before. The connections went straight from this room to the missile itself.

Another hour went by. She would have to act at last. But not yet. She looked at the key glittering before her in the white, bright light as though it were the enemy, or all the devils of hell. But she raised her arm, put her hand forward and took hold firmly.

When at last a faint hiss came from the loudspeaker, the knuckles of her hand, clutching the key, had turned white. But the voice that spoke was Daniel's. "All clear. Buzz is coming down to relieve you. Check him at the peephole before you release the door."

Her relief was so profound, the release from tension so great that she felt dizzy. Her hand had fallen from the key. For a moment she hung her head between her knees to recover her balance, and then she murmured a quiet prayer.

Buzz gave her a start when she peered out. His face was covered in grime, and there was a smear of blood on his forehead. He could not see her, but his face was relaxed and smiling. The smile grew broader when the door went up and she spoke.

"What a sight you are!"

"Yes, Mom," he said. "You look a bit frazzled yourself. Go on up to the barn. Lots of surprises."

Buzz was still Buzz. She could get no more from him.

The barn still smelled of cordite and was full of people. Fairfield and Rance, all smiles, together with some men introduced as Fairfield's aides.

"We came in by helicopter," the Colonel explained. "We'd learned where you were heading, and before we set off we heard stories of shooting round here."

There was no one within miles, Martha thought. But the Indians knew everything.

"So we piled in the whirly-birds and came out, but it was over by the time we got here." He looked at Daniel with more respect. "You have a good field officer."

"Oh, I was doing just great," he said with not a little sarcasm. "I let them get holed up in those rocks and couldn't budge them." Daniel was not pleased with himself. "It was Buzz and Hoffman who were the heroes."

Karen was shining. "They were just tremendous. We'd been here for hours and no one could move. We'd just pinned each other down. And Mr. Hoffman said to hold the door and he and Buzz put together the craziest bit of junk you ever saw."

Hans looked modestly pleased. "A length of pipe. Some dynamite I'd found, used for clearing rock, I suppose. A very simple ignitor. The only real work was hammering the front end so that the pinch was truly centered and Buzz did that. We mounted it here," he pointed to what had been the table, "and we had two wires leading back there—"

"A pocket rocket," Daniel said. "Blew them right into the sky."

"It actually landed a bit off course," Hans was apologetic. "There was no preset guidance. But it had more power than we expected."

"And it really hauled tail." Karen was enthusiastic. She sounded like Buzz. But Rance's attention was on Hans.

"I've been trying to think where I've seen you before," he said. "You're Hans Meister, aren't you? Mr. Hoffman! He laughed. "You're very cagey, all of you. Still, you're quite right. Need-to-know basis, all the way. That's the way we've been working, and successfully."

Daniel seemed to accept their presence amicably. There wasn't too much else he could have done. But Martha was aware of the significance of his asking her to go up to the barn. There was no question of them meeting in the installation itself, even on the upper level and certainly not in the Tomb Room, though it would have been useful to have the additional men to spell them. Karen's terror that had manifested when she had seen the dead missileer was such that she could neither go near, nor be in, either the room or the chamber door unless she herself carried what she called the panic box. It was bad policy, but they could do nothing about it. The mere sight of the door made her freeze, unable to move without it.

"Claustrophobia," Hans had said. "It affects a lot of would-be missile men."

The discussion was friendly enough, until they came to the wording of the ultimatum.

"Not an ultimatum, Martha. We must give them a basis for negotiation. They're here; they have the troops, the government; they're guarding our borders; we are in their hands."

Rance spoke. "I believe Mrs. Adams knows that the missile below us is no ordinary missile. The house genius here, Mr. Meister, had at least a hand in its design, I believe, and its payload is different from anything we've seen."

Fairfield looked very surprised and, for a moment, angry. His fair skin flushed, a scarlet tide rising from his collar to his crown. "I gather that the C-in-C has not been informed of everything, even by his national security advisor," he said dryly.

"I'm sorry, John," Rance said humbly. "But we had agreed on the most stringent application of need-to-know."

"Well, whatever it is," Fairfield went on, still looking ill-tempered, "it can't have been tested. They might be willing to risk it. Knowing that we are civilized human beings, wanting above all to save lives. We must be willing to compromise."

Martha listened carefully to his words, observed his fine, sensitive features, already restored to thoughtfulness after his quick outbreak of military pique. He would fail as Carmody had failed. He was a fine officer, a good man. But it would take an almighty power to rid the country of its new lords, the power of Magnanimity, or the threat of using that power. Fairfield, she was convinced, *could not do it*.

It was a relief when he and his men withdrew to set up quarters in the main house. "Can't my men relieve you at launch control?" he said.

"Not just yet," Hans said smoothly. "Nothing is in operating order. Young Adams and I are checking things over."

"We'll discuss the negotiations later," Fairfield said. "I'll arrange for a plane. You can catch Ulyanov himself in New York, fortunately. I think he's basically a reasonable man. They made the strike because it was a good opportunity to do so. After an election, we might have had another Reagan and they would have lost their chance. But now, with the China war on their hands . . ."

He spoke of arrangements for his men, bringing up provisions, gasoline and ammunition. "And fodder for your horses. Not much grazing round here." Karen had led them down and watered them before she'd had her breakfast. Already she was back at her post, on guard duty at the barn door. Rance nodded to her as the two men left, still discussing their arrangements, to look over the terrain. Martha was relieved to be left alone with Daniel.

"They seem to be taking it all right," Daniel said thoughtfully. She knew that he had been suspicious, not of Fairfield's loyalty, but of his willingness to give up his command. To Daniel's knife, and his leg holster, had been added a shoulder weapon—she was aware of the slight bulge under his loose shirt. The sentry had orders to challenge anyone entering the barn except members of their original party. "Routine," Daniel had announced. "Caution," he told Martha privately. "Just so that we know where they are."

"We might not have to bother with his plane," Daniel went on. "At least, no further than Cheyenne Mountain. From what Fairfield says he can get a man in."

Martha remembered the idea that had been driven out of her mind by all the turmoil. Was it foolish? What exactly was it that Buzz had said that night in New York? Armand . . . electronics . . .

"Where's Buzz?" she asked.

"Hans relieved him in the Tomb Room and he's on the upper level checking the transceiver."

"I'll just have a word with him," Martha said.

"Hurry back." He grinned. "We have to decide on the ultimatum, Mrs. A."

Before she went, Martha caught a glimpse of Karen at her post, flushed, eager, alert.

*   *   *

The tables and most of the chairs had been blown to bits
by the action of the pipe rocket. Daniel found her a
chair with no back but four legs. He squatted at her
feet, his dark head over her lap as they worked on the
message with a short pencil stub on the back of an old
envelope. The printed address stated "Barkham's Trading Post." The thought had to come: had many of Josh's
letters been written from this place?

How long the occupying force should be given to
leave took some consideration.

"Not so long that they can hang around, jockeying for
position," Martha said. "Twenty-four hours."

"A bit longer, be realistic," said Daniel. "Because
whatever the ultimatum is, you'll have to stick to it."

It was a long wrangle, and they both grew excited.
Daniel's mind went to the protection of his people,
which would return under the shelter of Magnanimity.
When the words came to Martha, brief, succinct, clear,
she wrote them down. Daniel peered, fumbled in his
pocket for the eyeglass he had long since lost, then
looked up, giving a shout of laughter.

His laughter rang round the barn, joyous, bright and
almost covered the other sound. Martha only recognized
the familiar, muted burst, as Daniel's head fell forward
and then back. Instinctively, she put her arms around
him and held his body to hers, but her arms were
swiftly covered in blood, and under their touch his shirt
sank into his ribcage in a way affronting the human
mind. He seemed to be quite dead and she lowered the
pitiful body to the floor. Then for one moment his eye
flickered open. He gave a smile, the ghost of his familiar grin, and raised his hand a few inches, in a last,
gallant gesture of farewell.

Rance stood in the door, a smoking pistol dangling at
his side.

"He was known as Bar-Lev," he said. "A most dangerous terrorist. I didn't have the chance to warn you. We had to wait to be sure what he was up to. In effect, he had come to take Magnanimity for himself."

Fairfield was behind him, almost at once. "Rance!"

"I had to take the opportunity and the responsibility, John. He's usually much too wily to catch off guard. And he had come too far."

Fairfield was horrified. "Martha, I'm so sorry it had to be done this way. I know he has been your protector; it must be a dreadful shock. But we've known since Kayenta who he really was. He was using you, Martha, to play his own game, and it had to stop here."

Karen was sobbing, trying to explain. Rance, pleading his years and infirmity, had asked her to check the roof. The girl brought up to politeness had obeyed. Her small breach of discipline had cost Daniel his life. It was a heavy burden for one not much more than a child.

Martha said nothing and John sighed. He put his hand on her shoulder briefly, and then gave the orders for the men to dig a grave. Bending over the body, Martha laid her head on the dead man's cheek in a last, tender embrace. Fairfield's sensitivity kept Rance and everyone else back until she stood, her back to the men and said, "You can take him now."

They would have dragged the body as earlier she had dragged the body of Perez's man, but under Fairfield's eyes they lifted it and bore it out with some dignity. They dug a shallow grave and when the body was placed in it, Martha came out, with a shawl wrapped about her to cover her bloody dress, into a sunset world where red rock reached up to a red sky.

"He was a Jew," she said, looking down at the grave, hastily covered in the sandy dirt. "I don't suppose anyone knows a Jewish prayer for the dead."

"He was an atheist," Rance replied.

The others had departed. A dead terrorist had no interest for them.

"No atheists in battle," Martha said. Bowing her head, she said the only words she knew. "For as much as it has pleased Almighty God of His great mercy to take unto Himself the soul of our brother here departed, we therefore commit his body to the ground, earth to earth, ashes to ashes, dust to dust in sure and certain hope . . ."

Rance's hand had not reached his gun when the bullet from Daniel's gun struck his brain.

" . . . of the Resurrection to eternal life, through our Lord Jesus Christ," Martha finished. She supposed it was blasphemy, and hoped to be forgiven.

—— XXXV ——

Fairfield's men came running at the shot and saw her with the gun smoking under the fringes of the shawl. The Colonel's hand warned them off.

"My God, Martha. The man only did what had to be done. Rance has been our strength, our mainstay."

"I'm sure he has," Martha said. "It was Rance who recognized you near Chicago, wasn't it? You didn't know him, did you John?"

"No," he said, "but . . ."

"And of all the people you've worked with, did anyone recognize him from before the surrender?"

"They wouldn't. He worked in Moscow."

"I believe he did. But for whom?"

"He's no double agent, Martha. He helped form the organization from the beginning."

"Not a double agent. A single Soviet agent." Virinsky's man. She should not have expected Fairfield to be outwitted quite so easily. "Rance helped you form the organization so that he could wrap it up any time he

427

wished. So much easier than a thousand freelances."
Her tongue was a lash.

"And you were the way to Magnanimity. They were
looking for you in Connecticut, and they found you
outside Chicago. By making you the leader of the Underground, they were certain I would come to you,
their little bird warm in their hands. He told you I had
knowledge of a special weapon, didn't he?"

"But even Walt suspected . . ."

"No. Walt suspected that I knew about the hidden
complex, but he didn't know about Magnanimity. No
living American knew that but me. Only the Russians
knew."

Fairfield was white under his tan and very shaken.
"If you're right . . ."

"She's right." Hans was beside her and his face was
grim. "Don't worry, Martha. Karen has agreed to take
my place in the Tomb Room, and Buzz has been advised. She won't make a mistake again. Rance *was* one
of them."

He looked down at the body with distaste. "When we
met in Kayenta, he had no suspicion of who I was; that
was obvious enough. Yet when he arrived here, he
knew. It troubled me. He made a call somewhere,
didn't he?"

"Mexican Water," Fairfield said slowly. "There were
problems finding a functioning telephone, but he didn't
want to use his transceiver. It was a long conversation."

"You've managed to kill the best man we had," Hans
said, with a savagery that Martha had never heard from
him. "No one could ever discover 'Daniel' but you
brought Rance here. Your whole organization has been
compromised."

Fairfield looked like a sick animal. But now he raised
his eyes.

"It's not quite terminal," he said. "I only followed
policy. Rance knew about the hidden bases, because
that was his special project. But he never knew my

people who were working with the Russians. He didn't press; it wasn't important enough, I suppose.

Fairfield could still function. His men were set to control the access points on the narrow roads and trails and flat stretches where helicopters might make a landing, but principally at the landing field at Oljeto. There was no talk of his people entering the launch complex. The Colonel had given up his command to Martha Adams. "I can still get someone to New York to deliver the ultimatum," he said. "When you have it ready."

Curtly, she laid out her plan. "The message will be transmitted at noon tomorrow, New York time, as the meeting starts. I have it ready," she said.

Virinsky had taken a group of picked men with him on the supersonic transport, a small group for discretion's sake. Borunukov was not to thunder in on this triumph for which he himself had worked so long. His man on the base was prepared effectively to incapacitate the Americans. He had been supplied with a drug, tasteless in itself, that added to their food or drink would render them useless for days. More troops could be called in from Dugway or Yuma and special guards from the Grand Canyon camp could be summoned at a moment's notice.

It was the great moment of his career. Tomorrow he would go back to announce his achievement at the meeting. New York, he decided suddenly, that should never be Ulyanovgrad. It was his city; the city of his great success. Virinskygrad had a better sound. They would owe him that.

How he would be cheered! He would have in his hands Meister, who had provided the Chinese with the missiles confounding the ABM systems and terrifying the Soviet Union. Bar-Lev, murderer of Lavrentin, who had thumbed his nose at the secret services of the world far too long. Virinsky would have control of the Doomsday weapon himself, and he would make an end of the woman who had nearly escaped him at last. In his great euphoria he had the radio operator transmit a coded message for Ulyanov; the Magnanimity base and the insurgent leader, Martha Adams, were in his hands.

Karen remained in the Tomb Room while Buzz, Hans and Fairfield worked out the last details. When Buzz had finished his labors, he left for Cheyenne Mountain. Martha had flinched at the thought of him there, but Fairfield had sworn that his men could hold him safe. Tomorrow, at noon, standard time, her message would go out. There was nothing to do now but wait to hear from Buzz.

Martha suddenly felt entombed herself. The grief she had crushed sprang up to claim her. Restless, she wandered outside and scanned the skies, but they were empty, silent. She stood for a while at Daniel's grave. She was still covered with his blood; she had no other garments. And she was not eager to cast them off. The stiff rasp against her skin was a reminder, an embrace. The tears dropped on her cheeks, unchecked, unheeded as a child's.

Daniel. He had become so very dear. So much loved. She would have taken him as a lover, but their meeting had come too soon. Passion and mourning were poor companions. But remembering that shattered body, aware of the spirit that could not be broken, she could have wished that it were otherwise, that the chilled and lonely Daniel could have warmed himself once more at the fire before he went into the dark. There, in the fading afterglow, under a crimson sky shading into lavender and grey, she said her last good-bye. Then she went down to the deepest level to take her turn until the morning.

With Virinsky away, the work at the Headquarters on First Avenue fell very heavily on Madame Paul. Virinsky had his "cabinet" to handle the running of the country, but in fact all decisions had to be referred to him. In his absence, he had appointed Madame Paul, his secretary, and his official chief aide to be in communication with him, and theirs was the responsibility for transmitting orders.

But suddenly, although Ulyanov and his suite had arrived, Virinsky could not be reached. He was still in transit. Madame Paul refused to be distracted, there was too much to do. Besides the usual work, there were the special security measures in the General Assembly building to be checked. With the greatest men of the Soviet Union together with most of the leaders of the rest of the world being gathered in one room, extraordinary measures had been taken. Not only must all potential intruders be kept out, but the building must be guarded from weapons based on land, in the sea or in the air. A whole flotilla was at anchor in New York Bay, the river was full of patrol boats, almost too many to allow for movement, lines of troops ringed the metropolis in concentric circles.

All employees who must be in the building on the great day were to be given security badges as they entered in the morning and fingerprint checks. Every precaution was taken. The weary Madame Paul, as thorough as always, felt a dull resentment. She was, after all, no great personage in the KGB. She had the work, the responsibility and yet her rank was far from the highest. Virinsky had promised her that she would be a Hero of the Soviet Union after that day. It did not seem enough. However she was not the first woman to have done the work while the men reaped the rewards, she thought, and went on with her tasks.

Virinsky was again a thundercloud, swelling with impatience. The landing facilities in the region were disgraceful. The supersonic had had to land at Deseret where he and his men were to transfer to another aircraft. They had been held up infuriatingly by his own orders on identification and processing. His position meant little to the local army men. The Under-Secretary, who was in effect Commissar of all that had been the United States, ironically was almost unknown here because of his dislike of public recognition. Apologies and aid were soon forthcoming, however, and Virinsky was provided with three of the newest, largest helicopters.

"And they can land on a dime," somebody boasted. However, Virinsky decided prudently to land at a small airstrip at Oljeto, where, he was assured, there would be jeeps that could complete his journey. It was then found that the helicopters had developed some mechanical faults. Work was begun immediately, but the delay stretched on hour after hour. The mechanics were all American nationals and Virinsky suspected that this was their form of sabotage. He would take care of them later.

While he waited, he spoke to his staff, though with the time difference it meant rousing Madame Paul from her bed. He was satisfied with the reports she made and told her that he would be back in time for the meeting, though he might miss the opening. "But no letting up of security," he warned. "Vigilance to the end."

Madame, who had exercised all possible vigilance, felt there was no reason to awaken her for such superfluous instruction. But she told him that his chief aide was at the camp in Central Park, inspecting its security, so that no dissidents could escape or be rescued while the eyes of the world were on the meeting, and Virinsky had a call put in to him there.

Central Park was large, and there were many areas now of encampment. The helicopters were ready by the time his aide was found and brought to the telephone, yet there were certain decisions to be made. Certain persons, it was decided, should be eliminated now for safety's sake. When the list was finished, Virinsky and his men went to the 'copters. But the pilots insisted on waiting for at least the pre-dawn light before they lifted off.

Very early on the moring of the 26th, Karen brought Martha coffee and took over the guarding of the key. It was a heroic act for the frightened girl, her amends for the death of Daniel. And for all her fears, the girl clutching the panic box was still trustworthy. She might be claustrophobic, but her courage was great.

Hans, on the upper level, gave her a cheerful smile. Buzz had sent the prearranged signal. He was in Cheyenne Mountain. Martha trembled, and prayed.

"Was it right to take the risk?"

"It was so close to one of their regular signals. Unless you were listening for it, no one would notice. No voice message. Get some sleep for a few hours."

But Martha could not sleep. She went out to get some air and to stretch her legs. In the moment when the greyness lifted to the sun's first rays, this place with its strange rocks springing up out of the desert floor seemed to her like the end of the world, the very edge of creation.

What was it Hans had said? She could not remember. But the words first heard long ago echoed in scraps and pieces in her mind.

"To this far region of the earth, this pathless wilderness . . .the high-ridged rocks." The words deepened her sense of horror. Climbing up to the top of a ridge, she scrambled and pulled herself along as though by sweat and effort she would drive away this daytime sense of nightmare, born, no doubt, of past griefs and future terrors. By noon that day she would send the message, and at any time thereafter, she might have a task to do.

The words she hadn't wanted to remember pounded through her head.

". . . The world is shaken . . . the roar of thunders reverberates, gleams the red levin and whirlwinds lick up the dust." She crushed her hands to her temples as though she could squeeze the thought away.

She had brought the glasses to scan the sky for aircraft, though Hans on the upper level had a scanner of his own. Her gaze swept over the sandy plain on the far side of the ridge and she caught her breath in eerie wonder.

Navahos by the hundreds were assembled on the plateau. In the center of the throng, a sapling was mounted, bearing strips of brightly-colored cloth. Standing by the tree was a tall, commanding man who seemed to be giving orders. Some sort of hut covered in skins faced the morning sun. Men in breechcloths filed inside in a slow parade and when they emerged they donned sacklike shirts decorated with painted circles, crescents and crosses, which they wore over buckskin leggings. The women wore the shirt also, and all passed by the leader and his helper who painted the same circles, crescents and crosses on each and every face. Then men and women alike fixed long feathers in their hair.

The dancers formed in circles. The leader raised his arms to heaven and began a long, lilting prayer. The people clasped hands. A strange, rhythmic chant began among them and was taken up by one group, then another. The song rose on the morning air. The bodies of the dancers reached up, crouched down and they began to circle, as the song grew louder and the dancing faster.

The leader gave a cry and a corresponding moan came from the rings of dancers. Some cut their bodies and smeared blood upon the tree. The leader called them to order and they reformed in their circles and were seated as the leader began to pray once more. Soon the dancing recommenced.

Martha closed her eyes. Were they dancing only in the hope that the white people would be going? Or from some deeper sense of fear calling for divine protection against disasters yet to come? She felt a great compassion, but would not alter her chosen course. Had the old gods once listened from the mountain tops, hearing the cries of men? If they had, they had not saved them. Disasters had fallen in their inexorable course. Who holds the helm of necessity . . .

She turned away and climbed down swiftly. That way madness lay. A rock fell and in the crash that followed, softened by the moaning chant, she heard what might have been the crack of gunfire, far away, beyond the plain with the gathered dancers. Sobered, she went to Fairfield and told him what she'd seen and heard.

The battle at Oljeto was short and bloody. The Americans, camouflaged, well-placed, and very much alive, had at the start all of the advantage of surprise. The men in the first helicopter were disposed of efficiently, though they were crack troops and took a toll of the small force. Virinsky's pilot, careful of his great passenger had lifted at once, prepared to retreat, but Virinsky was watching the action and ordered him to hover.

The men in the second machine had landed. Most of them were unscathed so far and they carried formidable fire power. The pilot turned to Virinsky.

"The rebels have spread themselves in the rocks. It could take several hours . . ."

Virinsky had no intention of waiting several hours. "Which way is the wind blowing?" he said.

"Southerly," the pilot answered.

"Then give the order to drop the gas," Virinsky said. "We'll wear masks."

The pilot was startled. "But, Comrade Under-Secretary, our men are down there."

He could see, clearly, two men crawling up in a brave, audacious maneuver bearing hand grenades against a well-placed machine gun.

Virinsky was already putting on his mask.

"Drop it," he said.

The pilot, grey-faced, obeyed orders. He tried not to look at his comrades on the ground. He had used this gas in Afghanistan and he knew all about it. There were whispers that Hitler's men had developed it, this gas that in a few moments turned a man to a blind, quivering, squeaking wreck, dying in a mess of his own excrement and vomit.

"Now, fly well east and find a spot nearer the destination."

The pilot soon saw a good landing place very close to his goal, the plateau behind the ridge that formed one side of this valley. But the Indians were assembled, performing their tribal rites. He had nothing but contempt for savages and their primitive nonsense, but odd stories had come from the reservation. Men in uniform were not welcome. Some had been known to disappear. It was promised that soon these places would be cleaned out, but he didn't like the look of this today. Yet the Under-Secretary could not be denied. After all, it was daytime, and his men were heavily armed. Besides, it was no sense searching for a small clearing in the rocks; there might be other parties of Americans, scattered about.

A strong gust of wind caused them to land in the center among the dancers close to the prayer tree. The Indians had been dancing since dawn and now many were leaping, falling and hurling themselves against the rocks. Most of them drew back as the machine descended, but the old man stood fast. His raised arms were sliced by the propellor and he fell at the foot of the tree. The pilot shuddered. Fortunately, the men were ready.

The Indians offered no resistance; though they were there in hundreds, they seemed drunk or dazed. They drew back to let the soldiers pass. Virinsky, too, was in a state of exaltation. He had glimpsed the swimming pool near the trading post. Huck had told more than she knew. He had the Doomsday weapon. Still, he and his guards waited prudently in the machine as the soldiers formed a double file through which the great man would proceed.

The early morning sun was dazzling. It was safe now to remove the masks and Virinsky, the last to do so, disentangled himself the better to see what was happening. He blinked his eyes to see a hundred knives flash in the sun, and a human tide swarm over his picked squad of troops armed with the most modern weapons known to man.

"Lift off," Virinsky told the pilot with great calm. "Bring her down on the other side of the ridge. You can just do it."

The pilot already had the machine in the air. If the Under-Secretary wanted the machine brought down in the road, with the chance of hitting one of those rocks or stones, he had no choice. There might be troops around that big house there. The Under-Secretary seemed to be without fear of any kind, but the pilot found himself praying to a God in whom he did not believe.

—— XXXVI ——

The great day dawned. The Anniversary Parade of the
October Revolution was still going on in Moscow. Mod-
els were being drawn through the streets as they were
in New York's Thanksgiving Parade, but these were not
the cartoon animals seen on that occasion. Instead there
was the reusable orbit-to-orbit shuttle, the Rocketo-
plan on its scram-jet booster, and the Soyuz Spacecraft
and Salyut Space Station. If the military knew that
some of this was merely a *pokazukha* at the moment,
the masses were suitably impressed. They needed something, for not even the Soviet control of news could
hide all of the losses they had taken in the China war.
But the crowds before the television cameras, who knew
their role, were cheering suitably. If some of them
muttered that it was time old Ulyanov took his place
next to his revered kinsman in the great Tomb, it was
not heard on the sound system. And they enjoyed the
floodlighting of this late parade that turned night into
day.

In New York the parade started early, to alternate with Moscow on the screens of the world. Ulyanov and Borunukov were in the lead cars, to be greeted by the Secretary-General at the building on First Avenue. It was a great day for the United Nations, even if it was to be its last in its present incarnation. After today, the name and most of its functions were to be given over to the new Comintern, while the rest would be absorbed in the new departments of state. The honeymoon period was over.

All the world's leaders were gathered together in the Great Hall of the General Assembly, together with their entourages, their country's delegations, to see and hear what the structure of the New Order was to be, and what was to be the fate of the world. Favored members of the public were admitted to certain seats, along with what was left of the stage and cinema, the press and academia. No invitations had been refused, for such refusal would have been noted and not forgotten.

At the entrance of Ulyanov, the satellite would pick up from the cameras in the Great Hall, and all coverage would switch from Red Square. Ulyanov was Premier now, as well as General-Secretary of the CPSU, since the ousting and subsequent death of Premier Tikhonov. This was his great day.

Security guards surrounded the hall, and were interspersed with the seated guests. Madame Paul, who knew that everything was in order, nevertheless walked to and fro, checking, rechecking every small detail. The television and radio people used their own sound systems, but the internal link-up was her responsibility, from the microphones of the speakers to the lines leading to the interpreters in their booths and back to the earpieces of everyone in the Great Hall. She walked about with her crew, making the last adjustments.

The only relief from her state of weary tension was the moment when she looked in one of the interpreters' booths and saw Armand Lesseps, fiddling with the wires, adjusting his own equipment as he liked to do.

He gave her his charming smile. "Bonjour, chère Madame. You don't mind that I take this booth for myself alone today." The interpreters usually shared, to save space. They had been rather squashed since the Trusteeship Council insisted on having translations into several American-Indian languages and this had caused a certain amount of friction in the booths. "We will give the French translation a chance."

It would be the only advantage for the French. Certainly against normal procedure but just this once . . . She gave him a smile that was her blessing and went on.

The incursion at Oljeto had been too sudden for the men to radio back to Fairfield. When he heard the helicopter coming, he ordered his men to hold their fire while he checked to see if it were friend or enemy. His force was thin, for he had stripped himself of men to guard the roads. Virinsky's guards opened fire from the helicopter and shot the sentries down, but not before the craft itself was hit. The pilot, descending, felt himself lose control as the machine suddenly accelerated forward and almost before he could feel fear his cabin smashed itself against a rock. He was unlucky. His neck was broken on impact, but his passengers were merely shaken up and extricated themselves without difficulty.

Fairfield and the two senior officers with him, all retirees in their sixties, retreated to the house, but they were no match for Virinsky's guards. The two officers were killed at once, but Fairfield, mortally wounded, and with his legs broken by bullets in the knees, lingered. The guard bent over him to make sure that he was dead.

"Come," Virinsky said, impatient. He would arrange to speak to Ulyanov from the firing capsule itself. A great surge of something like joy rose up in him.

The men moved off. Fairfield had fallen on the grenade he had been about to throw. His arms could still move a little but he could not lift himself enough to free it. His mind was dimming, but the image of Martha Adams came, clear and strong, her face with a look of astonished contempt at a man who refused to do his clear duty. His hand was on the pin. With an effort that he knew he could not make, he rolled over, pulled the pin and flung the grenade. One guard, who had been heartened by his master's exaltation, spread around the room, an exploded carcass. The other man lost an arm and a leg. Only Virinsky was untouched. He merely took the heavy pistol from the body of his close companion, and walked on.

Hans, on the upper level, had seen the helicopter's approach on his television viewer. No alarm had been sounded, so it must be some of Fairfield's men. But the moments passed and there was no confirming signal. Procedure demanded that without such confirmation the installation should be sealed. But he could not seal it. Martha was probably still in the barn. She was due to relieve Karen in just a few minutes. It was 9:40 local time, 16:40 Zulu time, in the language of the missile men, and 11:40 in New York. He scanned the firing capsule anxiously, but Karen was still there at the key. He punched in his viewer to the barn, but there was no one in sight. No one at all.

Virinsky was already in the barn. The presence of the sentries had made it obvious that this was the point of entry into the underground complex. His practiced gaze at once spotted the hidden cameras among the sheepskins. They were angled to the opening of the barn and he dropped down on his belly and wriggled to the place where the entrance must be, the wide shelves covering an area big enough for men and equipment to make a descent. He grunted in satisfaction as he found the

place and swung the shelves away. Before long he was
in the elevator bank of Magnanimity itself. He had
always known it was inevitable.

The doors of the Last Exit were up. Karen, tense, ran
past Martha as she approached down the corridor. The
girl was white and sweat glistened on her forehead.
Poor Karen, who could hardly bear to run through the
steel chamber. She would join Hans on the upper level.
Martha's hands were full. She had brought food and
drink enough for the forty-eight hours. This was to be
her vigil. There would be no rest for her; she was
encompassed by a dreadful solemnity. She would emerge
from that room free, or, she supposed, damned, but the
consequence would rest upon her soul and no other.

As one elevator cab brought Karen to the upper
level, the second brought Virinsky down. The car stopped
but did not open; the doors were on manual control.
While he searched the panel for the button, Karen
disappeared into the upper level Control Room. At her
word, Hans sealed off the entrance to the barn and
even the emergency exits. He peered anxiously at his
scanners but there was nothing outside except a raven
flying low and then, after a few moments, some blood-
smeared Indians staggering over the rocks, looking more
dazed than dangerous.

Virinsky looked down the corridor on the upper level.
This would not be the firing level; it was too close to
the surface. He punched the last button on the panel.
That would be the level of the firing capsule, and
perhaps of access to the missile itself. In a moment he
was on the lowest level, staring into the concrete depths.

In the blue, green and gold Assembly Hall of the United
Nations more than two thousand people were watching
the figures on the podium that was designed to be the
focal point of the great chamber. There were two figures instead of the usual three, but Ulyanov had the

place of honor in the center. He looked well enough to the audience in the hall and to the millions watching on their television screens. Makeup men had done their best and he seemed his usual self. Only his doctors knew that he had suffered a small stroke in Hall City.

The news was good. The last message from Virinsky—who should have been here at his side but would have to be forgiven—was that he himself, with his KGB troops, was taking possession of Magnanimity. The success could be announced. Honor at least would be saved, the old man told himself. He held onto the thought as objects seemed to wave and wander. The huge crowd turned to a great plain, bearing a crop of faces to be gathered for his need. He mistook the microphone before him for his water glass, but he recovered when the Marshal's gaze fell upon him, the Marshal, who seemed ten feet tall. Ulyanov was satisfied that it was Virinsky who had taken the Doomsday weapon: Virinsky, a safe man. But that thought brought its own terrors, for Virinsky was not here, nor had he been heard from that morning. The empty place at the Premier's side seemed itself a ghostly presence. But Virinsky would not lie. Constantin Virinsky would not be defeated by a woman.

Martha put her bundles down near the console and went to close the doors. Outside, in the corridor to the elevator a small object lay, dark against the concrete floor. Karen, in her terror, had dropped the panic box. Martha felt no anger, she understood. The night the girl had spent was full of anguish. "Such is the work wrought in the soul by this night that hides the hopes of the light of day."

She stepped through and retrieved the box quickly and straightened up, to see a man bearing a pistol that was trained upon her. She blinked. It might have been some paranoid mirage; the dust-covered, blood-spattered, ponderous figure looked so like Virinsky, the once Under-Secretary now said to be the dictator of the United States. But the gun was no mirage. Her own was heavy on her shoulder but she dare not make a move.

The gun was pointed at her head but the man's eyes were staring past her, past the Last Exit she had left open, to the room beyond, to focus on the console that held the final key.

His eyes moved back to her and he had no doubt. This was the heart of Magnanimity, and this was the woman. She was altered, reduced to nothing except eyes and arrogance, but unmistakable. This was Martha Adams.

He stepped forward; she shrank away. This was power. For the first time he knew true joy, full, rich, ecstatic. He allowed her to creep fearfully as he moved in for the kill. He was relishing the moment, then suddenly her head rose high—just as the doors came crashing down. It was to be his last glimpse of her. Martha would see him once again.

She, who could not leave a trapped animal, went back to the viewer to be sure. The face, full of terror, was unfamiliar now, but as the hands beat and scrabbled against the door, she had a glimpse of the forked thumb, and she turned her back and walked away.

She sat at the console, the microphone by her right hand, the key at her left. Sixty seconds to go. The red light flashed; the signal that the NORAD hook-up was active. Her message would reach the General Assembly; it would soon be known round the country and beyond.

It was written out on a sheet before her, this second Declaration of Independence, no noble-looking document, but a sheet of yellowed paper from Barkham's Trading Post, blotted by a leaky pen. But she did not need to read it. The words possessed her tongue.

Borunukov, all martial glitter, was his usual imposing self. He was once more in the area of his greatest victory, and here he could lick his wounds over his unexpected mauling at the hands of the Chinese. He had been hurt, but he could not be beaten. The power of the Soviets was still too great. And the greatest threat was gone. Ulyanov had officially informed him that the Adams woman, the leader of the insurgent forces, had been captured and the Magnanimity base secured. During the ceremonies, Virinsky, that useful bureaucrat, was to broadcast to them from the missile site. With this weapon, the Chinese threat was nothing. He would wipe them from the face of the earth. This had turned out after all to be the great day they had planned.

The Secretary-General of the United Nations, demoted from the podium to a seat on the floor, was just ending his unctious, long-drawn-out speech. Ulyanov, he noticed, looked ill under his make-up. He would be glad when this was over. Virinsky would have managed it much better. The Marshal, too, felt a certain surprise that Virinsky had not returned. He looked at his watch. The Secretary-General was running late. Just thirty seconds to go. At last he sat. Twenty seconds; Ulyanov would rise and the New Order would begin.

Martha was alone in that hidden place, with the trapped madman by her side, but she was not solitary. The dark night had passed. Josh, Daniel, and all the people who had loved this land were with her as the green light went on and she opened her lips to speak.

The Marshal disliked the earpiece that he believed detracted from the dignity of his appearance. There was the usual irritating, crackling noise. He saw Ulyanov's lips moving but heard no sound from him, and tried switching the channel. Perhaps the message from Virinsky at the Magna site was coming in. Then a voice came, a woman's voice, but certainly not the muted tone of an interpreter. It sounded through the headsets into every ear.

"I, Martha Adams, do hereby demand that all troops of the USSR and its satellites, together with their civilian personnel, begin at once to evacuate the United States of America and its territories." The voice rang from every loudspeaker round the Great Hall. "Such evacuation is to be completed within forty-eight hours of the receipt of this demand." It was thundering through the microphones and simultaneously out across the world.

"Any delay or failure to expedite and complete the said evacuation will result in the annihilation of the USSR from Smolensk to the Kolyma range."

Ulyanov collapsed, eyes protruding, tongue lolling, to the horror of his delegation. He could not speak or move, but in his mind one thought he had tried to bury rose and spread: Virinsky had lied and he had failed.

The voice went on, the voice of command.

"Only total and complete compliance will bring about Magnanimity."

The Marshal looked at his country's leader, prostrate upon the floor. The taking of the Doomsday weapon. His last *pokazhuka*, then. The insurgents had the base. The Adams woman controlled the key.

The message took less than a minute to deliver, but the words ended an era. Ulyanov's eyes glazed over. The words of a dead President had felled the second Lenin. The failure of Virinsky would bring down Kharkev, perhaps leaving the Soviet Union for the Marshal. Borunukov looked round the Great Hall at the milling crowd, the excited delegates, the terrified Russians and knew he must take charge. Forty-eight hours. With his SS18's he could obliterate everything west of the Rockies, but he could not be sure of stopping that woman. And he would not for a crippled half of the United States, bargain away all of Russia. He was a Russian after all and he did what had to be done.

* * *

By one p.m. that day Bruce Joshua Adams was relaying dispatches to the Magnanimity site. The great Russian lift-off had begun at McGuire Air Force base. To the woman in the capsule, there came a flood of relief and joy. For a moment her hand fell from the key and she was ready to spring up, exultant, but her lessons had been hard and she kept her vigil. Through the forty-eight hours, from every state the messages poured in, until on October 28th, at twelve noon, Eastern Standard time, she received the ultimate signal. The evacuation was complete. Martha Adams rose, shaken but still strong like her beloved United States. As she made her way to the surface, death touched her once more when she passed the body of Virinsky. But up above, tossing her bright hair, she walked out into the sunlight of the free land.